Snorri Sturluson

Edda

Prologue and *Gylfaginning*

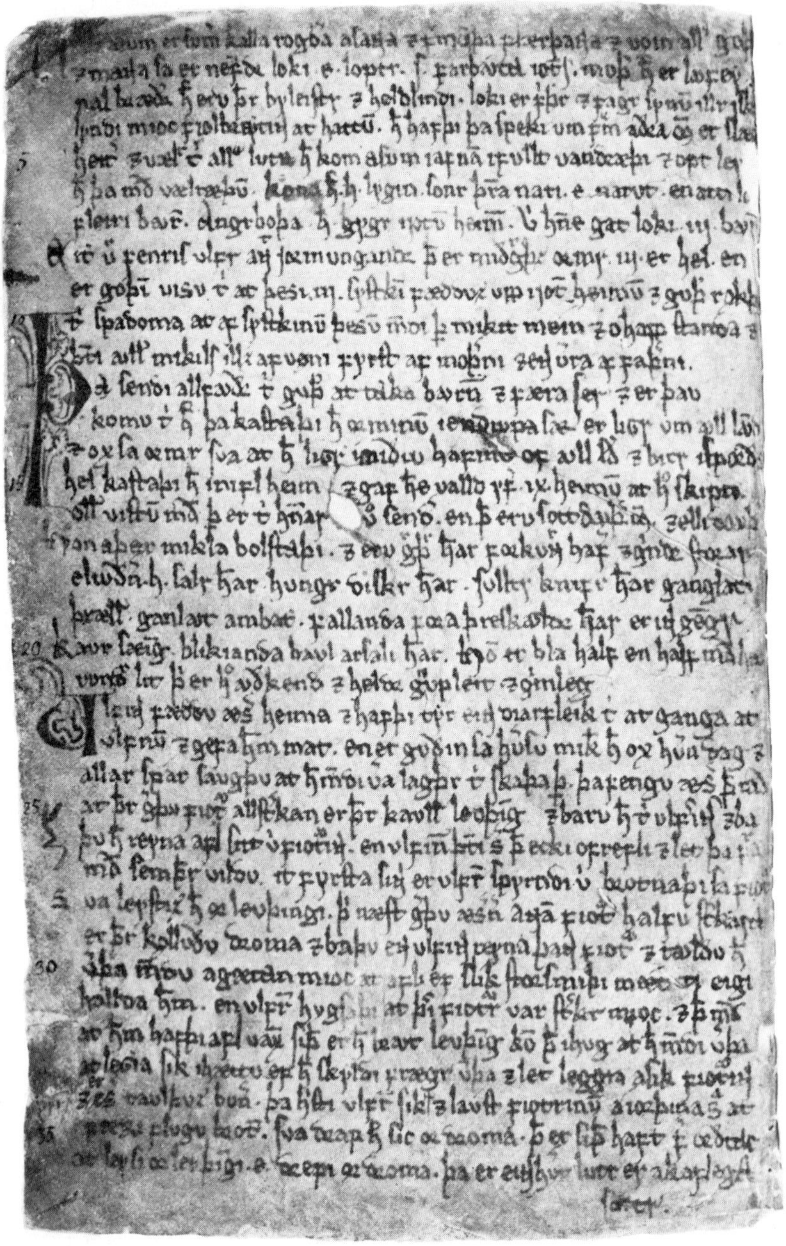

Codex Regius, fo. 7v (reduced)
(see pp. 26/34–28/1)

Snorri Sturluson

Edda

Prologue and *Gylfaginning*

Edited by
ANTHONY FAULKES

CLARENDON PRESS · OXFORD

1982

Oxford University Press, Walton Street, Oxford OX2 6DP
London Glasgow New York Toronto
Delhi Bombay Calcutta Madras Karachi
Kuala Lumpur Singapore Hong Kong Tokyo
Nairobi Dar es Salaam Cape Town
Melbourne Auckland
and associate companies in
Beirut Berlin Ibadan Mexico City

Published in the United States by
Oxford University Press, New York

© Anthony Faulkes 1982

British Library Cataloguing in Publication Data
Snorri Sturluson
Edda.
Part 1: Prologue and Gylfaginning.
1. Icelandic and Old Norse poetry – History and criticism
I. Title II. Faulkes, Anthony
839' .6'1009 PT7312 79–41803
ISBN 0-19-811175-4

Text set in 10/12 pt Linotron 202 Times, printed and bound
in Great Britain at The Pitman Press, Bath

Contents

Abbreviated references

AH *Gudesagn:* P. A. Munch, *Norrøne gude- og heltesagn*, rev. A. Holtsmark, Oslo 1967.

AH *Studier:* A. Holtsmark, *Studier i Snorres Mytologi*, Oslo 1964.

Akv: Atlakviða (*PE* 282–91).

Alv: Alvíssmál (*PE* 129–34).

AM 748 I and II 4to, Arnamagnæan Institute, Copenhagen, and Stofnun Árna Magnússonar, Reykjavík; printed in *SnE* II. 397–494, 573–627 (where the second is referred to as AM 1 e ß fol.); facsimile in *Fragments of the Elder and Younger Edda*, Copenhagen 1945 (Corpus Codicum Islandicorum Medii Aevi, XVII).

AM 757 a 4to, Arnamagnæan Institute, Copenhagen; printed in *SnE* II. 501–72.

Bdr: Baldrs draumar (*PE* 135–8).

Codex Regius of the eddic poems: GkS 2365 4to, Stofnun Árna Magnússonar, Reykjavík; printed in *PE*; facsimile in *Codex Regius of the Elder Edda*, Copenhagen 1937 (Corpus Codicum Islandicorum Medii Aevi, X).

Egils saga: ÍF II.

Elder Edda: see *PE* and Codex Regius.

Flateyjarbók: GkS 1005 fol., Stofnun Árna Magnússonar, Reykjavík; printed in *Flateyjarbok*, I–III, Christiania 1860–8; facsimile in Corpus Codicum Islandicorum Medii Aevi, I, Copenhagen 1930.

Fm: Fáfnismál (*PE* 219–26).

Grammatical Treatises: all four are edited in *SnE* II. 2–249. See also *Den første og anden grammatiske afhandling i Snorres Edda*, ed. V. Dahlerup and Finnur Jónsson, København 1886; *Den tredje og fjærde grammatiske afhandling i Snorres Edda*, ed. B. M. Ólsen, København 1884; *The First Grammatical Treatise*, ed. Hreinn Benediktsson, Reykjavík 1972; *First Grammatical Treatise*, ed. E. Haugen, London 1972.

Grm: Grímnismál (*PE* 75–89).

Gylf: Gylfaginning.

Hákonar saga Hákonarsonar, ed. Guðbrandur Vigfússon, London 1887; tr. G. W. Dasent, London 1894 (Rolls Series, Icelandic Sagas II and IV).

Hauksbók: AM 371, 544, 675 4to, Stofnun Árna Magnússonar, Reykjavík, and Arnamagnæan Institute, Copenhagen; ed. E. Jónsson and F. Jónsson, København 1892–6; facsimile in *Hauksbók,* Copenhagen 1960 (Manuscripta Islandica, 5). The text of *Vǫluspá* is in AM 544 4to, foll. 20–21^r.

Háv: Hávamál (PE 43–64).

Hdl: Hyndluljóð (PE 152–62).

Heiðreks saga: The saga of King Heiðrek the Wise, ed. and tr. C. Tolkien, London 1960.

HH: Helgakviða Hundingsbana hin fyrri (PE 179–89).

HH II: *Helgakviða Hundingsbana ǫnnur (PE* 190–201).

Hkr: Snorri Sturluson, *Heimskringla,* ed. Bjarni Aðalbjarnarson, Reykjavík 1941–51 (*ÍF* XXVI–XXVIII).

Hrbl: Hárbarðsljóð (PE 97–104).

Hym: Hymiskviða (PE 105–12).

ÍF: Íslenzk fornrit, I– , Reykjavík 1933–

J: Papp. fol. nr 38, Royal Library, Stockholm.

K: AM 755 4to, Stofnun Árna Magnússonar, Reykjavík.

Ls: Lokasenna (PE 113–23).

MRN: E. O. G. Turville-Petre, *Myth and Religion of the North,* London 1964.

N: NkS 1878 b 4to, Royal Library, Copenhagen.

Noreen, A., *Altisländische und Altnorwegische Grammatik,* 4th ed., Halle 1923 (cited by paragraph no.).

Od: Oddrúnargrátr (PE 276–81).

PE (Poetic Edda): Norrœnn Fornkvæði, Sæmundar Edda, ed. S. Bugge, Christiania 1867; see also AM 748 and Codex Regius above.

R: Gks 2367 4to, Royal Library, Copenhagen; printed in *SnE* I and *Edda Snorra Sturlusonar,* ed. Finnur Jónsson, København 1931; facsimile in *Codex Regius of the Younger Edda,* Copenhagen 1940 (Corpus Codicum Islandicorum Medii Aevi, XIV).

Rm: Reginsmál (Sigurðarkviða Fáfnisbana ǫnnur, PE 212–8).

Saxo Grammaticus, *Gesta Danorum*, ed. J. Olrik, H. Ræder, F. Blatt, Hauniæ 1931–57; see also *The first nine books of the Danish History of Saxo Grammaticus*, tr. O. Elton, London 1894, and Saxo Grammaticus, *The History of the Danes*, I, tr. P. Fisher, ed. H. E. Davidson, Cambridge 1979.

Sd: Sigrdrífumál (PE 227–36).

SG *Kommentar: Die Lieder der Edda*, ed. B. Sijmons and H. Gering, III: Kommentar, erste Hälfte: Götterlieder, Halle 1927.

Skáld: Skáldskaparmál (SnE I. 206–593).

Skj: Den norsk-islandske Skjaldedigtning, A I–II, B I–II, ed. Finnur Jónsson, København og Kristiania 1912–15.

Skm: Skírnismál (PE 90–6).

SnE: Edda Snorra Sturlusonar, I–III, Hafniæ 1848–87.

Sturlunga saga, ed. Guðbrandur Vigfússon, I–II, Oxford 1878; tr. J. H. McGrew and R. G. Thomas, New York 1970–4.

Sǫgubrot af fornkonungum, in *Sǫgur Danakonunga*, ed. C. af Petersens and E. Olson, København 1919–25, pp. 3–25.

T: MS No. 1374, University Library, Utrecht; ed. W. van Eeden, *De Codex Trajectinus van de Snorra Edda*, Leiden 1913, and Árni Björnsson, *Snorra Edda*, Reykjavík 1975.

Th: Thott 1494 4to, Royal Library, Copenhagen.

Tms: Trójumanna saga, ed. J. Louis-Jensen, Copenhagen 1963.

U: DG 11, University Library, Uppsala (Codex Upsaliensis); printed in *SnE* II. 250–396; facsimile in *Snorre Sturlasons Edda, Uppsala-Handskriften DG 11*, I, Stockholm 1962; the second volume of this work (Uppsala 1977) gives a diplomatic text.

Vm: Vafþrúðnismál (PE 65–74).

Vsp: Vǫluspá (PE 1–42).

W: AM 242 fol., Arnamagnæan Institute, Copenhagen; ed. Finnur Jónsson, *Edda Snorra Sturlusonar, Codex Wormianus*, København og Kristiania 1924; facsimile in *Codex Wormianus*, Copenhagen 1931 (Corpus Codicum Islandicorum Medii Aevi, II).

Ynglinga saga: Hkr I. 9–83.

Þrk: Þrymskviða (PE 124–8).

Introduction

Gylfaginning is the first part of Snorri Sturluson's *Edda*, and contains the most extensive and coherent account of Scandinavian mythology that exists from the Middle Ages. The prologue that accompanies it develops a surprisingly rational theory about the origin of heathen religions which is of great interest for the history of ideas in medieval Scandinavia. It is true that the value of the work for historians of religion is seriously impaired by the fact that the author was a Christian who lived at a time when the myths he describes had long since ceased to be believed in. His sources may have been unreliable, and his attitude to his material was clearly influenced both by his own religious beliefs and by his education and reading which were largely within the tradition of medieval European Christianity. But *Gylfaginning* remains a source of primary importance for the study of heathen Scandinavian tradition, without which other sources such as the poems of the *Elder Edda* and the *Danish History* of Saxo Grammaticus would give a much less comprehensible picture. Moreover the narratives in *Gylfaginning* are skilfully told and highly entertaining, with occasional touches of subtle humour and irony. The over-all structure of the work, both in the ordering of the narratives within it and in the handling of the frame story in which they are contained, also reveals artistry of a high order. It is therefore a pity that the work has been difficult of access, particularly to English students, and has been read mainly in extracts that give a poor impression of the work as a whole. The present edition attempts to remedy this, by presenting for the first time the complete text of this part of Snorri's *Edda* in normalized spelling with a comprehensive glossary and sufficient explanatory notes to enable the text to be understood. In order to keep the volume as compact as possible, only a minimum of comment on mythological matters has been included, and that is mostly to be found in the index of names.

Synopsis

The prologue begins with an account of how mankind forgot about their creator and began to worship nature; from this arose heathen religions (1–2). Then the author tells of Troy, and how descendants of the Trojans (the Æsir) migrated to Scandinavia and founded various dynasties, and were so prosperous that they came to be considered gods (3–11).

Gylfaginning opens with an anecdote of how a king in Sweden, Gylfi, was tricked of some of his land by one of the newcomers (1). He goes to visit the newcomers, disguised as a beggar and calling himself Gangleri, to find out whether their success was due to their own nature or to the gods they worshipped. He is welcomed, but told that his life depends on his proving himself wiser than them (2). His questions are answered by three speakers, Hár, Jafnhár, and Þriði, and he is told first about the king of their gods, All-father (3), then about the beginning of the world and the origin of the giants and the gods, of whom the chief, Óðinn, turns out to be the same as All-father, and the creation of men (4–9). He is told about night and day, sun and moon, the bridge of the gods (Bifrǫst), the golden age, the creation of dwarfs, the world-ash (Yggdrasill), the norns, the dwellings of the gods, the wind, summer and winter (10–19). There follow descriptions of each of the gods and goddesses in turn, including with Loki an account of his offspring Hel and the story of the binding of Fenriswolf, and with the goddesses the story of Freyr's wooing of Gerðr (20–37). Gylfi hears about Óðinn's hall (Valhǫll), the origin of Óðinn's horse Sleipnir (with the story of the giant builder of the gods' stronghold), and Freyr's ship Skíðblaðnir (38–43). Then follow two stories about Þórr, his expedition to the court of Útgarðaloki and his fishing for the Midgard serpent (44–8); the death of Baldr, his funeral, the attempt to get him back from Hel; and the capture and punishment of Loki (49–50). Finally Gylfi asks and is told about the twilight of the gods (*ragnarøkr*) in their last battle against the giants, the destruction of the world, and its subsequent renewal (51–3). Before he can ask more there is a loud crash and the Æsir and their hall disappear: they are unable to answer further questions and Gylfi has won the content of wisdom, but is cheated of his victory. He goes home and passes on the stories. The Æsir, however, decide to adopt the names of the gods in the stories they have told so that people will think that they themselves are the gods. The identities of the 'historical' Æsir, migrants to Scandinavia from Asia, and the mythical ones in the stories, which have been kept distinct up to this point, are thus finally merged, and the author ends by suggesting that the myths told of them are really allegories of events in the Trojan war (54).

The author

Snorri Sturluson (1179–1241) was one of the leading figures in Icelandic social and political life in the thirteenth century. He acquired great wealth and power and became deeply involved in the political turmoil in the country that led to the collapse of the legal and social organization that had existed since the settlement and eventually to loss of independence in 1262–4, when Iceland became subject to the Norwegian throne. He visited the Norwegian court in 1218–20 and again in 1237–9, and evidently agreed to try to further the interests of King Hákon Hákonarson (who ruled from 1217 to 1263) and of the king's father-in-law Earl Skúli in Iceland. In the end, however, Skúli rebelled against the king and was defeated and killed (1240), and Snorri also came under the king's displeasure. He was killed in his own cellar on the orders of his countryman Gizurr Þorvaldsson acting on the king's authority.

Snorri was well known as an important public figure (he was twice lawspeaker in the Icelandic parliament), and also as a poet; several poems by him are quoted in *Sturlunga saga, Hákonar saga Hákonarsonar*, and the third and fourth *Grammatical Treatises* (see *Skj* A II. 52–79). There is only an isolated contemporary reference to him as the author of historical writings (*Sturlunga saga*, I. 299), but there is fairly good evidence that he compiled *Heimskringla*, a history of the kings of Norway from legendary times to 1177, and a separate saga of S. Óláfr. It is also considered likely that he wrote *Egils saga*, the biography of Iceland's greatest poet, though there is no direct evidence for this.

Snorri's authorship of the *Prose Edda* is considered established by the rubric at the head of the text in U, which is probably the oldest extant manuscript, written in Iceland in the early fourteenth century:

Bók þessi heitir Edda. Hana hefir saman setta Snorri Sturluson eptir þeim hætti sem hér er skipat. Er fyrst frá Ásum ok Ymi, þar næst Skáldskapar-mál ok heiti margra hluta, síðast Háttatal er Snorri hefir ort um Hákon konung ok Skúla hertuga (This book is called Edda. Snorri Sturluson has compiled it in the manner in which it is arranged here. There is first told about the Æsir and Ymir, then Skáldskaparmál ('poetic diction') and (poetical) names of many things, finally Háttatal ('enumeration of metres or verse-forms') which Snorri has composed about King Hákon and Earl Skúli).

A separate heading to *Háttatal* in this manuscript again names Snorri as its author, and verses from *Háttatal* are quoted and ascribed to him in *Hákonar saga*, in the third *Grammatical Treatise*, and in the version of the second part of *Skáldskaparmál* in W. There is a reference to the prose commentary to *Háttatal* naming Snorri as its author in the preface to the *Grammatical Treatises* in W (*SnE* II. 8), and *Skáldskaparmál* is attributed to him in the fragmentary manuscript AM 748 I 4to, though there the attribution is immediately followed by a list of kennings that is not thought to be part of Snorri's work (*SnE* II. 427–8). The other independent manuscripts do not mention the author's name, and the earliest reference to his authorship of the work as a whole outside manuscripts that contain it is in the late sixteenth-century *Oddverja Annáll* under the notice of his death: 'Andlát Snorra Sturlusonar . . . hann samsetti Eddu . . .'.[1]

Snorri's authorship of the *Prose Edda* was upheld by the renaissance scholar Arngrímur Jónsson (1568–1648), and since his time it has generally been accepted without question. But the surviving manuscripts, which were all written more than half a century after Snorri's death, differ from each other considerably and it is not likely that any of them preserve the work quite as he wrote it. A number of passages in *Skáldskaparmál* especially have been thought to be interpolations, and this section of the work has clearly been subject to various kinds of revision in most manuscripts. It has also been argued that the prologue and the first paragraph and part of the last paragraph of *Gylfaginning* are not by Snorri, at least in their surviving forms. The prologue contains ideas clearly derived from the Christian Latin learning of medieval Europe, and also includes inaccurate scraps of classical material, while *Gylfaginning* (like *Heimskringla*) appears to belong to strictly native Scandinavian tradition. Continental books were, however, widely known in Iceland in the twelfth century, and educated lay Icelanders were not isolated from the learning of the Christian tradition. The prologue to *Gylfaginning* is a piece of philosophical speculation not unworthy of the author of the

[1] *Islandske Annaler indtil 1578*, ed. G. Storm, Christiania 1888, p. 481.

prologue to *Heimskringla*. Moreover it is a necessary introduction to *Gylfaginning* not only to set the scene for the dialogue within which its mythological stories are enclosed, but also to make clear the author's attitude to his material: Snorri was a Christian and needed to establish the relationship of his heathen mythology to his own beliefs. The prologue explains the nature and origins of the religion described in the body of the work. The first paragraph of *Gylfaginning* is not in U and is not strictly necessary to the narrative. It may have been an afterthought, but the anecdote appears also in *Heimskringla* (I. 14–15) in a form that implies that the version in *Gylfaginning* already existed. The end of the last paragraph of *Gylfaginning* is also lacking in U; it is a return to one of the themes of the prologue and the same arguments apply to both, though the meaning of the penultimate sentence is not entirely clear and may not be quite as the author intended.

It is not known when Snorri wrote the books that are ascribed to him, though *Háttatal* was presumably written shortly after his first visit to Norway, and may have been the first part of his *Edda* to be written. The compilation of the rest could have extended over many years; some of the inconsistencies in the work as it has survived may be due to its having been still in process of revision when the author died. *Heimskringla*, which is evidently an expansion of the separate saga of S. Óláfr, is in some respects a more mature work than the *Edda*, and the first part, *Ynglinga saga*, seems to have a reference to *Gylfaginning* (*Hkr* I. 16/4–5). This saga, like *Gylfaginning* and its prologue, deals with the origin of the Æsir, but whereas in the *Edda* they are treated partly as gods and partly as human beings who came to be worshipped as gods, in *Ynglinga saga* they are consistently dealt with from the euhemeristic viewpoint, as human ancestors of the kings of Norway; and in *Ynglinga saga* the author does not, as in the *Edda*, combine Norse traditions with classical and biblical material. His concern in *Heimskringla* is with history, not mythology.

Snorri was the first Icelandic prose writer whose background is known who was not a cleric, though his ecclesiastical predecessors had been by no means uninterested in secular learning and he and his lay contemporaries were deeply imbued with Christian learning. But his outlook, though Christian, was predominantly secular. He seems to have belonged to a group of writers with interests in poetry and history, though there is no evidence that he presided over a 'school' of poets and scholars. He was a friend of Styrmir Kárason, a priest whose writings included a saga about S. Óláfr and a version of *Landnámabók*; his nephews Sturla Þórðarson and Óláfr hvítaskáld were both poets (the latter also a subdeacon) and Sturla compiled several historical works, while Óláfr was the author of the third *Grammatical Treatise* (in which classical rhetorical theory is applied to Icelandic verse), and may have written *Knytlinga saga*, a history of the Danish kings modelled on *Heimskringla*. Sturla Sighvatsson, another of Snorri's nephews, is said to have spent time at Snorri's home at Reykjaholt seeing to the copying of his uncle's historical writings (*Sturlunga saga* I. 299).

Snorri's books are a product of a particular social and cultural background, but they are also links in traditions of scholarly writing on various subjects that continue through the whole medieval period. *Heimskringla* is the high point in the evolution of Icelandic historical writing about the kings of Norway. The *Edda* forms part of two lines of development. One of its main concerns is language, and in this respect it belongs with the *Grammatical Treatises*, the first of which was written in the twelfth century and is mainly about orthography, while the fourth was written in the fourteenth century and, like the third, is about the rhetoric of poetry. But Snorri's mythography is also part of a continuing tradition. Mythological poems were still being written in the twelfth century and probably even later, and there is a fragment of a treatise on heathen religions in the fourteenth-century manuscript AM 162 m fol. (*SnE* II. 635–6), though in origin parts of this may be older than *Snorra Edda*.[2] The date of the first written collection of eddic poems is uncertain, but the idea of collecting and editing them may well have been suggested by Snorri's work in *Gylfaginning*, and it may also have inspired some of the writers of heroic sagas (*fornaldar sǫgur*) to include mythological material in their stories.

Like many other Icelanders, Snorri was interested in the past of his own people and in the ideas that had contributed to the development of the Icelandic civilization he knew. As a mythographer he was concerned to show that the attitudes and beliefs of his forebears were rational if unenlightened, and as a critic of

[2] See Stefán Karlsson, 'Ættbogi Noregskonunga', *Sjötíu ritgerðir helgaðar Jakobi Benediktssyni*, Reykjavík 1977, pp. 677–704.

poetry to show their culture as a highly developed art. His personal interest in mythology is apparent not only from his authorship of *Gylfaginning* and *Ynglinga saga*. In an anecdote in *Hákonar saga* (pp. 172–3), he is said to have composed a verse about Óðinn for Earl Skúli; and it seems from *Sturlunga saga* (I. 300, 327) that he called his booth at the Alþingi 'Valhǫll'. His prologue to *Gylfaginning* reveals that he was not just interested in mythology because it was important for the understanding of scaldic poetry: he there appears not only as a mythographer but also as a historian of religion, and his attitude to the heathen religion is almost as interesting as the mythology itself.

It was love of the traditional poetry of Scandinavia that was the underlying reason for the composition of the *Edda* as a whole. All parts of it are concerned largely with the kinds of poetry that had been cultivated in the north from at least the ninth century; but it was written at a time when both eddic and scaldic verse were declining in popularity. New kinds of poetry were being introduced from the south, among which the ballad, with its simpler metres and themes, was to be the most influential. Whether or not Snorri felt that the traditional forms of poetry he knew were under threat, his *Edda* was clearly written to encourage the study and composition of scaldic verse of the old type. One of its achievements is that we have in it not only an invaluable aid to the comprehension of early Scandinavian poetry, but also the texts of many verses and the contents of many myths that would otherwise have been lost.

The title

The original meaning of the word 'edda' as the title of Snorri's book is unknown, but references in fourteenth-century poems to 'eddu list' and 'eddu reglur' (art of edda, rules of edda) make it clear that at least by then the word was understood to mean 'poetics'.[3] That the name was used of Snorri's book in the Middle Ages is shown by the rubric in U quoted above, and by references to *Skáldskaparmál* and the prologue to *Gylfaginning* in AM 757 a 4to (*SnE* II. 532–3), and it is the usual name by which the work is referred to from the sixteenth century onwards. None of the other medieval manuscripts has any heading (only W and U contain the

[3] See A. Faulkes, 'Edda', *Gripla*, ii, Reykjavík 1977, 32–9.

beginning of the text) and it is uncertain whether the name was given the work by Snorri himself.

Snorri's *Edda* has often been thought of more as a mythological work than as a treatise on poetry, and so the word 'edda' has sometimes been regarded as meaning 'mythology'. When, therefore, the collection of traditional poems in the Codex Regius, GkS 2365 4to, was discovered in the seventeenth century the name *Edda* was also applied to that. Many of the mythological poems in that collection were recognized as the sources of Snorri's mythology in *Gylfaginning*, and it thus seemed to be an earlier version of Snorri's work. It was attributed, certainly mistakenly, to Sæmundr the wise, and came to be known as *Sæmundar Edda* or the *Elder* or *Poetic Edda*, to distinguish it from *Snorra Edda*, which is sometimes called the *Younger* or *Prose Edda*. (It is not in fact certain that Snorri's book was not compiled before the eddic poems were first collected together and written down.) The term eddic poetry is now used of the kind of poetry found in GkS 2365 4to, while the kind of poetry Snorri was concerned with in *Skáldskaparmál* and *Háttatal* is called scaldic poetry.

The prologue has no title in the manuscripts, but the name *Gylfaginning* appears in U (only), not in the initial rubric but at the end of the prologue. This name, which means 'deception (or tricking) of Gylfi', refers to the way Gylfi is treated at the end of the framing narrative (cf. also 7/25–7); but it also relates to the deception whereby the 'historical' Æsir convince the world that they are gods, and is a reminder that the stories Gylfi hears and evidently believes are not held by the author to be true. As he wrote in *Skáldskaparmál* (*SnE* I. 224): 'Eigi skulu kristnir menn trúa á heiðin goð ok eigi á sannindi þessar sagnar annan veg en svá sem hér finsk í upphafi bókar' (Christians must not believe in heathen gods, or in the truth of this account in any other way than in accordance with what is said at the beginning of this book (i.e. in the prologue to *Gylfaginning*)).

The contents of Snorri's *Edda*

Snorri's *Edda* is primarily a treatise on poetry. It is in three main parts, with a prologue in the form of a narrative prelude to the first part, *Gylfaginning*.

The third part, *Háttatal*, consists of a poem in 102 stanzas composed by Snorri in praise of King Hákon and Earl Skúli, in which each stanza illustrates a structural, stylistic, or metrical variation, with a commentary in prose explaining the techniques involved. The commentary, at least to begin with, is in dialogue form, though the speakers have no names or personalities. One reason for thinking that this was the first part of the *Edda* to be written is that the commentary includes a short analysis of poetic diction (*SnE* i. 600–8) which would have been redundant after *Skáldskaparmál* was composed.

The central section, *Skáldskaparmál*, is also the longest. It is an ambitious attempt to give a comprehensive account of the techniques of poetic diction, particularly as found in scaldic verse, and Snorri richly illustrates his analysis with quotations (usually consisting of half-stanzas of four lines each) from the work of earlier poets, many of whose poems are only preserved in Snorri's quotations in his *Edda* and in *Heimskringla* and must have been known to him mainly from oral tradition. His analysis is divided into two main parts, dealing with kennings (periphrastic descriptions) and *heiti* (poetical names) respectively, and some manuscripts also include collections of *þulur* (versified lists of *heiti*) which were probably mostly composed in the twelfth century. These may not have been included by Snorri, but some of them were evidently known to him. *Skáldskaparmál* also contains some narrative passages in which stories that are supposed to lie behind some of the poetical expressions discussed in the theoretical part of the work are told, and a preliminary narrative tells of the mythical origin of the mead of poetical inspiration. Some quite long passages of early narrative verse are quoted in connection with these stories in some manuscripts, and these too may be interpolations, though again Snorri certainly knew and used the poems from which they are taken even if he did not himself include the quotations in full.

Like *Háttatal*, *Skáldskaparmál* is cast in dialogue form, but here the speakers are given names: Bragi, god of poetry, gives the information; Ægir the sea-god is his questioner; and there is an introduction that sets the scene of their conversation. But, as in *Háttatal*, the dialogue becomes perfunctory in the course of the work and is abandoned towards the end. It may be that the speakers in *Skáldskaparmál* too were originally anonymous and that the introduction and first few narratives, where the dialogue between Ægir and Bragi is properly maintained, is really a separate section of the work, added by Snorri later (from the seventeenth century onwards the name *Bragarœður*, 'speeches of Bragi', has sometimes been used to distinguish this section). At any rate the material in *Skáldskaparmál* has not been fully assimilated to the dialogue setting; Bragi gives some information about himself and Ægir in the third person, in one case telling a story in which they both appear that takes place after the conversation in which he tells it (*SnE* I. 336–8). Perhaps Snorri had intended to revise this section completely.

There are some references to *Gylfaginning* and its prologue in *Skáldskaparmál* (*SnE* I. 224–6, cf. II. 533; I. 260, 262, 264, 270, 346). Although these would seem to indicate that *Gylfaginning* was written first, they may be later additions (they are not in all manuscripts), indicating perhaps that Snorri had begun to revise *Skáldskaparmál* after writing *Gylfaginning*. In one place in *Gylfaginning* there seems to be a reference to a story in *Skáldskaparmál* (see note to 25/29–30 below).

Gylfaginning is the part of the *Edda* in which Snorri's narrative powers are at their most developed, and where the device of the dramatic dialogue form is used most consistently and successfully, and so it assumed that it was written last. It contains a series of stories about the Norse gods arranged chronologically to cover their history from the creation of the world to its end (the twilight of the gods) and subsequent rebirth. The relevance of this part to the rest of the *Edda* and to the purpose of the whole as an art of poetry is not immediately apparent, but it is likely that it is an extension of the narratives included in *Skáldskaparmál*, and is intended to present in a systematic way the entire mythological background to the numerous mythological terms that form part of the poetic language discussed in *Skáldskaparmál*. Scaldic verse, in the earlier stages of its development, had been closely associated with the heathen religion, in both its subject-matter and diction, and many early poets had believed that poetry was the gift of the heathen gods and had originated with them.[4] Nevertheless it is true that many of the stories in *Gylfaginning* have little to do with poetry and must have been included mainly for the sake of completeness, or even just to provide entertainment.

[4] See *Gylf*, pp. 25/20–23 and 34/15 below; *SnE* I. 266; *Hkr* I. 17; *ÍF* II. 256; and cf. G. Kreutzer, *Die Dichtungslehre der Skalden*, Meisenheim am Glan 1977, pp. 109 and 185–95.

Models and sources

There were no precedents for Snorri's *Edda* as a comprehensive treatise on the metre and diction of vernacular poetry either in Scandinavian literature or elsewhere in Europe. Irish is the only other language in which treatises existed on native poetry in the Middle Ages, and it is unlikely that Snorri knew any of those. Several *artes poeticae* were composed in France and England in the twelfth and thirteenth centuries, but these were primarily concerned with Latin poetry, and though acquaintance with some of them might have been one of the factors that prompted the writing of the *Edda*, Snorri's treatment does not have much in common with them.[5] *Háttatal*, however, is somewhat similar to the treatise *De centum metris* of Servius, and the manner of its commentary is reminiscent of some early rhetorical treatises, while a number of the distinctions made in it are rather like those of traditional Latin grammar.[6] But for this part of the *Edda* there was a forerunner closer at hand in *Háttalykill*, a poem said to have been composed in the twelfth century by the Orkney poet Rǫgnvaldr kali (Norwegian by origin) and the Icelander Hallr Þórarinsson in which various scaldic metres were exemplified.[7] It does not survive complete, but in 82 extant verses or fragments 41 different metres are used. It does not seem that any commentary existed, however, and Snorri's work is both more ambitious and more clearly theoretical and analytical.

Skáldskaparmál was also a pioneering work, though some of Snorri's terminology again may be based on that of Latin works on rhetoric and grammar, and the analysis of scaldic diction in it may be based on traditional theories worked out by earlier Icelandic poets.[8] In any case it may be assumed that the composition of the

[5] E. Faral, *Les Arts poétiques du XII*e *et du XIII*e *siècle*, Paris 1924.

[6] See *Grammatici Latini*, iv, ed. H. Keil, Lipsiae 1864, pp. 456–67; Fortunatianus, *Ars rhetorica*, iii.1, ed. C. Halm, *Rhetores Latini minores*, Lipsiae 1863, pp. 120–1; Snorri's *setning, leyfi, fyrirboðning* (*SnE* i. 594) seems to correspond to *pars praeceptiva, pars permissiva*, and *pars prohibitiva* in Latin grammar and rhetoric; see *Den tredje og fjærde grammatiske afhandling*, ed. B. M. Olsen, København 1884, p. xvi.

[7] *Háttalykill enn forni*, ed. Jón Helgason and A. Holtsmark, København 1941 (Bibliotheca Arnamagnæana, i).

[8] See Halldór Halldórsson, *Old Icelandic heiti in Modern Icelandic*, Reykjavík 1975, pp. 11–30. The self-consciousness of early Scandinavian poets is well revealed by G. Kreutzer, op. cit. (note 4 above). Cf. G. Turville-Petre, *Haraldr the Hard-ruler and his Poets*, London 1968, pp. 12–13.

work was preceded by a good deal of learned discussion with friends interested in poetic theory. But Snorri was the first to set a theory down in writing; he had successors in the authors of the third and fourth *Grammatical Treatises*, though their methods and aims were different from his. Before *Skáldskaparmál* there existed, as far as is known, only some versified lists of words, names, and kennings (*þulur*), probably intended as aids to memory for poets, and the poem *Alvíssmál* (*PE* 129–34); it is uncertain when these were first written down. The age of the short list of kennings in prose in the fragmentary manuscripts AM 748 I 4to and 757 a 4to (*SnE* II. 428–32, 511–15) is also unknown, but this too lacks any kind of theoretical analysis.

Gylfaginning is unique among the mythographical writings of the Middle Ages. Just as *Skáldskaparmál* and *Háttatal* are unusual not only in being in the vernacular, but also in being concerned with vernacular poetry, so *Gylfaginning* is the only medieval treatise that deals comprehensively with the gods of the Germanic races rather than the Greek and Roman ones. There are brief mentions of the Germanic gods in Anglo-Saxon in the homilies *De falsis diis* of Ælfric and Wulfstan, but their only similarity to Snorri's treatment is the use of the euhemeristic interpretation of heathen gods as being really human beings; and Snorri's work quite lacks their polemical attitude to heathendom.[9] His almost humanistic detachment and his respect for antiquity make him in fact much more like the Latin mythographers of the Middle Ages, although unlike them he is not much interested in allegorical or symbolic interpretation of myth.[10] Having given a blanket explanation of the origin and significance of his material in the prologue (a subject to which he returns at the end of *Gylfaginning* and in *Skáldskaparmál, SnE* I. 224–8), he narrates his myths (through the mouths of his characters) as myths, entirely without comment and without attempting to use them for any moral purpose. There are only occasional traces of a tendency towards

[9] *Homilies of Ælfric, A Supplementary Collection*, ed. J. C. Pope, II, Oxford 1968 (Early English Text Society No. 260), pp. 667–724; *The Homilies of Wulfstan*, ed. D. Bethurum, Oxford 1957, pp. 220–4. There is an Icelandic translation of the former in *Hauksbók* 1892–6, pp. 156–64; see A. Taylor, 'Hauksbok and Ælfric's De Falsis Diis', *Leeds Studies in English*, New Series, iii (1969), 101–9.

[10] See Fulgentius, *Mitologiae*, ed. R. Helm in *Fabii Planciadis Fulgentii V. C. Opera*, Lipsiae 1898; *Fulgentius the Mythographer*, tr. L. G. Whitbread, Ohio 1971; *Scriptores rerum mythicarum Latini tres*, ed. G. H. Bode, Cellis 1834.

allegorical interpretation in *Gylfaginning*, e.g. at 27/18–22 and 29/31–30/7, where Snorri indulges in the widespread medieval practice of etymologizing names. Otherwise the only 'significance' the stories have is aetiological, for instance when Þórr's drinking feat is said to have been the origin of the tides (43/16; other examples at 28/9–10, 47/39, 48/22, 49/4,16). In contrast the main purpose of other medieval mythographers was to reinterpret heathen (i.e. in their case classical) myths as moral allegories. Snorri's matter-of-fact approach is much closer to that of earlier (and less well known) mythographers like Hyginus (probably second century), while his attempt to fit mythological tradition into a historical framework in the prologue (and in *Ynglinga saga*) shows his attitude to have something in common with that of Peter Comestor and Saxo Grammaticus.[11]

For some of the narrative parts of his *Edda* (as for much of *Heimskringla*) Snorri was indebted to the scholarly historians of the previous generation in Iceland. The account of the migration of the Æsir from Asia to Scandinavia in the prologue to *Gylfaginning* and various stories in *Skáldskaparmál* are derived from *Skjǫldunga saga*. Only extracts from this saga now survive in Icelandic, but an idea of its contents can be gained from the Latin version made at the end of the sixteenth century by Arngrímur Jónsson.[12] Like *Snorra Edda* it was probably based on oral stories in verse and prose together with literary sources such as the writings of Sæmundr the wise. The migration story seems to have developed in emulation of traditions found in Roman, Frankish, and British writings about the foundation of western nations by

---

[11] *Hygini Fabvlae*, ed. H. I. Rose, Lvgdvni Batavorvm 1934; *The Myths of Hyginus*, tr. M. Grant, Lawrence, Kansas 1960; Peter Comestor, *Historia Scholastica*, J. P. Migne, Patrologia Latina 198, Parisiis 1855, cols. 1116, 1124, etc. One might also compare the presentation of classical myths in the *Ecloga* of Theodulus (ed. J. Osternacher, Ripariae 1902), also in dialogue form and widely known in the Middle Ages; and in the introduction to the *Hauksbók* version of *Trójumanna saga*, ed. J. Louis-Jensen, Copenhagen 1963, pp. 1–5, though this may be later than *Snorra Edda*. On etymology and aetiology in *Gylf* see A. Holtsmark, *Studier i Snorres mytologi*, Oslo 1964, pp. 78–81.

[12] *Arngrimi Jonae Opera Latine Conscripta*, ed. Jakob Benediktsson, Hafniæ 1950–7 (Bibliotheca Arnamagnæana, IX–XII), I. 333 ff. (cf. IV. 107–17); see Jakob Benediktsson, 'Icelandic traditions of the Scyldings', *Saga-Book of the Viking Society*, xv (1957–61), 48–66. A fragment thought to be derived from the beginning of the saga ('Upphaf allra frásagna') is printed in *Fornmanna sögur*, XI, Kaupmannahøfn 1828, pp. 412–14.

survivors of the fall of Troy.[13] The connection of the Æsir with
Asia appears in various learned Icelandic writers from Ari onwards in association with the euhemeristic interpretation of the
heathen gods as human kings and the myths told about them as
perverted history. This interpretation lies behind the Scandinavian
genealogies that go back to the gods, such as the one appended to
Ari's *Íslendingabók* (*ÍF* I. 27–8), as well as being implicit in many of
the narratives of Saxo Grammaticus.

Snorri used various genealogies, some of them in verse, like
Ynglingatal and *Háleygjatal* (*Skj*. A I. 7–15, 68–71); both are quoted
in *Ynglinga saga*, the latter also in *Skáldskaparmál* and the
prologue to *Gylfaginning*. Others were in tabular form, and some
of the genealogy in the prologue is derived from English genealo-
gical tables. In both England and Iceland in the Middle Ages
genealogy was a product of learned antiquarian activity rather
than popular lore.[14]

Snorri may also have known a now lost 'Sigurðar saga' (an
earlier version of *Vǫlsunga saga* than the one that survives), and
taken from it information for the prologue to *Gylfaginning* and
parts of *Skáldskaparmál*. His reference to *Sigurðar saga* in *Háttatal*
(*SnE* I. 646), however, may be to the story of Sigurðr in general
rather than to a particular written version.

The knowledge of the Troy story, such as it is, shown in the
prologue and last chapter of *Gylfaginning* and in *Skáldskaparmál*
probably came principally from *Trójumanna saga*, an Icelandic
account of the Trojan war based on Latin sources.[15] The earlier
part of the prologue contains ideas that seem to show the influence
of various Latin writings, though it is uncertain whether Snorri
knew these at first hand.[16] But his adoption of such ideas, as well
as his linking of Scandinavian prehistory with classical legend,
shows that he was intent on making the Scandinavian past part of

[13] See A. Faulkes, 'Descent from the gods', *Medieval Scandinavia*, 11 (not yet
published).

[14] See A. Faulkes, 'The genealogies and regnal lists in a manuscript in Resen's
library', *Sjötíu ritgerðir helgaðar Jakobi Benediktssyni*, Reykjavík 1977, pp. 177–90.

[15] See *Trójumanna saga*, ed. J. Louis-Jensen, Copenhagen 1963, p. xi; *Hauksbók* 1960, p. xv.

[16] See U. and P. Dronke, 'The prologue of the prose Edda: explorations of a
Latin background', *Sjötíu ritgerðir helgaðar Jakobi Benediktssyni*, Reykjavík 1977,
pp. 153–76; A. Faulkes, 'Pagan sympathy: attitudes to heathendom in the prologue
to Snorra Edda', in *Edda, A collection of essays*, Manitoba (not yet published).

the European past, and on fitting native traditions into a European context.

In using the dialogue form to present his material in the three main parts of his treatise, Snorri was following a practice almost standard in learned treatises in the Middle Ages; it appears for instance in the dialogues of Gregory the Great, in the *Elucidarius* of Honorius Augustodunensis (both of which existed in Icelandic translations in Snorri's time), and in *Konungs skuggsjá*.[17] But some of the poems of the *Elder Edda* also present mythological information in dialogue form, and with the older poems of this kind there can be no question of the influence of learned treatises. There seems to have been an ancient Scandinavian tradition of composing poems of mythological instruction as dialogues or dramatic monologues. The closest parallel to *Gylfaginning* is *Vafþrúðnismál* (which is also a contest of wisdom) in which Óðinn gives information about the gods in third-person narrative; but there are similar devices in several other eddic poems, such as *Grímnismál, Baldrs draumar*, and *Vǫluspá*. The presentation of the series of riddles in *Heiðreks saga*, too, is reminiscent of *Gylfaginning*, though in its present form the saga may have been compiled later than *Snorra Edda*. *Skáldskaparmál* and *Háttatal*, where the dialogue form is used rather perfunctorily, are much more like the learned treatises, but *Gylfaginning*, where it is used in a dramatic and effective way, is closer to the tradition of the dialogue poems. Snorri has even succeeded in differentiating the roles of Hár, Jafnhár, and Þriði, particularly at 8/33–9/5 and 36/27–37/2.

The actual story that forms the frame of *Gylfaginning* seems to be Snorri's invention, but in many respects, particularly the conclusion, it is like the episode of Þórr and Útgarðaloki (see 43/30–5) and may be based on it. Gylfi as an opponent of the Æsir in Sweden was probably suggested by the story of Gefjun and Gylfi embodied in the verse from Bragi's *Ragnarsdrápa* quoted at

[17] *Heilagra manna sǫgur*, ed. C. R. Unger, Christiania 1877, ii. 179–255; 'Brudstykker af den islandske Elucidarius', ed. Konráð Gíslason, *Annaler for Nordisk Oldkyndighed og Historie*, 1858, pp. 51–172; see the introduction to *The Arna-Magnæan Manuscript 674 A, 4to*, Copenhagen 1957 (Manuscripta Islandica, 4); *Konungs skuggsiá*, ed. L. Holm-Olsen, Oslo 1945. Both Alcuin, *De rhetorica* (*Rhetores Latini minores*, ed. C. Halm, Lipsiae 1863, pp. 523–50) and Aldhelm, *De metris* (*Opera*, ed. R. Ehwald, Berolini 1919, Monumenta Germaniae historica, Auctores Antiquissimi xv, pp. 59–204), also use dialogue form.

7/12–19; this may possibly have been in *Skjǫldunga saga*. The first
verse of *Hávamál* is quoted at the beginning of *Gylfaginning* and
there is an allusion to the last verse at the end (54/30), though it is
uncertain whether this poem existed in the form in which it
appears in *PE* before Snorri wrote *Gylfaginning*. Hár, Jafnhár,
and Þriði are all names of Óðinn in *Grímnismál*, but then so is
Gangleri, so the identification of the three representatives of the
Æsir in *Gylfaginning* with Óðinn is by no means certain. Nevertheless we are probably right to assume that Gylfi's three-in-one
informant is a trinity representing aspects of Óðinn, but it is then
the Óðinn of the prologue, the 'historical' euhemerized king of the
human Æsir in their migration from Tyrkland, not the god who
appears in the myths within the dialogue. It is only at the end of
Gylfaginning that the human Æsir deliberately identify themselves
with the gods.

Many of the stories told in *Gylfaginning* are based on poems of
the *Elder Edda*, and many verses from such poems are quoted
within the dialogue. *Vǫluspá*, the first poem in the Codex Regius,
contains a series of myths organized into a chronological scheme
beginning with creation and ending with the destruction of the
world and its renewal, and it is clearly on this poem that Snorri
based the outline of the plan of *Gylfaginning*, as well as a number
of the stories in it (the scheme is also, of course, like that of the
Bible). Besides *Vǫluspá*, the poems most frequently used are
Vafþrúðnismál and *Grímnismál*. The texts of Snorri's quotations
from eddic poems are in some places quite different from the other
texts we have of them, which are all in manuscripts written after
his time. It is possible that he used an earlier manuscript that is
now lost, but it may be that he knew the poems only from oral
tradition. As an attempt at a scholarly systematization of traditional legends, *Gylfaginning* is a result of the same antiquarian
movement that gave rise to the collecting and copying of traditional poems in the *Elder Edda*, and it is uncertain which came first.

Other eddic poems are also used occasionally, and in some cases
verses are quoted from poems that otherwise have not survived
(e.g. in the story of Njǫrðr and Skaði, 24/3–15). Some material is
derived from scaldic poems (see for example the note to 45/10),
but there are no quotations from scaldic verse within the dialogue
(two appear in the introductory frame story; cf. note to 34/16–24).
There is quite a lot of material, however, for which no source is

known (e.g. the story of Þórr and Útgarðaloki, pp. 37–43). Since Snorri does not quote every verse he uses when he is following known poems, many of the stories that do not survive elsewhere may be based on poems or parts of poems that are now lost. But it is also possible that oral stories in prose on mythological subjects existed in the thirteenth century, though little can be known for certain about them. A number of Snorri's stories are similar to ones told by Saxo Grammaticus and must have a common source which need not in every case have been in verse.

There is no reason to believe, however, that everything in *Gylfaginning* is derived from ancient tradition, whether oral or written. Snorri was a Christian and had only a scholar's and an artist's interest in mythology; he was preserving it for antiquarian not religious reasons. In *Heimskringla* he treated even his historical sources with a certain freedom, and clearly he would not have felt it wrong to depart from or expand his sources in *Gylfaginning* too if artistic or other considerations required it, and he would probably not have felt inhibited from inventing new stories or drastically altering old ones if he saw fit.

Moreover it is unlikely that Snorri gives a very accurate picture of Norse mythology as a whole. Both *Vǫluspá* and *Gylfaginning* treat heathen mythology in a systematic way which was surely alien from the nature of the heathen religion itself, which must have consisted rather of a disorganized body of conflicting traditions that was probably never reduced in heathen times to a consistent orthodoxy such as Snorri attempts to present. His account of it is coloured by his Christian education which would have taught him to expect a religion to be a system of coherent beliefs; and in other ways too it is clear that his Christian attitudes have influenced his presentation of heathen myth. At the beginning of *Gylfaginning* the heathen religion is presented as a perversion of the true faith, in accordance with the explanation of the origin of heathen religions given in the prologue, where they are said to have been developed by human beings using the 'earthly understanding' given them by God but without the benefit of spiritual wisdom. Several qualities attributed to Óðinn conform to the Christian conception of an almighty creator and giver of life and judge of mankind, but must be alien from actual ideas about Óðinn in heathen times (at any rate we find a rather different picture of him in *Ynglinga saga*). Snorri saw his heathen ancestors not as entirely misguided but as falling short of the truth, and their creed as a misguided reflection of Christian orthodoxy. He can hardly have taken his account of creation seriously (see especially 9/8), and it was evidently part of his purpose to reveal some of the limitations and childishness of heathen religion. Sometimes he has not even made much effort to reconcile contradictions between variant traditions (see note to 14/14–17; there are numerous other contradictions in *Gylfaginning* that may or may not be deliberate). He clearly enjoyed the comedy of some of his stories, which often seem almost parodies of popular lore (for instance the account of the origin of Naglfar, 50/4–7), and his irony is sometimes even directed against the principal figures of Norse mythology (e.g. at 36/28–31). There are also clear examples of his modification of tradition to accommodate it to Christian ideas, as when he puts the description of places of reward and torment after the account of *ragnarøkr* (on his use of this term see glossary), which as a consequence becomes very like the Christian doomsday, instead of before as in *Vǫluspá*. Snorri had an intimate knowledge of Norse mythology, but he did not reproduce that mythology unchanged, and his account needs to be handled with care by those who wish to use it to shed light on heathen religion.

Although within the dialogue in *Gylfaginning* the myths are presented as myths, without any imposed interpretation, the general treatment of mythology there is far from naïve. It is a scholarly systematization of traditional material which is incorporated into a European historical framework and adapted to a Christian scheme of ideas. The euhemeristic attitude to the gods, characteristic of historiography rather than theology in the Middle Ages, and the detached non-polemical treatment of myth mark the work as belonging to the humanistic tradition of learned Icelandic writing of the twelfth century as it was found in Ari and the author of *Skjǫldunga saga*; and the scholarly analysis and careful, schematized presentation of what must have been an amorphous mass of tradition in poetry and oral prose make the work comparable with that of the author of the first *Grammatical Treatise*. In narrative skill and stylistic assurance it can stand beside the best sagas of Icelanders, with which it shares also the device of presenting stories in prose with verses freely quoted as corroboration, some of them represented as being the actual comments of characters in the story. Like some *fornaldar sǫgur*,

Gylfaginning is largely a re-telling in prose of stories originally transmitted in verse. Moreover, the technique of the fictional narrator (and dramatized audience), which is rarely used elsewhere in medieval Icelandic prose narrative, and nowhere to such effect, adds considerable dimension and sophistication to the work.

Snorri shows a mixture of influences from the learned writings of the Christian Middle Ages and from the traditional northern world of myth and legend. But only a small part of his work can be considered a direct reflection of 'popular' lore. He writes in a literary way and much of his material is learned. Even the eddic poems he quotes so often may have come to him from an antiquarian library rather than from the lips of the people.

Manuscripts

There are four manuscripts with independent textual value that contain the prologue, *Gylfaginning*, *Skáldskaparmál*, and *Háttatal*. These are the Codex Regius (R, written about the middle of the first half of the fourteenth century), Codex Wormianus (W, written about the middle of the fourteenth century), Codex Trajectinus (T, written about 1600, but believed to be a copy of a medieval manuscript that no longer survives), and Codex Upsaliensis (U, written in the early fourteenth century). R and T have very similar texts, but W and U differ both from them and from each other, in some places quite considerably, both in wording and contents. The first leaf of R has been lost and it now lacks the beginning of the prologue (to 5/13 in this edition), and after *Háttatal* it has two poems, *Jómsvíkingadrápa* and *Málsháttakvæði*, which are not part of the *Edda*. T also lacks the beginning of the prologue (to 3/33) and the end of *Háttatal*. W includes long passages in the prologue that are not in the other manuscripts; these passages contain material from biblical and classical tradition and are thought to be interpolations. It also contains four *Grammatical Treatises* and part of the eddic poem *Rígsþula* (*PE* 141–51), which are not part of Snorri's *Edda*; but some narrative passages that appear in the first half of *Skáldskaparmál* in other manuscripts are lacking. The second half of *Skáldskaparmál* in W had been subject to extensive revision by a fourteenth-century redactor, but pages have been lost from this part of the manuscript and only fragments of this section now remain; the beginning and end of *Háttatal* are also missing. But where the contents of W correspond to R and T, it has a text more similar to them than to U.

The text in U is throughout very different from the others. It has been subject to extensive verbal shortening, with the result that in many places the text hardly makes sense. Various passages that are in the other manuscripts are lacking, and much of the material that is included is in a different order. *Háttatal* is incomplete. U also contains some miscellaneous material which, although it is not part of the *Edda*, is connected with Snorri Sturluson or reflects his interests, and could be derived from his papers. These are *Skáldatal* (a list of Scandinavian court poets, a version of which is also found in one of the manuscripts of *Heimskringla*), a genealogy of the Sturlung family to which Snorri belonged, a list of Icelandic lawspeakers ending with Snorri's name, and a version of the second *Grammatical Treatise*. Both W and U lack the *þulur* found at the end of *Skáldskaparmál* in R and T.

Fragments survive of three other medieval manuscripts that contain parts of *Skáldskaparmál* and *þulur*; it is impossible to say whether they once contained other sections of the work. The text in AM 748 II 4to, written about 1400, is very similar to that in R; here a second scribe has added a genealogy of the Sturlung family. AM 748 I 4to, written in the early fourteenth century, and AM 757 a 4to, written the late fourteenth century, contain parts of a redaction of *Skáldskaparmál* and a collection of *þulur* which are both rather different from what survives in other manuscripts, and they include an additional list of kennings that was probably not originally part of Snorri's *Edda*. AM 748 I 4to also contains part of a collection of eddic poems, parts of the third *Grammatical Treatise* and a fragment of a fifth, and the poem *Íslendingadrápa*; AM 757 a 4to has parts of the third *Grammatical Treatise* and various religious (Christian) poems. A fourth medieval fragment, AM 756 4to, written in the fifteenth century, contains parts of both *Gylfaginning* and *Skáldskaparmál* derived from W.

Independent texts of a good many of the scaldic verses in *Snorra Edda* are found in various other works, such as sagas of kings (including *Heimskringla*), sagas of Icelanders, and the *Grammatic-*

al Treatises. Most of the eddic poems quoted in *Gylfaginning* (including *Vsp, Vm,* and *Grm*) are found in the Codex Regius of the *Elder Edda*, written in the second half of the thirteenth century, and some (including *Grm* and part of *Vm*) are also in AM 748 I 4to (see above). There is another version of *Vǫluspá* in *Hauksbók* (early fourteenth century), but *Vǫluspá hin skamma* is only in *Flateyjarbók* (last quarter of the fourteenth century).

Numerous post-medieval manuscripts of the prose *Edda* exist. These are largely derived from the extant medieval manuscripts, but in some cases contain parts of the medieval versions that have since been lost, for example, some of the redaction of the second part of *Skáldskaparmál* in W and the beginning of the prologue in R. The texts in many of these later manuscripts have been subject to extensive alteration and interpolation, particularly in *Skáldskaparmál*, the section which in both the medieval and the renaissance period attracted most attention.

There has been much discussion as to whether U or R and T best preserve the *Edda* as it was written by Snorri, but there is little on which to base a rational judgement. U is probably the oldest manuscript (though only by a few years), and the material accompanying the *Edda* in U implies a close connection with Snorri himself; but the arrangement in this version seems, at least to most modern readers, less logical and artistic. Scholars are reluctant to attribute what seems to be an improvement in the version in R and T to scribal alteration, and yet if R and T are closer to the original it is difficult to see what could have prompted a scribe to alter an arrangement that seems satisfactory so as to produce the illogicality of U. A third possibility, which is attractive but incapable of proof, is that U is derived from a draft made by Snorri, in which he may have assembled his material on loose leaves, and that R and T (and W) are derived from a revised and perhaps expanded version also by Snorri. Both versions may then have been further altered by later hands. On the whole it seems best to admit that the manuscripts preserve various compilations based on the lost work of Snorri Sturluson, each of which has its own interest and value.

Attempts have also been made to establish a stemma of the relationships of the principal manuscripts, but these have resulted in little agreement.[18] While R, T, and AM 748 II 4to clearly form one group and AM 748 I 4to and AM 757 a 4to another, the relationships of these groups to W and U are more complicated than a conventional stemma can indicate. Moreover there are large parts of the text that are not in all manuscripts, and even when they run parallel there is often little verbal correspondence, especially between U and the others, and there is no reliable way of determining which manuscripts have the more original readings. Taking into account also the span of time and possible number of copies between the author's original and the earliest extant manuscripts, it is clear that it is impossible to reconstruct an archetype with any confidence. Therefore it seems best to base a text on a single manuscript, emending it from one of the others only where it fails to make acceptable sense. Of the medieval manuscripts that contain *Gylfaginning*, R has the most coherent text and shows the least signs of scribal alteration and has therefore been chosen as the basis of this edition. Minor slips of the pen have been corrected silently and odd letters lost through damage to the manuscript have been supplied, but all other departures from the text of R are noted in the textual notes. The beginning of the prologue (to 5/13) is supplied from seventeenth-century manuscripts (K, N, Th, J) derived from R when it was complete.[19] For R, W, U, and *PE* the facsimile editions have been used; readings from other manuscripts are based on photographs kindly provided by Stofnun Árna Magnússonar á Íslandi.

The spelling (in the text, textual notes, and quotations in introduction and general notes), punctuation, word-division, use of capitals, paragraph division, and arrangement of verse-lines are editorial, but account has been taken of the punctuation and capitalization of the manuscripts in the placing of full stops, and of the use of large and ornamental capitals in making paragraph divisions. In the parts of the text based on seventeenth-century manuscripts modern word-forms have been modified to conform

---

[18] See *De Codex Trajectinus van de Snorra Edda*, ed. W. van Eeden, Leiden 1913, introduction; F. W. Müller, *Untersuchungen zur Uppsala-Edda*, Dresden 1941; *Edda Snorra Sturlusonar*, ed. Finnur Jónsson, København 1931, pp. xvii ff. (and references there); D. O. Zetterholm, *Studier i en Snorre-text*, Stockholm 1949 (Nordiska texter och undersökningar, 17); Snorri Sturluson, *Edda*, ed. A. Holtsmark and Jón Helgason, København 1950, pp. viii f.

[19] See A. Faulkes, 'The Prologue to Snorra Edda, An Attempt at Reconstruction', *Gripla*, iii, Reykjavík 1979, 204–13.

to medieval usage. The chapter numbering of *SnE* I has been added in the margins; in the prologue the numbers are not consecutive because the additional passages in W are included in that edition.

Bibliography

The best sources for Snorri's life are *Íslendinga saga* (in *Sturlunga saga*) and *Hákonar saga Hákonarsonar*, both by his nephew Sturla; and the sagas about Guðmundr Arason (*Biskupa sögur*, Kaupmannahöfn 1858–78, I. 405–618, II. 1–187). There are good accounts of him and his work in the introductions to *The Stories of the Kings of Norway by Snorri Sturlason*, tr. W. Morris and Eiríkur Magnússon, IV, London 1905 (The Saga Library, VI); and to *Heimskringla*, part 1, *The Olaf Sagas*, tr. S. Laing, rev. J. Simpson, London 1964, and part 2, *Sagas of the Norse Kings*, tr. S. Laing, rev. P. Foote, London 1961; and in G. Turville-Petre, *Origins of Icelandic Literature*, Oxford 1953, pp. 220–9.

The most influential discussions of Snorri's work this century have been in Sigurður Nordal, *Snorri Sturluson*, Reykjavík 1920; H. Kuhn, 'Das Nordgermanische Heidentum in den ersten Christlichen Jahrhunderten', *Zeitschrift für deutsches Altertum*, 79 (1942), 133–66 (reprinted in *Kleine Schriften*, Berlin 1969–72, II. 296–326); W. Baetke, *Die Götterlehre der Snorra-Edda*, Berlin 1952; and A. Holtsmark, *Studier i Snorres Mytologi*, Oslo 1964. Little has been written in English, but there are useful introductions to the facsimile edition of R by E. Wessén and to that of W by Sigurður Nordal. There are bibliographies of the *Prose Edda* in *Islandica*, xiii (1920) and xxxvii (1955), which can be supplemented from the periodical bibliographies in *Acta Philologica Scandinavica* up to 1962, and *Bibliography of Old Norse–Icelandic Studies* from 1963 onwards; see also *Kulturhistorisk leksikon for nordisk middelalder*, III, København 1958, pp. 479–80. The most useful edition is still *SnE* I–III, the first volume of which contains a Latin translation. *Edda Snorra Sturlusonar*, ed. Finnur Jónsson, København 1931, is more convenient, but has many inaccuracies and inconsistencies and is difficult to use. The edition by A. Holtsmark and Jón Helgason, København 1950, includes only parts of the text of *Gylfaginning* and *Skáldskaparmál*.

There are two modern English translations, neither of them

complete: *The Prose Edda by Snorri Sturluson*, tr. A. G. Brodeur,
New York 1916 (reprinted 1960), which does not include *Háttatal*
and omits part of *Skáldskaparmál*; and *The Prose Edda of Snorri
Sturluson*, tr. J. I. Young, Cambridge 1954 (reprinted 1973),
which has an introduction by Sigurður Nordal, but translates only
the text of the edition of A. Holtsmark and Jón Helgason, with the
addition of the prologue to *Gylfaginning*.

The best handbook of Scandinavian mythology in English is
MRN; but J. de Vries, *Altgermanische Religionsgeschichte*, I–II,
Berlin 1935–7 (extensively revised ed. 1956–7), and, for individual
mythological names, *Kulturhistorisk leksikon* (see above) should
also be consulted. P. A. Munch, *Norse Mythology*, tr. S. B.
Hustvedt, New York 1926, gives a useful survey of the material
but lacks the up-to-date bibliographical references in the latest
revision of Munch's Norwegian text by A. Holtsmark (*Norrøne
gude- og heltesagn*, Oslo 1967). There is commentary on the
important mythological poem *Vǫluspá* in the edition by Sigurður
Nordal, tr. B. S. Benedikz and J. McKinnell, Durham 1978.

Snorri Sturluson

Edda

PART I

[Prologue]

Almáttigr guð skapaði himin ok jǫrð ok alla þá hluti er þeim   1
fylgja, ok síðarst menn tvá er ættir eru frá komnar, Adam ok Evu,
ok fjǫlgaðisk þeira kynslóð ok dreifðisk um heim allan. En er fram
liðu stundir, þá ójafnaðisk mannfólkit: váru sumir góðir ok rétt
trúaðir, en myklu fleiri snerusk eptir girndum heimsins ok órœktu   5
guðs boðorð, ok fyrir því drekti guð heiminum í sjávargangi ok
ǫllum kvikvendum heimsins nema þeim er í ǫrkinni váru með Nóa.
Eptir Nóa flóð lifðu átta menn þeir er heiminn bygðu ok kómu frá
þeim ættir, ok varð enn sem fyrr at þá er fjǫlmentisk ok bygðisk
verǫldin þá var þat allr fjǫlði mannfólksins er elskaði ágirni fjár ok   10
metnaðar en afrœktusk guðs hlýðni, ok svá mikit gerðisk af því at
þeir vildu eigi nefna guð. En hverr mundi þá segja sonum þeira frá
guðs stórmerkjum? Svá kom at þeir týndu guðs nafni ok víðast um
verǫldina fansk eigi sá maðr er deili kunni á skapara sínum. En eigi
at síðr veitti guð þeim jarðligar giptir, fé ok sælu, er þeir skyldu við   15
vera í heiminum. Miðlaði hann ok spekina svá at þeir skilðu alla
jarðliga hluti ok allar greinir þær er sjá mátti loptsins ok
jarðarinnar. Þat hugsuðu þeir ok undruðusk hverju þat mundi
gegna at jǫrðin ok dýrin ok fuglarnir hǫfðu saman eðli í sumum
hlutum ok var þó ólíkt at hætti. Þat var eitt eðli at jǫrðin var   20
grafin í hám fjalltindum ok spratt þar vatn upp ok þurfti þar eigi
lengra at grafa til vaz en í djúpum dǫlum. Svá eru ok dýr ok fuglar,
at jafnlangt er til blóðs í hǫfði ok fótum. Ǫnnur náttúra er sú
jarðar at á hverju ári vex á jǫrðunni gras ok blóm ok á sama ári
fellr þat allt ok fǫlnar. Svá eru ok dýr ok fuglar, at þeim vex hár ok   25
fjaðrar ok fellr af á hverju ári. Þat er hin þriðja náttúra jarðar þá er
hon er opnuð ok grafin þá grœr gras á þeiri moldu er efst er á
jǫrðunni. Bjǫrg ok steina þýddu þeir á móti tǫnnum ok beinum
kvikvenda. Af þessu skilðu þeir svá at jǫrðin væri kyk ok hefði líf
með nokkurum hætti, ok þat vissu þeir at hon var furðuliga gǫmul   30
at aldartali ok máttug í eðli. Hon fœddi ǫll kvikvendi ok hon
eignaðisk allt þat er dó. Fyrir þá sǫk gáfu þeir henni nafn ok tǫlðu
ættir sínar til hennar. Þat sama spurðu þeir af gǫmlum frændum
sínum at síðan er talið váru mǫrg hundruð vetra þá var in sama
jǫrð, sól ok himintungl. En gangr himintunglanna var ójafn, áttu   35
sum lengra gang en sum skemra. Af þvílíkum hlutum grunaði þá at

nokkurr mundi vera stjórnari himintunglanna sá er stilla mundi
gang þeira at vilja sínum, ok mundi sá vera ríkr mjǫk ok máttugr;
ok þess væntu þeir, ef hann réði fyrir hǫfuðskepnunum, at hann
mundi fyrr verit hafa en himintunglin; ok þat sá þeir, ef hann réði
5 gang himintunglanna, at hann mundi ráða skini sólar ok dǫgg
loptsins ok ávexti jarðarinnar er því fylgir, ok slíkt sama vindinum
loptsins ok þar með stormi sævarins. Þá vissu þeir eigi hvar ríki
hans var. Af því trúðu þeir at hann réð ǫllum hlutum á jǫrðu ok í
lopti, himins ok himintunglum, sævarins ok veðranna. En til þess
10 at heldr mætti frá segja eða í minni festa þá gáfu þeir nafn með
sjálfum sér ǫllum hlutum ok hefir þessi átrúnaðr á marga lund
2 breyzk svá sem þjóðirnar skiptusk ok tungurnar greindusk. En alla
hluti skilðu þeir jarðligri skilningu þvíat þeim var eigi gefin andlig
spekðin. Svá skilðu þeir at allir hlutir væri smíðaðir af nokkuru
15 efni.
3 Verǫldin var greind í þrjár hálfur. Frá suðri í vestr ok inn at
Miðjarðarsjá, sá hlutr var kallaðr Affrica. Hinn syðri hlutr þeirar
deildar er heitr ok brunninn af sólu. Annarr hlutr frá vestri ok til
norðrs ok inn til hafsins, er sá kallaðr Evropa eða Enea. Hinn
20 nyrðri hlutr er þar kaldr svá at eigi vex gras ok eigi má byggja. Frá
norðri ok um austrhálfur allt til suðrs, þat er kallat Asia. Í þeim
hlut veraldar er ǫll fegrð ok prýði ok eign jarðar ávaxtar, gull ok
gimsteinar. Þar er ok mið verǫldin; ok svá sem þar er jǫrðin fegri
ok betri at ǫllum kostum en í ǫðrum stǫðum, svá var ok mannfólk-
25 it þar mest tignat af ǫllum giptum, spekinni ok aflinu, fegrðinni
ok alls kostar kunnustu.
4 Nær miðri verǫldunni var gǫrt þat hús ok herbergi er ágætast
hefir verit, er kallat var Troja. Þat kǫllum vér Tyrkland. Þessi staðr
var myklu meiri gǫrr en aðrir ok með meira hagleik á marga lund
30 með kostnaði ok fǫngum er þar váru til. Þar váru tólf konung-
dómar ok einn yfirkonungr ok lágu mǫrg þjóðlǫnd til hvers
konungdóms. Þar váru í borginni tólf hǫfuðtungur. Þessir
hǫfðingjar hafa verit um fram aðra menn þá er verit hafa í verǫldu
um alla manndómliga hluti.
9 35 Einn konungr er þar var er nefndr Munon eða Mennon. Hann
átti dóttur hǫfuðkonungs Priami, sú hét Troan. Þau áttu son, hann
hét Tror, þann kǫllum vér Þór. Hann var at uppfœzlu í Thracia
með hertoga þeim er nefndr er Loricus. En er hann var tíu vetra þá
tók hann við vápnum fǫður síns. Svá var hann fagr álitum er hann
40 kom með ǫðrum mǫnnum sem þá er fíls bein er grafit í eik. Hár

hans er fegra en gull. Þá er hann var tólf vetra hafði hann fullt afl.
Þá lypti hann af jǫrðu tíu bjarnstǫkum ǫllum senn ok þá drap hann
Loricum fóstra sinn ok konu hans Lora eða Glora ok eignaði sér
ríkit Thracia. Þat kǫllum vér Þrúðheim. Þá fór hann víða um lǫnd
ok kannaði allar heims hálfur ok sigraði einn saman alla berserki   5
ok risa ok einn hinn mesta dreka ok mǫrg dýr. Í norðrhálfu heims
fann hann spákonu þá er Sibil hét, er vér kǫllum Sif, ok fekk
hennar. Engi kann at segja ætt Sifjar. Hon var allra kvenna fegrst,
hár hennar var sem gull. Þeira son var Loriði, er líkr var feðr
sínum, hans son var Einriði, hans son Vingeþórr, hans son   10
Vingenir, hans son Móða, hans son Magi, hans son Sescef, hans
son Beðvig, hans son Athra, er vér kǫllum Annan, hans son
Ítrmann, hans son Heremóð, hans son Scialdun, er vér kǫllum
Skjǫld, hans son Biaf, er vér kǫllum Bjár, hans son Jat, hans son
Guðólfr, hans son Finn, hans son Friallaf, er vér kǫllum Friðleif.   15
Hann átti þann son er nefndr er Voden, þann kǫllum vér Óðin.
Hann var ágætr maðr af speki ok allri atgervi. Kona hans hét
Frigida, er vér kǫllum Frigg. Óðinn hafði spádóm ok svá kona   10
hans, ok af þeim vísindum fann hann þat at nafn hans mundi uppi
vera haft í norðrhálfu heimsins ok tignat um fram alla konunga.   20
Fyrir þá sǫk fýstisk hann at byrja ferð sína af Tyrklandi ok hafði
með sér mikinn fjǫlða liðs, unga menn ok gamla, karla ok konur,
ok hǫfðu með sér marga gersemliga hluti. En hvar sem þeir fóru
yfir lǫnd, þá var ágæti mikit frá þeim sagt, svá at þeir þóttu líkari
goðum en mǫnnum. Ok þeir gefa eigi stað ferðinni fyrr en þeir   25
koma norðr í þat land er nú er kallat Saxland. Þar dvalðisk Óðinn
langar hríðir ok eignask víða þat land.

Þar setr Óðinn til lands gæzlu þrjá sonu sína; er einn nefndr
Veggdegg, var hann ríkr konungr ok réð fyrir Austr Saxalandi;
hans sonr var Vitrgils, hans synir váru þeir Vitta, faðir Heingests, 30
ok Sigarr, faðir Svebdegg, er vér kǫllum Svipdag. Annarr son
Óðins hét Beldegg, er vér kǫllum Baldr; hann átti þat land er nú
heitir Vestfal. Hans son var Brandr, hans son Frioðigar, er vér
kǫllum Fróða, hans son var Freovin, hans son Wigg, hans son
Gevis, er vér kǫllum Gavi. Inn þriði son Óðins er nefndr Siggi,   35
hans son Rerir. Þeir langfeðgar réðu þar fyrir er nú er kallat
Frakland, ok er þaðan sú ætt komin er kǫlluð er Vǫlsungar. Frá
ǫllum þessum eru stórar ættir komnar ok margar. Þá   11
byrjaði Óðinn ferð sína norðr ok kom í þat land er þeir kǫlluðu
Reiðgotaland ok eignaðisk í því landi allt þat er hann vildi. Hann   40

setti þar til landa son sinn er Skjǫldr hét, hans son hét Friðleifr, þaðan er sú ætt komin er Skjǫldungar heita, þat eru Danakonungar, ok þat heitir nu Jótland er þá var kallat Reiðgotaland.

Eptir þat fór hann norðr þar sem nú heitir Svíþjóð. Þar var sá
5 konungr er Gylfi er nefndr, en er hann spyrr til ferða þeira Asiamanna er Æsir váru kallaðir, fór hann móti þeim ok bauð at Óðinn skyldi slíkt vald hafa í hans ríki sem hann vildi sjálfr. Ok sá tími fylgði ferð þeira at hvar sem þeir dvǫlðusk í lǫndum, þá var þar ár ok friðr góðr, ok trúðu allir at þeir væri þess ráðandi, þvíat þat
10 sá ríkismenn at þeir váru ólíkir ǫðrum mǫnnum þeim er þeir hǫfðu sét at fegrð ok at viti. Þar þótti Óðni fagrir lands kostir ok kaus sér þar borgstað er nú heita Sigtúnir. Skipaði hann þar hǫfðingjum ok í þá líking sem verit hafði í Troja, setti tólf hǫfuðmenn í staðinum at dœma landslǫg, ok svá skipaði hann réttum ǫllum sem fyrr
15 hǫfðu verit í Troju ok Tyrkir váru vanir.

Eptir þat fór hann norðr þar til er sjár tók við honum, sá er þeir hugðu at lægi um ǫll lǫnd, ok setti þar son sinn til þess ríkis er nú heitir Nóregr. Sá er Sæmingr kallaðr, ok telja þar Nóregskonungar sínar ættir til hans ok svá jarlar ok aðrir ríkismenn, svá sem segir í
20 Háleygjatali. En Óðinn hafði með sér þann son sinn er Yngvi er nefndr, er konungr var í Svíþjóðu, ok eru frá honum komnar þær ættir er Ynglingar eru kallaðir. Þeir Æsir tóku sér kvánfǫng þar innan lands, en sumir sonum sínum, ok urðu þessar ættir fjǫlmennar, at umb Saxland ok allt þaðan um norðrhálfur
25 dreifðisk svá at þeira tunga, Asiamanna, var eigintunga um ǫll þessi lǫnd; ok þat þykkjask menn skynja mega af því at skrifuð eru langfeðga nǫfn þeira, at þau nǫfn hafa fylgt þessi tungu ok þeir Æsir hafa haft tunguna norðr hingat í heim, í Nóreg ok í Svíþjóð, í Danmǫrk ok í Saxland; ok í Englandi eru forn lands heiti eða staða
30 heiti þau er skilja má at af annarri tungu eru gefin en þessi.

[Gylfaginning]

Gylfi konungr réð þar lǫndum er nú heitir Svíþjóð. Frá honum er
þat sagt at hann gaf einni farandi konu at launum skemtunar sinnar
eitt plógsland í ríki sínu þat er fjórir øxn drœgi upp dag ok nótt.
En sú kona var ein af Ása ætt. Hon er nefnd Gefjun. Hon tók fjóra
øxn norðan ór Jǫtunheimum, en þat váru synir jǫtuns ok hennar, ok
setti þá fyrir plóg. En plógrinn gekk svá hart ok djúpt at upp leysti
landit, ok drógu øxninir þat land út á hafit ok vestr ok námu staðar
í sundi nokkvoru. Þar setti Gefjun landit ok gaf nafn ok kallaði
Selund. Ok þar sem landit hafði upp gengit var þar eptir vatn; þat
er nú Lǫgrinn kallaðr í Svíþjóð. Ok liggja svá víkr í Leginum sem
nes í Selundi. Svá segir Bragi skáld gamli:

> Gefjun dró frá Gylfa
> glǫð djúprǫðul ǫðla,
> svá at af rennirauknum
> rauk, Danmarkar auka.
> Báru øxn ok átta
> ennitungl þar er gengu
> fyrir vineyjar víðri
> valrauf, fjǫgur haufuð.

Gylfi konungr var maðr vitr ok fjǫlkunnigr. Hann undraðisk þat 20 2
mjǫk er Ásafólk var svá kunnigt at allir hlutir gengu at vilja þeira.
Þat hugsaði hann hvárt þat mundi vera af eðli sjálfra þeira, eða
mundi því valda goðmǫgn þau er þeir blótuðu. Hann byrjaði ferð
sína til Ásgarðs ok fór með laun ok brá á sik gamals manns líki ok
dulðisk svá. En Æsir váru því vísari at þeir hǫfðu spádóm, ok sá 25
þeir ferð hans fyrr en hann kom, ok gerðu í móti honum
sjónhverfingar. En er hann kom inn í borgina þá sá hann þar háva
hǫll, svá at varla mátti hann sjá yfir hana. Þak hennar var lagt
gyltum skjǫldum svá sem spánþak. Svá segir Þjóðólfr inn hvinverski at Valhǫll var skjǫldum þǫkð: 30

> Á baki létu blíkja,
> barðir váru grjóti,
> Sváfnis salnæfrar
> seggir hyggjandi.

Gylfi sá mann í hallar durunum ok lék at handsǫxum ok hafði sjau 35
senn á lopti. Sá spurði hann fyrr at nafni. Hann nefndisk Gangleri

ok kominn af refilstigum ok beiddisk at sœkja til náttstaðar ok
spurði hverr hǫllina ætti. Hann svarar at þat var konungr þeira.
'En fylgja má ek þér at sjá hann. Skaltu þá sjálfr spyrja hann
nafns.'

5   Ok snerisk sá maðr fyrir honum inn í hǫllina. En hann gekk
eptir, ok þegar lauksk hurðin á hæla honum. Þar sá hann mǫrg gólf
ok mart fólk, sumt með leikum, sumir drukku, sumir með vápnum
ok bǫrðusk. Þá litaðisk hann umb ok þótti margir hlutir ótrúligir
þeir er hann sá. Þá mælti hann:

10   'Gáttir allar
áðr gangi fram
um skygnask skyli
þvíat óvíst er at vita
hvar óvinir
15   sitja á fleti fyrir.'

Hann sá þrjú hásæti ok hvert upp frá ǫðru, ok sátu þrír menn,
sinn í hverju. Þá spurði hann hvert nafn hǫfðingja þeira væri. Sá
svarar er hann leiddi inn at sá er í inu nezta hásæti sat var konungr
ok heitir Hár, en þar næst sá er heitir Jafnhár, en sá ofarst er Þriði
20   heitir. Þá spyrr Hár komandann hvárt fleira er eyrindi hans, en
heimill er matr ok drykkr honum sem ǫllum þar í Háva hǫll. Hann
segir at fyrst vil hann spyrja ef nokkvorr er fróðr maðr inni. Hár
segir at hann komi eigi heill út nema hann sé fróðari, ok

'Stattu fram meðan þú fregn,
25   sitja skal sá er segir.'

3   Gangleri hóf svá mál sitt:
'Hverr er œztr eða elztr allra goða?'
Hár segir: 'Sá heitir Alfǫðr at váru máli, en í Ásgarði inum forna
átti hann tólf nǫfn. Eitt er Alfǫðr, annat er Herran eða Herjan,
30   þriðja er Nikarr eða Hnikarr, fjórða er Nikuz eða Hnikuðr, fimta
Fjǫlnir, sétta Óski, sjaunda Ómi, átta Bifliði eða Biflindi, níunda
Sviðarr, tíunda Sviðrir, ellipta Viðrir, tólfta Jálg eða Jálkr.'
Þá spyrr Gangleri: 'Hvar er sá guð, eða hvat má hann, eða hvat
hefir hann unnit framaverka?'
35   Hár segir: 'Lifir hann of allar aldir ok stjórnar ǫllu ríki sínu ok
ræðr ǫllum hlutum stórum ok smám.'
Þá mælir Jafnhár: 'Hann smíðaði himin ok jǫrð ok loptin ok alla
eign þeira.'
Þá mælti Þriði: 'Hitt er mest er hann gerði manninn ok gaf honum

ǫnd þá er lifa skal ok aldri týnask, þótt líkaminn fúni at moldu
eða brenni at ǫsku. Ok skulu allir menn lifa þeir er rétt eru siðaðir
ok vera með honum sjálfum þar sem heitir Gimlé eða Vingólf, en
vándir menn fara til Heljar ok þaðan í Niflhel, þat er niðr í inn
níunda heim.' 5

Þá mælir Gangleri: 'Hvat hafðisk hann áðr at en himinn ok jǫrð
væri gǫr?'

Þá svarar Hár: 'Þá var hann með hrímþursum.'

Gangleri mælti: 'Hvat var upphaf? Eða hversu hófsk? Eða hvat **4**
var áðr?' 10

Hár svarar: 'Svá sem segir í Vǫluspá:

Ár var alda
þat er ekki var.
Vara sandr né sær
né svalar unnir. 15
Jǫrð fansk eigi
né upphiminn,
gap var ginnunga
en gras ekki.'

Þá mælir Jafnhár: 'Fyrr var þat mǫrgum ǫldum en jǫrð var 20
skǫpuð er Niflheimr var gǫrr, ok í honum miðjum liggr bruðr sá er
Hvergelmir heitir, ok þaðan af falla þær ár er svá heita: Svǫl,
Gunnþrá, Fjǫrm, Fimbulþul, Slíðr ok Hríð, Sylgr ok Ylgr, Víð,
Leiptr; Gjǫll er næst Helgrindum.'

Þá mælir Þriði: 'Fyrst var þó sá heimr í suðrhálfu er Muspell heitir. 25
Hann er ljóss ok heitr. Sú átt er logandi ok brennandi, er hann ok
ófœrr þeim er þar eru útlendir ok eigi eigu þar óðul. Sá er Surtr
nefndr er þar sitr á lands enda til landvarnar. Hann hefir loganda
sverð, ok í enda veraldar mun hann fara ok herja ok sigra ǫll goðin
ok brenna allan heim með eldi. Svá segir í Vǫluspá: 30

Surtr ferr sunnan
með sviga lævi.
Skínn af sverði
sól valtíva.
Grjótbjǫrg gnata 35
en gífr rata.
Troða halir Helveg,
en himinn klofnar.'

Gangleri mælir: 'Hversu skipaðisk áðr en ættirnar yrði eða **5**
aukaðisk mannfólkit?' 40

Þá mælir Hár: 'Ár þær er kallaðar eru Élivágar, þá er þær váru

svá langt komnar frá uppsprettunni at eitrkvikja sú er þar fylgði harðnaði svá sem sindr þat er renn ór eldinum, þá varð þat íss, ok þá er sá íss gaf staðar ok rann eigi, þá héldi yfir þannig úr þat er af stóð eitrinu ok fraus at hrími, ok jók hrímit hvert yfir annat allt í
5   Ginnungagap.'

Þá mælti Jafnhár: 'Ginnungagap, þat er vissi til norðrs ættar, fyltisk með þunga ok hǫfugleik íss ok hríms ok inn í frá úr ok gustr. En hinn syðri hlutr Ginnungagaps léttisk móti gneistum ok síum þeim er flugu ór Muspellsheimi.'

10 Þá mælti Þriði: 'Svá sem kalt stóð af Niflheimi ok allir hlutir grimmir, svá var þat er vissi námunda Muspelli heitt ok ljóst, en Ginnungagap var svá hlætt sem lopt vindlaust. Ok þá er mœttisk hrímin ok blær hitans svá at bráðnaði ok draup, ok af þeim kviku-dropum kviknaði með krapti þess er til sendi hitann, ok varð
15 manns líkandi, ok var sá nefndr Ymir. En hrímþursar kalla hann Aurgelmi, ok eru þaðan komnar ættir hrímþursa, svá sem segir í Vǫluspá hinni skǫmmu:

Eru vǫlur allar
frá Viðólfi,
20   vitkar allir
frá Vilmeiði,
en seiðberendr
frá Svarthǫfða,
allir jǫtnar
25   frá Ymi komnir.

En hér segir svá Vafþrúðnir jǫtunn

hvaðan Aurgelmir kom
með jǫtna sonum
fyrst, inn fróði jǫtunn:

30   "Þá er ór Élivágum
stukku eitrdropar
ok óx unz ór varð jǫtunn,
þar eru órar ættir
komnar allar saman;
35   því er þat æ allt til atalt."'

Þá mælir Gangleri: 'Hvernig óxu ættir þaðan eða skapaðisk svá at fleiri menn urðu, eða trúir þú þann guð er nú sagðir þú frá?'

Þá svarar Hár: 'Fyr øngan mun játum vér hann guð. Hann var
40 illr ok allir hans ættmenn. Þá kǫllum vér hrímþursa. Ok svá er sagt

at þá er hann svaf, fekk hann sveita. Þá óx undir vinstri hǫnd
honum maðr ok kona, ok annarr fótr hans gat son við ǫðrum. En
þaðan af kómu ættir. Þat eru hrímþursar. Hinn gamli hrímþurs,
hann kǫllum vér Ymi.'

Þá mælir Gangleri: 'Hvar bygði Ymir eða við hvat lifði hann?' 5 6
'Næst var þat, þá er hrímit draup, at þar varð af kýr sú er
Auðhumla hét, en fjórar mjólkár runnu ór spenum hennar, ok
fœddi hon Ymi.'

Þá mælir Gangleri: 'Við hvat fœddisk kýrin?'

Hár segir: 'Hon sleikti hrímsteinana, er saltir váru. Ok hinn 10
fyrsta dag er hon sleikti steina kom ór steininum at kveldi manns
hár, annan dag manns hǫfuð, þriðja dag var þar allr maðr. Sá er
nefndr Búri. Hann var fagr álitum, mikill ok máttugr. Hann gat
son þann er Borr hét. Hann fekk þeirar konu er Bestla hét, dóttir
Bǫlþorns jǫtuns, ok fengu þau þrjá sonu. Hét einn Óðinn, annarr 15
Vili, þriði Vé. Ok þat er mín trúa at sá Óðinn ok hans brœðr munu
vera stýrandi himins ok jarðar; þat ætlum vér at hann muni svá
heita. Svá heitir sá maðr er vér vitum mestan ok ágæztan, ok vel
megu þér hann láta svá heita.'

Þá mælir Gangleri: 'Hvat varð þá um þeira sætt, eða hvárir váru 20 7
ríkari?'

Þá svarar Hár: 'Synir Bors drápu Ymi jǫtun. En er hann fell, þá
hljóp svá mikit blóð ór sárum hans at með því drektu þeir allri ætt
hrímþursa, nema einn komsk undan með sínu hýski. Þann kalla
jǫtnar Bergelmi. Hann fór upp á lúðr sinn ok kona hans ok helzk 25
þar, ok eru af þeim komnar hrímþursa ættir, svá sem hér segir:

> Ørófi vetra
> áðr væri jǫrð skǫpuð,
> þá var Bergelmir borinn;
> þat ek fyrst of man
> er sá hinn fróði jǫtunn
> á var lúðr of lagiðr.' 30

Þá svarar Gangleri: 'Hvat hǫfðusk þá at Bors synir, ef þú trúir at 8
þeir sé guð?'

Hár segir: 'Eigi er þar lítit af at segja. Þeir tóku Ymi ok fluttu í 35
mitt Ginnungagap, ok gerðu af honum jǫrðina, af blóði hans sæinn
ok vǫtnin. Jǫrðin var gǫr af holdinu en bjǫrgin af beinunum, grjót
ok urðir gerðu þeir af tǫnnum ok jǫxlum ok af þeim beinum er
brotin váru.'

Þá mælir Jafnhár: 'Af því blóði er ór sárum rann ok laust fór, þar 40

af gerðu þeir sjá þann er þeir gerðu ok festu saman jǫrðina, ok
lǫgðu þann sjá í hring útan um hana, ok mun þat flestum manni
ófœra þykkja at komask þar yfir.'

Þá mælir Þriði: 'Tóku þeir ok haus hans ok gerðu þar af himin ok
5 settu hann upp yfir jǫrðina með fjórum skautum, ok undir hvert
horn settu þeir dverg. Þeir heita svá: Austri, Vestri, Norðri, Suðri.
Þá tóku þeir síur ok gneista þá er lausir fóru ok kastat hafði ór
Muspellsheimi, ok settu á miðjan Ginnungahimin bæði ofan ok
neðan til at lýsa himin ok jǫrð. Þeir gáfu staðar ǫllum eldingum,
10 sumum á himni, sumar fóru lausar undir himni, ok settu þó þeim
stað ok skǫpuðu gǫngu þeim. Svá er sagt í fornum vísindum at
þaðan af váru dœgr greind ok áratal, svá sem segir í Vǫluspá:

> Sól þat ne vissi
> hvar hon sali átti.
15 Máni þat ne vissi
> hvat hann megins átti.
> Stjǫrnur þat ne vissu
> hvar þær staði áttu.

Svá var áðr en þetta væri of jǫrð.'
20 Þá mælir Gangleri: 'Þettu eru mikil tíðindi er nú heyri ek. Furðu
mikil smíð er þat ok hagliga gert. Hvernig var jǫrðin háttuð?'
Þá svarar Hár: 'Hon er kringlótt útan, ok þar útan um liggr hinn
djúpi sjár, ok með þeiri sjávar strǫndu gáfu þeir lǫnd til bygðar
jǫtna ættum. En fyrir innan á jǫrðunni gerðu þeir borg umhverfis
25 heim fyrir ófriði jǫtna, en til þeirar borgar hǫfðu þeir brár Ymis
jǫtuns, ok kǫlluðu þá borg Miðgarð. Þeir tóku ok heila hans ok
kǫstuðu í lopt ok gerðu af skýin, svá sem hér segir:

> Ór Ymis holdi
> var jǫrð of skǫpuð,
30 en ór sveita sjár,
> bjǫrg ór beinum,
> baðmr ór hári,
> en ór hausi himinn;

35 En ór hans brám
> gerðu blíð regin
> Miðgarð manna sonum,
> en ór hans heila
> váru þau hin harðmóðgu
40 ský ǫll of skǫpuð.'

Þá mælir Gangleri: 'Mikit þótti mér þeir hafa þá snúit til leiðar   9
er jǫrð ok himinn var gert ok sól ok himintungl váru sett ok skipt
dœgrum—ok hvaðan kómu menninir þeir er heim byggja?'
Þá svarar Hár: 'Þá er þeir Bors synir gengu með sævar strǫndu,
fundu þeir tré tvau, ok tóku upp tréin ok skǫpuðu af menn. Gaf   5
hinn fyrsti ǫnd ok líf, annarr vit ok hrœring, þriði ásjónu, málit ok
heyrn ok sjón; gáfu þeim klæði ok nǫfn. Hét karlmaðrinn Askr, en
konan Embla, ok ólusk þaðan af mannkindin þeim er bygðin var
gefin undir Miðgarði. Þar næst gerðu þeir sér borg í miðjum heimi
er kallaðr er Ásgarðr. Þat kǫllum vér Troja. Þar bygðu guðin ok   10
ættir þeira ok gerðusk þaðan af mǫrg tíðindi ok greinir bæði á
jǫrðunni ok í lopti. Þar er einn staðr er Hliðskjálf heitir, ok þá er
Óðinn settisk þar í hásæti þá sá hann of alla heima ok hvers manns
athæfi ok vissi alla hluti þá er hann sá. Kona hans hét Frigg
Fjǫrgvinsdóttir, ok af þeira ætt er sú kynslóð komin er vér kǫllum   15
Ása ættir, er bygt hafa Ásgarð hinn forna ok þau ríki er þar liggja
til, ok er þat allt goðkunnig ætt. Ok fyrir því má hann heita
Alfǫðr at hann er faðir allra goðanna ok manna ok alls þess er af
honum ok hans krapti var fullgert. Jǫrðin var dóttir hans ok kona
hans. Af henni gerði hann hinn fyrsta soninn, en þat er Ásaþórr.   20
Honum fylgði afl ok sterkleikr. Þar af sigrar hann ǫll kvikvendi.
'Nǫrfi eða Narfi hét jǫtunn er bygði í Jǫtunheimum. Hann átti   10
dóttur er Nótt hét. Hon var svǫrt ok døkk sem hon átti ætt til. Hon
var gipt þeim manni er Naglfari hét. Þeira son hét Auðr. Því næst
var hon gipt þeim er Annarr hét. Jǫrð hét þeira dóttir. Síðarst átti   25
hana Dellingr, var hann Ása ættar. Var þeira son Dagr. Var hann
ljóss ok fagr eptir faðerni sínu. Þá tók Alfǫðr Nótt ok Dag son
hennar ok gaf þeim tvá hesta ok tvær kerrur ok setti þau upp á
himin at þau skulu ríða á hverjum tveim dœgrum umhverfis
jǫrðina. Ríðr Nótt fyrri þeim hesti er kallaðr er Hrímfaxi, ok at   30
morni hverjum døggvir hann jǫrðina af méldropum sínum. Sá
hestr er Dagr á heitir Skinfaxi, ok lýsir allt lopt ok jǫrðina af faxi
hans.'
Þá mælti Gangleri: 'Hversu stýrir hann gang sólar ok tungls?'   11
Hár segir: 'Sá maðr er nefndr Mundilfœri er átti tvau bǫrn. Þau   35
váru svá fǫgr ok fríð at hann kallaði annat Mána en dóttur sína Sól,
ok gipti hana þeim manni er Glenr hét. En guðin reiddusk þessu
ofdrambi ok tóku þau systkin ok settu upp á himin, létu Sól keyra
þá hesta er drógu kerru sólarinnar þeirar er guðin hǫfðu skapat til
at lýsa heimana af þeiri síu er flaug ór Muspellsheimi. Þeir hestar   40

14   Gylfaginning
```

heita svá: Árvakr ok Alsviðr. En undir bógum hestanna settu
goðin tvá vindbelgi at kœla þá, en í sumum frœðum er þat kallat
ísarnkol. Máni stýrir gǫngu tungls ok ræðr nýjum ok niðum. Hann
tók tvau bǫrn af jǫrðunni, er svá heita: Bil ok Hjúki, er þau gengu
5   frá brunni þeim er Byrgir heitir, ok báru á ǫxlum sér sá er heitir
Sœgr, en stǫngin Simul. Viðfinnr er nefndr faðir þeira. Þessi bǫrn
fylgja Mána, svá sem sjá má af jǫrðu.'

12      Þá mælir Gangleri: 'Skjótt ferr sólin, ok nær svá sem hon sé
hrædd, ok eigi mundi hon þá meir hvata gǫngunni at hon hræddisk
10  bana sinn.'
    Þá svarar Hár: 'Eigi er þat undarligt at hon fari ákafliga, nær
gengr sá er hana sœkir. Ok øngan útveg á hon nema renna undan.'
    Þá mælir Gangleri: 'Hverr er sá er henni gerir þann ómaka?'
    Hár segir: 'Þat eru tveir úlfar, ok heitir sá er eptir henni ferr
15  Skǫll. Hann hræðisk hon ok hann mun taka hana, en sá heitir Hati
Hróðvitnisson er fyrir henni hleypr, ok vill hann taka tunglit, ok
svá mun verða.'
    Þá mælir Gangleri: 'Hver er ætt úlfanna?'
    Hár segir: 'Gýgr ein býr fyrir austan Miðgarð í þeim skógi er
20  Járnviðr heitir. Í þeim skógi byggja þær trǫllkonur er Járnviðjur
heita. In gamla gýgr fœðir at sonum marga jǫtna ok alla í vargs
líkjum, ok þaðan af eru komnir þessir úlfar. Ok svá er sagt at af
ættinni verðr sá einn mátkastr er kallaðr er Mánagarmr. Hann
fyllisk með fjǫrvi allra þeira manna er deyja, ok hann gleypir tungl
25  ok støkkvir blóði himin ok lopt ǫll. Þaðan týnir sól skini sínu ok
vindar eru þá ókyrrir ok gnýja heðan ok handan. Svá segir í
Vǫluspá:

        Austr býr in aldna
        í Járnviði
30      ok fœðir þar
        Fenris kindir.
        Verðr ór þeim ǫllum
        einna nokkurr
        tungls tjúgari
35      í trǫlls hami.

        Fyllisk fjǫrvi
        feigra manna,
        rýðr ragna sjǫt
        rauðum dreyra.
40      Svǫrt verða sólskin
```

of sumur eptir,
veðr ǫll válynd.
Vituð ér enn eða hvat?'

Þá mælir Gangleri: 'Hver er leið til himins af jǫrðu?'   13
Þá svarar Hár ok hló við: 'Eigi er nú fróðliga spurt. Er þér eigi   5
sagt þat at guðin gerðu brú til himins af jǫrðu ok heitir Bifrǫst?
Hana muntu sét hafa, kann vera at þat kallir þú regnboga. Hon er
með þrim litum ok mjǫk sterk ok ger með list ok kunnáttu meiri en
aðrar smíðir. Ok svá sem hon er sterk, þá mun hon brotna þá er
Muspells megir fara ok ríða hana, ok svima hestar þeira yfir stórar   10
ár. Svá koma þeir fram.'
Þá mælir Gangleri: 'Eigi þótti mér goðin gera af trúnaði brúna,
er hon skal brotna mega, er þau megu gera sem þau vilja.'
Þá mælir Hár: 'Eigi eru goðin hallmælis verð fyrir þessa smíð.
Góð brú er Bifrǫst, en engi hlutr er sá í þessum heimi er sér megi   15
treystask þá er Muspells synir herja.'
Þá mælti Gangleri: 'Hvat hafðisk Alfǫðr þá at er gǫrr var   14
Ásgarðr?'
Hár mælir: 'Í upphafi setti hann stjórnarmenn ok beiddi þá at
dœma með sér ørlǫg manna ok ráða um skipun borgarinnar. Þat   20
var þar sem heitir Iðavǫllr í miðri borginni. Var þat hit fyrsta þeira
verk at gera hof þat er sæti þeira standa í, tólf ǫnnur en hásætit þat
er Alfǫðr á. Þat hús er bezt gert á jǫrðu ok mest. Allt er þat útan
ok innan svá sem gull eitt. Í þeim stað kalla menn Glaðsheim.
Annan sal gerðu þeir, þat var hǫrgr er gyðjurnar áttu, ok var   25
hann allfagr. Þat hús kalla menn Vingólf. Þar næst gerðu þeir þat
at þeir lǫgðu afla ok þar til gerðu þeir hamar ok tǫng ok steðja ok
þaðan af ǫll tól ǫnnur. Ok því næst smíðuðu þeir málm ok stein ok
tré, ok svá gnógliga þann málm er gull heitir at ǫll búsgǫgn ok ǫll
reiðigǫgn hǫfðu þeir af gulli, ok er sú ǫld kǫlluð gullaldr, áðr en   30
spiltisk af tilkvámu kvennanna. Þær kómu ór Jǫtunheimum. Þar
næst settusk guðin upp í sæti sín ok réttu dóma sína ok mintusk
hvaðan dvergar hǫfðu kviknat í moldunni ok niðri í jǫrðunni svá
sem maðkar í holdi. Dvergarnir hǫfðu skipazk fyrst ok tekit
kviknun í holdi Ymis ok váru þá maðkar, en af atkvæði guðanna   35
urðu þeir vitandi mannvits ok hǫfðu manns líki ok búa þó í jǫrðu
ok í steinum. Moðsognir var dvergr ok annarr Durinn. Svá segir í
Vǫluspá:

    Þá gengu regin ǫll
    á rǫkstóla,   40

ginnheilug goð,
ok of þat gættusk
at skyldi dverga
drótt of skepja
5   ór brimi blóðgu
ok ór Bláins leggjum.
Þar mannlíkun
mǫrg of gerðusk,
dvergar í jǫrðu,
10   sem Durinn sagði.

Ok þessi segir hon nǫfn þeira dverganna:

Nýi, Niði,
Norðri, Suðri,
Austri, Vestri,
15   Alþjólfr, Dvalinn,
Nár, Náinn,
Nipingr, Dáinn,
Bifurr, Báfurr,
Bǫmbǫrr, Nori,
20   Óri, Ónarr,
Óinn, Mǫðvitnir,
Vigr ok Gandálfr,
Vindálfr, Þorinn,
Fili, Kili,
25   Fundinn, Váli,
Þrór, Þróinn,
Þekkr, Litr, Vitr,
Nýr, Nýráðr,
Rekkr, Ráðsviðr.

30 En þessir eru ok dvergar ok búa í steinum, en inir fyrri í moldu:

Draupnir, Dólgþvari,
Hǫrr, Hugstari,
Hleðjólfr, Glóinn,
Dóri, Óri,
35   Dúfr, Andvari,
Heptifili,
Hárr, Síarr.

En þessir kómu frá Svarinshaugi til Aurvanga á Jǫruvǫllu, ok er
40 kominn þaðan Lofarr; þessi eru nǫfn þeira:
Skirpir, Virpir,
Skafiðr, Ái,

Álfr, Ingi,
Eikinskjaldi,
Falr, Frosti,
Fiðr, Ginnarr.'

Þá mælir Gangleri: 'Hvar er hǫfuðstaðrinn eða helgistaðrinn   5 15
goðanna?'
Hár svarar: 'Þat er at aski Yggdrasils. Þar skulu guðin eiga dóma
sína hvern dag.'
Þá mælir Gangleri: 'Hvat er at segja frá þeim stað?'
Þá segir Jafnhár: 'Askrinn er allra tréa mestr ok beztr. Limar   10
hans dreifask yfir heim allan ok standa yfir himni. Þrjár rœtr
trésins halda því upp ok standa afar breitt. Ein er með Ásum, en
ǫnnur með hrímþursum, þar sem forðum var Ginnungagap. In
þriðja stendr yfir Niflheimi, ok undir þeiri rót er Hvergelmir, en
Níðhǫggr gnagar neðan rótna. En undir þeiri rót er til hrímþursa   15
horfir, þar er Mímis brunnr, er spekð ok mannvit er í fólgit, ok
heitir sá Mímir er á brunninn. Hann er fullr af vísindum fyrir því at
hann drekkr ór brunninum af horninu Gjallarhorni. Þar kom
Alfǫðr ok beiddisk eins drykkjar af brunninum, en hann fekk eigi
fyrr en hann lagði auga sitt at veði. Svá segir í Vǫluspá: 20

Allt veit ek Óðinn
hvar þú auga falt,
í þeim inum mæra
Mímis brunni.
Drekkr mjǫð Mímir   25
morgun hverjan
af veði Valfǫðrs.
Vituð þér enn eða hvat?

Þriðja rót askins stendr á himni, ok undir þeiri rót er brunnr sá er
mjǫk er heilagr er heitir Urðar brunnr. Þar eigu guðin dómstað   30
sinn. Hvern dag ríða Æsir þangat upp um Bifrǫst. Hon heitir ok
Ásbrú. Hestar Ásanna heita svá: Sleipnir er baztr—hann á Óðinn,
hann hefir átta fœtr; annarr er Glaðr, þriði Gyllir, fjórði Glær,
fimti Skeiðbrimir, sétti Silfrtoppr, sjaundi Sinir, átti Gils, níundi
Falhófnir, tíundi Gulltoppr, Léttfeti ellipti. Baldrs hestr var   35
brendr með honum. En Þórr gengr til dómsins ok veðr ár þær er
svá heita:

Kǫrmt ok Qrmt
ok Kerlaugar tvær,
þær skal Þórr vaða   40

dag hvern
er hann dœma skal
at aski Yggdrasils,
þvíat Ásbrú
5   brenn ǫll loga,
heilug vǫtn hlóa.'

Þá mælir Gangleri: 'Brenn eldr yfir Bifrǫst?'

Hár segir: 'Þat er þú sér rautt í boganum er eldr brennandi.
Upp á himin mundu ganga hrímþursar ok bergrisar ef ǫllum væri
10   fœrt á Bifrǫst þeim er fara vilja. Margir staðir eru á himni fagrir ok
er þar allt guðlig vǫrn fyrir. Þar stendr salr einn fagr undir askinum
við brunninn, ok ór þeim sal koma þrjár meyjar þær er svá heita:
Urðr, Verðandi, Skuld. Þessar meyjar skapa mǫnnum aldr. Þær
kǫllum vér nornir. Enn eru fleiri nornir, þær er koma til hvers
15   manns er borinn er at skapa aldr, ok eru þessar goðkunnigar, en
aðrar álfa ættar, en inar þriðju dverga ættar, svá sem hér segir:

Sundrbornar mjǫk
hygg ek at nornir sé,
eigut þær ætt saman.
20   Sumar eru Áskunnar,
sumar eru álfkunnar,
sumar dœtr Dvalins.'

Þá mælir Gangleri: 'Ef nornir ráða ørlǫgum manna, þá skipta
þær geysi ójafnt, er sumir hafa gott líf ok ríkuligt, en sumir hafa
25   lítit lén eða lof, sumir langt líf, sumir skamt.'

Hár segir: 'Góðar nornir ok vel ættaðar skapa góðan aldr, en
þeir menn er fyrir óskǫpum verða, þá valda því illar nornir.'

16   Þá mælir Gangleri: 'Hvat er fleira at segja stórmerkja frá
askinum?'

30   Hár segir: 'Mart er þar af at segja. Ǫrn einn sitr í limum
asksins, ok er hann margs vitandi, en í milli augna honum sitr
haukr sá er heitir Veðrfǫlnir. Íkorni sá er heitir Ratatoskr renn
upp ok niðr eptir askinum ok berr ǫfundarorð milli arnarins ok
Níðhǫggs. En fjórir hirtir renna í limum asksins ok bíta barr. Þeir
35   heita svá: Dáinn, Dvalinn, Duneyrr, Duraþrór. En svá margir
ormar eru í Hvergelmi með Níðhǫgg at engi tunga má telja. Svá
segir hér:

Askr Yggdrasils
drýgir erfiði
40   meira en menn viti.

Hjǫrtr bítr ofan
en á hliðu fúnar,
skerðir Níðhǫggr neðan.

Svá er sagt:

> Ormar fleiri　　　　　　　　　　　　　　　　5
> liggja und aski Yggdrasils
> en þat of hyggi hverr ósviðra afa.
> Góinn ok Móinn
> (þeir ró Grafvitnis synir),
> Grábakr ok Grafvǫlluðr,　　　　　　　　10
> Ófnir ok Sváfnir
> hygg ek at æ myni
> meiðs kvistum má.

Enn er þat sagt at nornir þær er byggja við Urðar brunn taka hvern
dag vatn í brunninum ok með aurinn þann er liggr um brunninn,　15
ok ausa upp yfir askinn til þess at eigi skyli limar hans tréna eða
fúna. En þat vatn er svá heilagt at allir hlutir þeir sem þar koma í
brunninn verða svá hvítir sem hinna sú er skjall heitir, er innan
liggr við eggskurn, svá sem hér segir:

> Ask veit ek ausinn,　　　　　　　　　　20
> heitir Yggdrasill,
> hár baðmr, heilagr,
> hvíta auri.
> Þaðan koma dǫggvar
> er í dali falla.　　　　　　　　　　　　25
> Stendr hann æ yfir grœnn
> Urðar brunni.

Sú dǫgg er þaðan af fellr á jǫrðina, þat kalla menn hunangfall, ok
þar af fœðask býflugur. Fuglar tveir fœðask í Urðar brunni. Þeir
heita svanir, ok af þeim fuglum hefir komit þat fugla kyn er svá　30
heitir.'

Þá mælti Gangleri: 'Mikil tíðindi kannþu at segja af himnum.　17
Hvat er þar fleira hǫfuðstaða en at Urðar brunni?'

Hár segir: 'Margir staðir eru þar gǫfugligir. Sá er einn staðr þar
er kallaðr er Álfheimr. Þar byggvir fólk þat er ljósálfar heita, en　35
døkkálfar búa niðri í jǫrðu, ok eru þeir ólíkir þeim sýnum en
myklu ólíkari reyndum. Ljósálfar eru fegri en sól sýnum, en
døkkálfar eru svartari en bik. Þar er einn sá staðr er Breiðablik er
kallaðr, ok engi er þar fegri staðr. Þar er ok sá er Glitnir heitir, ok

eru veggir hans ok steðr ok stólpar af rauðu gulli, en þak hans af
silfri. Þar er enn sá staðr er Himinbjǫrg heita. Sá stendr á himins
enda við brúar spǫrð, þar er Bifrǫst kemr til himins. Þar er enn
mikill staðr er Valaskjálf heitir. Þann stað á Óðinn. Þann gerðu
5 guðin ok þǫkðu skíru silfri, ok þar er Hliðskjálfin í þessum sal, þat
hásæti er svá heitir. Ok þá er Alfǫðr sitr í því sæti þá sér hann of
allan heim. Á sunnanverðum himins enda er sá salr er allra er
fegrstr ok bjartari en sólin, er Gimlé heitir. Hann skal standa þá er
bæði himinn ok jǫrð hefir farizk, ok byggja þann stað góðir menn
10 ok réttlátir of allar aldir. Svá segir í Vǫluspá:

> Sal veit ek standa
> sólu fegra
> gulli betra
> á Gimlé.
15 > Þar skulu dyggvar
> dróttir byggja
> ok of aldrdaga
> yndis njóta.'

Þá mælir Gangleri: 'Hvat gætir þess staðar þá er Surtalogi
20 brennir himin ok jǫrð?'
Hár segir: 'Svá er sagt at annarr himinn sé suðr ok upp frá
þessum himni, ok heitir sá himinn Andlangr, en hinn þriði
himinn sé enn upp frá þeim ok heitir sá Víðbláinn, ok á þeim himni
hyggjum vér þenna stað vera. En ljósálfar einir hyggjum vér at nú
25 byggvi þá staði.'
18 Þá mælir Gangleri: 'Hvaðan kemr vindr? Hann er sterkr svá at
hann hrœrir stór hǫf ok hann œsir eld en svá sterkr sem hann er þá
má eigi sjá hann. Því er hann undarliga skapaðr.'
Þá segir Hár: 'Þat kann ek vel segja þér. Á norðanverðum
30 himins enda sitr jǫtunn sá er Hræsvelgr heitir. Hann hefir arnar
ham. En er hann beinir flug þá standa vindar undan vængum
honum. Hér segir svá:

> Hræsvelgr heitir
> er sitr á himins enda,
35 > jǫtunn í arnar ham.
> af hans vængum
> kveða vind koma
> alla menn yfir.'

Þá mælir Gangleri: 'Hví skilr svá mikit at sumar skal vera heitt   **19**
en vetr kaldr?'

Hár segir: 'Eigi mundi svá fróðr maðr spyrja, þvíat þetta vitu
allir at segja, en ef þú ert einn orðinn svá fávíss at eigi hefir þetta
heyrt, þá vil ek þó þat vel virða at heldr spyrir þú eitt sinn ófróðliga   5
en þú gangir lengr duliðr þess er skylt er at vita. Svásuðr heitir sá
er faðir Sumars er, ok er hann sællífr svá at af hans heiti er þat
kallat svásligt er blítt er. En faðir Vetrar er ýmist kallaðr Vindlóni
eða Vindsvalr. Hann er Vásaðar son, ok váru þeir áttungar
grimmir ok svalbrjóstaðir, ok hefir Vetr þeira skaplyndi.'   10

Þá mælir Gangleri: 'Hverir eru Æsir þeir er mǫnnum er skylt at   **20**
trúa á?'

Hár segir: 'Tólf eru Æsir guðkunnigir.'

Þá mælir Jafnhár: 'Eigi eru Ásynjurnar óhelgari ok eigi megu
þær minna.'   15

Þá mælir Þriði: 'Óðinn er œztr ok elztr Ásanna. Hann ræðr
ǫllum hlutum, ok svá sem ǫnnur guðin eru máttug, þá þjóna
honum ǫll svá sem bǫrn fǫður. En Frigg er kona hans, ok veit hon
ørlǫg manna þótt hon segi eigi spár, svá sem hér er sagt at Óðinn
mælir sjálfr við þann Ás er Loki heitir: 20

"Œrr ertu Loki
ok ørviti,
hví ne legskaþu, Loki?
Ørlǫg Frigg
hygg ek at ǫll viti
þótt hon sjálfgi segi."   25

'Óðinn heitir Alfǫðr, þvíat hann er faðir allra goða. Hann heitir
ok Valfǫðr, þvíat hans óskasynir eru allir þeir er í val falla. Þeim
skipar hann Valhǫll ok Vingólf, ok heita þeir þá einherjar. Hann
heitir ok Hangaguð ok Haptaguð, Farmaguð, ok enn hefir hann   30
nefnzk á fleiri vega þá er hann var kominn til Geirrøðar konungs:

"Heitumsk Grímr
ok Ganglari,
Herjan, Hjálmberi,
Þekkr, Þriði,   35
Þuðr, Uðr,
Helblindi, Hár,
Saðr, Svipall,
Sanngetall,
Herteitr, Hnikarr,   40

Bileygr, Báleygr,
Bǫlverkr, Fjǫlnir,
Grímnir, Glapsviðr, Fjǫlsviðr,
Síðhǫttr, Síðskeggr,
5   Sigfǫðr, Hnikuðr,
Alfǫðr, Atríðr, Farmatýr,
Óski, Ómi,
Jafnhár, Blindi,
Gǫndlir, Hárbarðr,
10   Sviðurr, Sviðrir,
Jálkr, Kjalarr, Viðurr,
Þrór, Yggr, Þundr,
Vakr, Skilfingr,
Váfuðr, Hroptatýr,
15   Gautr, Veratýr.'''

Þá mælir Gangleri: 'Geysi mǫrg heiti hafi þér gefit honum.
Ok þat veit trúa mín at þetta mun vera mikill fróðleikr sá er hér
kann skyn ok dœmi hverir atburðir hafa orðit sér til hvers þessa
nafns.'
20   Þá segir Hár: 'Mikill skynsemi er at rifja vandliga þat upp. En þó
er þér þat skjótast at segja at flest heiti hafa verit gefin af þeim
atburð at svá margar sem eru greinir tungnanna í verǫldunni, þá
þykkjask allar þjóðir þurfa at breyta nafni hans til sinnar tungu til
ákalls ok bœna fyrir sjálfum sér, en sumir atburðir til þessa heita
25   hafa gerzk í ferðum hans ok er þat fœrt í frásagnir, ok muntu eigi
mega fróðr maðr heita ef þú skalt eigi kunna segja frá þeim
stórtíðindum.'
21   Þá mælir Gangleri: 'Hver eru nǫfn annarra Ásanna? Eða hvat
hafask þeir at? Eða hvat hafa þeir gert til frama?'
30   Hár segir: 'Þórr er þeira framast; sá er kallaðr Ásaþórr eða
Ǫkuþórr. Hann er sterkastr allra guðanna ok manna. Hann á
þar ríki er Þrúðvangar heita, en hǫll hans heitir Bilskirnir. Í þeim
sal eru fimm hundrað gólfa ok fjórir tigir. Þat er hús mest svá at
menn hafa gert. Svá segir í Grímnismálum:

35   Fimm hundrað gólfa
ok um fjórum tøgum,
svá hygg ek Bilskirni með bugum.
Ranna þeira
er ek ræfr vita,
40   míns veit ek mest magar.

Þórr á hafra tvá er svá heita: Tanngnjóstr ok Tanngrisnir; ok reið
þá er hann ekr, en hafrarnir draga reiðna. Því er hann kallaðr
Ǫkuþórr. Hann á ok þrjá kostgripi. Einn þeira er hamarrinn
Mjǫllnir er hrímþursar ok bergrisar kenna þá er hann kemr á lopt,
ok er þat eigi undarligt: hann hefir lamit margan haus á feðrum 5
eða frændum þeira. Annan grip á hann beztan, megingjarðar, ok
er hann spennir þeim um sik þá vex honum ásmegin hálfu. Inn
þriðja hlut á hann þann er mikill gripr er í. Þat eru járnglófar. Þeira
má hann eigi missa við hamars skaptit. En engi er svá fróðr at
telja kunni ǫll stórvirki hans, en segja kann ek þér svá mǫrg tíðindi 10
frá honum at dveljask munu stundirnar áðr en sagt er allt þat er ek
veit.'

Þá mælir Gangleri: 'Spyrja vil ek tíðinda af fleiri Ásunum.' 22

Hár segir: 'Annarr son Óðins er Baldr, ok er frá honum gott at
segja. Hann er beztr ok hann lofa allir. Hann er svá fagr álitum ok 15
bjartr svá at lýsir af honum, ok eitt gras er svá hvítt at jafnat er til
Baldrs brár. Þat er allra grasa hvítast, ok þar eptir mátþu marka
hans fegrð bæði á hár ok á líki. Hann er vitrastr Ásanna ok fegrst
talaðr ok líknsamastr, en sú náttúra fylgir honum at engi má
haldask dómr hans. Hann býr þar sem heitir Breiðablik. Þat er á 20
himni. Í þeim stað má ekki vera óhreint, svá sem hér segir:

> Breiðablik heita
> þar er Baldr hefir
> sér of gerva sali,
> í því landi
> er ek liggja veit 25
> fæsta feiknstafi.

Hinn þriði Áss er sá er kallaðr er Njǫrðr. Hann býr á himni þar **23**
sem heitir Nóatún. Hann ræðr fyrir gǫngu vinds ok stillir sjá ok
eld. Á hann skal heita til sæfara ok til veiða. Hann er svá auðigr ok 30
fésæll at hann má gefa þeim auð landa eða lausafjár er á hann heita
til þess. Eigi er Njǫrðr Ása ættar. Hann var upp fœddr í
Vanaheimum, en Vanir gísluðu hann goðunum ok tóku í mót at
Ásagíslingu þann er Hœnir heitir. Hann varð at sætt með goðunum
ok Vǫnum. 35

'Njǫrðr á þá konu er Skaði heitir, dóttir Þjaza jǫtuns. Skaði vill
hafa bústað þann er átt hafði faðir hennar—þat er á fjǫllum
nokkvorum þar sem heitir Þrymheimr—en Njǫrðr vill vera nær sæ.
Þau sættusk á þat at þau skyldu vera níu nætr í Þrymheimi, en þá

aðrar níu at Nóatúnum. En er Njǫrðr kom aptr til Nóatúna af
fjallinu þá kvað hann þetta:

> "Leið erumk fjǫll—
> varka ek lengi á,
> 5   nætr einar níu:
> úlfa þytr
> mér þótti illr vera
> hjá sǫngvi svana."

Þá kvað Skaði þetta:

> 10   "Sofa ek máttigak
> sævar beðjum á
> fugls jarmi fyrir:
> sá mik vekr
> er af víði kemr
> 15   morgun hverjan: már."

Þá fór Skaði upp á fjallit ok bygði í Þrymheimi ok ferr hon mjǫk á
skíðum ok með boga ok skýtr dýr. Hon heitir ǫndurguð eða
ǫndurdís. Svá er sagt:

> Þrymheimr heitir
> 20   er Þjazi bjó,
> sá hinn ámátki jǫtunn,
> en nú Skaði byggvir,
> skír brúðr guða,
> fornar toptir fǫður.

24 25   'Njǫrðr í Nóatúnum gat síðan tvau bǫrn. Hét sonr Freyr en
dóttir Freyja. Þau váru fǫgr álitum ok máttug. Freyr er hinn
ágætasti af Ásum. Hann ræðr fyrir regni ok skini sólar ok þar með
ávexti jarðar, ok á hann er gott at heita til árs ok friðar. Hann ræðr
ok fésælu manna. En Freyja er ágætust af Ásynjum. Hon á þann
30   bœ á himni er Fólkvangar heita, ok hvar sem hon ríðr til vígs þá á
hon hálfan val, en hálfan Óðinn, svá sem hér segir:

> Fólkvangr heitir,
> en þar Freyja ræðr
> sessa kostum í sal.
> 35   Hálfan val
> hon kýss á hverjan dag,
> en hálfan Óðinn á.

Salr hennar Sessrúmnir, hann er mikill ok fagr. En er hon ferr, þá ekr hon kǫttum tveim ok sitr í reið. Hon er nákvæmust mǫnnum til á at heita, ok af hennar nafni er þat tignarnafn er ríkiskonur eru kallaðar "fróvur". Henni líkaði vel mansǫngr. Á hana er gott at heita til ásta.'

Þá mælir Gangleri: 'Miklir þykkja mér þessir fyrir sér Æsirnir, ok eigi er undarligt at mikill kraptr fylgi yðr, er þér skuluð kunna skyn goðanna ok vita hvert biðja skal hverrar bœnarinnar. Eða eru fleiri enn goðin?'

Hár segir: 'Sá er enn Áss er Týr heitir. Hann er djarfastr ok bezt hugaðr ok hann ræðr mjǫk sigri í orrostum. Á hann er gott at heita hreystimǫnnum. Þat er orðtak at sá er "týhraustr" er um fram er aðra menn ok ekki sésk fyrir. Hann var vitr svá at þat er mælt at sá er "týspakr" er vitr er. Þat er eitt mark um djarfleik hans, þá er Æsir lokkuðu Fenrisúlf til þess at leggja fjǫturinn á hann, Gleipni, þá trúði hann þeim eigi at þeir mundu leysa hann fyrr en þeir lǫgðu honum at veði hǫnd Týrs í munn úlfsins. En þá er Æsir vildu eigi leysa hann þá beit hann hǫndina af þar er nú heitir úlfliðr, ok er hann einhendr ok ekki kallaðr sættir manna.

'Bragi heitir einn. Hann er ágætr at speki ok mest at málsnild ok orðfimi. Hann kann mest af skáldskap, ok af honum er bragr kallaðr skáldskapr, ok af hans nafni er sá kallaðr bragr karla eða kvenna er orðsnild hefir framar en aðrir, kona eða karlmaðr. Kona hans er Iðunn. Hon varðveitir í eski sínu epli þau er goðin skulu á bíta þá er þau eldask, ok verða þá allir ungir, ok svá mun vera allt til ragnarøkrs.'

Þá mælir Gangleri: 'Allmikit þykki mér goðin eiga undir gæzlu eða trúnaði Iðunnar.'

Þá mælir Hár ok hló við: 'Nær lagði þat ófœru einu sinni. Kunna mun ek þar af at segja, en þú skalt nú fyrst heyra nǫfn Ásanna fleiri.

'Heimdallr heitir einn. Hann er kallaðr hvíti Áss. Hann er mikill ok heilagr. Hann báru at syni meyjar níu ok allar systr. Hann heitir ok Hallinskíði ok Gullintanni: tennr hans váru af gulli. Hestr hans heitir Gulltoppr. Hann býr þar er heitir Himinbjǫrg við Bifrǫst. Hann er vǫrðr goða ok sitr þar við himins enda at gæta brúarinnar fyrir bergrisum. Þarf hann minna svefn en fugl. Hann sér jafnt nótt sem dag hundrað rasta frá sér. Hann heyrir ok þat er gras vex á jǫrðu eða ull á sauðum ok allt þat er hæra lætr. Hann hefir lúðr þann er Gjallarhorn heitir ok heyrir blástr hans í alla heima. Heimdalar sverð er kallat hǫfuð. Hér er svá sagt:

> Himinbjǫrg heita,
> en þar Heimdall kveða
> valda véum.
> 5 Þar vǫrðr goða
> drekkr í væru ranni
> glaðr hinn góða mjǫð.

Ok enn segir hann sjálfr í Heimdalargaldri:

> "Níu em ek mœðra mǫgr,
> 10 níu em ek systra sonr."

28 'Hǫðr heitir einn Ássinn. Hann er blindr. Œrit er hann styrkr. En vilja mundu goðin at þenna Ás þyrfti eigi at nefna, þvíat hans handaverk munu lengi vera hǫfð at minnum með goðum ok mǫnnum.

29 15 'Víðarr heitir einn, hinn þǫgli Áss. Hann hefir skó þjǫkkvan. Hann er sterkr næst því sem Þórr er. Af honum hafa goðin mikit traust í allar þrautir.

30 'Áli eða Váli heitir einn, sonr Óðins ok Rindar. Hann er djarfr í orrostum ok mjǫk happskeytr.

31 20 'Ullr heitir einn, sonr Sifjar, stjúpsonr Þórs. Hann er bogmaðr svá góðr ok skíðfœrr svá at engi má við hann keppask. Hann er ok fagr álitum ok hefir hermanns atgervi. Á hann er ok gott at heita í einvígi.

32 'Forseti heitir sonr Baldrs ok Nǫnnu Nepsdóttur. Hann á þann 25 sal á himni er Glitnir heitir, en allir er til hans koma með sakarvandræði, þá fara allir sáttir á braut. Sá er dómstaðr beztr með guðum ok mǫnnum. Svá segir hér:

> Glitnir heitir salr,
> hann er gulli studdr
> 30 ok silfri þakðr it sama,
> en þar Forseti
> byggvir flestan dag
> ok svæfir allar sakar.

33 'Sá er enn talðr með Ásum er sumir kalla rógbera Ásanna ok 35 frumkveða flærðanna ok vǫmm allra goða ok manna. Sá er nefndr Loki eða Loptr, sonr Fárbauta jǫtuns. Móðir hans er Laufey eða Nál. Brœðr hans eru þeir Býleistr ok Helblindi. Loki er fríðr ok fagr sýnum, illr í skaplyndi, mjǫk fjǫlbreytinn at háttum. Hann

hafði þá speki um fram aðra menn er slœgð heitir, ok vælar til allra
hluta. Hann kom Ásum jafnan í fullt vandræði ok opt leysti hann
þá með vælræðum. Kona hans heitir Sigyn, sonr þeira Nari eða
Narfi. Enn átti Loki fleiri bǫrn. Angrboða hét gýgr í 34
Jǫtunheimum. Við henni gat Loki þrjú bǫrn. Eitt var Fenrisúlfr, 5
annat Jǫrmungandr (þat er Miðgarðsormr), þriðja er Hel. En er
goðin vissu til at þessi þrjú systkin fœddusk upp í Jǫtunheimum ok
goðin rǫkðu til spádóma at af systkinum þessum mundi þeim mikit
mein ok óhapp standa ok þótti ǫllum mikils ills af væni, fyrst af
móðerni ok enn verra af faðerni. 10
    'Þá sendi Alfǫðr til guðin at taka bǫrnin ok fœra sér. Ok er þau
kómu til hans þá kastaði hann orminum í inn djúpa sæ er liggr um
ǫll lǫnd, ok óx sá ormr svá at hann liggr í miðju hafinu of ǫll lǫnd
ok bítr í sporð sér. Hel kastaði hann í Niflheim ok gaf henni vald
yfir níu heimum at hon skipti ǫllum vistum með þeim er til hennar 15
váru sendir, en þat eru sóttdauðir menn ok ellidauðir. Hon á þar
mikla bólstaði ok eru garðar hennar forkunnar hávir ok grindr
stórar. Eljúðnir heitir salr hennar, Hungr diskr hennar, Sultr kníf
hennar, Ganglati þrællinn, Ganglǫt ambátt, Fallanda Forað
þreskǫldr hennar er inn gengr, Kǫr sæing, Blíkjanda Bǫl ársali 20
hennar. Hon er blá hálf en hálf með hǫrundar lit—því er hon
auðkend—ok heldr gnúpleit ok grimlig.
    'Úlfinn fœddu Æsir heima, ok hafði Týr einn djarfleik til at
ganga at úlfnum ok gefa honum mat. En er guðin sá hversu mikit
hann óx hvern dag, ok allar spár sǫgðu at hann mundi vera lagðr til 25
skaða þeim, þá fengu Æsir þat ráð at þeir gerðu fjǫtur allsterkan er
þeir kǫlluðu Leyðing ok báru hann til úlfsins ok báðu hann reyna
afl sitt við fjǫturinn. En úlfinum þótti sér þat ekki ofrefli ok lét þá
fara með sem þeir vildu. It fyrsta sinn er úlfrinn spyrndi við
brotnaði sá fjǫturr. Svá leystisk hann ór Leyðingi. Því næst gerðu 30
Æsirnir annan fjǫtur hálfu sterkara er þeir kǫlluðu Dróma, ok
báðu enn úlfinn reyna þann fjǫtur ok tǫlðu hann verða mundu
ágætan mjǫk at afli ef slík stórsmíði mætti eigi halda honum. En
úlfrinn hugsaði at þessi fjǫturr var sterkr mjǫk, ok þat með at
honum hafði afl vaxit síðan er hann braut Leyðing. Kom þat í hug 35
at hann mundi verða at leggja sik í hættu ef hann skyldi frægr
verða, ok lét leggja á sik fjǫturinn. Ok er Æsir tǫlðusk búnir, þá
hristi úlfrinn sik ok laust fjǫtrinum á jǫrðina ok knúðisk fast at,
spyrnir við, braut fjǫturinn svá at fjarri flugu brotin. Svá drap hann
sik ór Dróma. Þat er síðan haft fyrir orðtak at leysi ór Leyðingi eða 40

drepi ór Dróma þá er einnhverr hlutr er ákafliga sóttr. Eptir þat
óttuðusk Æsirnir at þeir mundu eigi fá bundit úlfinn. Þá sendi
Alfǫðr þann er Skírnir er nefndr, sendimaðr Freys, ofan í Svart-
álfaheim til dverga nokkurra ok lét gera fjǫtur þann er Gleipnir
5 heitir. Hann var gjǫrr af sex hlutum: af dyn kattarins ok af skeggi
konunnar ok af rótum bjargsins ok af sinum bjarnarins ok af anda
fisksins ok af fogls hráka. Ok þóttu vitir eigi áðr þessi tíðindi, þá
máttu nú finna skjótt hér sǫnn dœmi at eigi er logit at þér: sét
muntþu hafa at konan hefir ekki skegg ok engi dynr verðr af hlaupi
10 kattarins ok eigi eru rœtr undir bjarginu, ok þat veit trúa mín at
jafnsatt er þat allt er ek hefi sagt þér þótt þeir sé sumir hlutir er þú
mátt eigi reyna.'
     Þá mælir Gangleri: 'Þetta má ek at vísu skilja at satt er. Þessa
hluti má ek sjá er þú hefir nú til dœma tekit, en hvernig varð
15 fjǫturrinn smíðaðr?'
     Hár segir: 'Þat kann ek þér vel segja. Fjǫturrinn varð sléttr ok
blautr sem silkirœma, en svá traustr ok sterkr sem nú skaltu heyra.
Þá er fjǫturrinn var fœrðr Ásunum, þǫkkuðu þeir vel sendimanni
sitt eyrindi. Þá fóru Æsirnir út í vatn þat er Ámsvartnir heitir, í
20 hólm þann er Lyngvi er kallaðr, ok kǫlluðu með sér úlfinn, sýndu
honum silkibandit ok báðu hann slíta ok kváðu vera nokkvoru
traustara en líkindi þœtti á fyrir digrleiks sakar, ok seldi hverr
ǫðrum ok treysti með handaafli, ok slitnaði eigi; en þó kváðu þeir
úlfinn slíta mundu. Þá svarar úlfrinn:
25   '"Svá lízk mér á þenna dregil sem ǫnga frægð munak af hljóta
þótt ek slíta í sundr svá mjótt band, en ef þat er gǫrt með list ok
væl, þótt þat sýnisk lítit, þá kemr þat band eigi á mína fœtr."
     'Þá sǫgðu Æsirnir at hann mundi skjótt sundr slíta mjótt
silkiband, er hann hafði fyrr brotit stóra járnfjǫtra,—"en ef þú fær
30 eigi þetta band slitit þá muntu ekki hræða mega goðin, enda
skulum vér þá leysa þik."
     'Úlfrinn segir: "Ef þér bindið mik svá at ek fæk eigi leyst mik þá
skollið þér svá at mér mun seint verða at taka af yðr hjálp. Ófúss
em ek at láta þetta band á mik leggja. En heldr en þér frýið mér
35 hugar þá leggi einnhverr hǫnd sína í munn mér at veði at þetta sé
falslaust gert."
     'En hverr Ásanna sá til annars ok þótti nú vera tvau vandræði ok
vildi engi sína hǫnd fram selja fyrr en Týr lét fram hǫnd sína hœgri
ok leggr í munn úlfinum. En er úlfrinn spyrnir, þá harðnaði bandit,
40 ok því harðara er hann brauzk um, því skarpara var bandit. Þá

hlógu allir nema Týr. Hann lét hǫnd sína. Þá er Æsirnir sá at
úlfrinn var bundinn at fullu, þá tóku þeir festina er ór var
fjǫtrinum er Gelgja heitir, ok drógu hana gǫgnum hellu mikla—sú
heitir Gjǫll—ok festu helluna langt í jǫrð niðr. Þá tóku þeir mikinn
stein ok skutu enn lengra í jǫrðina—sá heitir Þviti—ok hǫfðu þann 5
stein fyrir festar hælinn. Úlfrinn gapði ákafliga ok feksk um mjǫk
ok vildi bíta þá. Þeir skutu í munn honum sverði nokkvoru; nema
hjǫltin við neðra gómi, en efra gómi blóðrefill. Þat er gómsparri
hans. Hann grenjar illiliga ok slefa renn ór munni hans. Þat er á sú
er Ván heitir. Þar liggr hann til ragnarøkrs.' 10

Þá mælir Gangleri: 'Furðu illa barnaeign gat Loki, en ǫll þessi
systkin eru mikil fyrir sér. En fyrir hví drápu Æsir eigi úlfinn er
þeim er ills ván af honum?'

Hár svarar: 'Svá mikils virðu goðin vé sín ok griðastaði at eigi
vildu þau saurga þá með blóði úlfsins þótt svá segi spárnar at hann 15
muni verða at bana Óðni.'

Þá mælir Gangleri: 'Hverjar eru Ásynjurnar?' **35**

Hár segir: 'Frigg er œzt. Hon á þann bœ er Fensalir heita ok er
hann allvegligr. Ǫnnur er Sága. Hon býr á Søkkvabekk, ok er
þat mikill staðr. Þriðja er Eir. Hon er læknir beztr. Fjórða er 20
Gefjun. Hon er mær, ok henni þjóna þær er meyjar andask. Fimta
er Fulla. Hon er enn mær ok ferr laushár ok gullband um hǫfuð.
Hon berr eski Friggjar ok gætir skóklæða hennar ok veit launráð
með henni. Freyja er tignust með Frigg. Hon giptisk þeim manni
er Óðr heitir. Dóttir þeira heitir Hnoss. Hon er svá fǫgr at af 25
hennar nafni eru hnossir kallaðar þat er fagrt er ok gersemligt. Óðr
fór í braut langar leiðir, en Freyja grætr eptir, en tár hennar er gull
rautt. Freyja á mǫrg nǫfn, en sú er sǫk til þess at hon gaf sér ýmis
heiti er hon fór með ókunnum þjóðum at leita Óðs. Hon heitir
Mardǫll ok Hǫrn, Gefn, Sýr. Freyja átti Brísingamen. Hon er 30
kǫlluð Vanadís. Sjaunda Sjǫfn: hon gætir mjǫk til at snúa hugum
manna til ásta, kvenna ok karla. Af hennar nafni er elskuginn
kallaðr sjafni. Átta Lofn: hon er svá mild ok góð til áheita at hon
fær leyfi af Alfǫðr eða Frigg til manna samgangs, kvenna ok karla,
þótt áðr sé bannat eða þvertekit. Fyrir því er af hennar nafni lof 35
kallat, ok svá þat er lofat er mjǫk af mǫnnum. Níunda Vár: hon
hlýðir á eiða manna ok einkamál er veita sín á milli konur ok
karlar. Því heita þau mál várar. Hon hefnir ok þeim er brigða.
Tíunda Vǫr: hon er ok vitr ok spurul, svá at engi hlut má hana
leyna. Þat er orðtak at kona verði vǫr þess er hon verðr vís. Ellipta 40

Syn: hon gætir dura í hǫllinni ok lýkr fyrir þeim er eigi skulu inn
ganga, ok hon er sett til varnar á þingum fyrir þau mál er hon vill
ósanna. Því er þat orðtak at syn sé fyrir sett þá er hann neitar.
Tólfta Hlín: hon er sett til gæzlu yfir þeim mǫnnum er Frigg vill
5 forða við háska nokkvorum. Þaðan af er þat orðtak at sá er forðask
hleinir. Þrettánda Snotra: hon er vitr ok látprúð. Af hennar heiti er
kallat snotr kona eða karlmaðr sá er vitr maðr er. Fjórtánda Gná:
hana sendir Frigg í ymsa heima at eyrindum sínum. Hon á þann hest
er renn lopt ok lǫg, er heitir Hófvarfnir. Þat var eitt sinn er hon
10 reið at Vanir nokkvorir sá reið hennar í loptinu. Þá mælti einn:

"Hvat þar flýgr?
Hvat þar ferr
eða at lopti líðr?"

'Hon segir:

15   "Ne ek flýg
         þó ek fer
         ok at lopti líðk
         á Hófvarfni
         þeim er Hamskerpir
20   gat við Garðrofu."

'Af Gnár nafni er svá kallat at þat gnæfar er hátt ferr. Sól ok Bil
36 eru talðar með Ásynjum, en sagt er fyrr frá eðli þeira. Enn eru þær
aðrar er þjóna skulu í Valhǫll, bera drykkju ok gæta borðbúnaðar
ok ǫlgagna. Svá eru þær nefndar í Grímnismálum:

25   Hrist ok Mist
         vil ek at mér horn beri,
         Skeggjǫld ok Skǫgul,
         Hildr ok Þrúðr,
         Hlǫkk ok Herfjǫtur,
30   Gǫll ok Geirahǫð,
         Randgríð ok Ráðgríð
         ok Reginleif.
         Þær bera einherjum ǫl.

Þessar heita valkyrjur. Þær sendir Óðinn til hverrar orrostu. Þær
35 kjósa feigð á menn ok ráða sigri. Guðr ok Rota ok norn in yngsta
er Skuld heitir ríða jafnan at kjósa val ok ráða vígum. Jǫrð, móðir
Þórs, ok Rindr, móðir Vála, eru talðar með Ásynjum.
37   'Gymir hét maðr, en kona hans Aurboða. Hon var bergrisa

ættar. Dóttir þeira er Gerðr er allra kvenna er fegrst. Þat var einn dag er Freyr hafði gengit í Hliðskjálf ok sá of heima alla, en er hann leit í norðrætt þá sá hann á einum bœ mikit hús ok fagrt, ok til þess húss gekk kona, ok er hon tók upp hǫndum ok lauk hurð fyrir sér þá lýsti af hǫndum hennar bæði í lopt ok á lǫg, ok allir 5 heimar birtusk af henni. Ok svá hefndi honum þat mikla mikillæti er hann hafði sezk í þat helga sæti at hann gekk í braut fullr af harmi. Ok er hann kom heim, mælti hann ekki, hvárki svaf hann né drakk; engi þorði ok krefja hann orða. Þá lét Njǫrðr kalla til sín Skírni, skósvein Freys, ok bað hann ganga til Freys ok beiða 10 hann orða ok spyrja hverjum hann væri svá reiðr at hann mælir ekki við menn. En Skírnir kvazk ganga mundu ok eigi fúss, ok kvað illra svara vera ván af honum. En er hann kom til Freys þá spurði hann hví Freyr var svá hnipinn ok mælti ekki við menn. Þá svarar Freyr ok sagði at hann hafði sét konu fagra ok fyrir hennar 15 sakar var hann svá harmsfullr at eigi mundi hann lengi lifa ef hann skyldi eigi ná henni.

'"Ok nú skaltu fara ok biðja hennar mér til handa ok hafa hana heim hingat hvárt er faðir hennar vill eða eigi, ok skal ek þat vel launa þér." 20

'Þá svarar Skírnir, sagði svá at hann skal fara sendiferð en Freyr skal fá honum sverð sitt. Þat var svá gott sverð at sjálft vásk. En Freyr lét eigi þat til skorta ok gaf honum sverðit. Þá fór Skírnir ok bað honum konunnar ok fekk heitit hennar, ok níu nóttum síðar skyldi hon þar koma er Barey heitir ok ganga þá at brullaupinu 25 með Frey. En er Skírnir sagði Frey sitt eyrindi þá kvað hann þetta:

"Lǫng er nótt,
lǫng er ǫnnur,
hvé mega ek þreyja þrjár?
Opt mér mánaðr 30
minni þótti
en sjá hálf hýnótt."

'Þessi sǫk er til er Freyr var svá vápnlauss er hann barðisk við Belja ok drap hann með hjartar horni.'

Þá mælir Gangleri: 'Undr mikit er þvílíkr hǫfðingi sem Freyr er 35 vildi gefa sverð svá at hann átti eigi annat jafngott! Geysi mikit mein var honum þat þá er hann barðisk við þann er Beli heitir. Þat veit trúa mín at þeirar gjafar mundi hann þá iðrask.'

Þá svarar Hár: 'Lítit mark var þá at er þeir Beli hittusk. Drepa mátti Freyr hann með hendi sinni. Verða mun þat er Frey mun 40

þykkja verr við koma er hann missir sverðsins þá er Muspells synir
fara ok herja.'

38 Þá mælir Gangleri: 'Þat segir þú at allir þeir menn er í orrostu
hafa fallit frá upphafi heims eru nú komnir til Óðins í Valhǫll.
5 Hvat hefir hann at fá þeim at vistum? Ek hugða at þar skyldi vera
allmikit fjǫlmenni.'

Þá svarar Hár: 'Satt er þat er þú segir, allmikit fjǫlmenni er þar,
en myklu fleira skal enn verða, ok mun þó oflítit þykkja þá er
úlfrinn kemr. En aldri er svá mikill mannfjǫlði í Valhǫll at eigi má
10 þeim endask flesk galtar þess er Sæhrímnir heitir. Hann er soðinn
hvern dag ok heill at aptni. En þessi spurning er nú spyrr þú þykki
mér líkara at fáir muni svá vísir vera at hér kunni satt af at segja.
Andhrímnir heitir steikarinn en Eldhrímnir ketillinn. Svá er hér
sagt:

15   Andhrímnir lætr
        í Eldhrímni
        Sæhrímni soðinn,
        fleska bazt.
        En þat fáir vitu
20   við hvat einherjar alask.'

Þá mælir Gangleri: 'Hvárt hefir Óðinn þat sama borðhald sem
einherjar?'

Hár segir: 'Þá vist er á hans borði stendr gefr hann tveim úlfum
er hann á, er svá heita: Geri ok Freki. Ok ønga vist þarf hann: vín
25 er honum bæði drykkr ok matr. Svá segir hér:

        Gera ok Freka
        seðr gunntamiðr
        hróðigr Herjafǫðr,
        en við vín eitt
30   vápngafigr
        Óðinn æ lifir.

Hrafnar tveir sitja á ǫxlum honum ok segja í eyru honum ǫll
tíðindi þau er þeir sjá eða heyra. Þeir heita svá: Huginn ok
Muninn. Þá sendir hann í dagan at fljúgja um allan heim ok koma
35 þeir aptr at dǫgurðarmáli. Þar af verðr hann margra tíðinda víss.
Því kalla menn hann hrafna guð. Svá sem sagt er:

        Huginn ok Muninn
        fljúgja hverjan dag
        jǫrmungrund yfir.

Óumk ek Hugin
at hann aptr ne komi,
þó sjámk ek meir at Munin.'

Þá mælir Gangleri: 'Hvat hafa einherjar at drykk þat er þeim 39
endisk jafngnógliga sem vistin, eða er þar vatn drukkit?' 5
Þá segir Hár: 'Undarliga spyrðu nú at Alfǫðr mun bjóða til sín
konungum eða jǫrlum eða ǫðrum ríkismǫnnum ok muni gefa þeim
vatn at drekka, ok þat veit trúa mín at margr kemr sá til Valhallar
er dýrt mundi þykkjask kaupa vazdrykkinn ef eigi væri betra
fagnaðar þangat at vitja, sá er áðr þolir sár ok sviða til banans. 10
Annat kann ek þér þaðan segja. Geit sú er Heiðrún heitir stendr
uppi á Valhǫll ok bítr barr af limum trés þess er mjǫk er nafnfrægt
er Léraðr heitir, en ór spenum hennar rennr mjǫðr sá er hon fyllir
skapker hvern dag. Þat er svá mikit at allir einherjar verða
fulldruknir af.' 15
Þá mælir Gangleri: 'Þat er þeim geysi haglig geit. Forkunnar
góðr viðr mun þat vera er hon bítr af.'
Þá mælir Hár: 'Enn er meira mark at of hjǫrtinn Eikþyrni er
stendr á Valhǫll ok bítr af limum þess trés, en af hornum hans
verðr svá mikill dropi at niðr kemr í Hvergelmi, en þaðan af falla 20
ár þær er svá heita: Síð, Víð, Sekin, Ekin, Svǫl, Gunnþró, Fjǫrm,
Fimbulþul, Gipul, Gǫpul, Gǫmul, Geirvimul; þessar falla um Ása
bygðir. Þessar eru enn nefndar: Þyn, Vin, Þǫll, Bǫll, Gráð,
Gunnþráin, Nyt, Nǫt, Nǫnn, Hrǫnn, Vína, Veg, Svinn,
Þjóðnuma.' 25
Þá mælir Gangleri: 'Þetta eru undarlig tíðindi er nú sagðir þú. 40
Geysi mikit hús mun Valhǫll vera, allþrǫngt mun þar opt vera
fyrir durum.'
Þá svarar Hár: 'Hví spyrr þú eigi þess, hversu margar dyrr eru á
Valhǫll eða hversu stórar? Ef þú heyrir þat sagt þá muntu segja at 30
hitt er undarligt ef eigi má ganga út ok inn hverr er vill. En þat er
með sǫnnu at segja at eigi er þrøngra at skipa hana en ganga í
hana. Hér máttu heyra í Grímnismálum:

Fimm hundrað dura
ok of fjórum tøgum, 35
svá hygg ek á Valhǫllu vera.
Átta hundruð einherja
ganga senn ór einum durum
þá er þeir fara með vitni at vega.'

41   Þá mælir Gangleri: 'Allmikill mannfjǫlði er í Valhǫll. Svá njóta
trú minnar at allmikill hǫfðingi er Óðinn er hann stýrir svá miklum
her. Eða hvat er skemtun einherjanna þá er þeir drekka eigi?'
       Hár segir: 'Hvern dag þá er þeir hafa klæzk þá hervæða þeir sik
5   ok ganga út í garðinn ok berjask ok fellr hverr á annan. Þat er leikr
þeira. Ok er líðr at dǫgurðarmáli þá ríða þeir heim til Valhallar ok
setjask til drykkju, svá sem hér segir:

        Allir einherjar
        Óðins túnum í
10   hǫggvask hverjan dag.
        Val þeir kjósa
        ok ríða vígi frá,
        sitja meir um sáttir saman.

       En satt er þat er þú sagðir: mikill er Óðinn fyrir sér. Mǫrg dœmi
15 finnask til þess. Svá er hér sagt í orðum sjálfra Ásanna:

        "Askr Yggdrasils,
        hann er œztr viða,
        en Skíðblaðnir skipa,
        Óðinn Ása,
20   en jóa Sleipnir,
        Bifrǫst brúa,
        en Bragi skálda,
        Hábrók hauka,
        en hunda Garmr."'

42 25   Þá mælir Gangleri: 'Hverr á þann hest Sleipni? Eða hvat er frá
honum at segja?'
       Hár segir: 'Eigi kanntu deili á Sleipni ok eigi veiztu atburði af
hverju hann kom!—en þat mun þér þykkja frásagnarvert. Þat var
snimma í ǫndverða bygð goðanna, þá er goðin hǫfðu sett Miðgarð
30 ok gert Valhǫll, þá kom þar smiðr nokkvorr ok bauð at gera þeim
borg á þrim misserum svá góða at trú ok ørugg væri fyrir bergrisum
ok hrímþursum þótt þeir komi inn um Miðgarð. En hann mælir sér
þat til kaups at hann skyldi eignask Freyju, ok hafa vildi hann sól
ok mána. Þá gengu Æsirnir á tal ok réðu ráðum sínum, ok var þat
35 kaup gert við smiðinn at hann skyldi eignask þat er hann mælir til
ef hann fengi gert borgina á einum vetri, en hinn fyrsta sumars dag
ef nokkvorr hlutr væri ógjǫrr at borginni þá skyldi hann af
kaupinu. Skyldi hann af ǫngum manni lið þiggja til verksins. Ok er
þeir sǫgðu honum þessa kosti, þá beiddisk hann at þeir skyldu lofa

at hann hefði lið af hesti sínum er Svaðilfœri hét. En því réð Loki
er þat var til lagt við hann. Hann tók til hinn fyrsta vetrar dag at
gera borgina, en of nætr dró hann til grjót á hestinum. En þat þótti
Ásunum mikit undr hversu stór bjǫrg sá hestr dró, ok hálfu meira
þrekvirki gerði hestrinn en smiðrinn. En at kaupi þeira váru sterk   5
vitni ok mǫrg sœri, fyrir því at jǫtnum þótti ekki trygt at vera með
Ásum griðalaust ef Þórr kvæmi heim, en þá var hann farinn í
Austrveg at berja trǫll. En er á leið vetrinn, þá sóttisk mjǫk
borgargerðin ok var hon svá há ok sterk at eigi mátti á þat leita. En
þá er þrír dagar váru til sumars þá var komit mjǫk at borghliði. Þá   10
settusk guðin á dómstóla sína ok leituðu ráða ok spurði hverr
annan hverr því hefði ráðit at gipta Freyju í Jǫtunheima eða spilla
loptinu ok himninum svá at taka þaðan sól ok tungl ok gefa
jǫtnum. En þat kom ásamt með ǫllum at þessu mundi ráðit hafa sá
er flestu illu ræðr, Loki Laufeyjarson, ok kváðu hann verðan ills   15
dauða ef eigi hitti hann ráð til at smiðrinn væri af kaupinu, ok
veittu Loka atgǫngu. En er hann varð hræddr þá svarði hann eiða
at hann skyldi svá til haga at smiðrinn skyldi af kaupinu, hvat sem
hann kostaði til. Ok it sama kveld er smiðrinn ók út eptir grjótinu
með hestinn Svaðilfœra, þá hljóp ór skóginum nokkvorum merr at   20
hestinum ok hrein við. En er hestrinn kendi hvat hrossi þetta var
þá œddisk hann ok sleit sundr reipin ok hljóp til merarinnar, en
hon undan til skógar ok smiðrinn eptir ok vill taka hestinn, en
þessi hross hlaupa alla nótt ok dvelsk smíðin þá nótt. Ok eptir um
daginn varð ekki svá smíðat sem fyrr hafði orðit. Ok þá er   25
smiðrinn sér at eigi mun lokit verða verkinu, þá fœrisk smiðrinn í
jǫtunmóð. En er Æsirnir sá þat til víss at þar var bergrisi kominn,
þá varð eigi þyrmt eiðunum, ok kǫlluðu þeir á Þór, ok jafnskjótt
kom hann ok því næst fór á lopt hamarrinn Mjǫllnir, galt þá
smíðarkaupit ok eigi sól ok tungl, heldr synjaði hann honum at   30
byggva í Jǫtunheimum ok laust þat hit fyrsta hǫgg er haussinn
brotnaði í smán mola ok sendi hann niðr undir Niflhel. En Loki
hafði þá ferð haft til Svaðilfœra at nokkvoru síðar bar hann fyl. Þat
var grátt ok hafði átta fœtr, ok er sá hestr beztr með goðum ok
mǫnnum. Svá segir í Vǫluspá: 35

Þá gengu regin ǫll
á rǫkstóla,
ginnheilug goð
ok of þat gættusk,
hverr hefði lopt allt   40

       lævi blandit
       eða ætt jǫtuns
       Óðs mey gefna.

       Á gengusk eiðar,
5   orð ok sœri,
       mál ǫll meginlig
       er á meðal fóru.
       Þórr einn þat vann
       þrunginn móði.
10   Hann sjaldan sitr
       er hann slíkt of fregn.'

43   Þá mælir Gangleri: 'Hvat er at segja frá Skíðblaðni er hann er
       beztr skipa? Hvárt er ekki skip jafngott sem hann er eða jafn-
       mikit?'
15   Hár segir: 'Skíðblaðnir er beztr skipanna ok með mestum
       hagleik gerr, en Naglfari er mest skip, þat er á Muspell. Dvergar
       nokkvorir, synir Ívalda, gerðu Skíðblaðni ok gáfu Frey skipit.
       Hann er svá mikill at allir Æsir megu skipa hann með vápnum ok
       herbúnaði, ok hefir hann byr þegar er segl er dregit, hvert er fara
20   skal. En þá er eigi skal fara með hann á sæ þá er hann gǫrr af svá
       mǫrgum hlutum ok með svá mikilli list at hann má vefja saman
       sem dúk ok hafa í pung sínum.'

44   Þá mælir Gangleri: 'Gott skip er Skíðblaðnir, en allmikil
       fjǫlkyngi mun við vera hǫfð áðr svá fái gert. Hvárt hefir Þórr
25   hvergi svá farit at hann hafi hitt fyrir sér svá ríkt eða ramt at
       honum hafi ofrefli í verit fyrir afls sakar eða fjǫlkyngi?'
       Þá mælir Hár: 'Fár maðr vættir mik at frá því kunni segja, en
       mart hefir honum harðfœrt þótt. En þótt svá hafi verit at
       nokkvorr hlutr hafi svá verit ramr eða sterkr at Þórr hafi eigi sigr
30   fengit á unnit, þá er eigi skylt at segja frá, fyrir því at mǫrg dœmi
       eru til þess, ok því eru allir skyldir at trúa, at Þórr er mátkastr.'
       Þá mælir Gangleri: 'Svá lízk mér sem þess hlutar mun ek yðr
       spurt hafa er engi er til fœrr at segja.'
       Þá mælir Jafnhár: 'Heyrt hǫfum vér sagt frá þeim atburðum er
35   oss þykkja ótrúligir at sannir muni vera, en hér mun sjá sitja nær er
       vita mun sǫnn tíðindi af at segja, ok muntu því trúa at hann mun
       eigi ljúga nú it fyrsta sinn er aldri laug fyrr.'
       Þá mælir Gangleri: 'Hér mun ek standa ok hlýða ef nokkvorr
       órlaustn fær þessa máls, en at ǫðrum kosti kalla ek yðr vera
40   yfirkomna ef þér kunnið eigi at segja þat er ek spyr.'

Þá mælir Þriði: 'Auðsýnt er nú at hann vill þessi tíðindi vita þótt
oss þykki eigi fagrt at segja. En þér er at þegja.

'Þat er upphaf þessa máls at Qkuþórr fór með hafra sína ok
reið ok með honum sá Áss er Loki er kallaðr. Koma þeir at kveldi
til eins búanda ok fá þar náttstað. En um kveldit tók Þórr hafra   5
sína ok skar báða. Eptir þat váru þeir flegnir ok bornir til ketils.
En er soðit var þá settisk Þórr til náttverðar ok þeir lagsmenn. Þórr
bauð til matar með sér búandanum ok konu hans ok bornum
þeira. Sonr búa hét Þjálfi en Rǫskva dóttir. Þá lagði Þórr
hafrstokurnar útar frá eldinum ok mælti at búandi ok heimamenn   10
hans skyldu kasta á hafrstokurnar beinunum. Þjálfi, son búanda,
helt á lærlegg hafrsins ok spretti á knífi sínum ok braut til mergjar.
Þórr dvalðisk þar of nóttina, en í óttu fyrir dag stóð hann upp ok
klæddi sik, tók hamarinn Mjǫllni ok brá upp ok vígði
hafrstokurnar. Stóðu þá upp hafrarnir ok var þá annarr haltr eptra   15
fœti. Þat fann Þórr ok talði at búandinn eða hans hjón mundi eigi
skynsamliga hafa farit með beinum hafrsins. Kennir hann at
brotinn var lærleggrinn. Eigi þarf langt frá því at segja, vita megu
þat allir hversu hræddr búandinn mundi vera er hann sá at Þórr lét
síga brýnnar ofan fyrir augun; en þat er sá augnanna, þá hugðisk   20
hann falla mundu fyrir sjóninni einni samt. Hann herði hendrnar
at hamarskaptinu svá at hvítnuðu knúarnir, en búandinn gerði sem
ván var ok ǫll hjúnin, kǫlluðu ákafliga, báðu sér friðar, buðu at
fyrir kvæmi allt þat er þau áttu. En er hann sá hræzlu þeira þá gekk
af honum móðrinn ok sefaðisk hann ok tók af þeim í sætt bǫrn   25
þeira Þjálfa ok Rǫsku ok gerðusk þau þá skyldir þjónustumenn
Þórs ok fylgja þau honum jafnan síðan. Lét hann þar eptir hafra ok   **45**
byrjaði ferðina austr í Jǫtunheima ok allt til hafsins, ok þá fór hann
út yfir hafit þat it djúpa. En er hann kom til lands þá gekk hann
upp ok með honum Loki ok Þjálfi ok Rǫskva. Þá er þau hǫfðu litla   30
hríð gengit varð fyrir þeim mǫrk stór. Gengu þau þann dag allan til
myrks. Þjálfi var allra manna fóthvatastr. Hann bar kýl Þórs, en til
vista var eigi gott. Þá er myrkt var orðit leituðu þeir sér til
náttstaðar ok fundu fyrir sér skála nokkvorn mjǫk mikinn. Váru
dyrr á enda ok jafnbreiðar skálanum. Þar leituðu þeir sér náttbóls.   35
En of miðja nótt varð landskjálpti mikill, gekk jǫrðin undir þeim
skykkjum ok skalf húsit. Þá stóð Þórr upp ok hét á lagsmenn sína
ok leituðusk fyrir ok fundu afhús til hœgri handar í miðjum
skálanum ok gengu þannig. Settisk Þórr í dyrrin en ǫnnur þau váru
innar frá honum ok váru þau hrædd, en Þórr helt hamarskaptinu   40

ok hugði at verja sik. Þá heyrðu þau ym mikinn ok gný. En er kom
at dagan þá gekk Þórr út ok sér hvar lá maðr skamt frá honum í
skóginum ok var sá eigi lítill. Hann svaf ok hraut sterkliga. Þá
þóttisk Þórr skilja hvat látum verit hafði of nóttina. Hann spennir
5   sik megingjǫrðum ok óx honum ásmegin, en í því vaknar sá maðr
ok stóð skjótt upp. En þá er sagt at Þór varð bilt einu sinni at slá
hann með hamrinum, ok spurði hann at nafni. En sá nefndisk
Skrýmir.
'"En eigi þarf ek," sagði hann, "at spyrja þik at nafni. Kenni ek
10 at þú ert Ásaþórr. En hvárt hefir þú dregit á braut hanzka minn?"
'Seildisk þá Skrýmir til ok tók upp hanzka sinn. Sér Þórr þá at
þat hafði hann haft of nóttina fyrir skála, en afhúsit, þat var
þumlungrinn hanzkans. Skrýmir spurði ef Þórr vildi hafa fǫruneyti
hans, en Þórr játti því. Þá tók Skrýmir ok leysti nestbagga sinn ok
15 bjósk til at eta dǫgurð, en Þórr í ǫðrum stað ok hans félagar.
Skrýmir bauð þá at þeir legði mǫtuneyti sitt, en Þórr játti því. Þá
batt Skrýmir nest þeira allt í einn bagga ok lagði á bak sér. Hann
gekk fyrir of daginn ok steig heldr stórum. En síðan at kveldi
leitaði Skrýmir þeim náttstaðar undir eik nokkvorri mikilli. Þá
20 mælir Skrýmir til Þórs at hann vill leggjask niðr at sofna,—"en þér
takið nestbaggann ok búið til nótturðar yðr."
'Því næst sofnar Skrýmir ok hraut fast, en Þórr tók nestbaggann
ok skal leysa, en svá er at segja sem ótrúligt mun þykkja, at engi
knút fekk hann leyst ok engi álarendann hreyft svá at þá væri
25 lausari en áðr. Ok er hann sér at þetta verk má eigi nýtask þá varð
hann reiðr, greip þá hamarinn Mjǫllni tveim hǫndum ok steig fram
ǫðrum fœti at þar er Skrýmir lá ok lýstr í hǫfuð honum. En
Skrýmir vaknar ok spyrr hvárt laufsblað nakkvat felli í hǫfuð
honum, eða hvárt þeir hefði þá matazk ok sé búnir til rekna. Þórr
30 segir at þeir munu þá sofa ganga. Ganga þau þá undir aðra eik. Er
þat þér satt at segja at ekki var þá óttalaust at sofa.
'En at miðri nótt þá heyrir Þórr at Skrýmir hrýtr ok sefr fast svá
at dunar í skóginum. Þá stendr hann upp ok gengr til hans, reiðir
hamarinn títt ok hart ok lýstr ofan í miðjan hvirfil honum. Hann
35 kennir at hamars muðrinn søkkr djúpt í hǫfuðit. En í því bili
vaknar Skrýmir ok mælti:
'"Hvat er nú? Fell akarn nokkvot í hǫfuð mér? Eða hvat er títt
um þik, Þórr?"
'En Þórr gekk aptr skyndiliga ok svarar at hann var þá
40 nývaknaðr; sagði at þá var mið nótt ok enn væri mál at sofa. Þá

hugsaði Þórr þat, ef hann kvæmi svá í færi at slá hann it þriðja hǫgg, at aldri skyldi hann sjá sik síðan; liggr nú ok gætir ef Skrýmir sofnaði fast. En litlu fyrir dagan, hann heyrir þá at Skrýmir mun sofnat hafa, stendr þá upp ok hleypr at honum, reiðir þá hamarinn af ǫllu afli ok lýstr á þunnvangann þann er upp vissi. Søkkr þá 5 hamarrinn upp at skaptinu, en Skrýmir settisk upp ok strauk of vangann ok mælir:

'"Hvárt munu foglar nokkvorir sitja í trénu yfir mér? Mik grunar er ek vaknaða at tros nokkvot af kvistunum felli í hǫfuð mér. Hvárt vakir þú Þórr? Mál mun vera upp at standa ok klæðask. En 10 ekki eiguð þér nú langa leið fram til borgarinnar er kallat er Útgarðr. Heyrt hefi ek at þér hafið kvisat í milli yðvar at ek væra ekki lítill maðr vexti, en sjá skuluð þér þar stœrri menn ef þér komið í Útgarð. Nú mun ek ráða yðr heilræði: látið þér eigi stórliga yfir yðr. Ekki munu hirðmenn Útgarðaloka vel þola 15 þvílíkum kǫgursveinum kǫpuryrði. En at ǫðrum kosti hverfið aptr, ok þann ætla ek yðr betra af at taka. En ef þér vilið fram fara, þá stefnið þér í austr, en ek á nú norðr leið til fjalla þessa er nú munuð þér sjá mega."

'Tekr Skrýmir nestbaggann ok kastar á bak sér ok snýr þvers á 20 braut í skóginn frá þeim, ok eigi er þess getit at Æsirnir bæði þá heila hittask.

'Þórr fór fram á leið ok þeir félagar ok gekk fram til miðs dags. 46 Þá sá þeir borg standa á vǫllum nokkvorum ok settu hnakkann á bak sér aptr áðr þeir fengu sét yfir upp, ganga til borgarinnar ok 25 var grind fyrir borghliðinu ok lokin aptr. Þórr gekk á grindina ok fekk eigi upp lokit, en er þeir þreyttu at komask í borgina þá smugu þeir milli spalanna ok kómu svá inn, sá þá hǫll mikla ok gengu þannig. Var hurðin opin. Þá gengu þeir inn ok sá þar marga menn á tvá bekki ok flesta œrit stóra. Því næst koma þeir fyrir 30 konunginn Útgarðaloka ok kvǫddu hann, en hann leit seint til þeira ok glotti um tǫnn ok mælti:

'"Seint er um langan veg at spyrja tíðinda. Eða er annan veg en ek hygg, at þessi sveinstauli sé Ǫkuþórr? En meiri muntu vera en mér lízk þú. Eða hvat íþrótta er þat er þér félagar þykkisk vera 35 við búnir? Engi skal hér vera með oss sá er eigi kunni nokkurs konar list eða kunnandi um fram flesta menn."

'Þá segir sá er síðarst gekk, er Loki heitir: "Kann ek þá íþrótt er ek em albúinn at reyna, at engi er hér sá inni er skjótara skal eta mat sinn en ek." 40

'Þá svarar Útgarðaloki: "Íþrótt er þat ef þú efnir, ok freista skal
þá þessar íþróttar,"—kallaði útar á bekkinn at sá er Logi heitir
skal ganga á gólf fram ok freista sín í móti Loka. Þá var tekit trog
eitt ok borit inn á hallar gólfit ok fyllt af slátri. Settisk Loki at
5 ǫðrum enda en Logi at ǫðrum, ok át hvártveggi sem tíðast ok
mǿttusk í miðju troginu. Hafði þá Loki etit slátr allt af beinum en
Logi hafði ok etið slátr allt ok beinin með ok svá trogit, ok sýndisk
nú ǫllum sem Loki hefði látit leikinn.

'Þá spyrr Útgarðaloki hvat sá hinn ungi maðr kunni leika, en
10 Þjálfi segir at hann mun freista at renna skeið nokkvor við
einhvern þann er Útgarðaloki fær til. Hann segir, Útgarðaloki, at
þetta er góð íþrótt ok kallar þess meiri ván at hann sé vel at sér
búinn of skjótleikinn ef hann skal þessa íþrótt inna, en þó lætr
hann skjótt þessa skulu freista. Stendr þá upp Útgarðaloki ok gengr
15 út, ok var þar gott skeið at renna eptir sléttum velli. Þá kallar
Útgarðaloki til sín sveinstaula nokkvorn er nefndr er Hugi ok bað
hann renna í kǫpp við Þjálfa. Þá taka þeir it fyrsta skeið, ok er
Hugi því framar at hann snýsk aptr í móti honum at skeiðs enda.
Þá mælir Útgarðaloki:
20 '"Þurfa muntu, Þjálfi, at leggja þik meir fram ef þú skalt vinna
leikinn, en þó er þat satt at ekki hafa hér komit þeir menn er mér
þykkir fóthvatari en svá."

'Þá taka þeir aptr annat skeið, ok þá er Hugi kemr til
skeiðs enda ok hann snýsk aptr, þá var langt kólfskot til Þjálfa. Þá
25 mælir Útgarðaloki:
'"Vel þykki mér Þjálfi renna skeiðit, en eigi trúi ek honum nú at
hann vinni leikinn. En nú mun reyna er þeir renna it þriðja
skeiðit."

'Þá taka þeir enn skeið. En er Hugi er kominn til skeiðs enda ok
30 snýsk aptr, ok er Þjálfi eigi þá kominn á mitt skeiðit. Þá segja allir
at reynt er um þenna leik.

'Þá spyrr Útgarðaloki Þór hvat þeira íþrótta mun vera er hann
muni vilja birta fyrir þeim, svá miklar sǫgur sem menn hafa gǫrt
um stórvirki hans. Þá mælir Þórr at helzt vill hann þat taka til at
35 þreyta drykkju við einhvern mann. Útgarðaloki segir at þat má vel
vera ok gengr inn í hǫllina ok kallar skutilsvein sinn, biðr at hann
taki vítishorn þat er hirðmenn eru vanir at drekka af. Því næst
kemr fram skutilsveinn með horninu ok fær Þór í hǫnd. Þá mælir
Útgarðaloki:
40 '"Af horni þessu þykkir þá vel drukkit ef í einum drykk gengr

af, en sumir menn drekka af í tveim drykkjum. En engi er svá lítill drykkjumaðr at eigi gangi af í þrimr."

'Þórr lítr á hornit, ok sýnisk ekki mikit ok er þó heldr langt. En hann er mjǫk þyrstr, tekr at drekka ok svelgr allstórum ok hyggr at eigi skal þurfa at lúta optar at sinni í hornit. En er hann þraut 5 eyrindit ok hann laut ór horninu ok sér hvat leið drykkinum, ok lízk honum svá sem alllítill munr mun vera at nú sé lægra í horninu en áðr. Þá mælti Útgarðaloki:

'"Vel er drukkit, ok eigi til mikit. Eigi mundak trúa ef mér væri sagt frá at Ásaþórr mundi eigi meira drykk drekka, en þó veit ek at 10 þú munt vilja drekka af í ǫðrum drykk."

'Þórr svarar øngu, setr hornit á munn sér ok hyggr nú at hann skal drekka meira drykk ok þreytir á drykkjuna sem honum vansk til eyrindi, ok sér enn at stikillinn hornsins vill ekki upp svá mjǫk sem honum líkar. Ok er hann tók hornit af munni sér ok sér í, lízk 15 honum nú svá sem minna hafi þorrit en í inu fyrra sinni. Er nú gott berandi borð á horninu. Þá mælti Útgarðaloki:

'"Hvat er nú, Þórr? Muntu nú eigi sparask til eins drykkjar meira en þér mun hagr á vera? Svá lízk mér, ef þú skalt nú drekka af horninu hinn þriðja drykkinn sem þessi mun mestr ætlaðr. En 20 ekki muntu mega hér með oss heita svá mikill maðr sem Æsir kalla þik ef þú gerir eigi meira af þér um aðra leika en mér lízk sem um þenna mun vera."

'Þá varð Þórr reiðr, setr hornit á munn sér ok drekkr sem ákafligast má hann ok þreytir sem lengst at drykknum. En er hann 25 sá í hornit þá hafði nú helzt nokkut munr á fengizk. Ok þá býðr hann upp hornit ok vill eigi drekka meira. Þá mælir Útgarðaloki:

'"Auðsét er nú at máttr þinn er ekki svá mikill sem vér hugðum. En viltu freista um fleiri leika? Sjá má nú at ekki nýtir þú hér af."
30

'Þórr svarar: "Freista má ek enn of nokkura leika. En undarliga mundi mér þykkja þá er ek var heima með Ásum ef þvílíkir drykkir væri svá litlir kallaðir. En hvat leik vilið þér nú bjóða mér?"

'Þá mælir Útgarðaloki: "Þat gera hér ungir sveinar, er lítit mark 35 mun at þykkja, at hefja upp af jǫrðu kǫtt minn. En eigi mundak kunna at mæla þvílíkt við Ásaþór ef ek hefða eigi sét fyrr at þú ert myklu minni fyrir þér en ek hugða."

'Því næst hljóp fram kǫttr einn grár á hallar gólfit ok heldr mikill. En Þórr gekk til ok tók hendi sinni niðr undir miðjan 40

kviðinn ok lypti upp. En kǫttrinn beygði kenginn svá sem Þórr
rétti upp hǫndina. En er Þórr seildisk svá langt upp sem hann mátti
lengst þá létti kǫttrinn einum fœti ok fær Þórr eigi framit þenna
leik. Þá mælir Útgarðaloki:

5 ' "Svá fór þessi leikr sem mik varði: kǫttrinn er heldr mikill, en
Þórr er lágr ok lítill hjá stórmenni því sem hér er með oss."

'Þá mælir Þórr: "Svá lítinn sem þér kallið mik, þá gangi nú til
einnhverr ok fáisk við mik! Nú em ek reiðr!"

'Þá svarar Útgarðaloki ok litask um á bekkina ok mælti: "Eigi sé
10 ek þann mann hér inni er eigi mun lítilræði í þykkja at fásk við
þik." Ok enn mælir hann: "Sjám fyrst. Kalli mér hingat kerlinguna
fóstru mína Elli, ok fáisk Þórr við hana ef hann vill. Felt hefir hon
þá menn er mér hafa litizk eigi ósterkligri en Þórr er."

'Því næst gekk í hǫllina kerling ein gǫmul. Þá mælir Útgarðaloki
15 at hon skal taka fang við Ásaþór. Ekki er langt um at gera. Svá fór
fang þat at því harðara er Þórr knúðisk at fanginu, því fastara stóð
hon. Þá tók kerling at leita til bragða, ok varð Þórr þá lauss á
fótum, ok váru þær sviptingar allharðar, ok eigi lengi áðr en Þórr
fell á kné ǫðrum fœti. Þá gekk til Útgarðaloki, bað þau hætta
20 fanginu, ok sagði svá at Þórr mundi eigi þurfa at bjóða fleirum
mǫnnum fang í hans hǫll. Var þá ok liðit á nótt. Vísaði
Útgarðaloki Þór ok þeim félǫgum til sætis ok dveljask þar nátt-

47 langt í góðum fagnaði. En at morni þegar dagaði stendr Þórr upp
ok þeir félagar, klæða sik ok eru búnir braut at ganga. Þá kom þar
25 Útgarðaloki ok lét setja þeim borð. Skorti þá eigi góðan fagnað,
mat ok drykk. En er þeir hafa matazk þá snúask þeir til ferðar.
Útgarðaloki fylgir þeim út, gengr með þeim braut ór borginni. En
at skilnaði þá mælir Útgarðaloki til Þórs ok spyrr hvernig honum
þykkir ferð sín orðin, eða hvárt hann hefir hitt ríkara mann
30 nokkvorn en sik. Þórr segir at eigi mun hann þat segja at eigi hafi
hann mikla ósœmð farit í þeira viðskiptum.

' "En þó veit ek at þér munuð kalla mik lítinn mann fyrir mér, ok
uni ek því illa."

'Þá mælir Útgarðaloki: "Nú skal segja þér it sanna er þú ert út
35 kominn ór borginni, at ef ek lifi ok megak ráða þá skaltu aldri
optar í hana koma. Ok þat veit trúa mín at aldri hefðir þú í hana
komit ef ek hefða vitat áðr at þú hefðir svá mikinn krapt með þér,
ok þú hafðir svá nær haft oss mikilli ófœru. En sjónhverfingar hefi
ek gert þér, svá at fyrsta sinn er ek fann þik á skóginum kom ek til
40 fundar við yðr. Ok þá er þú skyldir leysa nestbaggann þá hafðak

bundit með grésjárni, en þú fant eigi hvar upp skyldi lúka. En því
næst laust þú mik með hamrinum þrjú hǫgg, ok var it fyrsta minzt
ok var þó svá mikit at mér mundi endask til bana ef á hefði komit.
En þar er þú sátt hjá hǫll minni setberg, ok þar sáttu ofan í þrjá dali
ferskeytta ok einn djúpastan, þar váru hamarspor þín. Setberginu 5
brá ek fyrir hǫggin, en eigi sátt þú þat. Svá var ok of leikana er þér
þreyttuð við hirðmenn mína. Þá var þat it fyrsta er Loki gerði.
Hann var mjǫk soltinn ok át títt, en sá er Logi heitir, þat var
villieldr ok brendi hann eigi seinna trogit en slátrit. En er Þjálfi
þreytti rásina við þann er Hugi hét, þat var hugr minn, ok var 10
Þjálfa eigi vænt at þreyta skjótfœri hans. En er þú drakt af horninu
ok þótti þér seint líða—en þat veit trúa mín at þá varð þat undr er
ek munda eigi trúa at vera mætti: annarr endir hornsins var út í
hafi, en þat sáttu eigi, en nú er þú kemr til sjávarins þá muntu sja
mega hvern þurð þú hefir drukkit á sænum." 15
'Þat eru nú fjǫrur kallaðar. Ok enn mælir hann:
'"Eigi þótti mér hitt minna vera vert er þú lyptir upp kettinum,
ok þér satt at segja þá hræddusk allir þeir er sá er þú lyptir af jǫrðu
einum fœtinum. En sá kǫttr var eigi sem þér sýndisk: þat var
Miðgarðsormr er liggr um lǫnd ǫll, ok vansk honum varliga 20
lengðin til at jǫrðina tœki sporðr ok hǫfuð. Ok svá langt seildisk
þú upp at skamt var þá til himins. En hitt var ok mikit undr um
fangit er þú stótt svá lengi við ok fell eigi meir en á kné ǫðrum fœti
er þú fekzk við Elli, fyrir því at engi hefir sá orðit, ok engi mun
verða ef svá gamall er at elli bíðr, at eigi komi ellin ǫllum til falls. 25
Ok er nú þat satt at segja at vér munum skiljask, ok mun þá betr
hvárratveggju handar at þér komið eigi optar mik at hitta. Ek mun
enn annat sinn verja borg mína með þvílíkum vælum eða ǫðrum
svá at ekki vald munuð þér á mér fá."
'En er Þórr heyrði þessa tǫlu greip hann til hamarsins ok bregðr 30
á lopt, en er hann skal fram reiða þá sér hann þar hvergi
Útgarðaloka. Ok þá snýsk hann aptr til borgarinnar ok ætlask þá
fyrir at brjóta borgina. Þá sér hann þar vǫllu víða ok fagra en ǫnga
borg. Snýsk hann þá aptr ok ferr leið sína til þess er hann kom aptr
í Þrúðvanga. En þat er satt at segja at þá hafði hann ráðit fyrir sér 35
at leita til ef saman mætti bera fundi þeira Miðgarðsorms, sem
síðan varð. Nú ætla ek engan kunna þér sannara at segja frá þessi
ferð Þórs.'
Þá mælir Gangleri: 'Allmikill er fyrir sér Útgarðaloki, en með **48**
vælum ok fjǫlkyngi ferr hann mjǫk. En þat má sjá at hann er mikill 40

fyrir sér at hann átti hirðmenn þá er mikinn mátt hafa. Eða hvárt hefir Þórr ekki þessa hefnt?'

Hár svarar: 'Eigi er þat ókunnigt, þótt eigi sé frœðimenn, at Þórr leiðrétti þessa ferðina er nú var frá sagt, ok dvalðisk ekki lengi
5 heima áðr hann bjósk svá skyndiliga til ferðarinnar at hann hafði eigi reið ok eigi hafrana ok ekki fǫruneyti. Gekk hann út of Miðgarð svá sem ungr drengr, ok kom einn aptan at kveldi til jǫtuns nokkurs; sá er Hymir nefndr. Þórr dvalðisk þar at gistingu of nóttina. En í dagan stóð Hymir upp ok klæddisk ok bjósk at róa
10 á sæ til fiskjar. En Þórr spratt upp ok var skjótt búinn ok bað at Hymir skyldi hann láta róa á sæ með sér. En Hymir sagði at lítil liðsemð mundi at honum vera er hann var lítill ok ungmenni eitt.

'"Ok mun þik kala ef ek sit svá lengi ok útarliga sem ek em
15 vanr."

'En Þórr sagði at hann mundi róa mega fyrir því frá landi at eigi var víst hvárt hann mundi fyrr beiðask at róa útan, ok reiddisk Þórr jǫtninum svá at þá var búit at hann mundi þegar láta hamarinn skjalla honum, en hann lét þat við berask þvíat hann hugðisk þá at
20 reyna afl sitt í ǫðrum stað. Hann spurði Hymi hvat þeir skyldu hafa at beitum, en Hymir bað hann fá sér sjálfan beitur. Þá snerisk Þórr á braut þangat er hann sá øxna flokk nokkvorn er Hymir átti. Hann tók hinn mesta uxann, er Himinhrjótr hét, ok sleit af hǫfuðit ok fór með til sjávar. Hafði þá Hymir út skotit nǫkkvanum. Þórr
25 gekk á skipit ok settisk í austrrúm, tók tvær árar ok røri, ok þótti Hymi skríðr verða af róðri hans. Hymir reri í hálsinum fram ok sóttisk skjótt róðrinn. Sagði þá Hymir at þeir váru komnir á þær vaztir er hann var vanr at sitja ok draga flata fiska, en Þórr kvezk vilja róa myklu lengra, ok tóku þeir enn snertiróðr. Sagði Hymir
30 þá at þeir váru komnir svá langt út at hætt var at sitja útar fyrir Miðgarðsormi. En Þórr kvezk mundu róa eina hríð ok svá gerði, en Hymir var þá allókátr. En þá er Þórr lagði upp árarnar, greiddi hann til vað heldr sterkjan ok eigi var ǫngullinn minni eða óramligri. Þar lét Þórr koma á ǫngulinn oxahǫfuðit ok kastaði fyrir
35 borð, ok fór ǫngullinn til grunns. Ok er þá svá satt at segja at engu ginti þá Þórr minnr Miðgarðsorm en Útgarðaloki hafði spottat Þór þá er hann hóf orminn upp á hendi sér. Miðgarðsormr gein yfir oxahǫfuðit en ǫngullinn vá í góminn orminum. En er ormrinn kendi þess, brá hann við svá hart at báðir hnefar Þórs skullu út á
40 borðinu. Þá varð Þórr reiðr ok fœrðisk í ásmegin, spyrndi við svá

fast at hann hljóp báðum fótum gǫgnum skipit ok spyrndi við
grunni, dró þá orminn upp at borði. En þat má segja at engi hefir
sá sét ógurligar sjónir er eigi mátti þat sjá er Þórr hvesti augun á
orminn, en ormrinn starði neðan í mót ok blés eitrinu. Þá er sagt
at jǫtunninn Hymir gerðisk litverpr, fǫlnaði, ok hræddisk er hann sá 5
orminn ok þat er særinn fell út ok inn of nǫkkvann. Ok í því bili er
Þórr greip hamarinn ok fœrði á lopt þá fálmaði jǫtunninn til
agnsaxinu ok hjó vað Þórs af borði, en ormrinn søktisk í sæinn. En
Þórr kastaði hamrinum eptir honum, ok segja menn at hann lysti af
honum hǫfuðit við grunninum. En ek hygg hitt vera þér satt at 10
segja at Miðgarðsormr lifir enn ok liggr í umsjá. En Þórr reiddi til
hnefann ok setr við eyra Hymi svá at hann steyptisk fyrir borð ok
sér í iljar honum. En Þórr óð til lands.'

Þá mælir Gangleri: 'Hafa nokkvor meiri tíðindi orðit með **49**
Ásunum? Allmikit þrekvirki vann Þórr í þessi ferð.' 15

Hár svarar: 'Vera mun at segja frá þeim tíðindum er meira þótti
vert Ásunum. En þat er upphaf þessar sǫgu at Baldr inn góða
dreymði drauma stóra ok hættliga um líf sitt. En er hann sagði
Ásunum draumana þá báru þeir saman ráð sín, ok var þat gert at
beiða griða Baldri fyrir alls konar háska, ok Frigg tók svardaga til 20
þess at eira skyldu Baldri eldr ok vatn, járn ok alls konar málmr,
steinar, jǫrðin, viðirnir, sóttirnar, dýrin, fuglarnir, eitr, ormar. En
er þetta var gert ok vitat, þá var þat skemtun Baldrs ok Ásanna at
hann skyldi standa upp á þingum en allir aðrir skyldu sumir skjóta
á hann, sumir hǫggva til, sumir berja grjóti. En hvat sem at var 25
gert, sakaði hann ekki, ok þótti þetta ǫllum mikill frami. En er
þetta sá Loki Laufeyjarson þá líkaði honum illa er Baldr sakaði
ekki. Hann gekk til Fensalar til Friggjar ok brá sér í konu líki. Þá
spyrr Frigg ef sú kona vissi hvat Æsir hǫfðusk at á þinginu. Hon
sagði at allir skutu at Baldri, ok þat at hann sakaði ekki. Þá mælir 30
Frigg:

'"Eigi munu vápn eða viðir granda Baldri. Eiða hefi ek þegit af
ǫllum þeim."

'Þá spyrr konan: "Hafa allir hlutir eiða unnit at eira Baldri?"

'Þá svarar Frigg: "Vex viðarteinungr einn fyrir vestan Valhǫll. 35
Sá er mistilteinn kallaðr. Sá þótti mér ungr at krefja eiðsins."

'Því næst hvarf konan á brut. En Loki tók mistiltein ok sleit upp
ok gekk til þings. En Hǫðr stóð útarliga í mannhringinum þvíat
hann var blindr. Þá mælir Loki við hann:

'"Hví skýtr þú ekki at Baldri?"' 40

'Hann svarar: "Þvíat ek sé eigi hvar Baldr er, ok þat annat at ek em vápnlauss."

'Þá mælir Loki: "Gerðu þó í líking annarra manna ok veit Baldri sœmð sem aðrir menn. Ek mun vísa þér til hvar hann stendr. Skjót
5 at honum vendi þessum."

'Hǫðr tók mistiltein ok skaut at Baldri at tilvísun Loka. Flaug skotit í gǫgnum hann ok fell hann dauðr til jarðar, ok hefir þat mest óhapp verit unnit með goðum ok mǫnnum. Þá er Baldr var fallinn þá fellusk ǫllum Ásum orðtǫk ok svá hendr at taka til hans,
10 ok sá hverr til annars, ok váru allir með einum hug til þess er unnit hafði verkit. En engi mátti hefna, þar var svá mikill griðastaðr. En þá er Æsirnir freistuðu at mæla þá var hitt þó fyrr at grátrinn kom upp svá at engi mátti ǫðrum segja með orðunum frá sínum harmi. En Óðinn bar þeim mun verst þenna skaða sem hann kunni mesta
15 skyn hversu mikil aftaka ok missa Ásunum var í fráfalli Baldrs. En er goðin vitkuðusk þá mælir Frigg ok spurði hverr sá væri með Ásum er eignask vildi allar ástir hennar ok hylli ok vili hann ríða á Helveg ok freista ef hann fái fundit Baldr ok bjóða Helju útlausn ef hon vill láta fara Baldr heim í Ásgarð. En sá er nefndr Hermóðr inn
20 hvati, sveinn Óðins, er til þeirar farar varð. Þá var tekinn Sleipnir, hestr Óðins, ok leiddr fram, ok steig Hermóðr á þann hest ok hleypti braut. En Æsirnir tóku lík Baldrs ok fluttu til sævar. Hringhorni hét skip Baldrs. Hann var allra skipa mestr. Hann vildu goðin fram setja ok gera þar á bálfǫr Baldrs. En skipit gekk
25 hvergi fram. Þá var sent í Jǫtunheima eptir gýgi þeiri er Hyrrokkin hét. En er hon kom ok reið vargi ok hafði hǫggorm at taumum þá hljóp hon af hestinum, en Óðinn kallaði til berserki fjóra at gæta hestsins, ok fengu þeir eigi haldit nema þeir feldi hann. Þá gekk Hyrrokkin á framstafn nǫkkvans ok hratt fram í fyrsta viðbragði svá
30 at eldr hraut ór hlunnunum ok lǫnd ǫll skulfu. Þá varð Þórr reiðr ok greip hamarinn ok myndi þá brjóta hǫfuð hennar áðr en goðin ǫll báðu henni friðar. Þá var borit út á skipit lík Baldrs, ok er þat sá kona hans Nanna Nepsdóttir þá sprakk hon af harmi ok dó. Var hon borin á bálit ok slegit í eldi. Þá stóð Þórr at ok vígði bálit með
35 Mjǫllni. En fyrir fótum hans rann dvergr nokkurr. Sá er Litr nefndr. En Þórr spyrndi fœti sínum á hann ok hratt honum í eldinn ok brann hann.

'En at þessi brennu sótti margs konar þjóð: fyrst at segja frá Óðni, at með honum fór Frigg ok valkyrjur ok hrafnar hans, en

Freyr ók í kerru með gelti þeim er Gullinbursti heitir eða
Slíðrugtanni. En Heimdallr reið hesti þeim er Gulltoppr heitir, en
Freyja kǫttum sínum. Þar kømr ok mikit fólk hrímþursa ok
bergrisar. Óðinn lagði á bálit gullhring þann er Draupnir heitir.
Honum fylgði síðan sú náttúra at hina níundu hverja nótt drupu af   5
honum átta gullhringar jafnhǫfgir. Hestr Baldrs var leiddr á bálit
með ǫllu reiði. En þat er at segja frá Hermóði at hann reið níu
nætr døkkva dala ok djúpa svá at hann sá ekki fyrr en hann kom til
árinnar Gjallar ok reið á Gjallar brúna. Hon er þǫkð lýsigulli.
Móðguðr er nefnd mær sú er gætir brúarinnar. Hon spurði hann at   10
nafni eða ætt ok sagði at hinn fyrra dag riðu um brúna fimm fylki
dauðra manna,

'"En eigi dynr brúin minnr undir einum þér ok eigi hefir þú lit
dauðra manna. Hví ríðr þú hér á Helveg?"

'Hann svarar at "ek skal ríða til Heljar at leita Baldrs. Eða hvárt   15
hefir þú nakkvat sét Baldr á Helvegi?"

'En hon sagði at Baldr hafði þar riðit um Gjallar brú, "en niðr
ok norðr liggr Helvegr."

'Þá reið Hermóðr þar til er hann kom at Helgrindum. Þá sté
hann af hestinum ok gyrði hann fast, steig upp ok keyrði hann   20
sporum. En hestrinn hljóp svá hart ok yfir grindina at hann kom
hvergi nær. Þá reið Hermóðr heim til hallarinnar ok steig af hesti,
gekk inn í hǫllina, sá þar sitja í ǫndugi Baldr bróður sinn, ok
dvalðisk Hermóðr þar um nóttina. En at morni þá beiddisk
Hermóðr af Helju at Baldr skyldi ríða heim með honum ok sagði   25
hversu mikill grátr var með Ásum. En Hel sagði at þat skyldi svá
reyna hvárt Baldr var svá ástsæll sem sagt er,

'"Ok ef allir hlutir í heiminum, kykvir ok dauðir, gráta hann, þá
skal hann fara til Ása aptr, en haldask með Helju ef nakkvarr
mælir við eða vill eigi gráta."   30

'Þá stóð Hermóðr upp, en Baldr leiðir hann út ór hǫllinni ok tók
hringinn Draupni ok sendi Óðni til minja, en Nanna sendi Frigg
ripti ok enn fleiri gjafar; Fullu fingrgull. Þá reið Hermóðr aptr leið
sína ok kom í Ásgarð ok sagði ǫll tíðindi þau er hann hafði sét ok
heyrt.   35

'Því næst sendu Æsir um allan heim ørindreka at biðja at Baldr
væri grátinn ór Helju. En allir gerðu þat, menninir ok kykvendin
ok jǫrðin ok steinarnir ok tré ok allr málmr, svá sem þú munt sét
hafa at þessir hlutir gráta þá er þeir koma ór frosti ok í hita. Þá er

sendimenn fóru heim ok hǫfðu vel rekit sín eyrindi, finna þeir í
helli nokkvorum hvar gýgr sat. Hon nefndisk Þǫkk. Þeir biðja
hana gráta Baldr ór Helju. Hon segir:

> "Þǫkk mun gráta
> 5   þurrum tárum
> Baldrs bálfarar.
> Kyks né dauðs
> nautka ek karls sonar:
> haldi Hel því er hefir.".

10   'En þess geta menn at þar hafi verit Loki Laufeyjarson er flest
hefir illt gert með Ásum.'

50   Þá mælir Gangleri: 'Allmiklu kom Loki á leið er hann olli fyrst
því er Baldr var veginn, ok svá því er hann varð eigi leystr frá
Helju. Eða hvárt varð honum þessa nakkvat hefnt?'

15   Hár segir: 'Goldit var honum þetta svá at hann mun lengi
kennask. Þá er guðin váru orðin honum svá reið sem ván var, hljóp
hann á braut ok fal sik í fjalli nokkvoru, gerði þar hús ok fjórar
dyrr at hann mátti sjá ór húsinu í allar áttir. En opt um daga brá
hann sér í laxlíki ok falsk þá þar sem heitir Fránangrsfors. Þá
20   hugsaði hann fyrir sér hverja væl Æsir mundu til finna at taka hann
í forsinum. En er hann sat í húsinu tók hann língarn ok reið á
ræxna svá sem net er síðan. En eldr brann fyrir honum. Þá sá hann
at Æsir áttu skamt til hans ok hafði Óðinn sét ór Hliðskjálfinni
hvar hann var. Hann hljóp þegar upp ok út í ána ok kastaði netinu
25   fram á eldinn. En er Æsir koma til hússins þá gekk sá fyrst inn er
allra var vitrastr, er Kvasir heitir. Ok er hann sá á eldinum
fǫlskann er netit hafði brunnit þá skilði hann at þat mundi væl vera
til at taka fiska, ok sagði Ásunum. Því næst tóku þeir ok gerðu sér
net eptir því sem þeir sá á fǫlska at Loki hafði gert. Ok er búit var
30   netit þá fara Æsir til árinnar ok kasta neti í forsinn. Helt Þórr enda
ǫðrum ok ǫðrum heldu allir Æsir ok drógu netit. En Loki fór fyrir
ok legsk niðr í milli steina tveggja. Drógu þeir netit yfir hann ok
kendu at kykt var fyrir ok fara í annat sinn upp til forsins ok kasta
út netinu ok binda við svá þungt at eigi skyli undir mega fara. Ferr
35   þá Loki fyrir netinu, en er hann sér at skamt var til sævar þá hleypr
hann upp yfir þinulinn ok rennir upp í forsinn. Nú sá Æsirnir hvar
hann fór, fara enn upp til forsins ok skipta liðinu í tvá staði, en
Þórr veðr þá eptir miðri ánni ok fara svá til sævar. En er Loki sér
tvá kosti—var þat lífs háski at hlaupa á sæinn, en hitt var annarr at

hlaupa enn yfir netit—ok þat gerði hann, hljóp sem snarast yfir netþinulinn. Þórr greip eptir honum ok tók um hann ok rendi hann í hendi honum svá at staðar nam hǫndin við sporðinn. Ok er fyrir þá sǫk laxinn aptrmjór.

'Nú var Loki tekinn griðalauss ok farit með hann í helli nokkvorn. Þá tóku þeir þrjár hellur ok settu á egg ok lustu rauf á hellunni hverri. Þá váru teknir synir Loka Váli ok Nari eða Narfi. Brugðu Æsir Vála í vargs líki ok reif hann í sundr Narfa bróður sinn. Þá tóku Æsir þarma hans ok bundu Loka með yfir þá þrjá steina—einn undir herðum, annarr undir lendum, þriði undir knésfótum—ok urðu þau bǫnd at járni. Þá tók Skaði eitrorm ok festi upp yfir hann svá at eitrit skyldi drjúpa ór orminum í andlit honum. En Sigyn kona hans stendr hjá honum ok heldr mundlaugu undir eitrdropa. En þá er full er mundlaugin þá gengr hon ok slær út eitrinu, en meðan drýpr eitrit í andlit honum. Þá kippisk hann svá hart við at jǫrð ǫll skelfr. Þat kallið þér landskjálpta. Þar liggr hann í bǫndum til ragnarøkrs.'

Þá mælir Gangleri: 'Hver tíðindi eru at segja frá um ragnarøkr? Þess hefi ek eigi fyrr heyrt getit.'

Hár segir: 'Mikil tíðindi eru þaðan at segja ok mǫrg. Þau in fyrstu at vetr sá kemr er kallaðr er fimbulvetr. Þá drífr snær ór ǫllum áttum. Frost eru þá mikil ok vindar hvassir. Ekki nýtr sólar. Þeir vetr fara þrír saman ok ekki sumar milli. En áðr ganga svá aðrir þrír vetr at þá er um alla verǫld orrostur miklar. Þá drepask brœðr fyrir ágirni sakar ok engi þyrmir fǫður eða syni í manndrápum eða sifjasliti. Svá segir í Vǫluspá:

> Brœðr munu berjask
> ok at bǫnum verðask,
> munu systrungar
> sifjum spilla.
> Hart er með hǫlðum,
> hórdómr mikill,
> skeggjǫld, skálmǫld,
> skildir klofnir,
> vindǫld, vargǫld,
> áðr verǫld steypisk.

Þá verðr þat er mikil tíðindi þykkja, at úlfrinn gleypir sólna, ok þykkir mǫnnum þat mikit mein. Þá tekr annarr úlfrinn tunglit, ok gerir sá ok mikit ógagn. Stjǫrnurnar hverfa af himninum. Þá er ok þat til tíðinda at svá skelfr jǫrð ǫll ok bjǫrg at viðir losna ór jǫrðu

upp, en bjǫrgin hrynja, en fjǫtrar allir ok bǫnd brotna ok slitna. Þá
verðr Fenrisúlfr lauss. Þá geysisk hafit á lǫndin fyrir því at þá snýsk
Miðgarðsormr í jǫtunmóð ok sœkir upp á landit. Þá verðr ok þat at
Naglfar losnar, skip þat er svá heitir. Þat er gert af nǫglum dauðra
5 manna, ok er þat fyrir því varnanar vert ef maðr deyr með
óskornum nǫglum at sá maðr eykr mikit efni til skipsins Naglfars
er goðin ok menn vildi seint at gert yrði. En í þessum sævargang
flýtr Naglfar. Hrymr heitir jǫtunn er stýrir Naglfara. En Fenrisúlfr
ferr með gapanda munn ok er hinn efri kjǫptr við himni en hinn
10 neðri við jǫrðu. Gapa mundi hann meira ef rúm væri til. Eldar
brenna ór augum hans ok nǫsum. Miðgarðsormr blæss svá eitrinu
at hann dreifir lopt ǫll ok lǫg, ok er hann allógurligr, ok er hann á
aðra hlið úlfinum. Í þessum gný klofnar himinninn ok ríða þaðan
Muspells synir. Surtr ríðr fyrst ok fyrir honum ok eptir bæði eldr
15 brennandi. Sverð hans er gott mjǫk. Af því skínn bjartara en af
sólu. En er þeir ríða Bifrǫst þá brotnar hon sem fyrr er sagt.
Muspells megir sœkja fram á þann vǫll er Vígríðr heitir. Þar kemr
ok þá Fenrisúlfr ok Miðgarðsormr. Þar er ok þá Loki kominn ok
Hrymr ok með honum allir hrímþursar, en Loka fylgja allir Heljar
20 sinnar. En Muspells synir hafa einir sér fylking; er sú bjǫrt mjǫk.
Vǫllrinn Vígríðr er hundrað rasta víðr á hvern veg.

'En er þessi tíðindi verða þá stendr upp Heimdallr ok blæss
ákafliga í Gjallarhorn ok vekr upp ǫll guðin ok eiga þau þing
saman. Þá ríðr Óðinn til Mímis brunns ok tekr ráð af Mími fyrir sér
25 ok sínu liði. Þá skelfr askr Yggdrasils ok engi hlutr er þá óttalauss á
himni eða jǫrðu. Æsir hervæða sik ok allir einherjar ok sœkja fram
á vǫlluna. Ríðr fyrstr Óðinn með gullhjálm ok fagra brynju ok geir
sinn er Gungnir heitir. Stefnir hann móti Fenrisúlf, en Þórr fram á
aðra hlið honum ok má hann ekki duga honum þvíat hann hefir
30 fullt fang at berjask við Miðgarðsorm. Freyr bersk móti Surti ok
verðr harðr samgangr áðr Freyr fellr. Þat verðr hans bani er hann
missir þess hins góða sverðs er hann gaf Skírni. Þá er ok lauss
orðinn hundrinn Garmr er bundinn er fyrir Gnipahelli. Hann er it
mesta forað. Hann á víg móti Tý ok verðr hvárr ǫðrum at bana.
35 Þórr berr banaorð af Miðarðsormi ok stígr þaðan braut níu fet. Þá
fellr hann dauðr til jarðar fyrir eitri því er ormrinn blæss á hann.
Úlfrinn gleypir Óðin. Verðr þat hans bani. En þegar eptir snýsk
fram Víðarr ok stígr ǫðrum fœti í neðra keypt úlfsins. (Á þeim fœti
hefir hann þann skó er allan aldr hefir verit til samnat: þat eru
40 bjórar þeir er menn sníða ór skóm sínum fyrir tám eða hæl. Því

skal þeim bjórum braut kasta sá maðr er at því vill hyggja at koma
Ásunum at liði.) Annarri hendi tekr hann inn efra keypt úlfsins ok
rífr sundr gin hans ok verðr þat úlfsins bani. Loki á orrostu við
Heimdall ok verðr hvárr annars bani. Því næst slyngr Surtr eldi yfir
jǫrðina ok brennir allan heim. Svá er sagt í Vǫluspá: 5

Hátt blæss Heimdallr
horn er á lopti.
Mælir Óðinn
við Míms hǫfuð.
Skelfr Yggdrasils   10
askr standandi,
ymr it aldna tré
en jǫtunn losnar.

Hvat er með Ásum?
Hvat er með álfum?   15
Ymr allr Jǫtunheimr.
Æsir ró á þingi.
Stynja dvergar
fyrir steindurum,
veggbergs vísir.   20
Vituð ér enn eða hvat?

Hrymr ekr austan
hefisk lind fyrir.
Snýsk Jǫrmungandr
í jǫtunmóði.   25
Ormr knýr unnir,
ǫrn mun hlakka,
slítr nái niðfǫlr,
Naglfar losnar.

Kjóll ferr austan,   30
koma munu Muspells
of lǫg lýðir,
en Loki stýrir.
Þar ró fíflmegir
með freka allir.   35
Þeim er bróðir
Býleists í fǫr.

Surtr ferr sunnan
með sviga lævi.
Skínn af sverði   40
sól valtíva.

Grjótbjǫrg gnata
en gífr rata,
troða halir Helveg
en himinn klofnar.

5   Þá kømr Hlínar
harmr annarr fram
er Óðinn ferr
við úlf vega,
en bani Belja
10   bjartr at Surti:
þar mun Friggjar
falla angan.

Gengr Óðins son
við úlf vega,
15   Víðarr of veg
at valdýri.
Lætr hann megi Hveðrungs
mund of standa
hjǫr til hjarta.
20   Þá er hefnt fǫður.

Gengr inn mæri
mǫgr Hlǫðynjar
nepr at naðri
níðs ókvíðnum.
25   Munu halir allir
heimstǫð ryðja
er af móði drepr
Miðgarðs véorr.

Sól mun sortna,
30   søkkr fold í mar.
Hverfa af himni
heiðar stjǫrnur.
Geisar eimi
ok aldrnari,
35   leikr hár hiti
við himin sjálfan.

Hér segir enn svá:

Vígríðr heitir vǫllr
er finnask vígi at
40   Surtr ok in svásu guð.

Hundrað rasta
hann er á hverjan veg.
Sá er þeim vǫllr vitaðr.'

Þá mælir Gangleri: 'Hvat verðr þá eptir er brendr er himinn ok **52**
jǫrð ok heimr allr ok dauð goðin ǫll ok allir einherjar ok allt 5
mannfólk? Ok hafið þér áðr sagt at hverr maðr skal lifa í
nokkvorum heimi um allar aldir?'

Þá segir Þriði: 'Margar eru þá vistir góðar ok margar illar. Bazt
er þá at vera á Gimlé á himni, ok allgott er til góðs drykkjar þeim
er þat þykkir gaman í þeim sal er Brimir heitir. Hann stendr ok á 10
himni. Sá er ok góðr salr er stendr á Niðafjǫllum, gjǫrr af rauðu
gulli. Sá heitir Sindri. Í þessum sǫlum skulu byggja góðir menn ok
siðlátir. Á Nástrǫndum er mikill salr ok illr ok horfa í norðr dyrr.
Hann er ok ofinn allr orma hryggjum sem vandahús, en orma
hǫfuð ǫll vitu inn í húsit ok blása eitri svá at eptir salnum renna 15
eitrár, ok vaða þær ár eiðrofar ok morðvargar, svá sem hér segir:

Sal veit ek standa
sólu fjarri
Nástrǫndu á.
Norðr horfa dyrr. 20
Falla eitrdropar
inn of ljóra.
Sá er undinn salr
orma hryggjum.
Skulu þar vaða 25
þunga strauma
menn meinsvara
ok morðvargar.

En í Hvergelmi er verst:

Þar kvelr Níðhǫggr 30
nái framgengna.'

Þá mælir Gangleri: 'Hvárt lifa nokkvor goðin þá? Eða er þá **53**
nokkvor jǫrð eða himinn?'

Hár segir: 'Upp skýtr jǫrðunni þá ór sænum ok er þá grœn ok
fǫgr. Vaxa þá akrar ósánir. Víðarr ok Váli lifa svá at eigi hefir 35
særinn ok Surtalogi grandat þeim, ok byggja þeir á Iðavelli, þar
sem fyrr var Ásgarðr. Ok þar koma þá synir Þórs, Móði ok Magni,
ok hafa þar Mjǫllni. Því næst koma þar Baldr ok Hǫðr frá Heljar.
Setjask þá allir samt ok talask við ok minnask á rúnar sínar ok

rœða of tíðindi þau er fyrrum hǫfðu verit, of Miðgarðsorm ok um Fenrisúlf. Þá finna þeir í grasinu gulltǫflur þær er Æsirnir hǫfðu átt. Svá er sagt:

> Víðarr ok Váli
> 5   byggja vé goða
> þá er sortnar Surtalogi.
> Móði ok Magni
> skulu Mjǫllni hafa
> Vingnis at vígþroti.

10   En þar sem heitir Hoddmímis holt leynask menn tveir í Surtaloga er svá heita: Líf ok Leifþrasir; ok hafa morgindǫggvar fyrir mat. En af þessum mǫnnum kemr svá mikil kynslóð at byggvisk heimr allr. Svá sem hér segir:

> Líf ok Leifþrasir;
> 15   en þau leynask munu
> í holti Hoddmímis.
> Morgindǫggvar
> þau sér at mat hafa,
> en þaðan af aldir alask.

20   Ok hitt mun þér undarligt þykkja er sólin hefir getit dóttur eigi ófegri en hon er, ok ferr sú þá stigu móður sinnar, sem hér segir:

> Eina dóttur
> berr Álfrǫðul
> áðr hana Fenrir fari.
> 25   Sú skal ríða
> er regin deyja
> móður braut mær.

En nú ef þú kant lengra fram at spyrja þá veit ek eigi hvaðan þér kemr þat, fyrir því at ǫngan mann heyrða ek lengra segja fram 30   aldarfarit. Ok njóttu nú sem þú namt.'

54   Því næst heyrði Gangleri dyni mikla hvern veg frá sér, ok leit út á hlið sér. Ok þá er hann sésk meir um þá stendr hann úti á sléttum velli, sér þá ǫnga hǫll ok ǫnga borg. Gengr hann þá leið sína braut ok kemr heim í ríki sitt ok segir þau tíðindi er hann hefir sét ok 35   heyrt. Ok eptir honum sagði hverr maðr ǫðrum þessar sǫgur.

En Æsir setjask þá á tal ok ráða ráðum sínum ok minnask á þessar frásagnir allar er honum váru sagðar, ok gefa nǫfn þessi hin sǫmu er áðr eru nefnd mǫnnum ok stǫðum þeim er þar váru, til þess at þá er langar stundir liði at menn skyldu ekki ifask í at allir væri einir, þeir Æsir er nú var frá sagt ok þessir er þá váru þau sǫmu nǫfn gefin. Þar var þá Þórr kallaðr—ok er sá Ásaþórr hinn gamli, sá er Qkuþórr—ok honum eru kend þau stórvirki er Þórr (Ector) gerði í Troju. En þat hyggja menn at Tyrkir hafi sagt frá Ulixes ok hafi þeir hann kallat Loka, þvíat Tyrkir váru hans hinir mestu óvinir.

5

General notes

p.6,l.26–7. 'from the fact that the names of their ancestors are written', i.e. from the names that are recorded in their genealogies, which could be seen to belong to the language of the 'Æsir'.

p.6,l.29–30. The reference seems to be to the existence of non-Germanic, í.e. Celtic, place-names in England. Snorri makes a comparable remark in *Hkr* i. 153; cf. *Fornmanna sögur*, xi, Kaupmannahøfn 1828, p. 412 (probably derived from the beginning of *Skjǫldunga saga*).

p.7,l.4. The Gefjun described here and in *Hkr* i. 14–15 has a different nature from the one mentioned at p.29,l.21, but there is no real conflict, because this is one of the human Æsir of the prologue, while the figures within the dialogue are the divine ones they worship. The Gefjun that appears in *Ls* 19–20 seems more like the one in this story. In various Icelandic versions of Latin writings Gefjun is used as an equivalent of Diana, though in the Norwegian biblical commentary in *Stjórn* (ed. C. R. Unger, Christiania 1862, p. 90) she is made equivalent to Venus. Cf. AH *Studier* 69–71.

p.7,l.12–19. This verse is thought to be part of Bragi's chief surviving poem *Ragnarsdrápa*, in which he described illustrations depicting various legends on a shield supposed to have been given him by Ragnarr loðbrók (see *SnE* i. 370, 374, 426, 436–8). It is also quoted in *Hkr* i. 15, but otherwise the poem is only preserved in manuscripts of *SnE* (see *Skj* A i. 1–4). A different interpretation of the first four lines, based on an emended text, is given by R. Frank, 'Old Norse Court Poetry, The Dróttkvætt Stanza', *Islandica*, xlii, Ithaca 1978, 108–10.

p.7,l.16. *ok* links *fjǫgur haufuð* and *átta ennitungl*, and the whole phrase is the object of *báru*.

p.7,l.27–8. Cf. p.39,l.24–5.

p.7,l.31–4 is also quoted in *Fagrskinna*, ed. Finnur Jónsson, København 1902–3, p. 17, and *Flateyjarbók*, i. 574, in both of which it is attributed, as here, to Þjóðólfr; and in *Hkr* i. 117, where it is attributed, probably correctly, to Þorbjǫrn hornklofi, a Norwegian poet who flourished around AD 900. It is though to be part of a poem known as *Haraldskvæði* or *Hrafnsmál* about Haraldr hárfagri (died *c*.940), and refers ironically to the rout of that king's opponents at the battle of Hafrsfjǫrðr (*c*.885), who are described as having used their shields to protect their backs as they fled.

Þjóðólfr of Hvinir in Norway was also associated with Haraldr hárfagri, and the poems *Haustlǫng* (quoted in *Skáld*) and *Ynglingatal* (quoted in Snorri's *Ynglinga saga*) are attributed to him. Cf. *Skáldatal*, *SnE* III. 273, and see *Skj* A I. 7–21.

p.7,l.36–p.8,l.1. Cf. *Vm* 8.

p.8,l.10–15 = *Háv* 1.

p.8,l.22–3. Cf. *Vm* 7. Gylfi is to demonstrate his wisdom by his ability to *ask* questions (cf. *Háv* 28, 63) and his opponents will be defeated if he can think of a question they cannot answer; cf. p.36,l.32–40 and note, and p.54,l.28–30.

p.8,l.24–5 are metrical enough to be arranged as verse, but whether they are a quotation, and if so from what, it is impossible to say. Cf. *Vm* 9, 11.

p.8,l.29–32. All these names, or variants of them, appear both in the *þula* of Óðinn names in *SnE* II. 472–3 and in the verses quoted from *Grm*, p.21,l.32–p.22,l.15 below. When there are alternative forms here, it is the second form that corresponds to *Grm* and the *þula*. In the version of this passage in U only one of each of the alternatives is given, again generally the second.

p.9,l.12–19 = *Vsp* 3. The differences from the *PE* texts are taken to imply different oral versions of the poem, but Snorri may have deliberately excluded Ymir at this point.

p.9,l.22–4. These rivers are among those listed in *Grm* 27–8. Cf. p.33,l.21–5 and note. On Gjǫll cf. p.47,l.9.

p.9,l.29. The phrase *endi veraldar* occurs only here in *Gylf*. From p.25,l.26 the word *ragnarøkr* is used.

p.9,l.31–8 = *Vsp* 52 (cf. p.51,l.38–p.52,l.4).

p.10,l.14. *þess* could be neuter, but nevertheless it seems likely that the origin of the *kraptr* is conceived as a personal agency (Alfǫðr or Surtr?).

p.10,l.18–25 = *Hdl* 33 (preserved in *Flateyjarbók*). Verses 29–44 of this poem are thought to have constituted what was apparently known to Snorri as *Vǫluspá hin skamma*.

p.10,l.27–35 = *Vm* 30–1; lines 27–9 is a question asked by Óðinn in the poem, who has assumed the name Gagnráðr (cf. the textual note to line 26); lines 30–5 are Vafþrúðnir's answer, and *órar* (line 33) refers to the giants, whose various family lines extend back in time and meet in a common progenitor (line 34).

p.11,l.16–19. Cf. p.3,l.36 ff., p.4,l.9 ff., and p.8,l.27–36: the name the Æsir have given to the almighty ruler whose existence they have deduced from natural phenomena by means of their *jarðlig skilning* is Óðinn, because that is the name of the greatest being they know, and they presume the two are identical; and Hár invites Gangleri to accept this identification. (At p.13,l.4–17 however, Alfǫðr/Óðinn appears again to be euhemerized as a human king, and even here he is far from eternal.) *Sá maðr* (line 18) relates to the following *er* clause which refers to Óðinn Borsson. In line 17 *hann* refers to *stýrandi*, and *svá* means the name Óðinn, as in line 18. Line 19 implies that if Gangleri is going to address the almighty he ought to address him by this name. This is thus the fullest answer yet to Gangleri's enquiry at p.8,l.27. Note that Óðinn Borsson, the god, is always distinct from Óðinn Friallafsson, the human king of the prologue.

The whole paragraph is the words of Hár. There is no justification for taking part of it as an interposition by the author, breaking into the dramatic framework to state his own belief. Snorri is imaginatively trying to re-create a heathen credo. Similarly *þér* (line 19) is not to be taken to refer to the reader: it means Gangleri primarily, though it may include his Scandinavian contemporaries generally.

p.11,l.27–32 = *Vm* 35. The speaker is Vafþrúðnir, the wise old giant.

p.11,l.35 ff. *Grm* 40–1, quoted at p.12,l.28–40, is the main source, but cf. *Vm* 21 and *Vsp* 4. See also p.3,l.18 ff.

p.12,l.1. The second *gerðu* is from the verb *gerða*.

p.12,l.2–3. Cf. p.37,l.29.

p.12,l.4 ff. Kennings based on these legends are mentioned in *Skáld* (*SnE* I. 314–16); see R. Meissner, *Die Kenningar der Skalden*, Bonn und Leipzig 1921, p. 104.

p.12,l.9–11. Snorri here distinguishes the stars that are 'fixed' (to the inverted bowl of the sky) from those that 'move' (planets, and perhaps comets and shooting stars).

p.12,l.11. The *forn vísindi* may be just eddic poems (e.g. *Vm* 23 and 25 as well as *Vsp* 6), but Snorri may also have had in mind twelfth-century Icelandic books on astronomy and the calendar such as that which survives in the Royal Library, Copenhagen as GkS 1812 4to (see *Äldsta delen af cod. 1812 4to Gml. Kgl. Samling*, ed. L. Larsson, København 1883, and *Alfræði íslenzk*, II, ed. N. Beckman and K. Kålund, København 1914–16). Cf. also *Genesis* I. 14.

p.12,l.13–18 = *Vsp* 5.

p.12,l.19. 'It was the same with the earth before this took place', or perhaps 'thus it was above the earth (i.e. in the sky) before this took place'. The words of *jǫrð* are only in R, but it is hard to see that the sentence makes better sense if they are omitted.

p.12,l.23–4. It is not quite clear on which side of the surrounding ocean the giants live. It is perhaps most natural to take it that they were on the inside, round the edge of the world inhabited by men, but the story of Útgarðaloki suggests that some at least lived beyond the ocean (p.37,l.28–9). Eddic poems provide no clear statement on this.

p.12,l.28–40 = *Grm* 40–1.

p.13,l.6. *hinn fyrsti* is presumably Óðinn; cf. *Vsp* 17–18. The vagueness of identification here is presumably because the author knew that *Vsp* has Hœnir and Lóðurr in place of Vili and Vé in this episode.

p.13,l.8. *þeim* is attracted into the case of the relative clause, and *mannkindin* is construed as if a plural (cf. *ólusk*).

p.13,l.10. *kallaðr* is abbreviated *kall* with a line and curl through *-ll*, as at p.14,l.23, p.19,l.35, 39, p.23,l.2, and elsewhere. The gender seems to be influenced by that of the complement *Ásgarðr*; *kǫlluð* (to agree with *borg*, as in W) would be more normal; T has *kallat*. Cf. p.30,l.7 and note, and p.39,l.11, where the neuter form is written. At p.4,l.27–8 W has *þat hús ok herbergi . . . er kǫlluð var Troja*; see also p.29,l.26 and note.

p.13,l.10–17. Here the gods worshipped by the human Æsir of the frame story are themselves euhemerized and represented as having lived on earth in the past (note the tense of *settisk* at p.13,l.13), and as being the ancestors of the human Æsir. Cf. p.8,l.28–9 and p.15,l.23. At p.20,l.5, however, Hliðskjálf is said to be in heaven.

p.13,l.20. Although the phrases *gera e-rri barn*, *gera barn af e-rri* occur in the sense 'beget a child on (with) s-one' (see J. Fritzner, *Ordbog over det gamle norske Sprog*, Oslo 1954, s.v. *barn* and *gera* 7), the phrase used here suggests 'make (a child) out of (in this case) earth', and the ambiguity may be intentional.

p.13,l.25. If Jǫrð here, as at p.13,l.19, is a personification of the earth, Snorri evidently knew more than one legend about her ancestry. Cf. p.3,l.29–33, and p.30,l.36.

p.13,l.31. The origin of dew; cf. p.19,l.24–9.

p.13,l.34 ff. Snorri appears to be combining several originally distinct aetiological stories about the sun and moon (night and day). Besides p.13,l.22–33, p.13,l.34–p.14,l.7, p.14,l.8–17, he has yet another account at p.12,l.7–19 (referred to at p.13,l.40). Note also p.54,l.20–7 and *SnE* I. 484. Some of these stories may represent popular tradition, others may have a more learned origin, or at least have been modified by learned speculation (and perhaps scaldic word-play?); cf. A. Holtsmark, 'Bil og Hjuke', *Maal og Minne*, 1945, 139–54. Only some parts of these accounts are represented in extant eddic poetry; cf. *Vm* 12, 14, 23, 25, *Grm* 37, 39, *Vsp* 5–6, 40, and the note to p.14,l.14–17. See also *SnE* II. 431/3–4 (not part of Snorri's work), which is perhaps part of a lost poem.

p.14,l.2. *í sumum frœðum*: i.e. presumably *Grm* 37; see note to p.12,l.11.

p.14,l.6. i.e. *stǫngin* (*heitir*) *Simul*. For *sá* (line 5) see *sár* (1) in glossary.

p.14,l.14–17. The two wolves are also mentioned in *Grm* 39 and (as

Skalli and Hatti) in one manuscript of *Heiðreks saga* (p. 81). The
statement here that the wolf that goes ahead of the sun will catch the
moon is only in R and W and could be an interpolation, though it is
repeated in all manuscripts at p.49,l.38. In any case it is probably only a
deduction from *Grm* 39 and *Vsp* 40 (quoted at p.14,l.28–35), where
tungl (here = sun) was probably taken by some medieval readers to
mean the moon. Mánagarmr (p.14,l.23) does not appear in other
sources and, unless he is the same as Hati Hróðvitnisson, must
represent a different tradition, though he may be merely Snorri's
rationalization of *Vsp* 40–1. Yet another version of the destruction of
the sun appears in *Vm* 46–7 (quoted at p.54,l.22–7), where it is Fenrir
who swallows it.

p.14,l.28–p.15,l.3 = *Vsp* 40–1. The second verse, like p.14,l.23–6
above, is a prophecy about *ragnarøkr*.

p.15,l.31. Cf. *Vsp* 8. The significance of this verse and the identity of the
three females are obscure in the poem, and Snorri does not offer any
clarification. But Jǫtunheimar symbolizes for him the forces of destruction and chaos that conflict with the order and civilization fostered by
the Æsir.

p.15,l.39–p.17,l.4 corresponds to *Vsp* 9, 10/5–8, 11–13, 15 and 16/1–4.
Vsp 10/1–4 and 14 are paraphrased in prose. Snorri's version differs
considerably from *PE*, but the fact that all the dwarf-lists (conflated as
they evidently are from several overlapping *þulur*) appear both in
Snorri's version and in the texts of *Vsp* in the Codex Regius of the eddic
poems and *Hauksbók* means that if they are an interpolation in *Vsp* the
interpolation was made at an early stage in the poem's textual history.
There is no textual evidence that they are spurious.

p.16,l.11. *hon* is the prophetess (*vǫlva*) who is the speaker in *Vsp*.

p.17,l.18. At p.25,l.40 Gjallarhorn is in the possession of Heimdallr (cf.
p.50,l.23). If *Heimdallar hljóð* in *Vsp* 27 means Gjallarhorn, it is there
said to be hidden under Yggdrasill.

p.17,l.21–8 = *Vsp* 28/7–14.

p.17,l.27. The meaning of *af veði* is obscure: p.17,l.18 suggests that
Snorri took it to be a vessel, and believed that this was Gjallarhorn. In
Vsp 27, however, the *veð* (presumably Óðinn's eye) seems to be
conceived as the source of the flow of mead, or something over which it
flows.

p.17,l.35. Baldr has not been mentioned before. For a moment Snorri
seems to have forgotten his dramatic framework, and that to Gangleri
Baldr will need an introduction (cf. p.23,l.14), though one would not of
course have been necessary for Snorri's contemporary readers. His
death and burial are related on pp. 45–7 below.

p.17,l.38–p.18,l.6 = *Grm* 29. The precise reason why Þórr has to walk and wade is not apparent either from the verse or from the prose.

p.18,l.11. *allt* is presumably adverbial, either with *þar . . . fyrir* 'everywhere there' or with *guðlig vǫrn* 'entirely, absolutely'.

p.18,l.17–22 = *Fm* 13. The speaker is the serpent Fáfnir. This is the only quotation in *Gylf* from an eddic poem usually classed as 'heroic' rather than 'mythological'. It may be that the verse was known to Snorri as part of another poem, but the content of this and other verses in *Fáfnismál* is mythological and Snorri may have considered the poem mythological as it stands.

p.18,l.34. *barr* normally means the foliage of conifers. But Snorri was not necessarily ignorant of the nature of the ash, which he would have known from his visits to Scandinavia. *Bíta barr* is an alliterating phrase, and *barr* may have been extended in reference, at any rate in poetry, to include all kinds of foliage (see glossary and cf. *SnE* I. 340: *barr eða lauf*). Alternatively, since Yggdrasill was evergreen (p.19,l.26) it may have been imagined to partake of the nature of a conifer.

p.18,l.38–p.19,l.13 = *Grm* 35 and 34. The conflicting information about the number of stags at p.18,l.34 is derived from *Grm* 33; *Grm* 32, 34, and 35 also conflict on the number of serpents (note Snorri's compromise at p.18,l.35–6). The reason for the apparent contradictions in *Grm* may be that the poem we have was compiled from variant versions of poetical myths, just as *Háv* included variant versions of gnomic utterances.

p.19,l.18. This idea may have been suggested by the so-called petrifying springs in Iceland which coat objects in their vicinity with a white deposit.

p.19,l.20–7 = *Vsp* 19. *æ* (line 26) can be taken either with *grœnn* (i.e. evergreen) or with *stendr*.

p.20,l.11–18 = *Vsp* 64.

p.20,l.22. *þessum himni* = 'our heaven (sky)', i.e. the one humans see; *annarr himinn* (line 21) = Andlangr; *þenna stað* line 24 = Gimlé.

p.20,l.24–5. i.e. no men are to be found in these places yet (cf. p.9,l.3). Presumably these heavens will be peopled with good men after the end of the world; cf. p.53,l.9.

p.20,l.33–8 = *Vm* 37.

p.21,l.3. *svá fróðr* i.e. as Gangleri claims to be.

p.21,l.13. The number twelve does not include Óðinn, and Þórr is number one (cf. *Annarr* p.23,l.14, *þriði* p.23,l.28). Loki, as an afterthought (p.26,l.34), makes a thirteenth. Cf. the beginning of *Skáld* (*SnE* I. 208) where the list of twelve Æsir similarly excludes Óðinn (and

Baldr and Hǫðr, though since Nanna is present among the Ásynjur this cannot be because the episode takes place after Baldr's death), but has in addition Hœnir, and includes Loki. In spite of the different terminology in U at p.22,l.28 (*goðanna eða Ásanna*) and p.22,l.31 (*sterkastr Ása ok allra guðanna ok manna*), it does not seem that Snorri intended to distinguish Æsir from other gods (i.e. Vanir), though the exclusion of the latter (i.e. Njǫrðr and Freyr) from the tally in *Gylf* would leave exactly twelve including Óðinn and Loki. But Njǫrðr is described as an Áss at p.23,l.28 (in all manuscripts, including U) in spite of the statement at p.23,l.32 (which R omits).

p.21,l.21–6. This seems to be a conflation of *Ls* 29/1,4–6, 21/1–2, and 47/3. Snorri may have known a different oral version of the poem from that preserved in *PE*, but the differences may be just due to his faulty memory.

p.21,l.29. Snorri seems to be identifying the *einherjar* in Valhǫll with the *rétt siðaðir menn* in Gimlé (p.9,l.3) by associating both places with Vingólf.

p.21,l.32–p.22,l.15 = *Grm* 46–50 and 54, but again with considerable differences. Cf. p.8,l.29–32 and note.

p.22,l.16–19, 24–5. Cf. *Grm* 48–50, where some of Óðinn's names are said to have arisen from his various adventures; such adventures are known from *PE*, *Skáld*, *Ynglinga saga*, and various heroic sagas (*fornaldar sǫgur*) which may have existed as oral tales in Snorri's time, and from some stories of hagiographic tendency associated with Óláfr Tryggvason, e.g. in *Flateyjarbók*. P.22,l.20–4 harks back to the explanation in the prologue, p.4,l.9–12.

p.22,l.30–1. The names Ásaþórr and Ǫkuþórr are probably here intended to distinguish this Þórr from Þórr son of Munon (p.4,l.37), as at p.55,l.3–4. Cf. p.13,l.20.

p.22,l.33–4. 'the biggest ever built': *menn* is here used in its widest non-specific sense as indefinite subject, and does not mean 'humans' as opposed to 'divine beings'; the statement paraphrases p.22,l.38–40.

p.22,l.35–40 = *Grm* 24. Óðinn is the speaker in the poem, and his (principal) son is Þórr (p.13,l.20).

p.23,l.18–19. See textual note. This sentence is concerned with attributes other than physical, so the emendation seems justified.

p.23,l.20. Breiðablik has already been mentioned (p.19,l.38) but this seems to have been forgotten; U adds 'þann stað er . . . fyrr er nefndr'.

p.23,l.22–7 = *Grm* 12.

p.23,l.33–5. The conflict between Æsir and Vanir is mentioned again in *Skáld* (*SnE* i. 216), and in *Vsp* 24, *Ls* 34, *Vm* 39; and in greater detail in

Ynglinga saga (*Hkr* I. 12), where it is almost divested of its mythical character.

More details about Njǫrðr's marriage are given in *Skáld* (*SnE* I. 212–14; cf. 262); see also *Ynglinga saga* (*Hkr* I. 21–2) and the verses of *Háleygjatal* quoted there. In Saxo Grammaticus, Book I, 8, the story of Haddingus and Regnilda appears to be a euhemerized version of the legend of Njǫrðr and Skaði, and the two verses Snorri quotes (p.24,l.3–15), though they are not recorded elsewhere in Old Norse, were evidently known to Saxo in some form. They presumably form part of an otherwise lost poem about Njǫrðr.

p.24,l.19–24 = *Grm* 11.

p.24,l.32–7 = *Grm* 14; cf. p.21,l.27–9. On Freyja's role here where Frigg might have been expected cf. *Egils saga* (*ÍF* II. 244) and *Sǫrla þáttr* (*Flateyjarbók*, I. 276). See also *SnE* I. 304, where Freyja is called *eigandi valfalls*. On the same page and at *SnE* I. 284 Frigg is said to be the owner of the bird-shape which in *Þrk* 3 and *SnE* I. 212 seems to belong to Freyja.

p.25,l.6–8. Gylfi here discovers the apparent answer to his question at p.7,l.22–3.

p.25,l.14–19. This story is told in more detail below, pp. 27–9.

p.25,l.29–30. Clearly a reference to the story of the loss of the apples and the near-disaster that resulted, told in *Skáld* (*SnE* I. 210–12); the *ek* refers perhaps as much to Snorri as to Hár. The reference does not necessarily mean that *Gylf* was written after *Skáld*, since it could have been added later, or perhaps means simply that Snorri was reserving the story for a later place in his work.

p.26,l.1. *hǫfuð* is the subject. The sentence is not in U here and really belongs in *Skáld*; see *SnE* I. 264 (where 'sem fyrr er ritat' presumably refers to the present passage in *Gylf*) and 538. The legend underlying these rather puzzling passages has not been preserved. Cf. *SnE* I. 608 (*Háttatal* 7) and II. 498–9; *ÍF* VII. 208 n.

p.26,l.2–7 = *Grm* 13.

p.26,l.8–10. Nothing more survives of *Heimdalargaldr*, though it is referred to again in *Skáld* (*SnE* I. 264) and Heimdallr's parentage is mentioned in the verse of Úlfr Uggason quoted at *SnE* I. 268. There is a later eddic-type poem known as *Hrafnagaldr Óðins* or *Forspjallsljóð* (*PE* 371–6).

p.26,l.12–14, 15. Cf. p.46 and p.50,l.37 ff. below.

p.26,l.28–33 = *Grm* 15.

p.27,l.10. A comma at *faðerni*, making *þá . . . sér* line 11 the main clause of the sentence beginning at line 6 might make the passage smoother, but all manuscripts indicate a major break at *faðerni* (new paragraph

RW, new sentence TU). The use of *ok* to introduce a main clause after a subordinate clause (line 9) is not uncommon (see *ok* in glossary).

p.27,l.15. 'over the nine worlds' (see *heimr* in glossary); i.e. all who died of sickness or old age in any of the nine worlds came under Hel's jurisdiction, though her actual authority was over the one of the nine to which all such people were obliged to go (Niflheimr).

p.27,l.18–20. The list is extended in U, and another more elaborate account is found in AM 748 I 4to (*SnE* II. 494: 'Frá híbýlum Heljar').

p.27,l.40–p.28,l.1. There seem, however, to be no examples of the use of these sayings in Old Icelandic.

p.28,l.5–12. There is a metrical version of the composition of Gleipnir in AM 748 I 4to and AM 757 a 4to (*SnE* II. 431–2 and 515).

p.29,l.26. Verb and participle are attracted into agreement with the complement *hnossir*. The subject is *þat er fagrt er* ('whatever is beautiful and valuable is called a *hnoss*'). According to the *þula* in *SnE* I. 557, Hnoss had a sister called Gersemi ('treasure, jewel').

p.29,l.28–9. Another attempt to explain the multiplicity of names for a single figure in Norse mythology. Cf. p.22,l.16–27 and note. There are more names for Freyja in the *þula* in *SnE* I. 557.

p.29,l.31. *Vanadís*: Freyja was technically not one of the Ásynjur, just as Njǫrðr and Freyr were not really Æsir (see p.23,l.32 and p.24,l.25–6 and cf. note to p.21,l.13).

p.30,l.7. *kallat* is written *kall* with abbreviation sign in R and W, cf. note to p.13,l.10; the neuter form is probably intended here since the participle relates to both a masculine and a feminine noun (*snotr* could be masculine or feminine, but not neuter), but note the masculine *sá*. U has *kǫlluð*.

p.30,l.11–20. These verses are only known from here.

p.30,l.25–33 = *Grm* 36 (the speaker is Óðinn).

p.30,l.38–p.31,l.26. There is a poetical version of this story in *Skm*; p.31,l.27–32 = *Skm* 42.

p.31,l.33–4. Freyr is in several places referred to as *bani* or *dólgr* (enemy) *Belja*, see p.52,l.9 (= *Vsp* 53) and *SnE* I. 262 (= *Háleygjatal*, 5) and 482, but nothing more is known of the story referred to. In *Haustlǫng*, 18, quoted at *SnE* I. 282, Beli is used as a characteristic name for one of the giants.

p.31,l.40–p.32,l.2. i.e. at *ragnarøkr*, see p.50,l.13–14, 30–2.

p.32,l.4. Cf. p.21,l.29 and note, p.24,l.31, and p.9,l.3 and p.15,l.26. There certainly seem to be inconsistencies, but one of them would be resolved if Vingólf/Gimlé is taken to be part of Valhǫll.

p.32,l.8–9. i.e. at *ragnarøkr*, when as many *einherjar* as possible will be

needed to help defend the gods from the wolf Fenrir and their other
enemies. This idea is also found in scaldic poetry, e.g. *Eiríksmál*
(*Skjaldevers*, ed. Jón Helgason, København 1962 (Nordisk filologi A
12), 22–3; E. V. Gordon, *An Introduction to Old Norse*, rev. A. R.
Taylor, Oxford 1957, 148–9).

p.32,l.11. *þessi spurning* (nominative) is not syntactically linked to the
rest of the sentence, since *þykki* is impersonal and *líkara* neuter, but it
is picked up by *hér* . . . *af* (concerning this matter) in the last clause.

p.32,l.15–20, 26–31, p.32,l.37–p.33,l.3 = *Grm* 18–20.

p.33,l.6–7. Cf. *Eiríksmál* (see note to p.32,l.8–9) and Eyvindr skáldaspillir's *Hákonarmál* (*Hkr* I. 186–97).

p.33,l.16–17. Gangleri's reply is unmistakably ironic. Thus Snorri draws
attention to the naïve aspects of the mythology he treats.

p.33,l.18–25. Cf. *Grm* 26–8. But at p.9,l.20–24 Hvergelmir was described as a spring (*bruðr*) which existed before Valhǫll and Eikþyrnir
did, and Snorri is evidently giving two incompatible versions of the
source of the rivers. Five of those named at p.33,l.21–5 are among
those listed at p.9,l.22–4 (though some in variant forms), and all the
names in both lists (or variants of them) are included in *Grm* 27–8.
Many also appear in the *þula* in *SnE* I. 575–8.

p.33,l.34–9 = *Grm* 23.

p.34,l.8–13 = *Vm* 41.

p.34,l.16–24 = *Grm* 44. The use of the plural *Ásanna* at p.34,l.15 is odd,
since Óðinn alone is the speaker in the poem. Hár may be referring to
its transmission. It is difficult to know whether Snorri seriously thought
that eddic poems were composed by the Æsir. But he carefully excludes
scaldic poems from the dialogue in *Gylf*, almost certainly because of the
anachronism of putting quotations from the work of historical poets
into the mouths of prehistoric characters. This implies that he thought
the eddic poems they do quote were composed in prehistoric times,
before the migration of the Æsir.

The human poet Bragi would fit rather uncomfortably into these
mythological surroundings, and it may be that it is the god Bragi who is
meant at p.34,l.22.

p.34,l.33–4. Freyja was particularly coveted by giants (cf. *Þrk* 8, 23, *Vsp*
25, *SnE* I. 270). The sun and moon are obviously included because of
Vsp 25/5–6, but it is uncertain whether Snorri is right to connect *Vsp*
25–6 (quoted at p.35,l.36–p.36,l.11; verse 26 also paraphrased at
p.35,l.28–30) with this story.

p.35,l.10. The builder was evidently not building the wall course by
course but to its full height a stretch at a time, starting at one end and
finishing at the other.

p.35,l.14–17. Cf. p.48,l.10–11 and p.27,l.2–3. Loki is tormented to make him speak (like Óðinn in the prose introduction to *Grm*) at *SnE* I. 284–6; cf. 210, 212, 340. At p.49,l.5 ff. his torture is retributive.

p.35,l.20–1. *hestr* and *merr* are the words for stallion and mare; *hross* normally denotes the species without distinction of sex. *Hvat hrossi þetta var:* 'what sort of horse it was', i.e. that it was a mare.

p.35,l.29–30. Cf. *Þrk* 32.

p.35,l.32. i.e. below the lowest world (see p.9,l.4–5 and *Vm* 43), such was the force of the blow.

p.35,l.33. *hann* = Loki. An eight-legged horse is depicted on picture-stones from Gotland made in the eighth or ninth centuries. See S. Lindqvist, *Gotlands Bildsteine* (Stockholm 1941–2) I. figs. 137 and 139. Cf. the riddle in *Heiðreks saga*, p. 44.

p.35,l.36–p.36,l.11 = *Vsp* 25–6.

p.36,l.16–17. These dwarfs appear also in *Skáld* (*SnE* I. 340) where the making of the ship is again mentioned. Cf. also *Grm* 43 (quoted at *SnE* I. 264). In *Ynglinga saga* (*Hkr* I. 18) Óðinn is said to own Skíðblaðnir.

p.36,l.31. The last four words relate both to *til þess* and to *því*. Snorri attributes to Hár the belief that there is an orthodoxy in the heathen religion. Cf. p.21,l.6, 11–12.

p.36,l.32–3. If Gangleri is right, he will have won the contest of wisdom; see p.8,l.23 and note, p.36,l.39–40, and cf. p.21,l.3 ff., p.22,l.26, p.44,l.3.

p.37,l.3–p.43,l.38. There is no poetical source extant for the story of Þórr and Útgarðaloki, but some motives in it appear in eddic poems: Þórr's taking refuge in a glove is referred to in *Hrbl* 26 (where the giant is called Fjalarr) and *Ls* 60, his inability to undo the food-bag in *Ls* 62, and the lameness of his goat in *Hym* 37 (but here Loki is made responsible and the context is different; the goats are mentioned several times in this poem). Þjálfi is only mentioned in one eddic poem (*Hrbl*), Rǫskva in none. A kenning for old age based on Þórr's wrestling with Elli is found in *Egils saga* verse 1 (*ÍF* II. 60), but this verse may not be as old as the saga claims.

p.37,l.7. *þeir lagsmenn* = Þórr and Loki, see glossary.

p.37,l.29. *hafit*: cf. p.12,l.2–3, 22–3, p.27,l.12–13, p.44,l.3–p.45,l.13. There is no explanation of how Þórr crossed it in RTW, though in U he is said to have swum. Perhaps he waded (cf. p.17,l.36 and p.45,l.13).

p.37,l.32. A foreshadowing of p.40,l.9 ff.

p.37,l.33. From here on the presence of Rǫskva in the party seems to be ignored; the pronoun *þau* still occurs sporadically (p.37,l.39–p.38,l.1, p.38,l.30), but *þeir* gradually supersedes it, and Rǫskva takes no further part in the action.

p.39,l.11. *kallat*: the masculine or feminine form would be more normal (cf. note to p.13,l.10).

p.39,l.17. *þann*, i.e. *kost* (alternative).

p.40,l.13–14. *hann* is the subject of *lætr* (= Útgarðaloki), *þessa* is the genitive with *freista*, *skulu* is impersonal; the direct speech equivalent of the clause is 'þessa skal skjótt freista' (cf. p.40,l.1–2).

p.40,l.30. *ok*: see *ok* in glossary and note to p.27,l.10.

p.40,l.35–6. *þat má vel vera*: 'that may well be', i.e. (presumably) that he is good at that, or that that is his chief accomplishment; or 'that will be fine'. On Þórr's drinking cf. *SnE* i. 270 and *Þrk* 24–5.

p.41,l.6. See note to p.40,l.30.

p.41,l.7. 'there must be a very little difference by which it is lower', i.e. it must be by a very small amount that it is lower.

p.41,l.22–3. 'than it seems to me will be the case with this one (game)'.

p.41,l.33. This is the first speech of Þórr to Útgarðaloki given in his own words, and he uses the 'polite' plural form of the pronoun (unless he is including all those present in his question), while Útgarðaloki consistently uses the 'familiar' singular form in addressing Þórr (cf. p.42,l.7, 32).

p.42,l.32. i.e. Þórr views his loss of future reputation as more serious than his present humiliation.

p.42,l.38. *hafðir*: perhaps an error for *hefðir* (so WT): 'and that you would have', 'and that you were going to have (brought us)'.

p.42,l.39. *kom ek*: i.e. it was I who came.

p.43,l.16. *Þat . . . kallaðar*: an aetiological aside. The *nú* makes it clear that it is not part of Útgarðaloki's speech, but whether the speaker is Þriði, or whether Snorri has for a moment broken through the dramatic frame of his story is perhaps open to doubt. *Ok . . . hann* must be spoken by Þriði, referring to Útgarðaloki.

p.43,l.24–5. *sá* corresponds logically, though not syntactically, to *ǫllum* (anacoluthon).

p.43,l.30–2. In lifting the hammer above his head with both hands, Þórr has for a moment had to take his eyes off Útgarðaloki. Note the similarity to the end of *Gylf*, where Gangleri, surprised by the sudden noise (p.54,l.31), for a moment takes his eyes off his interlocutors, and they disappear.

p.44,l.3. 'It is not unknown even (to those who) are not scholars': even those who are not scholars know this story—another comment on Gangleri's ignorance (cf. p.15,l.5, p.21,l.3, p.22,l.26, p.33,l.6, 29, p.34,l.27–8), and Hár does not on this occasion even need Þriði's help to tell it.

The following story figures in *Húsdrápa* and *Ragnarsdrápa* and other scaldic poems used by Snorri (see *SnE* i. 242–4, 252–8, 370, 412–14, 474–6, 504, ii. 499; *Skj* A i. 3–4, 6, 137, 140) as well as in *Hym*; see SG *Kommentar* 255–6. It is depicted on stones from Altuna (Uppland, Sweden), Hørdum (Hassing, Thisted, Denmark), and Gosforth, Cumberland (see *MRN*, plate 21; Einar Ó. Sveinsson, *Íslenzkar bókmenntir í fornöld*, i, Reykjavík 1962, pp. 343 and 346; P. Foote and D. M. Wilson, *The Viking Achievement*, London 1970, plate 26).

p.44,l.16. *fyrir því . . . at*: 'for this reason . . . that'.

p.45,l.10. *ek* = Hár. The hammer never misses (*SnE* i. 344), but on the other hand the Midgard serpent survives to fight at *ragnarøkr* (p.50,l.3). Snorri does not attempt to reconcile the two, but appeals to the existence of more than one version of the story. The first ('segja menn') is supported by Úlfr Uggason's *Húsdrápa* (*SnE* i. 258), which also supports the reading *hrǫnnunum* in WT for *grunninum*. The second version ('hitt') probably corresponded to Bragi's *Ragnarsdrápa* (cf. *SnE* i. 504), though the conclusion of the story in what survives of this poem is not quite clear. *Hym* also seems to be defective at this point in the story, but it differs from Snorri's account in that there Hymir survives the expedition.

p.45,l.16 ff. Baldr's death figures in Úlfr Uggason's *Húsdrápa* (*SnE* i. 234, 238, 240, 264, 428), *Vsp*, *Bdr*, and other poems. Saxo Grammaticus (Book III) includes a euhemerized version of the story.

p.46,l.7–8. 'that was the greatest disaster ever brought to pass'.

p.46,l.9. *fellusk . . . orðtǫk ok svá hendr*: zeugma.

p.46,l.26. 'The steed of the troll(-wife)' is a well-known kenning for wolf, possibly based on this story. See, for example, *Hkr* iii. 178 and *Orms þáttr Stórólfssonar*, verse 7 (*Flateyjarbók*, i. 528); and cf. *Hkr* iii. 177 and *Helgakviða Hjǫrvarðssonar*, prose after verse 30 (*PE* 176). A carved stone from Hunnestad, Skåne (Sweden), depicts a wolf as a mount, see *MRN*, plate 22. Cf. R. Meissner, *Die Kenningar der Skalden*, Bonn und Leipzig 1921, pp. 124–5.

p.46,l.29. The ship evidently had the prow facing up the beach and was launched stern first.

p.47,l.4. Cf. p.47,l.32, where Óðinn gets the ring back again. The inclusion of *síðan* (p.47,l.5), which T omits, makes this statement conflict with *Skáld*, *SnE* i. 344, where the ring is said to have had this property from the beginning. But there are other such contradictions in *SnE*, and it is not certain that *síðan* is an addition. Cf. also *Skm* 21 and *SnE* i. 354.

p.48,l.4–9. This verse is not found elsewhere, but it may be from an otherwise lost poem about the death of Baldr.

p.48,l.22. 'in the way in which nets have been ever since', an aetiological comment, like that at p.49,l.3–4.

p.48,l.39. *hitt*, i.e. the opposite course (*at . . . netit*); *annarr*, i.e. *lífs háski*.

p.49,l.5 ff. Loki's capture and punishment are related briefly, and with certain differences (particularly in the names of Loki's sons), in the concluding prose in *Ls*. There the episode is not connected with the death of Baldr.

p.49,l.16. 'That is what you call an earthquake': Hár's comment to Gangleri. Another aetiological aside.

p.49,l.20. *þau*: i.e. *tíðindi*.

p.49,l.27–36 = *Vsp* 45.

p.49,l.37 ff. The present tenses in this and the following passages of dialogue are to be taken as referring to future time. Up to p.49,l.17 all narratives have related to past events, though present tenses have often described actions continuing through the present (e.g. p.29,l.8–10, p.49,l.13–17).

p.49,l.37–9. Cf. p.14,l.14–17, 22–6, 34, p.54,l.24, and notes to p.13,l.34 ff. and p.14,l.14–17.

p.50,l.5–7. The syntax is rather unclear, but *fyrir því* probably relates to the *at*-clause, and the *ef*-clause explains the *varnan*, i.e. the warning is against letting (one ought not to let) a man die with uncut nails. Cf. *viðvǫrunarvert*, *ÍF* xii. 274.

p.50,l.16. Cf. p.15,l.9.

p.50,l.24. Cf. p.51,l.8–9 (*Vsp* 46); *Ynglinga saga*, *Hkr* i. 13 and 18; *Sd* 14.

p.50,l.31–2. Cf. p.31,l.22–3, p.31,l.40–p.32,l.2.

p.50,l.40. i.e. when shoes are being made and the shape is cut from a piece of leather, leaving waste scraps at the toes (*fyrir tám*: not 'for the toes') and heel, which would often be triangular in shape (*bjórar*).

p.51,l.6–p.52,l.36 = *Vsp* 46/5–8, 47/1–4, 48, 50–3, 55–7. There are considerable differences between the texts.

p.51,l.13. The *jǫtunn* here could be Fenrisúlfr (p.29,l.10, p.50,l.2), or Garmr (p.50,l.32–3; cf. *Vsp* 44, 49, 54, 58) or Loki (p.49,l.17, cf. p.26,l.36).

p.51,l.22 and p.51,l.33 conflict with p.50,l.8; p.51,l.31–2 with p.50,l.13–14. Snorri may have intentionally departed from the account in *Vsp*, and originally he may not have included all the verses here quoted (many of them are lacking in U), since their inclusion draws attention to the discrepancies.

p.52,l.5. Hlín is thought to have been another name for Frigg, in spite of p.30,l.4. Her first grief would have been the death of her son Baldr (see *SnE* i. 260, 304; *Ls* 27).

p.52,l.24. Both the Codex Regius of the eddic poems and the manuscripts of *SnE* have *ókvíðnum* (RW; *ókvíðjum* T; the text of *Hauksbók* is illegible here), and the word therefore relates to *naðri*: 'unafraid of shameful acts, not holding back from his wicked deed'. The emendation *ókvíðinn* (relating to *mǫgr*, i.e. *Þórr*) would give easier sense ('unashamed of disgrace, having no fear of belying his reputation') but has no manuscript support.

p.52,l.29–30. Cf. Arnórr Jarlaskáld (born *c*.1012), *Þorfinnsdrápa*, 24, quoted in *Skáld* (*SnE* i. 316):

> Bjǫrt verðr sól at svartri,
> søkkr fold í mar døkkvan.

It is usually assumed that Arnórr was influenced by *Vsp* rather than vice versa.

p.52,l.38–p.53,l.3 = *Vm* 18.

p.53,l.6–7. *Ok . . . aldir* may be a statement or reminder rather than a question.

p.53,l.8–13. Cf. p.9,l.2–3, p.20,l.7–18 and note to p.32,l.4. Óðinn himself does not survive *ragnarøkr*.

p.53,l.15 conflicts with p.53,l.21–2.

p.53,l.16. Cf. p.9,l.4–5, which also conflicts with p.27,l.14–16.

p.53,l.17–31 = *Vsp* 38–9. In the versions of *Vsp* in *PE* there is no mention of Hvergelmir, and Níðhǫggr seems to be at Nástrǫnd.

p.54,l.4–9 = *Vm* 51.

p.54,l.14–19 = *Vm* 45. The first line is syntactically incomplete; it is the answer to the question 'Hvat lifir manna . . .' in *Vm* 44, and the verb of the question has to be supplied in the answer.

p.54,l.22–7 = *Vm* 47. *berr* refers to future time. Cf. p.49,l.37–9 and note.

p.54,l.29. *þat* could refer either to the question ('how you will be able to ask such a question') or to the answer ('where you will get an answer from'). Cf. note to p.8,l.22–3.

p.54,l.30. Cf. *Háv* 164 and note to p.8,l.10–15.

p.54,l.31–3. Cf. note to p.43,l.30–2.

p.54,l.35. This is how the stories are supposed to have reached the author (cf. note to p.34,l.16–24). Snorri is on other occasions concerned to give a realistic explanation for the transmission of information, e.g. *Hkr* i. 298, ii. 358. See S. Nordal, *Snorri Sturluson* (Reykjavík 1920), pp. 201–2. Cf. also *Grettis saga* (*ÍF* vii. 205), *Ǫrvar-Odds saga* (ed. R. C.

Boer, Leiden 1888, pp. 194–5), *Njáls saga* (*ÍF* XII. 330–1), *Orms þáttr Stórólfssonar*, ch. 8 (*Flateyjarbók*, I. 529).

p.54,l.38. *þar*, i.e. in Scandinavia, to men of their own company and to the localities in their new homeland. Cf. p.6,l.24–30 and notes.

p.55,l.2. *er nú var frá sagt*, i.e. the Æsir about whom stories have been told in *Gylf* (*er áðr eru nefnd*, p.54,l.38). Their names and exploits are now being attributed by a deliberate policy of deception to the 'historical' Æsir ('þessir' p.55,l.2) emigrant from Asia, to whom Gangleri has been talking, so that the local people and their descendants would believe them to be identical.

p.55,l.3–4. i.e. someone there was given the name of Þórr, that is the name that had belonged to the original (god) Þórr (Qkuþórr), and to him were attributed the deeds of (H)ector of Troy, which were supposed to be symbolically represented in myths relating to Qkuþórr (see *SnE* I. 226–8); cf. p.4,l.35–p.5,l.9.

p.55,l.5–7. i.e. the uncomplimentary myths about Loki are supposed to derive from Turkish (i.e. Trojan, and hostile) accounts of Ulysses.

Textual notes

The text (from 5/13) is based solely on R: readings from other manuscripts are only quoted when the text of R is incoherent or has obvious omissions. Verses from eddic and scaldic poems are also printed (and glossed) in the form in which they appear in R, and there is no attempt at a critical text.

The text of the first part of the prologue is based on K. The only medieval heading preserved is that in U (see Introduction)   3/1 skapaði] *NJWU*; skóp *K*   3/2 tvá] *NJW*; þá *K*   3/4 þá] *NJW; K omits*   3/6 ok (1)] *NJW; K omits*   3/7 í ǫrkinni váru] *NJW*; váru í ǫrkinni *K*   3/8–9 ok kómu . . . ættir] *NJW; K omits*   3/9 þá] *NW*; þegar *K*   3/10 allr] *NJWU*; mestr *K*   3/11 afrœktusk] *JW*, afrœktisk *U*; afrœktu *K*   3/13 Svá] *NThJW*; Ok svá *K*   3/14 eigi (1)] *W*, ei *NThJ*; engi *K*   3/15 jarðligar giptir] *NJWU*; veraldligar giptur *K*   3/16 Miðlaði hann] *JW*; Hann miðlaði *K*   spekina] *NTh*, spekinni *K*   at] *NJW; K omits*   3/18 Þat] *NThJWU*; Þó *K*   3/19 saman] *NThJWU*; sam *K*   3/20 hætti] *NThJW*; háttum *K*   at (2)] *NJW*, er *K*   3/21 ok (1)] *NJWU*; þá *K*   vatn upp] *NJW*; upp vatn *K*   3/23 ok] *NThJW*; sem *K*   ǫnnur náttúra er sú] *NJWU*; Sú er ǫnnur náttúra *K*   3/24 á jǫrð- unni gras] *JW*; gras á jǫrðu *K*   3/25 at] *NThJWU; K omits*   3/26–8 Þat er . . . jǫrðunni] *based on N; K omits*   3/26 er (2)] *JW; N omits*   3/27 þá] *ThJWU*; at þá *N*   moldu] *ThJWU*; jǫrðu eða moldu *N*   3/28 á] *NThJ*; í *K*   3/29 svá] *NWU; K omits*   3/31 í] *NJW*; at *K*   3/32 –4/6 Fyrir . . . jarðarinnar] *based on N; K omits*   3/32 nafn] *ThJW*; nǫfn *N*   3/33 Þat] *here T begins*   gǫmlum frændum] *JWT*, feðrum *N*   3/34 váru] *JWT*; var *N*   3/35 himintungl] *JWT*; tungl himins *N*   4/1 nokkurr] *ThJWTU*; einnhverr *N*   4/2 sá] *JWTU*; hann *N*   ríkr mjǫk] *ThT*; mjǫk ríkr *N*   ok máttugr] *ThJWT*; máttugr ok mikill *N*   4/3 þess] *JWT*; þessu *N*   ef] *JWT*; er *N*   réði] *ThJT*; réð *NW*   hǫfuðskepnunum] *JWT*; hǫfuðskepnunni *N*   4/6 ávexti] *ThJWT*; atvexti *N*   4/6–9 er . . . veðranna] *T; KNTh omit*   4/11–12 ok hefir . . . greindusk] *WT; KNTh omit*   4/13 þeir] *JT*; þeir af *K*   4/14 spekðin] *WT*; skynsemð *K*   4/19 sá] *JWT; K omits*   eða Enea] *JWTU*, eða Evea *Th*, eða Ena *N; K omits*   4/20 byggja] *NThJWU*; byggja sǫkum frosta *K*   4/21 austrhálfur] *NJWT*; austrhálfu *K*   kallat] *NWT*, kǫlluð *K*   4/22 ávaxtar] *JW*, ávǫxtr *NTh; K omits*   4/23 verǫldin] *NJWTU*; verǫld *K*   ok (2)] *NThJWTU*; en *K*   4/23–4 fegri ok betri] *NJWT*; betri ok fegri ok gnœgri *K*   4/25 giptum] *ThJW*; giptunum *K*   aflinu] *ThWT*; aflinu ok *K*   4/26 kun- nustu] *W*, kunnastinnar *T*, kunnáttu *NThJ*; kunstum *K*   4/28 Troja] *NThJWT*; Troju *K*   4/29 gǫrr] *NThJWT; put after* hagleik *in*

K meira] *JWT*; myklu meira *K* marga lund] *NThJWT*; margar lundir
K 4/34 manndómliga] *NThJWT*; veraldliga *K* 4/35 Mennon] *WT*,
Menon *K* 4/36 hǫfuðkonungs] *NThJW*, hǫfuðkonungsins *KT* 4/37
uppfœzlu] *NJWT*; uppvexti ok uppfœzlu *K* 4/40 er (2)] *ThJWT*; var
K 5/2 Þá . . . senn] *NWT; K omits* 5/4 Thracia] *JWT*; Thraciam
K 5/5 allar] *NThT; KW omit* alla] *ThJWT; K omits* 5/6 heims]
JWT; heimsins *K* 5/9–13 Þeira . . . Scialdun] *based on Th; K and N
omit* 5/9 Loriði] *WT*; Hleriði *Th* feðr] *JWT*; fǫður *Th* 5/10 var]
JWT; Th omits Einriði] *T*; Irides er vér kǫllum Indriða
Th Vingeþórr] *JWU*; Vingþórr *Th* 5/11 Vingenir] *JWTU*; Hnikarr
Th hans son Móða] *JWU*, hans son Móði *T; Th omits* Magi] *JWU*;
Majus er vér kǫllum Magna *Th* Sescef] *T*; Leifr *Th* 5/12 Beðvig]
WU; Bǫðvígi *Th* hans son Athra] *JWTU; Th omits* er] *JWTU*; en
Th 5/13 Ítrmann] *WU*; Trógranni *Th* Heremóð] *JWT*; Hermóðr
Th Scialdun] *JWTU*; Skaðvígi *Th* er] *here R begins* 5/15 hans
son Finn] *WT; no longer legible in R* Friallaf] *WT (altered from* Frilleif
in T); Fiarllaf *R* 5/34 Freovin] *W*; Freovit *R* Wigg] Uuigg *or* Yvigg
R; Yvigg *W*, Uuig *T* 5/35 er vér k-] *W; hole in R* 5/36 Rerir] *WU*;
Verir *R* 6/2 -min e-] *W; hole in R* 6/9 þat] *WT; R omits* 6/12
Skipaði] *WTU*, Skipa *R* 6/17 til] *WTU; R omits* 7/1 *There is no
medieval heading in RWT; the name* Gylfaginning *is from the heading in
U.* 7/4 af] *WT; at R* 7/8 -un landi-] *WT; hole in R* 8/19 sá (1)]
WT; R omits 8/35 allar] *WT; hole in R* 9/4 í Ni-] *WTU; hole in
R* 9/12 alda] *WTU*; halda *R* 9/23 Fjǫrm] *W*; Fjǫrni *U*, Fǫrm *RT;
cf. 33/21* Fimbulþul] *written as two words in RT and split over line
division in W; cf. 33/22* 9/32 lævi] *WU*; leifi *RT; cf. 51/39*

10/3 úr] *WT*; en *R* 10/7 hǫfugleik] *WTU; written* hǫf|leik *over line
division R* 10/26 *RT add* Þá spurði Gangleri *after* jǫtunn (*the name
abbreviated* G. *in T; perhaps for* Gagnráðr?—*see explanatory note to
10/27–35*) 10/36 *R adds* saman *after* ættir 11/1 at] *WT; hole in
R* 11/11 dag] *WU; R omits* 11/19 þér] *WT; R has the abbreviation
for* þeir 11/23 *R adds* þú *after* drektu 12/9 eldingum] *TU*; eldinum
R 12/31 bjǫrg] *WT*; bjǫrgr *R* 13/5 menn] *written with the abbreviation for* mǫnnum *R* 13/7 ok (2)] *WT; hole in R* 13/19 fullgert] *WT*;
fullt gert *R* 13/20 þat] *WT*; þar *R* 13/24 Auðr] *WTU*; Uðr
R 13/35 át-] *WTU; hole in R* 14/20 Já- (1)] *WU; hole in R* 15/2
veðr] *W*; verðr *RTU* 15/25 gerðu] *written twice in R* 15/29–30 ok
ǫll reiðigǫgn] *WT; R omits* 15/37 -ǫso-] *WTU; hole in R* 16/4 dr-]
WTU; hole in R 16/20 Óri] *W*; Órinn *T*, Órr *U; R omits* 16/39–40
er kominn] *WU*; eru komnir *R* 17/2 Eikinskjaldi] *as one word U*
(*spelt* -skjalli), Eikinn, Skjaldi *R; split over line division WT* 17/7 *R has*
Ydrasils *here and at 18/3; elsewhere* Yggdrasils 17/22 þú] *WTU*;
á *R* 17/23 í] *WTU*; ór *R* 17/25 mjǫð] *WTU*; mǫð *R* 17/27 veði]
WTU, veiði *R* 17/35 Léttfeti] *WTU*; Léttfet *R* 17/36 dómsins]

WT; dóms síns *R*   18/11 er] *WU*; eru *RT*   vǫrn] *WT*, vǫtn
R   19/13 meiðs] *WU*; meðs *RT*   19/14 við] *WTU; R omits*   19/16
eigi] *WTU; R omits*   19/21 Yggdrasill] *WTU*; Yggdrasils *R*   19/26
grœnn] *WT*; grunn *R*   19/29 býflugur] *WTU*; blýflugur *R*   19/33 -fuð-]
WTU; hole in R
   20/4 -skjálf] *WTU*; -skjaf *R*   20/22 Andlangr] *WT*; Andlang
R   21/12 á] *WTU; R omits*   21/21 -rr e-] *WTU; hole in R*   21/28–9
-eim sk-] *WTU; hole in R*   21/33 Ganglari] *W*; Gangari *RT*, Gangleri
U   22/1 Bil-] *WTU*; Til- *R*   22/20 upp] *WTU; R omits*   22/22
atburð] *WT*; atburðr *R*   23/4 á lopt] *WTU; R omits*   23/13 ek]
WTU; R omits   23/18 fegrð] *WTU; hole in R*   á (1)] *WTU; R
omits*   23/18–19 fegrst talaðr] *WTU*; fegrstr taliðr *R*   23/32 Eigi . . .
ættar] *WU; R omits*   23/39 nætr] *WTU*; vetr *R*   24/1 aðrar] *T*; aðra
R   24/4 á] *WT; R omits*   24/10 máttigak] máttak *R*, mátka T, ne
mátta *W*   24/27 skini] *WTU*; skiln *R*   25/3 tignar-] *WTU; R
omits*   25/14 *R adds* hans *after* eitt   25/16 en] *WTU*; er *R*   25/18
úlfliðr] *WTU*; úlfriðr *R*   25/36 at] *WTU*; ok *R*   26/20 Ullr] *WTU*;
Ulli *R*   26/31 þar] *U and PE*; þat *RT*, þá *W*   26/32 flestan] *WT*;
flestum *R*   26/37 Helblindi] *WTU*; Heldlindi *R*   27/3 Sigyn] *W*
(*spelt* Sygin) *and T*; Lygin *R*   Nari] *WTU; R perhaps has* Nati   27/15
R perhaps has skipta, *in which case* skyldi *should be supplied before the
word* (*thus WTU*)   27/19 Ganglǫt] *W*; Ganlǫt *RT*   Forað] *WTU*;
Fora *R*   27/38–9 ok knúðisk . . . fjǫturinn] *WT* (*though T has*
spyrndi); *R omits, but has* spyrnir við *in the margin and a caret sign after*
sik *in line 38*   27/39 fjarri] *TU*; færri *R*   28/5 sex] *WU*; fimm *RT*
(*Roman numerals*)   28/8 at (1)] *WTU*; ok *R*   28/9 hafa] *WTU; R
omits*   29/10 Þar] *WTU*; Þá *R*   29/22 Fulla] *WT*; Fua *R*
   30/3 ósanna] *WTU*; ásanna *R*   30/17 líðk] *T*; líðr *RW*   30/36
-nan] *WTU; hole in R*   30/37 eru] *WU; hole in R*   31/4 lauk] *written
twice in R*   31/6 heimar] *WT; R omits*   31/34 drap] *WT*; diarp
R   32/10 Sæ(h)rímnir] *WTU*; Sæmnir *R*   32/11 apt-] *WU; hole in
R*   32/12 af] *WT; R omits*   32/19 En] *WTU*; at *R*   32/27 -tamiðr]
WT; -tamigr *R*   32/34 sendir] *WTU*; sendi *R*   33/18 Eikþyrni] *W*;
Eirþyrni *R*   33/19 hans] *WU; RT omit*   33/24 Veg] *W*; Vog
RT   34/24 Garmr] *WU*; Gramr *RT*   34/36 einum] *WT*; enum
R   35/1 at hann] *WT; R omits*   36/24 Hvárt *is written with a large
capital in RWU, and T also indicates a major break at this point*   36/27
Þá] *WT*; Þar *R*   36/30 eigi] *WTU; R omits*   36/36 mun (1)] *T*; munu
R   37/5 þar] *WT; R has the abbreviation for* þeir   37/23 ok] *WT*; at
R   37/31 dag] *WT; R omits*   39/12 Útgarðr] *WTU*; Útgarð *R*   39/21
eigi] *TU; RW omit*   39/35 þat er] *WT; R omits*
   40/21 þeir] *WT; written with the abbreviation for* þér *in R*   40/23
kemr] *WTU*; kominn *R*   40/26 þykki mér Þjálfi] *WTU*; þykkja mér þit
R   40/40 í] *WTU; R omits*   41/15 í] *U; R omits*   41/25 þreytir]

WU; þrýtr *R*   42/1 beygði kenginn] *WTU*; baugði kengit (*or* hangit) *R*   42/2 seildisk] *WT*; seldisk *R*   42/8 einnhverr] *WTU*; einnhvern *R*   42/21 í] *WT*; á *R*   43/1 eigi] *WU; RT omit*   43/6 þér] *WT; R omits*   43/9 trogit en slátrit] *WT*; slátrit en trogit *R*   43/23 er þú stótt . . . fœti] *WT; R omits*   43/35 En] *WT*; at *R*   43/37 þér] *WT; written with the abbreviation for* þeir *in R*   44/3 -menn] *W*; *R has the abbreviation for* -mǫnnum   44/4 frá] *WT; R omits*   44/10 á] *WT; R omits*   44/35 grunns] *WTU*; brunns *R*   44/36 minnr] *WT; R omits*   44/40 svá] *WU; R omits*   45/24 standa] *WT*; standi *R*   46/14 þeim mun] *W*; þeimun *R*   46/20 er] *WT*; en *R*   46/33 af] *WT*; á *R*   46/36 fœti sínum] *WT*; fœtum *R*   46/38 at (1)] *WT; R omits, and* þessa (*without preposition*) *may have been intended*   47/13 minnr] *WU*; jafnmjǫk *RT*   48/8 karls sonar] *W*, karlsonar *T*; kaldsonar *R*   48/9 haldi] *WTU*; hafi *R*   48/26 eldinum] *WT*; eldinn *R*   49/3 nam] *WTU*; naf *R*   49/8 sundr] *WTU; hole in R*   49/10 *R may have had* egg- *before* steina, *like U; the edge of the page is damaged*

50/17 þann vǫll] *WT*; þingvǫll *R*   50/18 Þar] *WTU*; Þá *R*   50/20 einir] *WTU*; yfir *R*   50/24 ríðr] *WTU*; reið *R*   50/28 Gungnir] *W*; Gugnir *RT*   50/39 hefir (2)] *WTU; omitted from the text in R, but was added in the margin; there is a caret sign in the text*   51/8 Mælir] *WU*; Mey *R*   51/26 knýr] *WT*; kýr *R*   51/29 Naglfar] *WT*; Naglfal *R*   51/39 lævi] *W*; leifi *RT* (*cf. 9/32*)   52/6 harmr] *T*; hamr *RW*   52/25 halir] *WT*; hallir *R*   52/26 heimstǫð] *WT*; heimsteið *R*   53/8 segir Þriði] *TU*, svarar Þriði *W; illegible in R*   53/9 á Gimlé] *TU*; á Gimlein (*i.e.* á Gimlé inn?) *R*   allgott] *WT*; allt gott *R*   53/30 Þar] *WTU*; Þá *R*   54/1 of (2)] *T*, um *W; R has the sign for* ok   54/7 Móði] *WTU*; Megi *R*   54/18 sér] *so PE*; er *R, W omits*   54/27 *The abbreviation for* -ir *may be written after* braut *in R; WTU have* brautir   55/4–5 er Þórr gerði í Troju *R, with* Ector *written between the lines above* Þórr; *WT have* er Ector gjǫrði í Troju

Glossary

All words except common pronouns are glossed, but only select references are given. † before a word or its explanation indicates that the usage is specifically poetical. Idiomatic usages of prepositions and adverbs are generally explained under the verbs with which they are associated. The following abbreviations are used:

a.	adjective	*neg.*	negative
abs(ol).	absolute(ly)	*nom.*	nominative
acc.	accusative	*num.*	numeral
adv.	adverb(ial)	*OE*	Old English
art.	article	*ord.*	ordinal
aux.	auxiliary	*o-self*	oneself
comp.	comparative	*p.*	past
conj.	conjunction	*pers.*	person
dat.	dative	*pl.*	plural
def.	definite	*poss.*	possessive
e-m	einhverjum	*pp.*	past participle
e-n	einhvern	*prep.*	preposition(al)
e-s	einhvers	*pres. (p.)*	present (participle)
e-t	eitthvert	*pret. pres.*	preterite-present
e-u	einhverju	*pron.*	pronoun
f.	feminine	*rel.*	relative
gen.	genitive	*sg.*	singular
imp.	imperative	*s-one*	someone
impers.	impersonal	*s-thing*	something
indecl.	indeclinable	*subj.*	subjunctive
inf.	infinitive	*subst.*	substantive
interrog.	interrogative	*sup.*	superlative
intrans.	intransitive	*sv.*	strong verb
irreg.	irregular	*trans.*	transitive
m.	masculine	*vb.*	verb
md.	middle voice	*wv.*	weak verb
n.	neuter		

†-a *neg. suffix* with vbs.; *vara* 9/14; with 2nd pers. pron. *ne legskaþu* (double neg. for emphasis) 21/23; combined with 1st pers. pron. *varka* 24/4, *máttigak* 24/10, *nautka* 48/8. See **-k**.

á (1) pres. of **eiga**.

á (2) *f.* river 9/22,41.

á (3) *prep.* (1) with acc., on, onto 7/24, 28/34; †separated from its noun (*lúðr*) 11/32; in, into 12/8, 18/9; at 41/3, 45/25; to 23/30, 41/12; up to 39/26; along (a road) 46/17; *á lopt* into the air 23/4; as regards, with

regard to 23/18; of manner, in 4/11, 21/31; of time, on 24/36, through
35/8, 42/21. (2) with dat., in, on 3/27, 7/36, 8/15, 23/20; †postposition
24/11; at 9/28; about 3/14; over 43/29; from in 48/29; on, with 35/3,
44/37; with parts of the body, belonging to 23/5; of time, in 3/24, 13/29,
within 34/31. (3) as adv., in (it) 41/19; on (them) 24/4; to 25/3; *þar á* on
it 46/24.

áðr *adv.* previously, before, earlier 9/10, 38/25, 53/6; above (in a book)
54/38; *áðr . . . nú* already . . . now 28/7. As conj., before 8/11, 44/5;
with dat. of length of time 11/28 (correlative with *þá*); implying
purpose, in order that 36/24, 39/25; *áðr* (. . .) *en* before 9/6,39, until, if
(. . . not), had not 46/31.

af *prep.* with dat., from 3/29, 31/5; away from 5/21; off 41/36, 46/27;
because of 4/8,18, 27/10; in 5/17; by (agent) 29/36, 31/6, (instrument,
cause) 15/31; by means of 5/19, 13/32; as a result of 22/21; from
(origin) 34/27; from among 7/4, 14/22 (2); (made) of 15/30, out of 4/14,
11/36; (full) of 17/17; (filled) with 40/4; (name) after 25/21 (2); about,
concerning 19/32; *vera af* originate from 25/3, forfeit 34/37; *af ǫllu afli*
with (using) all his strength 39/5, cf. 52/27; *af því at* as conj., from (by)
this (fact, circumstance) that 6/26. As adv., off 3/26, 25/18; from (it)
33/15, from (them) 12/27, 27/9 (1); about it 36/36; *þar* (. . .) *af* from it
11/6, from this 12/1, by means of this 13/21, about it 18/30, about them
11/35; *þaðan af* from them 13/8, from there or that 9/22, 13/11, by
means of this or these 12/12, 15/28, from that origin, from this 30/5; *hér*
(. . .) *af* in this 41/30, about this 32/12.

afar *adv.* very, extremely 17/12.

afhús *n.* side room 37/38, 38/12.

afi *m.* grandfather; man; †*hverr ósviðra afa* any old fool 19/7.

afl (1) *n.* strength 4/25, 13/21; sometimes physical strength as opposed to
supernatural power 36/26; *honum hafði a. vaxit* his strength had grown
27/35.

afl (2) *m.* forge 15/27.

afrœkjask (kt) *wv. md.* neglect 3/11.

aftaka *f.* deprivation, loss 46/15.

ágirni *f.* greed (with gen., for s-thing) 3/10, 49/25.

agnsax *n.* bait-knife (a knife for cutting bait) 45/8.

ágæti *n.* glory 5/24.

ágætr *a.* outstanding, excellent (*af e-u* or *at e-u* in s-thing) 5/17, 25/20;
renowned (for) 27/33; sup., most excellent 4/27, 11/18, 24/27.

áheit *n.* prayer 29/33.

aka (ók) *sv.* drive (with dat. of vehicle or draught animals) 23/2, 25/2,
47/1.

ákafliga *adv.* mightily 29/6; with great speed 14/11; with great zeal, strenuously 28/1; fervently 37/23; sup. *sem ákafligast má hann* as hard as he can 41/25.

ákall *n.* invocation 22/24.

akarn *n.* acorn 38/37.

akr *m.* cornfield 53/35.

ala (ól) *sv.* nourish; md., be produced, begotten 13/8, 54/19; *alask við* feed on, live on 32/20.

álarendi *m.* strap-end 38/24.

albúinn *a.* (*pp.*) quite prepared, ready and able (*at gera e-t* to do s-thing) 39/39.

aldarfar *n.* the course of the world (of history), progress of time 54/30.

aldartal *n.* count of time, age 3/31.

†aldinn *a.* aged 51/12; *in aldna* the aged one (f.) 14/28.

aldr *m.* life, course of (one's) life, destiny 18/13,26; *allan a.* throughout all time 50/39.

†aldrdagar *m.pl.* life-days; *of aldrdaga* for ever and ever 20/17.

aldri *adv.* never 9/1; *a. er* never will there be 32/9.

†aldrnari *m.* nourisher of life, i.e. fire 52/34.

†álfkunnr *a.* descended from (of the race of) elves 18/21.

álfr *m.* elf 18/16, 51/15.

álit *n.* appearance; dat. pl., in appearance 4/39, 11/13.

allfagr *a.* very beautiful 15/26.

allgóðr *a.* very good; n. as adv. or subst. *allgott er e-m til e-s* there is plenty of s-thing for s-one 53/9.

allharðr *a.* very violent 42/18.

alllítill *a.* very small 41/7.

allmikill *a.* very great 32/6, 34/2; a very great deal of 36/23; *a. fyrir sér* see **mikill**; n. as subst., a great deal 25/27, 48/12.

allógurligr *a.* very terrible 50/12.

allókátr *a.* very unhappy, uncheerful 44/32.

allr *pron. a.* all 3/1,16; (a, the) whole 3/10, 9/30, 11/12; all the 40/6; every 8/10; all (other) 5/20; all kinds of 5/17, 47/38; *hann . . . allr* it all (i.e. all over, entirely) 53/14; pl., they all 21/18, 26/26, 27/9, everyone 6/9, 21/4, 23/15; *ǫllum senn* all together 5/2; *ǫllum . . . þeim er* for all who 18/9; *alls þess er* of all that which 13/18; gen.pl. with sup., (fairest) of all 20/7; *allt* everything 3/32, 17/21 (all about where, or adv., completely); *þat allt* all that 10/35, 13/17. As adv., completely, all the way 6/24, 10/4; *allt til* all the way to 4/21, (of time) right on up to 25/25; everywhere 18/11 (see note).

allsterkr *a.* very strong 27/26.

allstórr *a.* very great; dat.pl. as adv., very mightily 41/4.

allvegligr *a.* very glorious 29/19.

allþrǫngr *a.* very crowded 33/27.

almáttigr *a.* almighty 3/1.

†**ámáttugr** *a.* very powerful (usually with supernatural power), very terrible; weak form *ámátki* 24/21.

ambátt *f.* female slave 27/19.

andask (að) *wv. md.* die 29/21.

andi *m.* breath 28/6.

andligr *a.* spiritual 4/13.

andlit *n.* face 49/12,15.

†**angan** *n.* delight; *a. Friggjar* = Óðinn 52/12.

annarr *pron. a.* and *num.* other 4/24, 6/19; another, a second 3/23, 8/29, 48/39 (sc. *lífs háski*); the other 51/4; the second 4/18, 5/31; a different 6/30, 38/15; anyone else 46/13; *annarr en* other than, besides 15/22; *annat* s-thing else 33/11; *þvíat . . . ok þat annat at* because . . . and because of this also 46/1; one (of two) 13/36, 37/15; *ǫðrum fæti* with one foot 38/27, 50/38, cf. 51/2; *annarr . . . a.* the one . . . the other 11/2, 40/5, 48/31; *hverr til annars* at each other 46/10; *hverr ǫðrum* to each other 28/23; *hvert upp frá ǫðru* one above the other 8/16; pl., others 4/29, 18/16; *allir aðrir* all the others 45/24; *þær aðrir er* those others who 30/23; *ǫnnur þau* the others 37/39; *ǫnnur guðin* the other gods 21/17, cf. 49/38; *aðra menn þá er* (all) other men who 4/33; *aðrir þrír* three other 49/24; *aðrar níu* the second nine 24/1.

aptann *m.* evening (the latter part of the day, from mid-afternoon onwards) 32/11, 44/7.

aptr *adv.* back 24/1, 32/35; again (or in the reverse direction?) 40/23; *lúka a.* close 39/26.

aptrmjór *a.* tapering behind 49/4.

ár (1) *adv.* early; †*ár alda* far back in time 9/12.

ár (2) *n.* year 3/24; prosperity (of the land) 6/9, 24/28.

ár (3) *f.* oar 44/25,32.

ár (4) pl. of **á (2)**.

áratal *n.* count of years 12/12.

ársali *m.* bed-hangings 27/20.

Ásagísling *f.* the Æsir's (giving in) hostage 23/34.

ásamt *adv.* together; *e-t kemr á. með e-m* s-one reaches agreement about s-thing 35/14.

ásjóna *f.* appearance, shape; face 13/6.

aska *f.* ashes 9/2.

askr *m.* ash (tree) 17/7, 34/16.

†Áskunnr *a.* descended from (of the race of) the Æsir 18/20.

ásmegin *n.* divine (Áss-) strength 23/7 (*honum* his), 38/5, 44/40.

ást *f.* love; pl. 46/17; relationship of love 29/32; i.e. love affairs? 25/5.

ástsæll *a.* beloved, popular 47/27.

at (1) *prep.* with dat., at 18/3, 19/33; in 8/28, 30/13, †postposition 52/39; in, i.e. obtainable from 44/12; into 10/4; to 9/1, 46/38; up to 27/24, 35/20; as far as 4/16, 39/6; against 52/10; on 37/22; (of time) at 32/35, in 42/23, to 34/6; in (respect of) 4/24; as regards 26/38; about 33/3; with 7/35; in accordance with 4/2, 46/6 (2); as 7/2 (2), 23/33, 25/17. As adv., there 46/34; in it 31/39; in this 33/18; *at þar er* up to where 38/27; *eigi at síðr* none the less 3/15.

at (2) *particle with inf.* to, in order to 29/29, 46/38 (2); for the purpose of 40/15; *til at* so as to 12/9; *hvat er at segja* what is to be told 17/9.

at (3) *conj.* that 3/9,13; so that 6/24; in order that 13/29; in that, by this that 44/1; with comp., *því . . . at* the . . . in that 7/25; *þat (. . .) at* this, that 5/19, 6/27, 45/30; *af því at* because 6/26; *til þess at* so that 4/10; with *at* repeated 55/1; *sá . . . at* such (of such a kind) that 6/8, 23/19, 35/33; *engi sá . . . at* no one . . . such that 43/24–5; *þau er . . . at* such that . . . that they 6/30; *svá at* so that 5/24; †*at . . . ne* lest . . . not 33/2; *þá . . . at* if (under those circumstances that) 14/9, 43/27; correlative with *svá* 11/1, with *fyrir því* 13/18.

át see **eta**.

†atall *a.* terrible 10/35.

atburðr *m.* event 36/34; *a. til* event giving rise to 22/18,24; circumstance 22/22; *atburðir af hverju hann kom* circumstances of his origin 34/27.

atganga *f.* attack; *veita atgǫngu* start to assail 35/17.

atgervi *f.* accomplishments 5/17, 26/22.

athæfi *n.* activity (cf. *hafask at*) 13/14.

atkvæði *n.* decree 15/35.

átrúnaðr *m.* belief, religion 4/11.

átt *f.* direction, region 9/26, 48/18, 49/22 (cf. **ætt**).

átta (1) see **eiga**.

átta (2) *num.* eight 3/8, 7/16.

átti (1) see **eiga**.

átti (2) *ord. num.* (the) eighth 8/31, 17/34, 29/33.

áttungr *m.* member of a (certain) family line; *þeir áttungar* those two members of the family 21/9 (cf. **ætt**).

auðigr *a*. rich 23/30.

auðkendr *a*. (*pp*.) easily recognizable 27/22.

auðr *m*. wealth (with gen., of or in s-thing) 23/31.

auðsénn *a*. (*pp*.) obvious 41/28 (cf. **sjá**).

auðsýnn *a*. evident 37/1.

auga *n*. eye 17/20, 18/31 (*honum* his), 37/20.

auka (jók) *sv*. increase, pile up 10/4 (impers. or intrans.; or *hvert* could be the object and *hrímit* the subject); pres. *eykr* adds, contributes 50/6; weak p. md. *aukaðisk* increased, became numerous 9/40 (cf. 3/3 *fjǫlgaðisk*, 3/9 *fjǫlmentisk*).

auki *m*. increase, addition (with gen., to s-thing) 7/15 (in apposition to *djúprǫðul*: 'which became an addition').

aurr *m*. mud 19/15,23.

ausa (jós) *sv*. with dat., pour 19/16; *a. e-t e-u* drench, lave s-thing with s-thing 19/20.

austan *adv*. from the east 51/22,30; *fyrir a.* with acc., to the east of 14/19.

austr (1) *n*. the east 39/18.

austr (2) *adv*. in the east 14/28; to the east 37/28.

austrhálfa *f*. eastern region 4/21.

austrrúm *n*. baling-seat (the rowing-seat in the lowest part of the boat, rear of centre) 44/25.

ávǫxtr *m*. growth, produce 4/6,22, 24/28 (dependent on *fyrir* 24/27).

báðir *a. pron.* (*n*. **bæði**) both 37/6, 44/39.

†baðmr *m*. tree 12/32 (generic sg.), 19/22.

baggi *m*. pack, bundle 38/17.

bak *n*. back; *á baki* on their backs 7/31; *á bak sér* on(to) his back 38/17, 39/20, onto their backs 39/25.

bál *n*. pyre 46/34, 47/4.

bálfǫr *f*. funeral, cremation 46/24; pl. 48/6.

banaorð *n*. news of s-one's death; *bera b. af e-m* i.e. kill s-one 50/35.

band *n*. band 28/26,27,30; bond 49/11,17, 50/1.

bani *m*. death 14/10, 33/10; slayer 51/4, 52/9; cause of death (*e-m* for s-one) 43/3; *hans b.* the cause of his death 50/31; *verða at bana e-m* cause s-one's death 29/16, 50/34; *verðask at bǫnum* slay each other 49/28.

banna (að) *wv*. forbid 29/35.

barn *n*. child 13/35, 21/18.

barnaeign *f*. the having of children; family 29/11.

barr *n.* needles (of a pine tree), but in the alliterative phrase *bíta barr* apparently the foliage of any tree taken as food 18/34, 33/12. (In modern Icelandic the word can also mean 'bud'.)

batt see **binda**.

baztr *a. sup.* best 17/32, 32/18, 53/8.

beðr *m.* (*gen.* **beðjar**) bed 24/11.

beiða (dd) *wv.* ask, bid (*e-n* s-one) 15/19 (with inf.); *b. e-n orða* try to get s-one to speak 31/10; *b. e-s e-m* ask for s-thing for s-one 45/20. Md., ask for o-self, beg (with noun clause) 34/39, 47/24 (*af e-m* from or of s-one); *beiðask e-s* ask for s-thing for o-self 17/19; with inf., ask that one may 8/1, 44/17.

bein *n.* bone 3/28, 11/37; ivory 4/40.

beina (d) *wv.* set in motion; *b. flug* exert o-self to fly 20/31.

beita *f.* bait 44/21.

bekkr *m.* bench, platform 39/30, 42/9; *útar á bekkinn* down to the lower end of the bench 40/2.

bera (bar) *sv.* carry 18/33, 29/23; have on one's body 7/16; take 27/27; bring 30/26; serve 30/23,33; *b. til ketils* i.e. put on to cook, boil 37/6; *berandi borð* a margin for carrying (space between top of liquid and rim of vessel so that it can be carried without spilling) 41/17; bear, endure 46/14; give birth to 35/33, 54/23 (future time); *b. e-n at syni* bear s-one as one's son 25/33; *vera borinn* be born 11/29, 18/15; *b. saman ráð sín* take counsel together 45/19; impers. *berr saman fundi* a meeting (confrontation) takes place (*þeira* between them) 43/36. Md. *við berask* be prevented; *láta e-t við berask* (decide to) refrain from s-thing 44/19.

bergrisi *m.* mountain giant 18/9, 23/4.

berja (barða) *wv.* beat, strike, pound (instrument in dat.) 7/32, 45/25; thrash 35/8; md., fight 8/8, 31/33 (*við e-n* with s-one); fight against each other 49/27.

berserkr *m.* berserk 5/5, 46/27 (cf. *Heiðreks saga* 5, 93; the berserk cult · was particularly associated with the cult of Óðinn. The connection with bears suggests shamanistic practices. See also *Ynglinga saga, Hkr* I. 17).

betr *adv. comp.* better 43/26.

betri *a. comp.* better 4/24, 33/9, 39/17; with dat., better than 20/13.

beygja (gð) *wv.* bend; *b. kenginn* bend (into) an arch, arch the back 42/1.

bezt *adv. sup.* best, most 25/10.

beztr *a. sup.* the best 15/23, 23/15; with gen. pl. 17/10, 36/13, (with def. art.) 36/15; very good, of the best kind 29/20; predicative, which is very valuable 23/6.

bíða (beið) *sv.* undergo, experience, suffer 43/25.

biðja (bað) *sv.* ask, order (with *at*-clause) 40/36, 44/10; *b. e-n e-s* pray to
s-one for s-thing (to be granted); *hvert b. skal hverrar bœnarinnar* which
one to address each (kind of) prayer to 25/8; *b. e-s e-m* beg for s-thing
for s-one 46/32; *b. sér e-s* beg for s-thing for o-self 37/23; with acc. and
inf., ask, tell s-one to do s-thing 27/27, 28/21; *bæði þá heila hittask*
wished them to meet again happily, i.e. bade farewell 39/21; with gen.,
ask in marriage 31/18,24 (*e-m* for s-one).

bik *n.* pitch 19/38.

bil *n.* moment 38/35, 45/6 (*er* when, at which).

bilt *n. a. as adv.* in the phrase *e-m verðr bilt* one is afraid, hesitates, lacks
the determination (*at gera e-t* to do s-thing) 38/6. The phrase perhaps
originally implied being paralysed with fear, terror-striken.

binda (batt) *sv.* tie (up), bind 28/2, 38/17; *b. þungt við* tie heavy weights
on (i.e. to the bottom of the net), weight down heavily 48/34.

birta (t) *wv.* make light; reveal, display 40/33; md., be illuminated 31/6.

bíta (beit) *sv.* bite 18/34, 25/18 (*af* off); *b. á* take bites from (on, of) 25/25;
b. af take bites from 33/19; *b.í* hold by the teeth 27/14.

bjarg *n.* rock 3/28, 11/37; mountain 28/6,10.

bjarnstaka *f.* bear-skin 5/2.

bjartr *a.* bright 23/16, 50/20; comp. 20/8; comp. n. as adv. 50/15.

bjó see **búa**.

bjóða (bauð) *sv.* offer (*e-m e-t* s-one s-thing) 41/33, 46/18; challenge
(s-one to s-thing) 42/20; *b. e-m til sín* invite s-one to stay with one 33/6;
b. e-m til e-s með sér invite s-one to share s-thing 37/8; with *at*-clause,
offer 6/6, 37/23, suggest 38/16; with inf., offer 34/30; *b. upp* hand back,
give up 41/26.

bjórr *m.* a triangular piece of (waste) leather 50/40, 51/1.

bjǫrn *m.* bear 28/6.

blanda (blétt) *sv.* mix, defile, taint (*e-u* with s-thing) 36/1.

blár *a.* black, livid 27/21.

blása (blés) *sv.* blow 50/22, 51/6; with dat., breathe out, blow out s-thing
45/4, 50/11.

blástr (rs) *m.* blast 25/40.

blautr *a.* soft 28/17.

bliðr *a.* dear, kind, friendly 12/36; pleasant 21/8.

blíkja (bleik) *sv.* glitter, gleam 7/31.

blindr *a.* blind 26/11, 45/39.

blóð *n.* blood 3/23, 11/23.

blóðrefill *m.* point of a sword 29/8.

blóðugr *a.* bloody 16/5.

blóm *n.* flower 3/24.

blóta (að) *wv.* worship, sacrifice to 7/23.

blær *m.* air-stream 10/13.

boðorð *n.* commandment 3/6.

bogi *m.* bow 24/17; (rain)bow 18/8.

bogmaðr *m.* archer 26/20.

bógr *m.* shoulder 14/1.

bólstaðr *m.* dwelling-place, mansion 27/17.

borð *n.* (1) table 32/23, 42/25. (2) the margin by which the liquid in a vessel is below the rim 41/17. (3) side of ship, gunwale 44/40; *af borði* off, away from the gunwale 45/8; *fyrir b.* overboard 44/35.

borðbúnaðr *m.* table-ware, articles used for eating and drinking 30/23.

borðhald *n.* fare 32/21.

borg *f.* city, stronghold (= Troy) 4/32; (= Ásgarðr) 7/27, 54/33; (= Ásgarðr inn forni) 13/9, 15/20; castle (= Útgarðr) 39/11,24, 42/27; fortification, rampart (around Valhǫll) 34/31, 35/3, (= Miðgarðr) 12/24.

borgargerð *f.* the building of the fortification 35/9.

borghlið *n.* gateway, entrance to the fortification 35/10, 39/26.

borgstaðr *m.* site for a town or castle 6/12.

brá (1) see **bregða**.

brá (2) *f.* eyelash, eyelid 12/25,35, 23/17.

bráðna (að) *wv.* melt 10/13.

bragð *n.* trick, feint 42/17.

bragr *m.* (1) a name for poetry 25/21 (the complement, not the subject). (2) paragon (with gen., among), chief, one outstanding (among) 25/22.

braut *f.* road, way 54/27; *á b., í b., á brut, braut* as adv., away, off 26/26, 29/27, 45/37, 46/22.

bregða (brá) *sv.* with dat., move (with a swift movement); *b. á lopt, b. upp* lift up, wave in the air 37/14, 43/30; *b. e-u fyrir e-t* move s-thing into the path of s-thing 43/6; *b. e-m (sér) í líki e-s* change (turn) s-one (o-self) into the form of s-thing 45/28, 48/18, 49/8; *b. e-u á sik* put on o-self, assume 7/24; intrans. *b. við* react, move back, jerk away 44/39.

breiðr *a.* broad; n. as adv., widely 17/12.

brenna (1) (brann) *sv.* intrans., burn, be consumed by fire 4/18, 9/2; pres. p., burning 9/26, 18/8, 50/15 (see AH *Studier* 29, 85).

brenna (2) (d) *wv.* trans., burn 9/30, 17/36, 20/20.

brenna (3) *f.* burning, funeral 46/38.

breyta (tt) *wv.* with dat., alter, change (*til* in accordance with, to suit) 22/23; md., change 4/12.

brigða (ð) *wv.* fail to keep one's word 29/38.

brim *n.* surf 16/5.

brjóta (braut) *sv.* break (trans.) 11/39, 27/35; break down, destroy 43/33; smash 46/31; md. *brjótask um* struggle 28/40.

bróðir *m.* (*pl.* **brœðr**) brother 11/16, 26/37, 47/23.

brot *n.* fragment 27/39.

brotna (að) *wv.* break (intrans.) 15/9, 27/30, 35/32.

brú *f.* bridge 15/6, 20/3, 34/21.

bruðr, brunnr *m.* spring, well 9/21, 14/5, 17/16, 19/14.

†brúðr *f.* bride 24/23.

brullaup *n.* wedding 31/25.

brún *f.* (*pl.* **brýnn**) eyebrow 37/20.

brunnr = bruðr.

brut = braut.

brynja *f.* coat of mail 50/27.

búa (bjó) *sv.* dwell 14/19, 19/36; *b. til e-s* prepare for s-thing, get on with s-thing (*yðr* for yourself) 38/21. Md., prepare (o-self to do s-thing), get ready 44/9; *búask til* (*at gera e-t*) prepare, begin (to do s-thing) 38/15; *búask til ferðarinnar* set out 44/5. See **búinn**.

búandi *m.* householder, farmer 37/5,10.

†bugr *m.* bend; *með bugum* all included 22/37.

búi *m.* = **búandi** 37/9.

búinn *pp.* (of **búa**) ready 27/37, 44/10; finished 48/29; *b. at* ready to, about to 42/24; *var búit at hann mundi* he was on the point of 44/18; *b. at sér of e-t* endowed with s-thing 40/13; *b. til* ready for 38/29; *b. við* proficient in 39/36.

búsgǫgn *n. pl.* household effects 15/29.

bústaðr *m.* dwelling-place 23/37.

býfluga *f.* bee 19/29.

bygð *f.* dwelling, settlement; a place to live 13/8; colonization 34/29; *til bygðar* to live in 12/23; pl., areas inhabited by (with gen.) 33/23.

byggja, byggva (gð) *wv.* inhabit 3/8, 13/3; live in 13/16, 20/9 (future time?), 20/25; abs., live (i.e. have a home) 4/20, 11/5; *b. í* live in 35/31; *b. á* live on 53/36. Md., become settled 3/9, 54/12.

býr *pres.* of **búa**.

byrja (að) *wv.* begin; *b. ferð sína, b. ferðina* set out, depart (*af* from) 5/21, 37/28.

byrr *m.* fair (favourable) wind 36/19.

bæði *adv.* (*conj.*) both 12/8, 23/18; *fyrir honum ok eptir bæði* (there was) both in front of him and behind him 50/14. Cf. **báðir**.

bœn *f.* prayer, petition 22/24, 25/8.

bœr *m.* farm, estate, dwelling 24/30, 29/18, 31/3.

daga (að) *wv.* dawn 42/23.

dagan *f.* dawn 32/34, 38/2.

dagr *m.* day 11/11, 17/8; acc. sg. *dag* in a day 7/3, by day 25/38; *þann dag allan* throughout the day 37/31; *um daga* in the daytime 48/18; *eptir um daginn* the next day 35/25.

dalr *m.* (*acc. pl.* **dali** and **dala**) valley 3/22, 43/4.

dauði *m.* death 35/16.

dauðr *a.* dead 46/7, 50/4, 53/5 (sc. *eru*); inanimate 47/28.

deild *f.* section 4/18.

deili *n. pl.* details (*á* of) 3/14, 34/27. (According to AH *Studier* 84 the equivalent of Latin *ratio*.)

deyja (dó) *sv.* die 3/32, 14/24, 50/5.

digrleikr *m.* thickness 28/22.

diskr *m.* plate 27/18.

djarfleikr *m.* boldness 25/14, 27/23 (*til at* enough to).

djarfr *a.* bold 26/18; sup., 25/10.

djúpr *a.* deep 3/22, 12/23; n. as adv. 7/6, 38/35; sup. (i.e. deeper than the other two) 43/5.

†djúprǫðull *m.* sun or circle of deep, i.e. gold or jewel or island (construe as object of *dró*, in apposition to *auka*) 7/13 (cf. *Hkr* I. 15 16).

dómr *m.* judgement, sentence, decree 23/20; (judicial) court 15/32 (see **rétta**), 17/7,36.

dómstaðr *m.* place of judgement, court 17/30, 26/26.

dómstóll *m.* seat of judgement 35/11 (cf. **rǫkstóll**).

dóttir *f.* daughter 4/36, 11/14; †female descendant 18/22.

draga (dró) *sv.* draw, pull 7/7, 13/39; drag 38/10, 48/31; catch (fish with a line) 44/28; *d. segl* hoist sail 36/19; *d. upp* pull up, plough up 7/3.

draumr *m.* dream 45/18,19.

dregill *m.* ribbon 28/25.

dreifa (ð) *wv.* (with dat.) scatter; (with acc.) besprinkle, bespatter 50/12; md., disperse, spread 3/3, 17/11; impers. 6/25.

dreki *m.* dragon 5/6.

drekka (drakk) *sv.* drink 8/7, 17/18; *d. af* drink from 40/37, 43/11, drain 41/1,11,19.

drekkja (kt) *wv.* with dat., drown 3/6, 11/23.

drengr *m.* youth 44/7.

drepa (drap) *sv.* kill 5/2, 11/22; strike, smite 27/39, 28/1 (impers., one knocks (s-thing)); md., kill each other 49/24.

dreyma (ð) *wv.* impers. *e-n dreymir e-t* s-one dreams s-thing 45/18.

†dreyri *m.* gore 14/39.

drífa (dreif) *sv.* drive (intrans.) 49/21.

drjúpa (draup) *sv.* drip 10/13, 49/15.

dropi *m.* drip, dripping, series of drops 33/20.

†drótt *f.* company 16/4, 20/16.

†drýgja (gð) *wv.* carry out; endure 18/39.

drykkja *f.* drink 30/23, 34/7; (the act of) drinking 40/35, 41/13.

drykkjumaðr *m.* drinker, man of prowess in drinking 41/2.

drykkr *m.* drink 8/21, 32/25; (the act of) drinking 41/6,25; draught 40/40, 41/18.

drœgi p. subj. of **draga**.

duga (ð) *wv.* with dat., help 50/29.

dúkr *m.* cloth 36/22.

duna (að) *wv.* thunder, rumble 38/33.

dur- see **dyrr**.

dveljask (dvalðisk) *wv. md.* stop, stay 5/26, 37/13; be delayed, be put a stop to 35/24; *d. munu stundirnar* much time will be taken up (whiled away) 23/11.

dvergr *m.* dwarf 12/6, 16/3 (gen. pl.), 16/9.

†dyggr *a.* trusty, good 20/15.

dylja (dulða) *wv.* conceal, dissemble, disguise; md. (reflexive) 7/25; pp. *duliðr e-s* ignorant of s-thing 21/6.

dynja (dunða) *wv.* rumble, resound, clatter 47/13.

dynr *m.* noise (*e-s* made by s-thing) 28/5,9; pl. 54/31.

dýr *n.* (wild) animal 3/19,25, 24/17.

dyrr *f. pl.* (*n. pl.* 37/39) doorway 37/35; doorways 33/29; gen. *dura* 30/1, 33/34; dat. *duru(nu)m* 7/35, 33/28.

dýrr *a.* dear; n. as adv., at a high price 33/9.

dœgr *n.* day (period of 12 hours); pl., day(s) and night(s) 12/12, 13/3; *á hverjum tveim dœgrum* every 24 hours 13/29.

dœma (ð) *wv.* judge; adjudge, decide 15/20; *d. lǫg* administer laws 6/14; intrans., pass judgement 18/2.

dœmi *n.* example; s-thing on which to base a judgement (*dómr*), origin, explanation, underlying story 22/18; (piece of) evidence (*til e-s* to prove s-thing) 28/8, 34/14, 36/30.

dǫgg *f.* dew 19/24,28; precipitation in general? 4/5.

dǫgurðarmál *n.* dinner-time 32/35, 34/6 (the main meal was taken early in the day in the Middle Ages).

dǫgurðr *m.* dinner 38/15.

døggva (gð) *wv.* bedew 13/31.

døkkálfar *m. pl.* dark elves 19/36,38 (see **ljósálfar** and Svartálfaheimr in index of names).

døkkr *a.* dark 13/23, 47/8.

eða *conj.* or, and 4/10, 8/29, 25/28; linking two parts of a question, and 8/33, 9/39, 10/36; *hvárt . . . eða* 7/22; linking a question to a statement, but 25/8, 34/3, 48/14; *kona eða karlmaðr* whether woman or man 25/23.

eðli *n.* nature, characteristic(s) 3/19,20,31, 7/22, 30/22.

ef *conj.* if 4/3, 11/33; correlative with *þá* 18/23, 21/4, 28/26, 40/40, with *þar* 39/13; in case 35/7; on condition that 46/18 (2); whether 8/22, 36/38, 38/13.

efna (d) *wv.* perform, carry out (successfully) 40/1.

efni *n.* material, substance 4/15, 50/6.

efri *a. comp.* upper 29/8, 50/9, 51/2.

efstr *a. sup.* uppermost 3/27.

egg *f.* edge 49/6.

eggskurn *n.* egg-shell 19/19.

eggsteinn *m.* edged (sharp) stone 49/10, textual note.

ei *neg. adv.* not 3/14, textual note.

eiðr *m.* vow, promise, oath 29/37, 35/17.

eiðrofi *m.* oathbreaker 53/16.

eiga (átta) *pret. pres. vb.* have 3/35, 8/29; hold 17/7; own 17/32; possess 13/32, 54/3; get (possession of) 24/30,37; have as children 13/22, 27/4; be married to 4/36, 13/25; be master of 8/2, 17/17; rule 5/32; †with suffixed neg. *eigut* they have not 18/19; *e. skamt til* be a short way off from 48/23; *e. undir* have dependent on (at the mercy of), risk on 25/27.

eigi *neg. adv.* not 3/12,21.

eigintunga *f.* native tongue, mother tongue 6/25.

eign *f.* property, wealth (with gen., consisting in) 4/22; belongings, contents, attributes: *alla e. þeira* everything in them 8/38.

eigna (að) *wv.* take possession of (*sér* for o-self) 5/3; md., get possession of, take to o-self 3/32, 5/27, (as wife) 34/33; get for o-self, win, earn 34/35, 46/17.

eik *f.* oak 4/40, 38/19,30.

eimi *m.* steam 52/33.

einhendr *a.* one-handed 25/19.

einherjar *m. pl.* the warriors in Valhǫll, champions 21/29, 30/33 (lit. united warriors? unique warriors? those who fight alone?).

einkamál *n.* private agreement 29/37.

einn *a., num.*, and *pron.* (1) one 3/20, 7/3; one of them 43/5; with gen. or *af*-phrase, one of 7/4, 23/3; with pl. noun *ór einum durum* from one doorway 33/38; a 54/22; a certain 7/2, 14/19; *e. sá staðr* a certain place 19/38; *e. Ássinn* one of the Æsir 26/11; *einum fœtinum* the one of its legs 43/19; with sup., the very . . . -est: *e. hin mesta* a particularly great 5/6; *sá e. mátkastr* that one especially mighty 14/23; *einna nokkurr* one special one, one in particular 14/33; the same 46/10; identical 55/2. (2) alone 21/4, 27/23; *e. saman* all alone, on his own 5/5; *einir sér* of their own, separate, 'alone to themselves' 50/20; *gull eitt* nothing but gold, pure gold 15/24; *undir einum þér* under just you 47/13; *e. samt* just by itself 37/21; only 20/24, 24/5, 44/13.

einnhverr *pron. a.* a certain 28/1; someone 28/35, 42/8; *einhvern mann* some person 40/35; *einhvern þann er* someone whom 40/11.

einvígi *n.* single combat 26/23.

eira (ð) *wv.* with dat., spare, not harm 45/21,34.

eitr *n.* poison 10/4, 45/4.

eitrá *f.* river of poison 53/16 (cf. AH *Studier* 31).

eitrdropi *m.* drop of poison 10/31, 49/14 (acc. pl. or dat. sg., collective; cf. **dropi**), 53/21 (cf. AH *Studier* 31).

eitrkvikja *f.* poisonous (or icy) flow (or fermentation? suppuration? cf. AH *Studier* 31) 10/1.

eitrormr *m.* poisonous snake 49/11.

ekr pres. of **aka**.

ekki *pron.*, n. of **engi**.

eldask (d) *wv. md.* grow old 25/25.

elding *f.* fiery body (i.e. such as stars and planets) 12/9.

eldr *m.* fire 9/30, 20/27; flames 46/30; pl. 50/10; furnace (for smelting) 10/2.

elli *f.* old age 43/25.

ellidauðr *a.* who has died of old age 27/16.

ellipti *ord. num.* (the) eleventh 8/32, 17/35, 29/40.

elska (að) *wv.* love 3/10.

elskugi *m.* love 29/32.

elztr *a. sup.* eldest 8/27, 21/16.

en *conj.* but, and 3/12, 6/5; beginning a sentence, now 7/4, 19/17; only sometimes a full adversative, as at 16/30 (2), 16/39, 17/19, 18/24,26, 43/33; with comparatives, than 3/22, 4/24; *áðr* (. . .) *en*, *fyrr en* before 7/26, 9/6,39, until 5/25, 15/30; *áðr en* had not 46/31; *annarr* (. . .) *en*, *fleiri* (. . .) *en* other than, besides 6/30, 15/22, 19/33; *framar en* to a greater extent than 25/23; *heldr* (. . .) *en* rather than that 21/6, 28/34.

enda *conj.* and so, and of course 28/30.

endask (d) *wv. md.* last, be sufficient (*e-m* for s-one) 32/10, 33/5; be enough (*til* to bring about, to become) 43/3.

endi *m.* end 9/28, 20/3, 40/18; (of time) 9/29.

endir *m.* end 43/13.

engi, øng- *pron. a.* (*acc. sg. m.* **engi, engan, øngan**) no one 5/8, 23/9; no 10/39, 38/23; *engi . . . fegri staðr* no fairer place 19/39; *engi . . . dómr hans* none of his judgements (decisions) 23/19; *engi . . . sá* (there is) no one (no, not a) 15/15, 39/39, 43/24, 45/2; n. *ekki* nothing 9/13, 23/21; no 9/19, 44/6, 49/23; as adv., not 25/13, 28/30, 49/22; dat. sg. n. *øngu*, *engu* nothing 41/12; with comp., no (less) 44/35.

enn *adv.* still 38/40, 45/11; also 29/22, 33/23; yet (or yet more) 15/3; further 41/31; again 3/9, 27/32, 43/28; yet again 40/29; in addition 20/2,3; moreover, as well 19/14, 41/14; in the future 32/8; with comp., still, even 27/10, 29/5, yet 25/9; *enn á fleiri vega* in still more ways 21/30.

†ennitungl *n.* forehead-star, i.e. eye 7/17.

epli *n.* apple 25/24.

eptir *prep.* (1) with dat., after 14/14, 45/9; behind 50/14; for, to fetch 35/19, 46/25; along, through 18/33, 48/38; over 40/15; in accordance with 13/27; *e. því sem* in imitation of that which 48/29; *e. honum* based on his account 54/35. (2) with acc., after (of time) 3/8, 6/16. (3) as adv., afterwards 15/1; *e. um daginn* the next day 35/24; after, in pursuit 35/23; *ganga e.* follow 8/6; behind 37/27; *vera e.* remain, be left 7/9; *grætr e.* remains behind weeping, or weeps for (him) 29/27; *þar e.* from this 23/17; *e. er* as conj., after 53/4.

eptri *a. comp.* hinder 37/15.

er *rel. particle* and *conj.* (1) who, which, that 3/2, 4/6; with pron., *sá* (. . .) *er* 8/19, 9/25, *þat* (. . .) *er* 4/27, 6/17, 35/31 (such that; similarly *þau er* 6/30); *þat er* that part which 10/6, what 36/40; *allt þat er* everything that 25/39; *til þess er* until 43/34; *þeim er* to whom 13/8; *sjá þann er* the sea with which 12/1. (2) introducing noun clause, that 8/39, 25/3 (2), 31/7,

45/27; *þat . . . er* that . . . (in) that 7/21, 9/21, 50/31; *þat er* this, that (i.e. when) 9/13, 29/36, 31/40, how 45/6; *þat er gras vex* grass growing 25/38. (3) where 23/26, 24/20, 44/28, 52/39; when 3/3, 20/31; while 48/21; if, since 15/13 (twice); since, seeing that 25/7, 28/29; in that 18/24; with adv. *þá* (. . .) *er, er . . . þá* when 3/9, 4/38, 13/2; *þegar er* immediately that, when 36/19; *síðan er* after 3/34, since 27/35; *nú . . . er* now that 42/34; *þar* (. . .) *er* where 6/12, 7/17 (as); *þangat er* to where 44/22; *þar fyrir er* over where 5/36; *þar til er* until 6/16; *hvárt er* whether 31/19; *því harðara er* the harder that 28/40.

†**tér** = **þér** 15/3, 51/21.

erfiði *n*. trouble, hardship, suffering 18/39.

eski *n*. box (made of ash) 25/24; (containing personal possessions) 29/23.

eta (át) *sv*. eat 38/15, 39/39.

eykr pres. of **auka**.

eyra *n*. ear 32/32, 45/12.

eyrindi *n*. (1) errand, business 8/20 (purpose in coming); *sitt e.* result of his errand 31/26; *þakka e-m sitt e.* thank s-one for carrying out one's errand 28/19; pl., mission 48/1; *at eyrindum* on errands 30/8. (2) breath 41/6,14.

fá (fekk) *sv*. get, obtain 17/19 (object understood), 31/24; become subject to 11/1; have (children) 11/15; adopt, hit on (a course of action) 27/26; give, supply 36/39; *fá sér* find o-self 44/21; *fá e-m e-t* give s-one s-thing 31/22, 32/5; *fá e-m í hǫnd* put into s-one's hand, hand to s-one 40/38; *fá til* provide, procure 40/11; with gen., marry 5/7, 11/14; with pp., be able, manage (to do s-thing), get (s-thing done) 28/2, 36/30, 39/25; *svá at ek fæk eigi* (see -**k**) so that I cannot 28/32; *áðr svá fái gert* in order to (be able to) make such a thing 36/24. Md. *fásk um* react violently, make a fuss 29/6; be obtained, achieved (*á* in it) 41/26; grapple, wrestle 42/8, 43/24.

faðerni *n*. paternity, the nature of one's father 13/27, 27/10.

faðir *m*. (*gen. sg.* **fǫður** 4/39; *dat. sg.* **feðr** 5/9, **fǫður** 21/18; *dat. pl.* **feðrum** 23/5) father 5/30, 13/18.

fagnaðr *m*. entertainment, cheer 33/10, 42/25; *í góðum fagnaði* with hospitable treatment 42/23.

fagr *a*. (*f*. **fǫgr**) beautiful 4/39, 11/13; fine, excellent 6/11, 50/27; pleasant, decent 37/2; *eru á himni fagrir* in heaven are beautiful, are in heaven which are beautiful 18/10; comp. *fegri* 4/23, with dat. *sólu fegra* fairer than the sun 20/12; sup. *fegrstr* 20/8; n. as adv. 23/18.

fall *n*. fall 43/25.

falla (fell) *sv*. fall 3/25, 19/25; 2nd pers. sg. p. *fell* 43/23; fall down 37/21,

38/28; (die) 11/22, 52/12; flow (down) 9/22, 33/20; *fellr hverr á annan* each falls on (attacks) the other, or they fall one on top of (after) another 34/5. Md. *e-t fellsk e-m* s-thing fails s-one 46/9 ('they were speechless').

fálma (að) *wv.* grope; *f. e-u til* grope, fumble at (it) with s-thing 45/7.

falslauss *a.* without deceit or trickery; n. as adv. 28/36.

fang *n.* grip, hold; *hafa fullt f.* have one's hands full 50/30; wrestling bout 42/15,21; wrestling 42/16,20; pl., materials, resources 4/30.

fár *a.* few; *f. maðr* few men, it is a rare man (that) 36/27; pl. as subst. *fáir* few people 32/12,19.

fara (fór) *sv.* go 6/6, 7/24; travel 5/4, 5/23; pres. p. *farandi* vagrant 7/2; extend (?) 30/21; flow 11/40; with a., go around (in a certain way) 29/22; with adv., fare, get on (in a certain way) 36/25, turn out 42/5; with acc., travel, go on (an errand, one's way, etc.) 31/21, 43/34, 54/21, suffer 42/31, overtake, catch 54/24; *f. ok herja* go and harry 9/29, similarly 15/10, 31/23, cf. **taka**; with inf., go to, set forth to (do s-thing) 52/7, with *at* and inf. 33/39; *f. á meðal* pass between (people), be transacted 36/7; *f. með* take 44/24 (*var farit með hann* he was taken 49/5), sail (a ship), drive (animals, a vehicle) 36/20, 37/3 (was driving); *f. með e-u, e-m* treat, do (with it or him) 27/29, treat, handle s-thing 37/17, use, deal in, practise s-thing 43/40; *f. saman* succeed each other, follow each other without a break 49/23; md., perish, pass away 20/9.

fast *adv.* hard 27/38, 38/22; firmly, tightly 47/20; deeply 38/32, 39/3.

fastr *a.* firm; comp. n. as adv. 42/16.

fávíss *a.* having little knowledge 21/4.

fax *n.* mane 13/32.

fé *n.* (*gen.* **fjár**) wealth 3/10,15.

feð- see **faðir**.

fegrð *f.* beauty 4/22,25, 6/11, 23/18.

fegr- see **fagr**.

feigð *f.* the coming of death 30/35.

feigr *a.* close to death, doomed, dying 14/37.

†feiknstafr *m.* horror-rune, evil intent 23/27.

fela (fal, fólginn) *sv.* hide; deposit 17/22; *vera í fólgit* be contained in 17/16; *f. sik* and md. *felask* take refuge, go into hiding 48/17,19.

félagi *m.* companion 38/15; *ok þeir félagar* (he) and his companions 39/23, 42/22,24.

fella (d) *wv.* fell, lay low 42/12; knock down 46/28.

ferð *f.* journey 5/21, 7/23; travelling 7/26; movements 6/8; expedition

45/15; 'faring', how one gets on, experience 42/29, 44/4; behaviour, dealings (*til* towards, with) 35/33; pl., travels 22/25, arrival 6/5.

ferskeyttr *a.* (*pp.*) square 43/5.

festa (st) *wv.* fix 4/10, 29/4; *f. saman* fasten together 12/1.

festr *f.* cord, halter 29/2 (i.e. the free end), 29/6.

fésæla *f.* wealth, prosperity 24/29.

fésæll *a.* wealthy 23/31.

fet *n.* pace 50/35.

†**fíflmegir** *m. pl.* monstrous brood 51/34 (cf. **mǫgr**).

fíll *m.* elephant 4/40.

fimbulvetr *m.* mighty winter 49/21.

fimm *num.* five 22/33, 33/34.

fimti *ord. num.* (the) fifth 8/30, 17/34, 29/21.

fingrgull *n.* gold ring (for the finger) 47/33.

finna (fann) *sv.* find, meet 5/7, 13/5; discover 5/19, 28/8; notice 37/16; *f. til* discover, think up, invent (for a certain purpose) 48/20. Md., be found 3/14; exist 9/16, 34/15; meet each other 52/39.

fiski *f.* fishing; *róa til fiskjar* go fishing 44/10.

fiskr *m.* fish 28/7, 44/28, 48/28.

fjall *n.* mountain 23/37, 39/18; *í fjalli* on or in a mountain 48/17 (the *hús* may be a cave).

fjalltindr *m.* mountain top 3/21.

fjár see **fé**.

fjara *f.* low tide 43/16.

fjarri *adv.* far away (*e-u* from s-thing) 27/39, 53/18.

fjórði *ord. num.* (the) fourth 8/30, 17/33, 29/20.

fjórir *num.* (*n.* **fjǫgur**) four 7/19, 22/33, 33/35.

fjórtándi *ord. num.* (the) fourteenth 30/7.

fjǫðr *f.* feather 3/26.

fjǫlbreytinn *a.* changeable, capricious 26/38.

fjǫlði *m.* multitude 5/22; *allr f.* the majority 3/10.

fjǫlgask (að) *wv. md.* multiply 3/3.

fjǫlkunnigr *a.* skilled in magic 7/20.

fjǫlkyngi *f.* magic, witchcraft 36/24, 43/40.

fjǫlmennask (t) *wv. md.* become peopled, become full of people 3/9.

fjǫlmenni *n.* crowd (of people) 32/6,7.

fjǫlmennr *a.* containing many people 6/24.

fjǫr *n.* (*dat.* **fjǫrvi**) life; body, flesh, blood? 14/24,36.

fjǫturr *m*. fetter, shackle 25/15, 50/1.

flá (fló) *sv*. skin 37/6.

flatr *a*. flat 44/28.

fleginn *pp*. of **flá**.

fleiri *a. comp*. (*dat. pl*. **fleiri, fleirum**) more 3/5, 10/37; further, other 25/31, 42/20; *hvárt fleira* (n.) *er eyrindi hans* whether he had any further business 8/20; *hvat . . . fleira* (with partitive gen.) what other 18/28, 19/33 (*en* than, besides).

flesk *n*. meat (pork) 32/10,18.

flestr *a. sup*. most, nearly every 12/2, 22/21; = all 39/30; *flestan dag* i.e. always 26/32; *flest* (adv.?) *hefir illt gert* has done most evil (or evil most) 48/10.

flet *n*. boards (of a hall, i.e. the wooden platforms or 'benches' used for seating) 8/15.

fljóta (flaut) *sv*. float; be launched? 50/8.

fljúga, fljúgja (flaug) *sv*. fly 10/9, 13/40, 32/34.

flóð *n*. flood 3/8.

flokkr *m*. herd 44/22.

flugr *m*. flight 20/31.

flytja (flutta) *wv*. carry, transport 11/35, 46/22 (in both cases object understood).

flærð *f*. deceit, fraud 26/35.

fogl = **fugl**.

†fold *f*. earth 52/30.

fólgit *pp*. of **fela**.

fólk *n*. people 8/7; race (of creature) 19/35; host 47/3.

forað *n*. evil, destructive creature, monster 50/34.

forða (að) *wv*. save, enable to escape (*við e-u* from s-thing) 30/5; md., avoid, escape 30/5.

forðum *adv*. formerly, once 17/13.

forkunnar *adv*. exceptionally 27/17, 33/16.

forn *a*. ancient 6/29, 12/11, 24/24 (former?); *(h)inn forni* the old (as opposed to the new one) 8/28, 13/16.

fors *m*. waterfall 48/21,33.

fóstra *f*. foster-mother, nurse 42/12.

fóstri *m*. foster-father 5/3.

fóthvatr *a*. fleet of foot; comp. 40/22, sup. 37/32.

fótr *m*. (*pl*. **fœtr**) foot or leg 3/23, 11/2, 17/33; dat. sg. *fœti* 37/16; *á kné ǫðrum fœti* on his knee with one leg, i.e. onto one knee 42/19.

frá *prep*. with dat., from 3/8, 10/19 (descended from); †after the noun 34/12; about 5/24, 18/28; elliptical, with gen., from the abode of 53/38; *skamt frá* a little way from 38/2; *innar frá* on the inside of 37/40; *útar frá* beyond 37/10; *upp frá* above 20/23; *suðr frá* to the south of 20/21. As adv., from 3/2; about (it) 36/30, 41/10; *inn í frá* inwards on from there (there was) 10/7.

fráfall *n*. death ('decease') 46/15.

fram *adv*. forward 38/26, 46/25, 50/28; on (distance) 39/11; into the water 46/29; forward, out 46/21; up, out in front 8/24; through (a door, into the presence of those inside) 8/11; in the front 44/26; in front of him 48/25; of time, by 3/3, on 39/23 (2); *lengra fram* (information about events) further on in time 54/28,29; *um fram* with acc., beyond, to a greater extent than 5/20, 27/1, superior to 4/33, 25/12 (*vera um fram* excel, surpass).

framar *adv. comp*. ahead (*því* so far) 40/18; *f. en* more than, beyond, in excess of 25/23.

framast *adv. sup*. most outstanding 22/30.

framaverk *n*. deed of distinction, achievement 8/34.

†framgenginn *a*. (*pp*.) departed (i.e. dead) 53/31.

frami *m*. fame, glory; *til frama* to achieve glory: *hvat . . . til frama* what glorious deeds 22/29; advantage, benefit, or distinction, honour 45/26.

framstafn *m*. prow 46/29.

frásagnarverðr *a*. worth the telling, worth making a story about 34/28.

frásǫgn *f*. narrative, story 22/25, 54/37.

fregna (frá) *sv*. ask 8/24; hear, learn 36/11.

freista (st) *wv*. with gen., make trial of, put to the test 40/1,14; *f. sín* try one's prowess 40/3; *f. um* (*of*) *e-t* have a try at (with) s-thing 41/29,31; with inf., attempt 40/10, 46/12; *f. ef* try if, see if 46/18.

†freki *m*. wolf (= Fenrir) 51/35.

fremja (framða) *wv*. perform, carry out 42/3.

friðr *m*. peace 6/9, 24/28; amnesty, quarter, grace 37/23, 46/32.

fríðr *a*. beautiful 13/36, 26/37.

frjósa (fraus) *sv*. freeze (*at* into) 10/4.

fróðleikr *m*. (fund of) knowledge, learning; *mikill f. sá er kann* a great deal of learning which would know (i.e. he would need great learning who could explain) 22/17.

fróðliga *adv*. intelligently, learnedly, like a learned man 15/5 (i.e. you are not well-informed if you need to ask that; cf. **fróðr, fræði**).

fróðr *a*. wise, having knowledge 8/22, 10/29, 11/31; well-informed 21/3; learned 22/26, 23/9; comp. 8/23.

frost *n.* frost 47/39, 49/22 (pl.; cf. also 4/20, textual note).

fróva *f.* lady 25/4 (a loan-word from Low German; cf. *frúva*, *Hkr* I. 25).

frumkveði *m.* originator (with gen., the first to speak with or disseminate s-thing) 26/35.

frýja (frýða) *wv.* disparage, cast aspersions on (*e-s*); *f. e-m hugar* question s-one's courage 28/34.

frægð *f.* fame 28/25.

frægr *a.* famous 27/36.

frændi *m.* relative 3/33, 23/6.

frœði *n. pl.* records, sources 14/2 (referring to *Grm*).

frœðimaðr *m.* learned man, scholar, man of wide knowledge 44/3.

fugl, fogl *m.* bird 3/19, 28/7.

fulldrukkinn *a.* (*pp.*) quite satisfied with drink 33/15.

fullgera (ð) *wv.* accomplish, bring into being 13/19.

fullr *a.* full 49/14, 50/30; *f. af* full of 17/17, 31/7; complete, absolute 27/2; full-grown, fully developed 5/1; *at fullu* thoroughly 29/2.

fúna (að) *wv.* rot, decay 9/1, 19/2, 19/17.

fundr *m.* meeting 43/36 (*þeira Miðgarðsorms* between him and M.); *til fundar við e-n* to meet s-one 42/40.

fundu p. pl. of **finna**.

furðu *adv.* amazingly 12/20, 29/11.

furðuliga *adv.* terribly 3/30.

fúss *a.* willing, eager 31/12 ('but (that he was) not eager, but without eagerness').

fyl *n.* foal 35/33.

fylgja (gð) *wv.* with dat., accompany 14/7, 42/27; *þar fylgði* accompanied them 10/1; attend 6/8; i.e. serve 37/27; take 8/3; appertain to 23/19, 47/5; belong to 3/2, 6/27; be a property of, be a characteristic of 13/21, 25/7; depend upon 4/6 (*því = skini ok dǫgg*).

fylki *n.* division (in an army), host, troop 47/11 (cf. '*fylki eru fimtigi*', *SnE* I. 534).

fylking *f.* troop, division, army, battle array 50/20.

fylla (t) *wv.* fill (*e-t* s-thing; *e-s, e-u*, or *af e-u* with s-thing) 33/13 ('with which it fills'), 40/4; md., fill o-self, become full (*e-u* or *með e-u* with s-thing) 10/7, 14/24,36 (future).

fyr = fyrir.

fyrir *prep.* (1) with acc., in front of 7/6, 37/20; into the presence of 39/30; into the way of (to ward off) 43/6; (of time) before 39/3; *f. austan, f. vestan* to the east, west of 14/19, 45/35; for, on account of 3/32, 15/14,

49/3; *f. e-s sakar* see **sǫk**; in respect of, against 30/2; as, in place of 54/11. (2) with dat., in front of 31/5, 33/28, i.e. across 39/26; ahead of 8/5, 14/16; in the presence of 40/33; at, by, near 50/40; on behalf of 22/24, 50/24; *ráða f.* rule over 4/3, 5/29; against 12/25, 34/31, 45/20; because of 37/21, 50/36, after noun 24/12; *f. hví* why 29/12; *f. því* (. . . *at*) for this reason (. . . that) 3/6, 13/17, 29/35, 50/5; *f. því at* because 17/17, 35/6, 54/29; *mikill* (*lítill, minni*) *f. sér* of great (little, less) account or importance 25/6, 41/38, 42/32. (3) as adv., in front 8/15, 48/31; ahead 38/18; *vera f.* be there, in the way 48/33; *þar . . . f.* around them, protecting them 18/11; *þar f. er* over where 5/36; *f. innan* on the inside 12/24; in exchange, in payment 37/24.

fyrr *adv. comp.* before 3/9; formerly 53/37; previously 6/14; on previous days 35/25; above (in the book) 30/22, 50/16; *gera e-t fyrr* be the first to do s-thing 44/17; *spyrja e-n fyrr* be the first to ask s-one, accost s-one by asking 7/36; *var hitt þó fyrr* yet the first thing that happened was 46/12; *fyrr* (. . .) *en* as conj., before 4/4, earlier than (with dat. of length of time) 9/20, until 5/25, 17/20, 25/16, 28/38.

fyrri (1) *a. comp.* former 16/30; previous 41/16, 47/11 (i.e. the day before yesterday? the other day?).

fyrri (2) *adv.* in front, ahead 13/30.

fyrrum *adv.* formerly, once upon a time 54/1.

fyrst *adv. sup.* first 8/22, 9/25; originally 10/29, 15/34; firstly, primarily 27/9; *f. . . . ok svá* firstly . . . and also 48/12.

fyrstr *a. sup.* (usually weak) first 11/11, 13/6, (strong) 50/27.

fýsask (t) *wv. md.* desire, be eager 5/21.

færri *a. comp.* fewer 27/39, textual note.

fæstr *a. sup.* fewest, very few 23/27.

fœða (dd) *wv.* feed (trans.) 3/31, 11/8; give birth to or nurse, foster 14/21 (*at sonum* as her sons), 14/30; bring up 27/23; *f. upp* bring up, raise 23/32; md., feed or be born (*af* from) 19/29; *fœðask við* live on 11/9; *fœðask upp* be brought up, bred 27/7.

fœra (ð) *wv.* bring 27/11, 28/18; *f. á lopt* raise in the air 45/7; *f. í frásagnir* make the subject of narratives 22/25. Md. *fœrask í* put o-self, fly into (a passion) 35/26, put on, imbue o-self with, summon up 44/40.

fœri *n.* range (from which s-thing can be done), opportunity, chance (to do s-thing); *koma í f.* get a chance 39/1.

fœrr *a.* passable; *ef ǫllum væri fœrt* if it was possible for everyone to go 18/10; *f. til* (with inf.) capable of (doing s-thing), able to 36/33.

fœtr see **fótr**.

fǫlna (að) *wv.* grow pale 45/5; fade 3/25.

fǫlski *m.* paleness (of ash lying in the form of s-thing burnt) 48/27,29.

fǫr *f.* journey, expedition 46/20; *vera í f. e-m* be in company with s-one 51/37.

fǫruneyti *m.* company, companionship 38/13, 44/6.

gamall *a.* old 3/30, 5/22; belonging to ancient times, primitive, original? 11/3, 14/21; as surname, (*hinn*) *gamli* the old (i.e. belonging to ancient times) 7/11, 55/4.

gaman *n.* pleasure, amusement; *e-t þykkir g. e-m* s-one takes pleasure in s-thing 53/10.

ganga (1) (gekk) *sv.* go 7/6,21; walk 17/36; move 37/36; be (going) 39/38; (continue to) be 21/6; pass, come (of time) 49/23; *g. leið sína* go one's way 54/33; with inf., *g. sofa* go to sleep 38/30; *g. vega* advance to fight 52/13; *g. á e-t* enter into s-thing, begin 34/34; *g. af e-m* pass from s-one (of a mood) 37/24; impers. *gengr af* it is drained 40/40, 41/2; *g. at e-m* attack s-one 52/21; *g. at e-u* allow o-self to take part in s-thing 31/25; *g. eptir* follow 8/5; *g. fram* move (forward, i.e. down the beach) 46/24, go on, forward 39/23, out 40/3; *áðr gangi fram* before one goes through (a door) 8/11 (see **fram**); *g. fyrir e-u* go in front of s-thing, draw s-thing 7/17; impers. *er inn gengr* where one enters 27/20; *g. til* approach 41/40, 42/7, go up 42/19; *g. upp* be lifted up 7/9, go ashore 37/29. Md. *gangask á* be disregarded, broken, gone back on 36/4.

ganga (2) *f.* course 12/11, 14/3; going, motion 14/9, 23/29.

gangr *m.* movement, course 3/35, 4/5, 13/34.

gap *n.* abyss 9/18.

gapa (ð) *wv.* gape 29/6, 50/9,10.

garðr *m.* fence, wall 27/17; enclosed place, courtyard 34/5.

gátt *f.* door-opening 8/10.

gefa (gaf) *sv.* give (*e-m e-t*) 3/32, 7/2; give away 31/36; apply 54/37; *e-t er gefit* (*e-m*) s-thing is given, granted (to s-one) 4/13, (a name) is taken, derived 6/30; *er þá váru . . . gefin* to whom then were given 55/3; *þeim er bygðin var gefin* to whom a dwelling-place was given 13/9 (see note); give in marriage 36/3 (pp. agreeing with direct object; *ætt* is indirect obj.); *g.* (*e-u*) *stað*(*ar*) stop (s-thing) 5/25, 10/3.

gegna (d) *wv.* with dat., mean 3/19.

geirr *m.* spear 50/27.

geisa (að) *wv.* rage, surge 52/33.

geit *f.* (she-) goat 33/11,16.

gelti see **gǫltr**.

gera (ð) *wv.* (*pp.* **gerr, gǫrr, gjǫrr**; *imp.* **gerðu** 46/3) do 15/13, 37/22; perform 7/26; act 46/3; make 15/27, 27/26; build 4/27, 34/30; create 9/7; pp., finished 50/7; *bezt gert* the best that has been built 15/23; pp.

agreeing with direct object *gerva* 23/24; *var þat* (sc. *ráð*) *gert* it was decided 45/19; g. *af* 13/20 see note; g. *af sér* make (s-thing) of o-self, achieve distinction, be successful (*um e-t* in s-thing) 41/22; g. *at* do (about s-thing), try 45/26; *ekki er langt um at g.* there is not a great deal to say about it 42/15. Md. (1) take place 13/11, 22/25; *svá mikit gerðisk af því* this went so far 3/11. (2) become 37/26, 45/5; be created, come into being (*mannlíkun* as subject, *dvergar* in apposition) or be made into, turn into (*mannlíkun* as complement) 16/8.

gerða (ð) *wv.* fence around (cf. **garðr**); *er þeir gerðu* with which they contained, enclosed 12/1.

gersemligr *a.* costly, precious 5/23, 29/26.

geta (gat) *sv.* (1) beget (used of either parent) 11/13, 54/20; g. *við e-m* beget on s-one 11/2, 27/5. (2) with gen., mention, speak of 49/19; *eigi er þess getit* the story does not mention 39/21; guess, suppose, presume 48/10.

geysask (t) *wv. md.* rush, flow furiously 50/2.

geysi *adv.* mighty, extremely 18/24, 22/16 (probably colloquial; sometimes used ironically, e.g. 33/16?).

†-gi *neg. suffix* 21/26.

†gífr *n.* troll (-wife) 9/36, 52/2.

gimsteinn *m.* gemstone 4/23.

gin *n.* mouth 51/3.

gína (gein) *sv.* open the mouth (*yfir* over, round, at) 44/37.

ginna (t) *wv.* make a fool of 44/36.

†ginnheilagr *a.* most holy (magically, supernaturally holy?) 16/1, 35/38.

†ginnunga gen. pl. (or sg.?) of the mighty spaces? 9/18; cf. *ginning* illusion, magical deception; perhaps 'filled with magic power'? (cf. AH *Gudesagn* 24).

gipt *f.* gift 3/15, 4/25.

gipta (1) *f.* good fortune 3/15, textual note.

gipta (2) (pt) *wv.* give in marriage 13/24, 35/12; md. with dat., marry 29/24.

girnd *f.* desire 3/5.

gísla (að) *wv.* give as hostage 23/33.

gisting *f.* being a guest; *at gistingu* as a guest 44/8.

gjalda (galt) *sv.* pay 35/29; repay, requite: *goldit var honum þetta* he was repaid for this 48/15.

gjǫf *f.* gift 31/38, 47/33.

gjǫrr *pp.* of **gera**.

glaðr *a.* happy 7/13, 26/7.

gleypa (t) *wv.* swallow 14/24, 49/37, 50/37 (the meaning is future in all three instances).

glotta (tt) *wv.* smile ironically or derisively; *g. um tǫnn* grin showing the teeth, i.e. insincerely 39/32.

gnaga (að) *wv.* gnaw 17/15.

†gnata (að) *wv.* clash, crash 9/35, 52/1.

gneisti *m.* spark 10/8, 12/7.

gnógliga *adv.* abundantly 15/29.

gnúpleitr *a.* with drooping face 27/22.

gnýja (gnúða) *wv.* roar, rage 14/26 (future).

gnýr *m.* noise (usually of wind, waves, etc.) 38/1; uproar 50/13.

gnæfa (að) *wv.* tower high up 30/21.

gnœgri *a. comp.* more abundant, better supplied (*at* with) 4/23–4, textual note.

goð *n. pl.* (heathen) gods 8/27, 9/29; referring to Æsir as opposed to Vanir 23/33,34, to gods as opposed to men 5/25, 13/18, 26/13,35, 35/34, 46/8, 50/7, 53/5; cf. **guð** and note to 21/13 (at 13/18 and 17/6 R may have *u* rather than *o*).

goðkunnigr *a.* divine, descended from gods 13/17, 18/15; spelt *guð-* 21/13 (*Æsir guðkunnigir* Æsir who are of divine ancestry or nature).

goðmǫgn *n. pl.* divine powers 7/23.

góðr *a.* good 3/4, 15/15; *góð til áheita* well-disposed towards prayers or good for praying to 29/33; *gott skeið at renna* a good running course 40/15; n. as subst. or adv. *er gott (e-m)* it is good (for one) 24/28, 25/4,11; *gott at segja* good (things) to be told 23/14; *er gott til e-s* there is plenty of s-thing 37/33 ('food was not easy to come by'); *inn góði* as surname, the good 45/17.

goldit *pp.* of **gjalda**.

gólf *n.* (earth) floor (in the centre of the hall, as opposed to the boarded platforms or benches down the sides of the hall) 40/3,4, 41/39; room, compartment, alcove (section of the building marked off by pillars) 8/6, 22/33,35.

gómr *m.* gum (*e-m* of s-one) 29/8, 44/38.

gómsparri *m.* gum-prop 29/8 (*sparri*: a length of wood to hold s-thing apart).

grafa (gróf) *sv.* dig 3/21,22,27; pp., inlaid 4/40.

granda (að) *wv.* with dat., harm 45/32, 53/36.

grár *a.* grey 35/34, 41/39.

gras *n.* grass 54/2; vegetation 3/24, 4/20, 9/19; plant 23/16,17.

Glossary

gráta (grét) *sv.* weep 29/27, 47/30; shed tears 47/39; *g. e-n* weep for s-one 47/28; *g. e-t tárum* weep tears for, at, because of s-thing 48/4.

grátr *m.* weeping 46/12, 47/26.

greiða (dd) *wv.* with *til* (adv.) prepare, put in order, get ready for use 44/32.

grein *f.* branch, division 22/22; particular, detail 3/17, 13/11 (the gen. *loptsins ok jarðarinnar* at 3/17–18 presumably mean the same as *á jǫrðunni ok í lopti* at 13/11–12).

greina (d) *wv.* divide 4/16; distinguish, make distinct 12/12; md., divide into branches 4/12.

grenja (jað) *wv.* howl 29/9.

grésjárn *n.* iron wire? magic wire? puzzle lock? 43/1 (the first element is thought to be a loan-word from Old Irish *grés* m. handicraft).

grið *n.* truce; pl., assurances of safety, immunity (*fyrir* from, in respect of) 45/20.

griðlauss *a.* without a (sworn) truce, assurances or guarantee of safety or inviolability; without quarter 49/5; n. as adv. 35/7.

griðastaðr *m.* place of sanctuary (inviolability) 29/14, 46/11 ('it was such an inviolable place, a place of such sanctuary').

grimligr *a.* fierce-looking 27/22.

grimmr *a.* grim 10/11 (vb. to be understood), 21/10.

grind *f.* (barred) gate 39/26, 47/21; pl. *grindr* 27/17.

grípa (greip) *sv.* grasp 38/26, 45/7; *g. til* snatch up 43/30; *g. eptir* make a grab at or for (as s-thing passes) 49/2.

gripr *m.* precious possession 23/6; *er mikill g. er í* which is very valuable 23/8.

grjót *n.* stones (collective) 7/32, 11/37, 35/3, 45/25.

grjótbjǫrg *n. pl.* rocky precipices 9/35, 52/1.

gróa (greri) *sv.* grow 3/27.

gruna (að) *wv.* impers. *e-n grunar* one suspects (wonders if, thinks s-thing likely) 3/36, 39/9.

grunnr *m.* bottom (of sea) 44/35, 45/10; *g. e-u* bottom of s-thing 19/26, textual note.

grœnn *a.* green (in leaf) 19/26, 53/34.

guð *m.* when sg., God 3/1,13; m. also at 8/33 (= Óðinn), gender uncertain at 10/37,39 (= Ymir) and 32/36 (= Óðinn; cf. **ǫndurguð**). Elsewhere n. pl. (= heathen gods, generally the Æsir; cf. **goð**) 11/34, 13/10 etc.

guðkunnigr = **goðkunnigr.**

guðligr *a.* divine 18/11.

gull *n.* gold 4/22, 15/24; *gulli betra* better than gold 20/13; *gulli studdr* supported by gold, i.e. golden pillars, or with walls of gold? 26/29.

gullaldr *m.* golden age 15/30.

gullband *n.* gold band 29/22.

gullhjálmr *m.* golden helmet 50/27.

gullhringr *m.* gold ring (bracelet) 47/4,6 (cf. **fingrgull**).

gulltafla *f.* golden piece (for a game like chess or draughts) 54/2.

†**gunntamiðr** *a.* (*pp.*) accustomed (trained) to battle 32/27 (epithet of Óðinn).

gustr *m.* blowing 10/7.

gyðja *f.* goddess 15/25.

gýgr *f.* giantess 14/19, 27/4, 46/25.

gyltr *a.* (*pp.*) gilded, golden 7/29.

gyrða (ð) *wv.* tighten a (horse's) girth 47/20 (the animal in acc., *hann*).

gæta (tt) *wv.* with gen., look after 29/23, 30/23; protect 20/19; guard 30/1, 46/27; *g. e-s fyrir e-m* guard s-thing against s-one 25/36; *g. til* take pains, be concerned (to do s-thing) 29/31; *g. ef* keep watch, pay attention (to see) whether 39/2. Md., concern o-self, deliberate, take counsel (*of* about) 16/2, 35/39.

gæzla *f.* keeping, guardianship, guard 25/27; *sett til gæzlu yfir* given the function of guarding 30/4; *setja til lands gæzlu* put in charge of the country 5/28.

gǫfugligr *a.* noble (in appearance), stately, magnificent 19/34.

gǫgnum, í gǫgnum *prep.* with acc., through 29/3, 45/1, 46/7.

gǫltr *m.* pig (boar) 32/10; dat. sg. *gelti* 47/1.

gǫrr (*n.* **gǫrt**) *pp.* of **gera**.

haf *n.* sea 4/19 (Mediterranean), 7/7 (Baltic), 43/14; ocean 27/13, 37/28 (the ocean encircling the earth); pl. 20/27.

hafa (ð) *wv.* have 3/19, 9/28; have in one's possession 53/38; get 26/16, 36/19; keep 36/22; bring 6/28, 31/18; with pp. 4/28 ('which was the most splendid there has ever been'), 7/9; with inf., have available for a certain purpose 32/5; *h. at e-u* use as (for) s-thing 33/4, 46/26, 54/18 (*sér* for themselves); *h. at minnum* remember 26/13; *h. fyrir e-t* use as, make serve as s-thing 27/40, 29/5; *hafa e-n* (*e-t*) *með sér* take, keep s-one (s-thing) with one 5/21, 6/20, be endowed with s-thing 42/37; *h. e-n nær e-u* bring s-one close to s-thing 42/38; *h. e-t til e-s* use s-thing for s-thing 12/25; *h. e-t til* have sufficient of s-thing 27/23; *vera haft uppi* be remembered, famous 5/20; *h. e-t við* use, employ s-thing on (it), for a certain purpose 36/24. Md. *hafask at* do, be (-come) engaged in 9/6,

11/33, 45/29; *hvat hafask þeir at* what is their occupation 22/29; *hafask lind fyrir* hold a shield in front of o-self 51/23.

hafr (rs) *m*. (he-) goat 23/1, 37/3, 44/6.

hafrstaka *f*. goat-skin 37/10,11,15.

haga (að) *wv*. with *til* (adv.) contrive (things), arrange it (that) 35/18.

hagleikr *m*. skill 4/29; workmanship, ingenuity 36/16.

hagliga *adv*. skilfully 12/21.

hagligr *a*. handy (*e-m* for s-one), beneficial, useful 33/16.

hagr *m*. convenience, advantage, benefit (*á* in it) 41/19.

halda (helt) *sv*. with dat., hold 27/33, 48/30; *haldi Hel því er hefir* let Hel keep what she has 48/9; *h. á e-u* hold s-thing in the hand 37/12; *h. upp* support 17/12. Md., stay, remain, be kept 47/29; be kept safe 11/25; remain valid, be fulfilled 23/20.

hálfa *f*. region, continent 4/16, 5/5.

hálfr *a*. half 27/21; half share of 24/31; *sjá hálf hýnótt* half this night of waiting 31/32; dat. sg. n. *hálfu* with comp., twice as, much (more) 27/31, 35/4; *vaxa hálfu* double, increase enormously 23/7.

hallmæli *n*. blame 15/14.

†halr *m*. man 9/37, 52/3,25.

háls *m*. bow (of a ship) 44/26.

haltr *a*. lame (with dat., in s-thing) 37/15.

hamarr *m*. hammer 15/27, 23/3.

hamarskapt *n*. handle of hammer 37/22,40.

hamarspor *n. pl*. prints, marks of a hammer 43/5.

hamr *m*. shape, form 14/35, 20/31.

handaafl *n*. strength of the hands 28/23.

handan *adv*. from beyond (see **heðan**) 14/26.

handaverk *n. pl*. handiwork 26/13.

handsax *n*. short sword, knife 7/35.

hang *n*. coil (of a serpent), loop of back 42/1, textual note (reading uncertain, and the word is not recorded elsewhere).

hanzki *m*. glove, mitten (i.e. a glove with a thumb but no divisions for the fingers) 38/10,11,13.

happskeytr *a*. who is a good shot 26/19.

hár (1) *n*. hair 3/25, 11/12.

hár (2) *a*. tall, high 3/21, 19/22; acc. sg. f. *háva* 7/27, nom. pl. m. *hávir* 27/17; n. as adv. 30/21, loud(ly) 51/6.

harðfœrr *a*. difficult to overcome, negotiate, deal with 36/28.

†**harðmóðigr** *a.* hard-hearted, stern, cruel 12/39.

harðna (að) *wv.* grow hard, set 10/2; grow tough 28/39.

harðr *a.* hard, tough 50/31; n. as adv., hard 38/34, 44/39; strongly 7/6, 47/21; calamitous, full of trouble 49/31; comp. n. as adv. 28/40, 42/16.

harmr *m.* sorrow, unhappiness 31/8; grief 46/13, 52/6.

harmsfullr *a.* full of sorrow, miserable 31/16.

háski *m.* danger 30/5, 45/20; *lífs h.* mortal danger 48/39.

hásæti *n.* throne 8/16, 15/22.

hátt n. of **hár (2)**.

hátta (að) *wv.* arrange, construct 12/21.

háttr *m.* (*dat. sg.* **hætti**) kind, type 3/20; *með nokkurum hætti* in some way 3/30; pl., habits, activity, behaviour 26/38.

haufuð = hǫfuð.

haukr *m.* hawk 18/32, 34/23.

hauss *m.* skull 12/4,34, 23/5, 35/31.

háv- see **hár (2)**.

heðan *adv.* hence; *h. ok handan* to and fro 14/26.

hefja (hóf) *sv.* lift 41/36, 44/37; begin, open (a speech) 8/26; md., begin; *hversu hófsk* how did everything begin 9/9.

hefna (d) *wv.* take vengeance 46/11; *h. e-m* take vengeance on s-one (*e-s* for s-thing) 29/38, 48/14; *h. e-s* get one's own back for s-thing 44/2; impers. *er hefnt e-s* s-one is avenged 52/20; *hefnir e-m e-t* s-one pays (is punished) for s-thing 31/6.

heiðr *a.* bright (unclouded) 52/32 (i.e. even though there are no clouds).

heilagr *a.* (inflected **helg-**) holy 17/30, 25/33, 31/7.

heili *m.* brain 12/26,38.

heill *a.* whole, unharmed 8/23, 32/11; *bæði þá heila* (acc. pl.) *hittask* said they wished them (Skrýmir and the Æsir) to have a happy reunion 39/22.

heilræði *n.* salutary advice 39/14.

heim *adv.* home 31/8, 35/7; back 31/19; *h. til* back to 34/6, up to, in to 47/22; *h. í* back to 46/19.

heima *adv.* at home 27/23, 41/32.

heimamaðr *m.* member of (one's, *e-s*) household 37/10.

heimill *a.* free, at s-one's service (with dat. of person); *h. er matr honum* he was welcome to food 8/21.

heimr *m.* world 3/5, 9/30; *norðr hingat í heim* north to this part of the world 6/28; the inhabited world 12/25, 53/5; one of the nine worlds of northern mythology 9/5,25, 53/7, pl. 13/13,40, 30/8. The number is traditional (see 9/5, 27/15, *Vsp* 2, *Vm* 43) though they are nowhere listed and nowhere systematically described. They presumably include Ásgarðr, Miðgarðr, Vanaheim(a)r, Álfheimr, Jǫtunheim(a)r, Niflheimr or Niflhel, Muspellsheimr, and perhaps Svartálfaheimr and Gimlé, or possibly Útgarðr; cf. the 'heavens', 20/21–5 and *SnE* I. 592–3, II. 485–6.

†**heimstǫð** *f.* the world, the world of time 52/26.

heit *n.* promise 31/24 (with suffixed art.).

heita (hét) *sv.* (1) (*pres.* **heitir**) be called 4/36, 7/1; *heitir* is the name of a place 24/19,32, sometimes with a pl. n., e.g. 25/35 ('in a place called H.'), contrast 6/12, 20/2 (cf. note to 29/26); *ok heitir* and it is called, which is called 15/6; *Gymir hét maðr* there was a man called G. 30/38. (2) (*pres.* **heitr**) call out (*á* to) 37/37, pray (to) 25/3; *h. á e-n til e-s* pray to s-one, invoke s-one for (concerning) s-thing 23/30, 25/5. Md. *heitumsk* I call myself 21/32.

heiti *n.* name 6/29, 21/7.

heitr *a.* hot 4/18, 9/26.

héla (d) *wv.* freeze (over) 10/3.

heldr *adv. comp.* rather (often with the suggestion of litotes) 27/22, 38/18, 41/3; quite 44/33; better, more easily 4/10; instead 35/30; *h. . . . en* rather . . . than 21/5; *h. en . . . þá* rather than that . . . (instead) 28/34.

helg- see **heilagr**.

helgistaðr *m.* holy place 17/5.

hella *f.* slab (of stone) 29/3, 49/6.

hellir *m.* cave 48/2, 49/5.

helzt *adv. sup.* most of all 41/26; chiefly, most willingly of all 40/34.

hendi, hendr dat. sg. and nom. acc. pl. of **hǫnd**.

hér *adv.* here 36/38, 39/36; to this place 40/21; in this matter 22/17; in the following examples (evidence) 28/8; in the following quotation 10/26, 11/26; *hér af* from this (game) 41/29; *hér . . . af* about this 32/12; *hér inni* in here 39/39, 42/10; *hér . . . nær* at hand, close by 36/35.

herbergi *n.* lodging, dwelling-place 4/27.

herbúnaðr *m.* war equipment 36/19.

herða (ð) *wv.* squeeze, grip, clench 37/21.

herðar *f. pl.* shoulders 49/10.

herja (að) *wv.* wage war 9/29, 15/16, 32/2.

hermaðr *m.* warrior 26/22.

herr *m.* host, army 34/3.

hertogi *m.* duke 4/38.

hervæða (dd) *wv.*, *h. sik* put on armour 34/4, 50/26.

hestr *m.* (male) horse, stallion 13/28, 25/34; steed 46/27,28.

heyra (ð) *wv.* hear 12/20, 21/5; *h. e-n segja* hear s-one tell 54/29; *h. sagt* hear tell 36/34; *h. e-t sagt* hear s-thing said, hear about s-thing 33/30; *h. getit e-s* hear tell of s-thing 49/19; impers. *heyrir e-t* one hears s-thing, s-thing is audible 25/40.

heyrn *f.* hearing 13/7.

himinn *m.* heaven (often in phrase *himinn ok jǫrð*) 3/1, 8/37; *himins* in heaven 4/9; sky 9/38, 12/4; *upp frá þessum himni* above this sky of ours 20/22; pl., the heavens (places in heaven?—but cf. 20/21–4) 19/32.

himintungl *n. pl.* heavenly bodies 3/35, 13/2.

hingat *adv.* to this place 6/28, 31/19, 42/11.

hinn (*n.* **hitt**) *art.* and *pron.* the 4/17,19; *hitt* this on the contrary, the opposite 33/31; the opposite course 48/39; followed by an *er*-clause, this also, this other thing 43/17,22, but this, this moreover 8/39; with another pron. for emphasis, *sá hinn* with a. and noun 11/31, 12/39, 35/31 (*er* such that); *hinn þriðja drykkinn* 41/20, similarly 44/23; *þessi hin sǫmu* 54/37; *einn hinn mesta* 5/6; *hans hinir mestu* 55/7. Cf. **inn**.

hinna *f.* membrane 19/18.

hirðmaðr *m.* a member of s-one's (*e-s*) *hirð* or following; retainer 39/15, 40/37, 43/7, 44/1.

hirtir see **hjǫrtr**.

hiti *m.* heat 10/13,14, 47/39; (= flames) 52/35.

hitt (1) see **hinn**. (2) *pp.* of **hitta**.

hitta (tt) *wv.* meet, come across 42/29; visit 43/27; hit upon, discover 35/16; *h. fyrir sér* find (s-thing) opposing one, come up against (s-thing of a certain kind) 36/25. Md., meet each other 39/22; *er þeir Beli hittusk* when he and B. met (i.e. joined battle) 31/39.

hjá *prep.* with dat., near, beside 43/4, 49/13; compared with 24/8, 42/6.

hjálp *n.* help 28/33.

hjarta *n.* heart 52/19.

hjó see **hǫggva**.

hjón, hjún *n.* member of a household 37/16,23.

hjǫlt *n. pl.* hilt 29/8.

†hjǫrr *m.* sword 52/19.

hjǫrtr *m.* (*pl.* **hirtir**) stag 18/34, 31/34, 33/18.

†hlakka (að) *wv.* screech with joy (anticipation) 51/27.

hlaup *n.* running 28/9.

hlaupa (hljóp) *sv.* run 11/23 (flow), 14/16; gallop 35/20,24; jump, leap 47/21, 48/24; rush 48/39; push, force one's way (*fótum* with the feet) 45/1; *h. af* jump off, dismount from 46/27; *h. at* rush up to 39/4.

hleina (d) *wv.* lie low, take refuge? 30/6 (not recorded elsewhere; cf. OE *hlinian, hlænan*).

hleypa (t) *wv.* with dat., make (a horse) gallop 46/22 (sc. *honum*).

hlið *f.* (*dat.* **hliðu**) side 19/2; *á aðra h. e-m* on one side of s-one 50/13; *líta út á h. sér* look out to one side (sideways), turn one's eyes 54/32.

hljóta (hlaut) *sv.* get 28/25.

†hloá *vb.* boil, rush, be turbulent? 18/6 (not recorded elsewhere).

hlunnr *m.* pieces of wood forming a slipway 46/30.

hlutr *m.* part 4/17, 10/8; piece 36/21; thing 3/1, 4/34, 28/11; *engi h. er sá* there is nothing 15/15; *allir hlutir* with gen., everything to do with, in (s-thing) 4/9.

hlýða (dd) *wv.* listen (*á* to) 29/37; *h. ef* listen (to find out) whether 36/38.

hlýðni *f.* obedience (*e-s* to s-one) 3/11.

hlæja (hló) *sv.* laugh 29/1; *h. við* laugh at what is said 15/5, 25/29.

hlær *a.* warm, mild 10/12.

hnakki *m.* the back of the head 39/24.

hnefi *m.* fist 44/39, 45/12.

hnipinn *a.* (*pp.*) downcast, depressed 31/14.

hnoss *f.* treasure, precious ornament 29/26.

hof *n.* temple 15/22.

hóf see **hefja**.

hold *n.* flesh 11/37, 12/28.

hólmr *m.* (small) island 28/20.

holt *n.* wood or (in Iceland) a small stony hill 54/10,16.

hórdómr *m.* (sexual) depravity, immorality, especially adultery 49/32.

horfa (ð) *wv.* face, point (*í* towards) 53/13,20; extend (*til* towards, to) 17/16.

horn *n.* (1) corner 12/6. (2) (drinking) horn 17/18, 30/26; horn of a stag 33/19; (musical instrument) 51/7.

hrafn *m.* raven 32/32, 46/39.

hráki *m.* spit 28/7.

hratt see **hrinda**.

hreyfa (ð) *wv.* move, shift (trans.) 38/24.

hreystimaðr *m.* man of valour, man of action 25/12.

hríð *f.* period of time; *litla h.* for a short time 37/31; *eina h.* for a while 44/31; *langar hríðir* for a long while 5/27.

hrím *n.* rime 10/4, 11/6; pl., layers of rime? 10/13.

hrímsteinn *m.* rime-stone 11/10.

hrímþurs *m*. frost-giant 9/8, 10/15.

hrína (hrein) *sv*. whinny, neigh (*við* at s-thing) 35/21.

hrinda (hratt) *sv*. with dat., push, thrust 46/29,36.

hringr *m*. circle 12/2; (arm-) ring, bracelet 47/32 (cf. **fingrgull**).

hrista (st) *wv*. shake 27/38.

hrjóta (hraut) *sv*. (1) snore 38/3,22,32. (2) fly 46/30.

†hróðigr *a*. triumphant 32/28.

hross *n*. horse (of either sex) 35/24; *hvat hrossi* what sort of horse, i.e. what sex of horse 35/21.

hryggr *m*. back, spine; of serpents, body 53/14,24.

hrynja (hrunða) *wv*. fall down 50/1.

hræða (dd) *wv*. make afraid 28/30; pp. *hræddr* afraid 14/9, 35/17; md., be afraid of (with acc.) 14/9,15; become afraid, panic 43/18, 45/5.

hræzla *f*. terror 37/24.

hrœra (ð) *wv*. move, stir (trans.) 20/27.

hrœring *f*. motion, ability to move (or emotion?) 13/6.

hugaðr *a*. (*pp*.) endued with courage; *bezt h*. most courageous 25/11.

hugr *m*. mind, thought(s) 29/31, 43/10; *kom þat í hug* it occurred to him 27/35; mind, attitude, feeling (*til e-s* towards s-one) 46/10; courage 28/35.

hugsa (að) *wv*. consider 3/18, 7/22; think to o-self 27/34; determine 39/1; *h. fyrir sér* turn over in one's mind, ponder, think out 48/20.

hunangfall *n*. honey-dew 19/28.

hundr *m*. dog 34/24, 50/33.

hundrað *n*. (*pl*. **hundrað** and **hundruð**) hundred (with partitive gen.) 3/34, 22/33; as a. (indecl.) 50/21.

hurð *f*. door 31/4, 39/29.

hús *n*. house, building 4/27, 15/23; dwelling, chamber, cave? 48/17,21,25 (see under **fjall**).

hvaðan *adv*. whence, where . . . from 10/27, 15/33, 54/28; interrog. 13/3, 20/26.

hvar *adv*. where 4/7, 8/14; *sá h. hann fór* saw him go 48/36; *sér h. lá maðr* saw a man lying 38/2; *til h*. towards where 46/4; *h. sem* wherever, correlative with *þá* 5/23 ('whatever countries they travelled through'), 6/8 ('whatever countries they stopped in'), 24/30. Interrog. 8/33, 11/5, 17/5.

hvárki *adv*. neither 31/8.

hvárr *pron*. each (of two) 50/34, 51/4; interrog., which (of two), pl., which side, which party 11/20.

hvárt *adv.* whether 38/28; *þat . . . h.* 7/22, 47/26; *h. er* as conj., whether 31/19; interrog., introducing direct questions (pleonastic) 32/21, 36/13.

hvártveggi *pron. a.* each (of two) 40/5; gen. pl., of both (of us) 43/27.

hvass *a.* sharp, keen, strong 49/22.

hvat *pron.* what (in both direct and indirect questions) 15/3, 38/37, 44/20; *við h.* on what 11/5; *h. leið* what was happening, how it was going on 41/6; *h. er* what is the matter 41/18, 51/14; *hvat . . . þat er* what . . . which 33/4; with partitive gen., what 8/33, how much 12/16, what sort of 39/35; *h. þeira íþrótta* which of those accomplishments (of his) 40/32; *h. er fleira stórmerkja* what further remarkable things are there 18/28; with dat., what kind of 35/21 (i.e. what sex of), 41/33; *h. látum* what the cause of the noises 38/4; *h. sem* whatever 35/18, 45/25.

hvata (að) *wv.* with dat., hasten (trans.) 14/9.

hvatr *a.* bold, active, swift 46/20.

hvé *adv. interrog.* how 31/29.

hverfa (hvarf) *sv.* go away, disappear 49/39, 52/31; *h. á brut* go off, vanish 45/37; *h. aptr* turn back 39/16.

hvergi *adv.* nowhere, on no occasion 36/25; nowhere = not at all 46/25 ('refused to move'), 47/22; *þar h.* nowhere there 43/31.

hvernig *adv.* how 42/28; interrog. 10/36, 12/21, 28/14.

hverr *pron.* (*acc. sg. m.* **hvern, hverjan**) (1) each (of more than two) 3/24, 34/10; every 13/29, 30/34; *sér til hvers þessa nafns* to each of these names individually 22/18; *hina níundu hverja* every ninth 47/5; with partitive gen., every, any 19/7, each 28/37; with forms of *annarr*: *h. annan* each other 35/11, *h. ǫðrum* one to another 28/22, *hvert yfir annat* one (layer) on top of the other 10/4, *hvert upp frá ǫðru* one above the other 8/16. (2) who, which (of indefinite number) 8/2, 25/8; what 8/17, 43/15 ('how great a'), *þat . . . hverju* 3/18; *hverjum* with whom 31/11; *af hverju* from what origin 34/28; *h. sá væri . . . er* who there was . . . who 46/16; *h. er* whoever 33/31. (3) interrog., who, which 3/12, 8/27; what 14/18; *hverir eru Æsir þeir er* who (or which) are the Æsir whom 21/11.

hversu *adv.* how 27/24, 37/19; *h. mikill* how much, what (a) great 46/15, 47/26; interrog. 9/9,39, 13/34.

hvert *adv.* whither; *h. er* (to) wherever 36/19.

hvessa (t) *wv.* sharpen; *h. augun á* fix with a piercing gaze 45/3.

hví *pron.* (dat. of **hvat**) why 21/1, 31/14; *fyrir hví* for what reason 29/12.

hvinverskr *a.* from Hvinir (Kvinesdal in the south of Norway) 7/29.

hvirfill *m.* crown (of the head); *í hvirfil honum* on his crown 38/34.

hvítna (að) *wv.* whiten (intrans.) 37/22.

hvítr *a.* white 19/18, 23/16; declined weak 19/23, 25/32; sup. 23/17.

hyggja (hugða) *wv.* think 18/18, 39/34; *þat h. menn* it is believed 55/5; *en þat of hyggi* than imagine, expect it ('than it would have been thought by') 19/7; *ek hugða* I should have thought 32/5; sometimes with subject of *at*-clause before main vb. 20/24, 21/25 (cf. 6/17); intend, determine 41/4,12; with *at* and inf., intend, prepare (to do s-thing) 38/1; *vilja h. at e-u* be concerned about s-thing, think s-thing important, wish to take thought about s-thing 51/1; pres. p. *hyggjandi* thoughtful, sensible (referring scornfully to warriors saving themselves by flight) 7/34; with acc. and inf., think s-thing is s-thing 20/24, 45/10; *svá hygg ek vera* thus I believe there are 33/36; with inf. understood 22/37 ('this I believe B. to consist of'). Md. with inf., think that one (will do s-thing) 37/20; with *at* and inf., intend, plan (to do s-thing) 44/19.

hylli *f.* favour, goodwill 46/17.

hýnótt *f.* night(s), period of waiting before a wedding; *sjá hálf h.* half such a wedding eve (or 'this half-wedding night', when one partner is absent?) 31/32.

hýski *n.* household, family 11/24.

hæll *m.* (1) heel 50/40; *á hæla e-m* on s-one's heels, immediately behind s-one 8/6. (2) anchoring peg or post 29/6.

hæri *a. comp.* higher (cf. **hár**); n. as adv., more loudly 25/39.

hætta (1) (tt) *wv.* with dat., stop, make an end of 42/19.

hætta (2) *f.* danger; *leggja sik í hættu* take some risk 27/36.

hætti see **háttr**.

hættligr *a.* boding danger 45/18.

hættr *a.* dangerous 44/30.

hœgri *a. comp.* right (as opposed to left) 28/38, 37/38.

hǫfðingi *m.* ruler 4/33, 8/17; lord, prince 31/35, 34/2.

hǫfuð, haufuð *n.* head 3/23, 7/19, 11/12; *í h. e-m* on s-one's head 38/27, 39/9.

hǫfuðkonungr *m.* supreme king 4/36 (cf. **yfirkonungr** 4/31).

hǫfuðmaðr *m.* leader, ruler 6/13.

hǫfuðskepna *f.* (natural) element 4/3.

hǫfuðstaðr *m.* chief place, most important (cult) centre 17/5, 19/33 (see AH *Studier* 60).

hǫfuðtunga *f.* chief language 4/32.

hǫfugleikr *m.* heaviness 10/7.

hǫgg *n.* blow 35/31, 39/2, 43/2.

hǫggormr *m.* poisonous snake, viper 46/26.

hǫggva (hjó) *sv.* strike; cut 45/8; *h. til* aim blows 45/25. Md. (reciprocal) fight 34/10.

†**hǫlðr** *m*. man 49/31.

hǫll *f*. hall, palace 7/28, 22/32.

hǫnd *f*. arm 11/1, 31/4; hand 25/17, 28/35; *hendi sinni* with his hand 41/40; *á hendi sér* on his hand 44/37; *í hendi honum* in his hand 49/3; *fellusk (þeim) hendr* i.e. they were paralysed 46/9; *e-m til handa* for s-one, on s-one's behalf 31/18; *hvárratveggju handar* on the side of each (party), for both our sakes 43/27; *til hœgri handar* on the right hand side 37/38.

hǫrgr *m*. sanctuary (generally not a building) 15/25.

hǫrund *f*. flesh 27/21.

í *prep*. (1) with acc., into 4/16 (1), 7/27, 9/4, 11/35, 35/12; to 4/16 (2), 43/35; towards 39/18; in 6/13 (1); on 15/32; onto 27/14 (1), 39/9, 50/38; when faced with 26/17; as, for 37/25; *í alla heima* as far as, throughout all worlds 25/40; *þar í brunninn* into that spring 19/17; of time, on, in, at 37/13, 48/33, during 54/10 (dat.?). (2) with dat., in 3/6,19; from in 19/15; with names, of, who lives at 24/25; in or on 48/17 (see **fjall**); *í þeim stað kalla menn* that place is called 15/24 (see **staðr**); as regards, in respect of 49/25; of time, on 41/16, in, at 9/29, 38/35, 46/29; *í því* at that moment 38/5. (3) as adv., in (it) 15/22, 36/26, 41/15; into it 46/34; about (it) 55/1; *þann er . . . í* in which 23/8; *þar ofan í* down in it 43/4.

iðrask (að) *wv. md*. repent (*e-s* of s-thing) 31/38.

ifask (að) *wv. md*. doubt, be in doubt (*í* about s-thing) 55/1.

íkorni *m*. squirrel 18/32.

il *f*. sole of the foot 45/13.

illa *adv*. badly; with difficulty 42/33; not at all 45/27.

illiliga *adv*. horribly 29/9.

illr *a*. evil 10/40, 18/27; unpleasant 24/7, 31/13; n. as subst., evil 27/9, 29/13.

inn (1) *adv*. in 27/20, 30/1; inwards 10/7; inside 8/18; inland 4/16; *inn í* (inside) into 7/27, 40/36.

inn (2) (*n*. **it**) *pron. art*. the 5/35, 8/18; with a. after noun 7/29, 30/35; combined with demonstrative for additional emphasis *í þeim inum* 17/23, *þau in fyrstu* (sc. *tíðindi*) 49/20, *þat it fyrsta* the first thing (NB *leikr* is m.) 43/7; *it þriðja skeiðit* 40/27; treble demonstrative for ironic emphasis *hafit þat it djúpa* 37/29 (see note). Cf. **hinn**.

inna (t) *wv*. perform (i.e. with success) 40/13.

innan *adv*. on the inside, within 15/24; *i. við* on the inside of 19/18; *fyrir i.* on the inside, on the inner edge 12/24; with following gen. *þar i. lands* within that country (those countries) 6/23.

innar *adv. comp*. further in 37/40.

inni *adv*. inside, within 8/22; *hér i.* in here 39/39, 42/10.

ísarnkol *n*. bellows 14/3; cf. *Grm* 37, where it is probably to be understood as analogous to the bellows of a forge.

íss *m*. ice 10/2,3,7.

it n. of **inn (2)**.

íþrótt *f*. accomplishment, feat 39/35, 40/1.

jafn *a*. equal; n. as adv., equally well, just as well (*sem* as) 25/38.

jafna (að) *wv*. compare; *j. e-u til e-s* liken s-thing to s-thing, i.e. call s-thing after s-thing 23/16.

jafnan *adv*. always, continually 27/2, 30/36; for ever 37/27.

jafnbreiðr *a*. just as wide (*e-u* as s-thing) 37/35 ('and it was as wide as the whole width of the hall').

jafngnógliga *adv*. as abundantly, with as great sufficiency (*sem* as) 33/5.

jafngóðr *a*. equally good (*sem* as) 31/36, 36/13.

jafnhǫfugr *a*. equal in weight, of the same weight (as itself) 47/6.

jafnlangt *n. a.* as *adv*., equally far 3/23.

jafnmikill *a*. equally large 36/13.

jafnmjǫk *adv*. as much 47/13, textual note.

jafnsannr *a*. equally true 28/11.

jafnskjótt *n. a.* as *adv*. immediately 35/28.

jarðligr *a*. earthly 3/15,17; worldly (as opposed to *andligr*) 4/13.

jarl *m*. jarl, earl 6/19, 33/7.

jarmr *m*. crying 24/12.

járn *n*. iron 45/21.

járnfjǫturr *m*. iron fetter 28/29.

járnglófar *m. pl.* iron gloves 23/8 (cf. *SnE* I. 284–8).

játa (tt) *wv*. say yes, agree (*e-u* to s-thing) 38/14,16; acknowledge (*e-n e-t* s-one to be s-thing) 10/39.

jaxl *m*. back tooth, molar 11/38.

†jór *m*. (male) horse 34/20.

jǫrð *f*. earth, world 3/1, 15/4; the ground 5/2, 15/33, 27/38; earth = soil 11/37; land as opposed to sea 12/1,21; personified 13/19 (cf. Jǫrð in index of names).

†jǫrmungrund *f*. the mighty earth 32/39.

jǫtunmóðr *m*. a giant fury 35/27, 50/3, 51/25.

jǫtunn *m*. giant 7/5, 10/24; with name 10/26, 11/15, 12/26; = Loki or Fenrisúlfr? 51/13.

-k *enclitic pron.* = *ek*, *munak* 28/25, *líðk* 30/17, *mundak* 41/9,36, *megak* 42/35, *hafðak* 42/40; with *ek*, *ek fæk* 28/32; with suffixed neg. -*a* and *ek*, *varka ek* 24/4, *nautka ek* 48/8; *ek máttigak* 24/10 (emended; cf. Noreen 531 note 1); *erumk* = *eru mér* 24/3.

kala (kól) *sv.* impers. with acc., one gets cold, freezes 44/14.

kaldr *a.* cold 4/20, 21/2; n. as subst. 10/10.

kalla (að) *wv.* (1) call: with two acc., call a person or a place s-thing 10/15,40, 12/26, (with pron. and a.) say that s-one is s-thing 42/7; assert, declare, reckon (s-thing or s-one to be s-thing) 36/39, 41/33, 42/32; *kallar þess meiri ván* declares it more likely 40/12; *er svá kallat* it is said 30/21; *vera kallaðr* be called, be known as 4/17, 6/6; pp. agreeing with complement rather than subject 7/10, 13/10, 29/26 (see note); *ekki kallaðr* not said to be, said not to be 25/19; *Heimdalar sverð er kallat hǫfuð* the head is called H.'s sword 26/1; name, give a name to 55/3; *e-t er kallat* s-thing takes its name (from s-thing) 29/36. (2) call out 37/23, 40/2; summon 28/20 (2), 31/9; *k. á* call on, invoke 35/28; *k. til* (adv.) summon 46/27.

kanna (að) *wv.* explore, get to know 5/5.

kanntu, kannþu = *kannt þú*, see **kunna**.

kapp *n.* rivalry, competition, race; pl. 40/17.

karl *m.* man, male 5/22, 25/22, 29/32; old man (Óðinn) 48/8.

karlmaðr *m.* male 13/7, 25/23, 30/7.

kasta (að) *wv.* with dat., throw 27/12, 37/11; object understood 12/27, 39/20; cast (a net) 48/30,33; impers. *kastat hafði* had been thrown 12/7.

kaup *n.* terms, bargain (*við* with) 34/35; (agreed) reward, payment 34/33; making of agreement 35/5; *vera af kaupinu* forfeit his reward 35/16.

kaupa (keypta) *wv.* buy, pay for 33/9.

kengr *m.* (**keng** *n.* textual note) bow, arch (see **beygja**) 42/1.

kenna (d) *wv.* recognize, know, perceive, feel 23/4, 35/21; be able to tell, realize 37/17, 38/9; with gen., feel 44/39; *k. e-t e-m* attribute s-thing to s-one 55/4. Md., feel (it) 48/16.

keppask (t) *wv. md.* compete (*við e-n* with s-one) 26/21.

kerling *f.* old woman 42/11,14; the old woman 42/17.

kerra *f.* chariot 13/28,39, 47/1.

ketill *m.* cooking-pot 32/13, 37/6.

ketti dat. sg. of **kǫttr**.

keyptr = **kjǫptr**.

keyra (ð) *wv.* drive 13/38; *k.* (*hest*) *sporum* drive (a horse) on with spurs, spur (a horse) on 47/20.

kind *f.* kind(red), (member of a certain) race; in poetry, child: *Fenris* *kindir* = wolves, possibly literally F.'s offspring 14/31.

kippa (t) *wv.* snatch; md. *kippask við* flinch, jerk away, be convulsed (in reaction to s-thing) 49/15.

kjóll *m.* a kind of ship 51/30.

kjósa (kaus) *sv.* choose 24/36; *k. sér* choose for o-self 6/11; *k. e-t á e-n* allot s-one s-thing 30/35; *k. val* choose (i.e. decide) who shall be slain (cf. **valkyrja**) 30/36, select one's victim, kill 34/11.

kjǫptr, keyptr *m.* jaw 50/9,38, 51/2.

kljúfa (klauf) *sv.* cleave; pp. *klofinn* cloven, split (vb. to be understood) 49/34.

klofna (að) *wv.* split (intrans.) 9/38, 50/13, 52/4.

klæða (dd) *wv.* dress; *k. sik* or md. *klæðask* get dressed 34/4, 37/14.

klæði *n. pl.* clothing 13/7.

kné *n.* knee 42/19, 43/23.

knésfót *f.* hough, the back of the knee 49/11.

knífr *m.* knife 27/18, 37/12.

knúi *m.* knuckle 37/22.

knútr *m.* knot 38/24.

knýja (knúða) *wv.* beat, churn up 51/26; md., exert o-self, struggle (*at e-u* in, with, at s-thing) 27/38, 42/16.

kólfskot *n.* (distance of) arrow shot, bowshot 40/24 (*kólfr* is a blunt-headed arrow; the more usual term is *ǫrskot*).

koma (kom) *sv.* come 4/40, 7/27; arrive 7/26; come (from), originate (*af* from) 13/3, 34/28; descend (from) 3/2, 5/37; *at hann komi* that he will come 8/23; *ok kominn* and (said he had) come 8/1; *kom ok reið* came riding 46/26; *svá kom* thus it came about 3/13; *komandinn* the newly arrived one 8/20; *láta k.* put, fasten 44/34; *k. e-m* bring s-one 27/2, 43/25 (compel); *k. e-u á leið* bring s-thing about 48/12; *k. á* find its mark, hit 43/3; *k. at* reach 35/10; *er kom at dagan* when dawn arrived 38/1; *k. fram* come to pass, happen 52/5, proceed, go on, advance, come ashore? 15/11; *k. fyrir* be paid in compensation, atone 37/24; *k. saman* converge, unite 10/34; *k. upp* come out, be emitted 46/12; *k. við* (*verr*) suit (worse), be (less) convenient, proper, advantageous (*er* that) 32/1. Md., bring o-self, manage to go, get (somewhere) 12/3, 39/27; *komask undan* get away, escape 11/24.

kona *f.* woman 5/22, 7/2; female 13/8, 25/23 (1,2); wife 5/3, 11/14, 25/23 (3).

konar *m.* gen. sg. in phrases *alls k.* of all kinds 45/20, *nokkurs k.* of some kind 39/37, *margs k.* many kinds of 46/38.

konungdómr *m.* kingdom 4/30,32.

konungr *m.* king 4/35, 8/18; as title after name 7/20, 21/31.

kosta (að) *wv.* impers. *e-n kostar e-t til* it costs s-one s-thing (for it, to do it) 35/19.

kostgripr *m.* treasure, special possession, favourite thing 23/3.

kostnaðr *m.* expense; expensive decoration? 4/30.

kostr *m.* (good) quality 4/24; *alls kostar* all kinds of 4/26; *at ǫðrum kosti* otherwise, alternatively, as a second choice 36/39, 39/16; (difficult) choice, alternative, possibility 48/39; pl., terms, conditions 34/39; *lands kostir* geographical conditions 6/11; *ráða sessa kostum* arrange the facilities, decide on the allocation of seats (i.e. who shall be admitted) or on the arrangement of the seats (and the fare?) 24/34.

kraptr *m.* (physical) strength 42/37; (creative) power 10/14, 13/19, 25/7.

krefja (krafða) *wv.* demand (*e-n e-s* s-thing of s-one) 45/36; *k. e-n orða* try to speak with s-one 31/9.

kringlóttr *a.* circular, disc-shaped 12/22 (*hon* = the inhabited earth, *orbis terrarum*).

kunna (kann, kunna; *kanntu, kannþu = kannt þú*) *pret. pres. vb.* know (nearly always with reference to ability to give information) 3/14, 22/18; be able to, i.e. have the knowledge to (with inf.) 20/29, 22/26, (with *at* and inf.) 5/8, 25/29; be able to perform 39/36; know how to (with inf.) 40/9, (with *at* and inf.) 41/37; *kann vera at* maybe 15/7.

kunnandi *f.* ability, accomplishment (s-thing one knows how to do) 39/37.

kunnátta *f.* (technical) knowledge, skill, expertness 4/26, textual note, 15/8.

kunnigr *a.* having supernatural knowledge and ability 7/21.

kunnusta *f.* knowledge, ability 4/26.

kunst *f.* art, accomplishment 4/26, textual note.

kvánfang *n.* match, woman to be a wife 6/22.

kveða (kvað) *sv.* say; †with unexpressed indefinite subject, *kveða* they say (with acc. and inf.) 20/37, 26/3; in prose often refers to speaking in verse 24/2,9, 31/26; with acc. and inf. 28/23, 31/13, with inf. understood 35/15, with acc. understood 28/21. Md. with inf., say that one will do s-thing 31/12, 44/28,31.

kveðja (kvadda) *wv.* speak to, greet 39/31.

kveld *n.* evening (the end of the day, nightfall) 11/11, 35/19, 44/7 (cf. **aptann**).

kvelja (kvalða) *wv.* torment, torture 53/30.

kvenna gen. pl. of **kona**.

kviðr *m.* belly 42/1.

kvikna (að) *wv.* be generated, come to life 15/33; impers. *kviknaði* there was a quickening, a coming to life 10/14.

kviknun *f.* quickening, coming to life 15/35.

kvikudropi *m.* flowing drop; pl., fermenting fluid? 10/13.

kvikvendi, kykvendi *n.* living being, creature 3/7,29,31, 13/21; pl., animals (as opposed to men) 47/37.

kvisa (að) *wv.* whisper 39/12.

kvistr *m.* branch 19/13, 39/9.

kvæmi p. subj. of **koma**.

kykr *a.* alive 3/29, 48/7; animate 47/28; n. as subst., s-thing alive 48/33.

kykvendi = **kvikvendi**.

kýll *m.* bag (for food) 37/32.

kyn *n.* family, species 19/30.

kynslóð *f.* progeny 3/3, 54/12; family line 13/15.

kýr *f.* cow 11/6,9.

kýss pres. of **kjósa**.

kœla (d) *wv.* cool 14/2.

kǫgursveinn *m.* child in arms, puppy 39/16 (cf. *Hrbl* 13, where Þórr uses the word of Hárbarðr. The literal meaning is unknown; cf. *kǫgurbarn*, also used derogatively, in *Ǫrvar-Odds saga*, ed. R. C. Boer, Leiden 1888, p. 120, and *Mariu saga*, ed. C. R. Unger, Christiania 1871, p. 1056).

kǫpuryrði *n.* overbearing speech, uppish speech, cheekiness 39/16.

kǫttr *m.* cat 25/2, 28/5, 41/36.

kømr = *kemr*, pres. of **koma**.

lá see **liggja**.

lagðr, lagiðr *pp.* of **leggja**.

lágr *a.* short 42/6.

lagsmaðr *m.* companion, fellow 37/37; *ok þeir lagsmenn* and (both) the companions, i.e. he and his companion with him 37/7.

lágu p. pl of **liggja**.

land *n.* land 7/7, 12/23 (pl.); country 5/4, 6/26; district? 6/29; territory (pl.) 7/1; *þar til landa* over those territories 6/1; land as opposed to sea 50/2; shore 44/16, 45/13.

landskjálpti *m.* earthquake 37/36, 49/16.

landslǫg *n. pl.* laws of the land 6/14.

landvǫrn *f.* defence of the land 9/28.

langfeðgar *m. pl.* ancestors, (male) family line 5/36, 6/27.

langr *a.* long 5/27, 18/25; n. as subst. or adv., far 10/1, a long way 29/4; *segja langt* speak at length 37/18, *gera langt um* make a long tale about it 42/15.

láta (lét) *sv.* (1) lose 29/1, 40/8. (2) make a noise 25/39; say, declare (with inf., that s-thing shall be done) 40/13; *l. yfir sér* behave, express o-self (in a certain manner), put on a certain manner 39/14. (3) let, allow (with acc. and inf., s-one to do s-thing) 11/19 ('agree to call him that'), 27/28, 44/11, 46/19; with inf. in passive sense, allow s-thing to be done 27/37, 28/34; make s-thing do s-thing, cause s-one or s-thing to do s-thing 7/31, 13/38, have s-thing done 42/25; *lét eigi* did not allow (or cause) 31/23; *l. gera* have made 28/4; *l. koma* put 44/34; *l. kalla e-n* have s-one summoned 31/9; cause to be (with pp.) 32/15; *l. eptir* leave behind 37/27; *l. fram* put forward 28/38.

látprúðr *a.* courtly in behaviour 30/6.

látum dat. pl. of **læti**.

laufsblað *n.* leaf of foliage, a single leaf 38/28.

laun (1) *f.* secrecy 7/24.

laun (2) *n. pl.* reward, payment 7/2.

launa (að) *wv.* reward (*e-m e-t* s-one for s-thing) 31/20.

launráð *n.* secret counsel, secret thought 29/23.

lausafé *n.* moveable wealth, money 23/31.

laushárr *a.* with flowing (unbound) hair 29/22.

lauss *a.* free 50/2,32; not still, not fixed, unsteady 42/17; uncontrolled 12/7; unconfined 11/40. Comp., less tight 38/25.

lax *m.* salmon 49/4.

laxlíki *n.* the shape, form of a salmon 48/19.

leggja (lagða, *pp.* **lagðr, lagiðr)** *wv.* lay, put 11/32, 25/15; place 25/16, 27/36; deposit 17/20; build 15/27; cover (*e-u* with s-thing) 7/28; *l. sik fram* put o-self out, make an effort, take pains 40/20; *nær lagði þat ófæru* it brought disaster close 25/29; *l. e-t til við e-n* grant s-thing to s-one, agree to s-thing with s-one (include in the conditions) 35/2; *vera lagðr til* be set to, destined to (cause) 27/25; *l. upp* ship (oars) 44/32. Md., lay o-self, lie (down) 38/20, 48/32; stop, be silent 21/23 (*legsk-a-þú*, with suffixed neg. and 2nd pers. pron.).

leggr *m.* leg, bone of leg (or arm) 16/6.

leið (1) *f.* way 15/4; *fara l. sína* go (on) one's way 43/34; *fara fram á l.* continue on one's way 39/23; *ek á nú norðr l.* my way now lies to the north 39/18; distance 39/11; *langar leiðir* long distances 29/27; *koma e-u á l., snúa e-t til leiðar* bring s-thing about 13/1, 48/12.

leið (2) p. of **líða**.

leiða (dd) *wv.* lead, conduct 8/18, 46/21.

leiðr *a.* hateful 24/3.

leiðrétta (tt) *wv.* put right, achieve redress for 44/4.

leika (lék) *sv.* play; perform 40/9; juggle (*at* with) 7/35; of flames, play 52/35.

leikr *m.* game, sport 8/7, 34/5; competition, contest 40/8, 41/22; *hvat leik* (dat.) what sort of contest 41/33.

leita (að) *wv.* with gen., look for 29/29; try to find, try to fetch 47/15; try to think of 35/11; *l. e-m e-s* seek out, find s-thing for s-one 37/35, 38/19; *l. á* assault, (take by) storm 35/9; *l. sér til e-s* try to find o-self s-thing 37/33; *l. til e-s* try (to use), resort to s-thing 42/17; *l. til ef* try whether, seek an opportunity for 43/36. Md. *leitask fyrir* explore, feel one's way 37/38.

lemja (lamða) *wv.* strike, lame, damage, crush (*e-t á e-m* s-one's s-thing) 23/5.

lén *n.* reward, emoluments, wealth, success 18/25.

lendir *f. pl.* loins 49/10.

lengð *f.* length; *lengðin* his length 43/21.

lengi *adv.* long 31/16, 43/23; for a long time 24/4, 44/4, i.e. for ever 26/13, 48/15; *eigi lengi* it was not long 42/18.

lengr *adv. comp.* for a longer time, any longer 21/6.

lengri *a. comp.* longer 3/36; n. as adv., further 3/22, 29/5; *lengra fram* further on in time 54/28,29.

lengst *adv. sup.* furthest 42/3; *sem l.* as long as possible 41/25.

létta (tt) *wv.* with dat., lift 42/3. Md., become free of moisture, clear up (of the sky) 10/8.

leyfi *n.* permission (*til* for) 29/34.

leyna (d) *wv.* hide (*e-t e-n* s-thing from s-one) 29/40. Md., take refuge, lie hid 54/10,15.

leysa (t) *wv.* untie, undo 38/14,24, 42/40; release, free 25/16, 27/2; redeem 48/13; uproot 7/6 (impers., was uprooted?); impers. (subj.) *leysi* one gets (s-thing) free 27/40. Md., free o-self, get free 27/30.

lið *n.* people, following, retinue 5/22, 50/25; troop, company, number 48/37; help (*til* for, towards, in) 34/38, 35/1; *at liði e-m* to s-one's assistance 51/2.

líða (leið) *sv.* move 30/13,17 (with suffixed pron., cf. **-k**); impers., progress (or drain away, of the liquid?) 43/12; *hvat leið drykkinum* how the drinking was getting on (how it was going with regard to the drinking) 41/6; of time, pass 3/4, 55/1; impers. *líðr at e-u* it gets near to s-thing, s-thing approaches 34/6; *á leið vetrinn = leið á vetrinn* (acc.) the winter passed by, drew to a close 35/8; *var liðit á nótt* the night was far spent, advanced 42/21.

liðsemð *f.* help, assistance 44/12.

líf *n.* life 3/29, 13/6.

lifa (ð) *wv.* live 3/8, 9/2; *l. við* live on (as sustenance) 11/5, 32/31.

liggja (lá) *sv.* lie 19/6; be situated 7/10, 9/21; lie concealed? 23/26; be found 19/19; extend 27/12, 43/20; *l. (þar) til* belong to (it), be subject to (it) 4/31, 13/16.

lík *n.* corpse 46/22,32.

líka (að) *wv.* with dat., please; *sem honum líkar* as he would like, as he wants 41/15; *e-t líkar e-m vel (illa)* s-one likes (dislikes) s-thing 25/4, 45/27.

líkami *m.* body 9/1.

líkandi *n.* form 10/15.

líki *n.* body, shape, appearance 7/24, 15/36; form 14/22, 49/8.

líkindi *n. pl.* likelihood; *en l. þætti á* than appeared probable 28/22.

líking *f.* pattern; *í þá líking sem* in imitation of the way that 6/13; *gera í l. e-s* follow s-one's example 46/3.

líknsamastr *a. sup.* most kind, merciful, gracious 23/19.

líkr *a.* like (*e-m* to s-one) 5/9; comp. 5/24; comp., more likely, very likely (*at* that) 32/12.

limar *f. pl.* branches 17/10, 33/19.

lind *f.* shield (of lime wood) 51/23.

língarn *n.* linen yarn, flaxen thread 48/21.

list *f.* art 15/8, 28/26, 36/21; skill 39/37.

líta (leit) *sv.* look 31/3, 39/31 (*til* at). Md., appear, seem (*e-m* to s-one) 39/35, 42/13; impers. *lízk e-m (svá) sem* it looks to s-one as if 36/32, 41/7,15,22; *e-m lízk á e-t* s-thing looks to one (*svá sem* as if) 28/25.

litask (að) *wv. md., l. um(b)* look around 8/8, 42/9.

lítill *a.* little 18/25, 41/35; small 38/3, 41/33; thin 28/27; short (of time) 37/30; poor, insignificant, inadequate 41/1; *l. vexti* of small stature 39/13; *l. fyrir sér* of small account (cf. **mikill**) 42/32; n. as subst., little 11/35; *litlu fyrir* shortly before 39/3.

lítilræði *n.* s-thing beneath one's dignity, a demeaning act (*í* in it) 42/10.

litr *m.* colour 15/8, 27/21, 47/13.

litverpr *a.* changeable (changed) in colour 45/5.

ljóri *m.* roof-opening (for smoke and light), skylight 53/22.

ljósálfar *m. pl.* light elves 19/35,37, 20/24 (there is no source older than Snorri for the distinction of light and dark elves; cf. AH *Studier* 37).

ljóss *a.* light, bright 9/26, 10/11, 13/27.

ljósta (laust) *sv.* strike 35/31, 45/9; knock 49/6; with dat. of instrument 27/38; *l. í, á* strike at, against, onto 38/27, 39/5; *l. e-n hǫgg* strike s-one a blow 43/2.

ljúga (laug) *sv.* lie 36/37; impers. passive *er logit at þér* you have been lied to 28/8.

lof *n.* (1) glory 18/25. (2) permission 29/35.

lofa (að) *wv.* (1) praise 23/15, 29/36 ('and similarly when things are praised highly'). (2) permit 34/39.

loga (að) *wv.* burn (intrans.); pres. p., flaming 9/26,28.

logi *m.* flame; dat. sg., in, with flame(s) 18/5.

lokinn *pp.* of **lúka**.

lokka (að) *wv.* lure, entice, trick 25/15.

lopt *n.* air, sky 4/9, 10/12; *loptsins* in the sky 3/17; pl., sky, skies 8/37, 14/25, 50/12; *í lopt, á lopt* into the sky, into the air, aloft 12/27, 23/4; *á lopti* in the air, aloft 7/36, 51/7; *at lopti* in the air or into the air? 30/13,17.

losna (að) *wv.* become free, untied 50/4, 51/13; *l. upp* become uprooted 49/40.

lúðr (rs) *m.* (1) trumpet 25/40. (2) coffin or cradle (with prep. *á*) 11/32 (probably coffin, but evidently associated by Snorri with *ǫrk* which could mean both coffin and ark, and this seems to have led to his interpreting the verse as referring to a Norse deluge); ark 11/25. Cf. AH *Gudesagn* 25.

lúka (lauk) *sv.*, *l. fyrir e-m* close against s-one 30/1; *l. fyrir sér* open (to enter) 31/4; *l. aptr* shut 39/26; *l. upp* open 39/27; *hvar upp skyldi l.* where the opening was 43/1; *l. e-u* finish s-thing: *eigi mun lokit verða verkinu* the job would not be finished 35/26. Md., shut itself, slam to 8/6.

lund *f.* manner, way 4/11,29.

lustu p. pl. of **ljósta**.

lúta (laut) *sv.* bow the head 41/5 (i.e. to begin a second draught); *l. ór e-u* stand up from s-thing, cease to bend over s-thing 41/6.

lýðir *m. pl.* people, followers, subjects, troops 51/32.

lypta (pt) *wv.* with dat., lift 5/2, 42/1, 43/17.

lýsa (t) *wv.* illuminate 12/9, 13/40; impers. *lýsir* it shines, light is shed 23/16, 31/5; *lýsir e-t* light is shed over s-thing 13/32.

lýsigull *n.* shining gold, gold that emits light (shines in the dark) 47/9 (cf. *SnE* I. 336; *Grettis saga*, *ÍF* VII. 57).

lysti p. subj. of **ljósta**.

†**læ** *n.* (*dat. sg.* **lævi**) destruction, that which destroys (with gen.); *sviga læ* destroyer of sticks, kenning for fire 9/32, 51/39; = darkness 36/1.

lægi p. subj. of **liggja**.

lægri *a. comp.* lower (in level) 41/7.

læknir *m.* physician 29/20.

lærleggr *m.* upper leg, thigh-bone, ham-bone 37/12.

læti *n.* noise 38/4.

lǫgr *m.* sea 51/32; *lopt ok lǫg* 30/9, 31/5, 50/12.

má (ð) *wv.* with dat., damage, eat away, destroy 19/13.

maðkr *m.* maggot, grub, worm 15/34,35.

maðr *m.* person 5/17, 18/15, 50/5; man 7/24, 11/2; human being(s) 8/39 ('man', generic sg.); being 11/18; *eigi sá m. er* no one who 3/14; *flestum manni* to most people 12/2; pl., people 3/8, 4/33; men 30/35; *þeir menn er* any men who 40/21; *mǫnnum* for men (people) 18/13; as indefinite subject 18/40; *kalla menn* i.e. is called 15/24, 19/28; *svá at menn hafa gert* ever made 22/34.

mál *n.* (1) time (with inf., to do s-thing) 39/10; *m. at sofa* time for sleep, i.e. not yet time to get up 38/40. (2) speech, conversation 8/26; power of speech 13/6 (with def. art.); language 8/28; agreement, contract 36/6; transaction 29/38; affair, matter, case 30/2, 36/39, 37/3.

málmr *m.* metal 15/28,29, 45/21, 47/38.

málsnild *f.* eloquence 25/20.

man see **muna**.

mánaðr *m.* month 31/30.

máni *m.* moon 12/15, 34/34.

manndómligr *a.* human 4/34.

manndráp *n.* killing, homicide 49/25.

mannfjǫlði *m.* number (multitude) of people 32/9, 34/1.

mannfólk *n.* mankind 53/6; with art. 3/4,10, 9/40; people 4/24.

mannhringr *m.* circle of people 45/38.

mannkind *f.* mankind 13/8 (construed as n. pl.).

mannlíkan *n.* human form, being in human shape 16/7.

mannvit *n.* human intelligence 17/16; as cognate object *vitandi mannvits* conscious with human intelligence 15/36.

mansǫngr *m.* love song, erotic verse 25/4.

már *m.* gull 24/15.

margr *a.* (*n.* **mart**) many 3/34, 9/20; with sg. noun, many a 4/11, 23/5; *m. sá* many a one 33/8; n. as subst., a lot 18/30,31 (gen.), 36/28.

mark *n.* sign (*um e-t* of s-thing) 25/14; importance, significance (*at e-u* in s-thing) 31/39, 41/35; *m. at of e-t* something of importance regarding s-thing 33/18.

marka (að) *wv.* note, infer 23/17.

†marr *m.* sea 52/30.

mart n. of **margr.**

matask (að) *wv. md.* eat; *hafa matazk* have finished one's meal 38/29, 42/26.

matr *m.* food 8/21, 27/24; meal 37/8.

mátti see **mega.**

máttr *m.* might, power, ability 41/28, 44/1.

máttugr *a.* mighty 3/31, 4/2, 24/26; sup. *mátkastr* 14/23, 36/31.

mátþu = *mátt þú,* see **mega.**

með *prep.* (1) with dat., with 3/7, 29/24 (1); (instrument) 9/30, 38/7, 43/1; by means of 10/14, 27/3, 47/1; in company with 15/20, 37/4; living with 9/8; along with, as well as 10/28; including 22/37; equally with (next to?) 29/24 (2); among 4/40, 46/16, (i.e. for) 49/31; *með sjálfum sér* among themselves 4/10; between 23/34; carrying 36/18, 40/38; *vera með* have 15/8; *með einum hug til* of one mind towards 46/10; *hafa með sér* see **hafa;** engaged in 8/7; *fara með* treat 37/17, act with 43/39; (of place) by, along 12/23, 13/4; against 33/39 (error for *við?*—so W and U); (accompanying circumstances) in 3/30, with 50/5,9; regarding 51/13,14. (2) with acc., taking 35/20, 50/27; *koma með* bring 26/25; *fara með* take 36/20, 37/3 (drive). (3) as adv., as well, with it 19/15, 40/7; *ok þat með* and this also 27/34; *þar með* also 4/7; with (by means of) them 49/9; *fara með* treat (it), do with (it) 27/29, take (it) 44/24.

meðal, á m. *prep.* between; as adv., between (them) 36/7.

meðan *adv.* meanwhile 49/15; as conj., while 8/24.

mega (má, mátta) *pret. pres. vb.* be able, can 7/28, 36/18; *máttu, mátþu* you can 23/17, 28/8; subj. *mega ek, megak* can I, I can 31/29, 42/35; *máttigak* I was not able (see **-k, -a**) 24/10; may 11/19, 40/35; be permitted 23/21; have the right to 13/17, 22/26; with neg., must 23/9; *eigi mátti* did not have the opportunity 45/3; *m. minna* have less power 21/14; *hvat má hann* what power has he 8/33; *sem hann mátti lengst* as he could furthest, as the furthest he could 42/2. Impers., be possible 48/34; *má* one can 4/20, 6/30; *mátti, mætti* one could 3/17, 4/10; *hann* (acc.) *má vefja* it can be folded 36/21; *eigi mátti* it was impossible 35/9.

megi (1) pres. subj. of **mega. (2)** dat. sg. of **mǫgr.**

megin *n.* might, power 12/16.

megingjarðar *f. pl.* girdle of might 23/6, 38/5.

meginligr *a.* mighty, solemn 36/6.

megir nom. pl. of **mǫgr**.

†**meiðr** *m*. tree (= Yggdrasill) 19/13.

mein *n*. injury 27/9; mischief, source of harm 49/38; handicap (*e-m* for s-one) 31/37.

meinsvari *a*. (weak declension only) perjured, who swears falsely 53/27 (not a synonym of *eiðrofi* 53/16, which probably refers specifically to breakers of vows: *meinsvari* is a more inclusive term).

meir *adv. comp*. more (in degree) 14/9, 33/3, 40/20; further 43/23, 54/32; from then on, after that, or once more, still 34/13 (or *m. um* the more?).

meiri *a. comp*. greater 4/29 (2), 18/40; larger 4/29 (1), 39/34; more important 45/14; *með list ok kunnáttu meiri* with greater art and skill 15/8; n. as subst., more, a greater amount 41/19,27; n. as adv., to a greater extent 50/10.

méldropi *m*. drop (of foam) from a horse's bit 13/31.

mergr *m*. marrow 37/12.

merr *f*. mare 35/20,22.

mest *adv. sup*. most 4/25; most of all, especially 25/20.

mestr *a. sup*. greatest 5/6, 11/18 (see **vita**), 17/10; the biggest 15/23, 22/40; of greatest significance 8/39; *hefir þat mest óhapp verit unnit* (predicative) this (deed) was done (so as to be) the greatest misfortune, this was the unluckiest deed ever done 46/8; *it mesta* of the greatest kind 50/34; n. as subst. (or adv.) *mest af skáldskap* most about poetry (i.e. more than anyone else) 25/21.

metnaðr *m*. glory 3/11.

mey, meyjar acc. sg. and nom. acc. pl. of **mær**.

miðla (að) *wv*. share out, distribute 3/16.

miðr *a*. (*n*. **mitt**) mid, middle of 4/23,27, 38/32; *í honum miðjum* in the middle of it 9/21.

mikill *a*. much 5/24, 11/23; a great deal of 49/32, 50/6; numerous 54/12; big, large 25/1, 42/5; great 5/22, 31/6, 45/26; severe 49/22; important 12/20, 46/11; *m. fyrir sér* mighty, of great importance or power, a great man (person) 25/6, 29/12, 34/14; n. as subst. or adv., much 3/11, 13/1, 21/1; dat. sg. *myklu* with comp., much, by far, many 3/5, 4/29, 32/8.

mikillæti *n*. arrogance 31/6 (*er* in which, which consisted in the fact that).

mildr *a*. gentle, kind 29/33.

milli, í m., á m. *prep*. with gen., between 18/31, 39/28, 48/32; *sín á m.* between themselves, between each other 29/37; as adv. 49/23.

minjar *f. pl*. keepsake, token, souvenir, reminder 47/32.

minn *a*. my 38/10.

minnask (t) *wv. md.* recall, call to mind, discuss 15/32; *m. á e-t* 53/39, 54/36.

minni (1) *n.* memory 4/10; *hafa at minnum* keep in memory, as s-thing to remember 26/13.

minni (2) *a. comp.* less 25/37; shorter 31/31; less mighty 44/33; *m. fyrir sér* a person of less significance (cf. *mikill*) 41/38; n. as subst. or adv., less 21/15, 41/16, 43/17.

minnr *adv.* less 44/36, 47/13.

minztr *a. sup.* least, smallest 43/2.

missa (1) *f.* loss (*e-m* for s-one) 46/15.

missa (2) (t) *wv.* with gen., be without 23/9, 32/1, 50/32.

misseri *n.* season, period of six months (or year?) 34/31.

mistilteinn *m.* mistletoe 45/36,37, 46/6.

mitt n. of **miðr** 11/36.

mjólká *f.* river of milk 11/7.

mjór *a.* slender 28/26,28.

mjǫðr *m.* mead 17/25, 26/7, 33/13.

mjǫk *adv.* very (with adjectives) 4/2, 17/30, 26/19; very much 7/21, 29/36; much, far 41/14; very nearly 35/10; often 24/16; a lot, particularly (i.e. this is his or her characteristic role) 25/11, 29/31, 43/40.

móðerni *n.* descent on the mother's side 27/10.

móðir *f.* (*pl.* **mœðr**) mother 26/9,36, 54/21,27 (gen. sg.).

móðr *m.* fury 36/9, 37/25, 52/27.

mold *f.* soil, earth (as substance) 3/27, 9/1, 15/33, 16/30.

moli *m.* small fragment; *í smán mola* (sg. collective) into bits 35/32.

morðvargr *m.* murderer 53/16,28.

morgindǫgg *f.* morning dew 54/11,17.

morgunn *m.* morning 17/26, 24/15; dat. sg. *morni* 13/31, 42/23, 47/24.

móti, á m., **í m.** *prep.* with dat., against 40/3, 50/30; towards 50/28; to meet 6/6, 40/18; in the face of, on the side facing 10/8; *gera e-t í m. e-m* receive s-one with s-thing 7/26; *þýða á m.* see **þýða**; *í mót* as adv., in exchange 23/33; back (to meet his gaze) 45/4.

muðr *m.* (inflected **munn-**) mouth 25/17, 50/9; *í munn mér* into my mouth 28/35, similarly 29/7, 41/12,15; striking face or edge of hammer 38/35.

muna (man, munða) *pret. pres. vb.* remember 11/30.

†mund *f.* hand; dat. (instrumental) sg., with his hand 52/18.

mundlaug *f.* hand basin 49/13.

munn see **muðr**.

munr *m.* difference (*at* by which) 41/7,26; *þeim mun* (with sup.) *sem* by so much . . . in that, to this degree . . . that 46/14; *fyr øngan mun* by no means, certainly not 10/39.

munu (mun, munda) *pret. pres. vb.* (1) indicating future time: will 9/29, 14/15; be about to 38/30; with vb. to be understood, it will be 43/26 (2); p. tense *mundi* future in the past, would 5/19, 48/20, was to 3/12; *myndi* would have, was about to 46/31; *munak* (see **-k**) I shall 28/25; *muntu = munt þú* 28/30; p. inf. *mundu* would 27/32, 44/31. (2) indicating probability, *mun, muni, myni* will 12/2, 19/12, must 11/16,17, 33/17; would need 36/24; with vb. to be understood, must be 41/20; *muntu vera* you must be 39/34; *muntþu hafa* you have surely 28/9; *hvárt munu sitja* can there be sitting 39/8; *vera mun at segja frá þeim tíðindum* I daresay there are tidings to be told 45/16; p. tense, would 7/22,23, 18/9; must 4/1,2; might 3/18; might well 26/12; *eigi mundak* (see **-k**) I would not have 41/9,36; p. inf., would 28/24, 37/21.

myklu see **mikill**.

myrkr *a.* dark 37/33; n. as subst. 37/32.

mæla (t) *wv.* say 8/9,37; speak (*til* to) 31/8, 42/28; *þat er mælt* they say 25/13; *m. til* demand 34/35; *m. e-t sér til kaups* stipulate s-thing as one's payment 34/32; *m. við e-n* speak to s-one, say to s-one 21/20, 31/11, talk with s-one (s-thing)? 51/8; *m. við* (adv.) be opposed (to s-thing), object 47/30.

mær *f.* (*pl.* **meyjar**) maiden, virgin 18/12, 25/33, 29/21, 54/27 (the subject, with *sú* 54/25); acc. sg. *mey* †girl, i.e. wife, beloved 36/3.

†mærr *a.* renowned, splendid, excellent 17/23, 52/21.

mœtask (tt) *wv. md.* (reciprocal) meet each other 10/12 (sg. with pl. subject), 40/6.

mǫgr *m.* (*pl.* **megir**) son 26/9, 52/22; *míns magar* that of my (i.e. Óðinn's) son (i.e. Þórr) 22/40; dat. sg. *megi* (with *hjarta*) 52/17. In the phrase *Muspells megir* 15/10, 50/17 the word could mean 'men, troop' (cf. 51/31–2), but cf. 15/16, 32/1, 50/14,20.

mǫrk *f.* forest 37/31.

mǫtuneyti *n.* food-sharing; *leggja m. sitt* pool their food, put all their food together 38/16.

ná (ð) *wv.* with dat., get (possession of), possess 31/17.

†naðr (rs) *m.* adder, serpent; = Miðgarðsormr 52/23.

nafn *n.* name 3/13,32; generic sg. 4/10.

nafnfrægr *a.* famous; *er mjǫk er nafnfrægt* whose name is well-known 33/12.

nagl *m.* nail (of the body) 50/4,6.

nakkvarr (*n.* **nakkvat**) = **nokkurr**.

nákvæmr *a.* close; attentive; sup. *nákvæmust mǫnnum til á at heita* (the) most convenient (approachable) for people to pray to 25/2.

námunda *prep.* with dat., close to, to the neighbourhood of 10/11.

†**nár** *m.* corpse; acc. pl. *nái* 51/28, 53/31.

náttból *n.* night-quarters 37/35.

náttlangt *adv.* all night 42/22.

náttstaðr *m.* lodging-place for the night 8/1, 37/5.

náttúra *f.* nature, characteristic quality, property 3/23 (cf. **eðli**), 3/26, 23/19, 47/5.

náttverðr *m.* supper 37/7 (cf. **nótturðr**).

†**ne** *neg. adv.* not 12/13,15,17; reinforcing suffixed neg. *-a* 21/23.

né *conj.* nor 9/14,15,17, 31/9; without a neg. preceding 48/7.

neðan *adv.* below 12/9, 19/3; from below, underneath 17/15; up(wards) 45/4.

neðri *a. comp.* lower 29/8, 50/10,38.

nefna (d) *wv.* name, call 4/35, 5/16; mention 54/38; speak the name of 3/12, 26/12; *er nefndr* is the name of 14/6, 47/10; *þessar eru enn nefndar* these are the names of others 33/23. Md. *nefndisk* said his name was 7/36, 38/7; *hefir hann nefnzk á fleiri vega* he called himself by various (other) names 21/31.

neita (að) *wv.* say no; *þá er hann* (*maðr* T, W, and U) *neitar* when one denies 30/3.

nema (1) *conj.* except 3/7, 29/1; with inf. 14/12; introducing a clause, except that 11/24; with subj., without, except by 46/28, if . . . not, unless 8/23.

nema (2) (nam) *sv.* take; *n. staðar* stop, come to rest 7/7, (get a grip) 49/3; *n. við e-u* push against, be stuck against 29/7; learn, acquire knowledge 54/30 ('may the knowledge you have acquired do you good').

†**nepr** *a.* with difficulty? dying? 52/23.

nes *n.* headland 7/11.

nest *n.* food for a journey 38/17.

nestbaggi *m.* food-bag, knapsack 38/14,21, 39/20, 42/40.

net *n.* net 48/22,24,27,34, 49/1.

netþinull *m.* the rope along the (top) edge of a net 49/2.

neztr *a. sup.* (*cf.* **neðri**) lowest 8/18.

nið *n.* darkening, waning of the moon 14/3.

níð *n.* insult, imputation of dishonour 52/24.

†**niðfǫlr** *a.* pale as rust? or as the waning moon? darkly pale? 51/28 (with ǫrn).

niðr *adv*. down, downwards 9/4, 18/33, 47/17.

niðri *adv*. down 15/33, 19/36.

níu *num*. nine 23/39, 25/33.

níundi *ord. num*. (the) ninth 8/31, 17/34.

njóta (naut) *sv*. with gen., enjoy 20/18; get benefit from 48/8 (*nautka* = *naut-ek-a*, see **-a**), imp. *njóttu* (= *njót þú*) 54/30; subj. *svá njóta* (*ek*) *trú minnar at* by my faith (salvation) 34/1; impers. *ekki nýtr sólar* the sun does no good, there is no sunshine 49/22.

nokkurr, nokkvorr, nakkvarr *pron. a*. a certain, some (or other) 3/30, 7/8; any 8/22, 34/37; anyone 36/38, 47/29; *n. mundi vera stjórnari* there must be some controller 4/1; with def. art., any of the 53/32; *ór skóginum nokkvorum* from the wood that happened to be nearby or from somewhere in the wood 35/20; *einna n*. one in particular 14/33; n. as adv. *nokkut, nakkvat* somewhat 41/26, at all 47/16, 48/14; dat. of degree with comp., somewhat 28/21, 35/33.

norðan *adv*. from the north; *n. ór . . .* from *. . .* in the north 7/5.

norðanverðr *a*. northern, northerly 20/29.

norðr (1) *n*. north 4/19, 10/6.

norðr (2) *adv*. north, northwards 5/26, 6/4, 39/18.

norðrhálfa *f*. the northern region (often referring to Europe), the northern continent 5/6,20; pl. 6/24.

norðrætt *f*. northerly direction 31/3.

norn *f*. norn 18/14,18,23,26,27, 19/14, 30/35.

nótt *f*. (*pl*. **nætr**) night 23/39, 31/24,27, 37/13; acc. sg., in a night 7/3, by night 25/38.

nótturðr *m*. supper (= **náttverðr**) 38/21.

nú *adv*. now 12/20, 15/5; just now 10/37, 28/14; in a moment 28/17, 31/18; at present 20/24; *nú it fyrsta sinn* now for the first time 36/37; referring to time of author 5/26,32, to time of fictional narrator 43/16; correlative with *er* 41/16 (1), 42/34 (now that); *er . . . þá . . . nú* 41/26; *nú er . . . þá* 43/14; *áðr . . . nú* 28/8.

ný *n*. new moon, waxing of the moon 14/3.

nyrðri *a. comp*. more northerly 4/20.

nýta (tt) *wv*. derive benefit (*af* from), be successful (in), get somewhere (with) 41/29; md., thrive, be successful 38/25.

nývaknaðr *a*. (*pp*.) just awoken 38/40.

nær *adv*. close, near 14/11, 47/22; nearly 14/8; as prep. with dat., near (to) 4/27, 23/38, 42/38.

næst *adv*. (*sup*.) next 11/6; *þar n., því n*. next to him 8/19, next after that 13/9,24; *sterkr n. því sem Þórr er* almost equal in strength to Þórr 26/16.

næstr *a. sup.* closest (*e-u* to s-thing), next (to) 9/24.

nætr pl. of **nótt**.

nǫkkvi *m.* row-boat 44/24, 45/6; equivalent to *skip* 46/29 (cf. also 44/25, 45/1).

nǫs *f.* nostril 50/11.

óask (að) *wv. md.* be afraid for, about (*at . . . ne* lest . . . not) 33/1.

óð see **vaða**.

óðul *n. pl.* property inherited as of right; homeland; *eiga þar ó.* be native there 9/27.

†of (1) *adv.* pleonastic with verbs in verse 11/30,32, 12/29,40, 36/11 etc.

of (2) *archaic prep.* (later replaced by *um* and *yfir*) with acc. (1) of place, over, across 39/6, 44/6; through, over 45/6, 53/22; throughout 13/13, 20/6; around 27/13; above or on? 12/19 (or as sense 3 below); *of veg* forward 52/15. (2) of time, through(out) 8/35; during 15/1, 38/4; at about 37/36. (3) subject, concerning 33/18; about 16/2, 54/1; with 40/13, 43/6; *freista of* try at 41/31. (4) †with dat. *ok of fjórum tøgum* 33/35 (cf. 22/36): perhaps adv. (quasi-comp.), 'beyond that, more than that by forty', rather than 'over forty'.

ofan *adv.* above 12/8, 19/1; from above, i.e. down 28/3, 37/20; *þar o. í* down in it 43/4.

ofarst *adv. sup.* uppermost 8/19.

ofdramb *n.* arrogance 13/38.

ófegri *a. comp.* less beautiful 54/21.

ofinn *pp.* (of *vefa*) woven (with dat., out of, with s-thing) 53/14 (serpents were twisted in the walls, or the walls were woven out of serpents; cf. 53/23).

oflítill *a.* too small 32/8.

ofrefli *n.* superiority in power (*e-m* over s-one), something beyond one's strength 27/28, 36/26.

ófriðr *m.* hostility 12/25.

ófróðliga *adv.* ignorantly 21/5.

ófúss *a.* reluctant 28/33.

ófœra *f.* s-thing impossible to traverse, an impossible undertaking 12/3; peril, disastrous situation 25/29, 42/38.

ófœrr *a.* impassable, untraversable (*e-m* by s-one) 9/27.

ógagn *n.* disadvantage, mischief 49/39.

ógjǫrr *a.* (*pp.*) undone, unfinished 34/37.

ógurligr *a.* terrible 45/3.

óhapp *n.* misfortune, disaster 27/9, 46/8.

óhelgari *a. comp.* less holy 21/14.

óhreinn *a.* impure, evil 23/21.

ójafn *a.* unequal, diverse 3/35; n. as adv., unequally, unfairly 18/24.

ójafnask (að) *wv. md.* become unequal, diverse 3/4.

ok *adv. and conj.* and 3/1, 9/21; also 3/16,22 (1); besides 42/21; *taka ok* see **taka**; indicating accompanying circumstances, with 29/22 (2), 48/17 (2) ('and there were . . .'), 49/23, but 31/12; *ok kominn* and (said he had) come 8/1; *svá hart ok yfir* so hard over, so hard and (high) over, so strongly and in such a way over 47/21; pleonastic, introducing main clause and correlative with *er* 27/9 (2), 40/30, 41/6 (3), 49/1; correlative with *þá er* 10/14 (see note to 27/10 and *Den første og anden grammatiske afhandling i Snorres Edda*, ed. V. Dahlerup and Finnur Jónsson, København 1886, p. 78; J. Fritzner, *Ordbog over det gamle norske Sprog*, Kristiania 1886–96, under **ok** *conj.* 9).

ók see **aka**.

ókunnigr *a.* unknown, secret 44/3.

ókunnr *a.* unknown, strange 29/29.

†ókvíðinn *a.* unafraid (*e-s* of s-thing), unconcerned, not anxious (about) 52/24.

ókyrr *a.* unquiet, violent 14/26.

ólíkr *a.* unlike 3/20 (note the n. form: 'it was different, there was dissimilarity'); with dat., unlike to, different from 6/10, 19/36; comp. 19/37.

olli see **valda**.

ólusk see **ala**.

ómaki *m.* trouble, inconvenience 14/13.

opinn *a.* open 39/29.

opna (að) *wv.* (cut) open 3/27.

opt *adv.* often 27/2, 31/30.

optar *adv. comp.* again, more than this once 41/5, 42/36, 43/27.

ór *prep.* with dat., from 7/5, 10/9; out of 10/2,30, (material) 12/28, 16/5,6; from among 14/32; coming from, leading from 29/2 (with *fjǫtrinum*); as adv., out of them 10/32.

óramligri *a. comp.* less mighty-looking 44/34.

órar = *várar*, see **várr**.

orð *n.* word 34/15, 46/13; pledged word 36/5; pl., speech, conversation 31/9,11.

orðfimi *f.* skill in words, command of language 25/21.

orðinn *pp.* of **verða**.

orðsnild *f.* eloquence 25/23.

orðtak *n.* saying 25/12, 27/40, 29/40, 30/3,5; pl., speech 46/9.

órlaustn *f.* solution, answer (*e-s* to s-thing) 36/39.

ormr *m.* serpent 18/36, 19/5, 45/22, 49/12, 53/14,24; = Miðgarðsormr 27/12,13, 44/37,38, 45/2,4,6,8, 50/36, 51/26.

orrosta *f.* battle 25/11, 26/19.

órœkja (kt) *wv.* neglect, fail to heed 3/5.

ósáinn *a.* (*pp.*) unsown, without being sown 53/35.

ósanna (að) *wv.* refute 30/3.

óskasonr *m.* adopted son 21/28.

óskorinn *a.* (*pp.*) uncut 50/6 (cf. **skera**).

óskǫp *n. pl.* misfortune, evil fate, curse 18/27.

ósterkligri *a. comp.* less strong-looking 42/13.

ósviðr *a.* not clever, foolish 19/7.

ósœmð *f.* loss of honour, loss of face 42/31.

ótrúligr *a.* unbelievable, incredible 8/8, 38/23; *ótrúligir at sannir muni vera* incredible that (they) can be true, unlikely to be true 36/35 (the construction seems to be a mixture of 'which it seems to us incredible that can be true' and 'which seem to us incredible').

ótta *f.* the last part of the night, the time just before dawn 37/13.

óttalauss *a.* unafraid 50/25; *ekki var óttalaust at sofa* it was not possible to sleep without fear, securely 38/31.

óttask (að) *wv. md.* be afraid 28/2.

óvinr *m.* enemy 8/14, 55/7.

óvíss *a.* uncertain 8/13 ('one cannot know with certainty').

óx see **vaxa**.

oxahǫfuð *n.* ox-head 44/34,38.

plógr *m.* plough 7/6.

plógsland *n.* plough-land, acre, the amount of land that can be ploughed in a certain time 7/3.

prýði *f.* splendour 4/22.

pungr *m.* purse 36/22.

ráð *n.* counsel 45/19 (see **bera**); *taka r. af* consult 50/24; scheme, plan, course of action 27/26, 35/16 (*til at* so that, by which); *leita ráða* discuss what to do 35/11; *ráða ráðum sínum* take counsel, hold a conference 34/34, 54/36.

ráða (réð) *sv.* (1) with dat., control 4/5, 8/36; rule 7/1, 18/23; determine,

assign 30/35,36; have power over 24/28; be the cause of 35/15; *vera e-s
ráðandi* be responsible for s-thing 6/9; *r. því er* (or *at*) bring it about (by
one's advice) that, be responsible for the decision that (to) 35/1,12,14;
abs., have one's way 42/35; *r. ráðum* see **ráð**. (2) with preps. *r. fyrir* rule
over 4/3, 5/29, control 23/29; *r. fyrir sér* determine, make up one's
mind 43/35; *r. um* decide about, be in charge of 15/20. (3) with acc.,
advise; *r. heilræði* give good advice (*e-m* to s-one) 39/14.

ragna gen. of **regin**.

ragnarøkr (rs) *n.* twilight of the powers 25/26, 29/10, 49/17,18. This is the
word consistently used (sometimes spelt with -*kk*-) in *Snorra Edda* and
(once) in *Ls*. Other eddic poems however use the form *ragna rǫk*, doom
of the powers.

ramr *a.* (physically) strong, powerful (but sometimes referring to magical
power) 36/29; *n.* as subst., *svá ramt* something so powerful, such power
36/25.

†rann *n.* building 22/38 (gen. pl., with *mest*), 26/6.

rás *f.* race, running 43/10.

rata (að) *wv.* (1) travel about, be abroad. (2) fall. In this text the word
occurs only at 9/36 and 52/2 and it is uncertain which meaning was
intended.

rauðr *a.* red (of blood) 14/39, (of fire) 18/8, (of gold) 20/1, 29/28, 53/11.

rauf *f.* hole 49/6.

refilstigr *m.* trackless way? secret path? 8/1.

†regin *n. pl.* (divine) powers 12/36, 14/38, 15/39, 54/26.

regn *n.* rain 24/27.

regnbogi *m.* rainbow 15/7.

reið (1) *f.* carriage, chariot 23/1, 25/2, 37/4, 44/6; riding 30/10 (2).

reið (2) p. of **ríða**.

reiða (dd) *wv.* lift, swing (a weapon) 38/33, 39/4; *r. fram* swing down and
forward, i.e. strike 43/31; *r. til* (adv.) swing up or round, bring forward
45/11.

reiðask (dd) *wv. md.* be(come) angry (*e-m*, *e-u* with s-one or at s-thing)
13/37, 44/17.

reiði *n.* harness, trappings 47/7.

reiðigǫgn *n. pl.* utensils (cf. *reiða* f., service) or riding equipment (cf. *reið*
f., riding) 15/30.

reiðr *a.* angry (*e-m* with s-one) 31/11, 38/26.

reip *n.* rope; pl., tackle 35/22.

reka (rak) *sv.* pursue, fulfil (an errand) 48/1.

rekja (rakða) *wv.* trace; *r. spádóma til at* discover prophecies implying that 27/8.

rekkja *f.* (*gen. pl.* **rekna**) bed 38/29.

renna (1) (d) *wv.* slip, glide, slide 48/36, 49/2.

renna (2) (rann; *3rd pers. sg. pres.* **renn, rennr**) *sv.* run 10/2, 11/7; with acc., run (gallop) over or through 30/9; *r. skeið* run a race or course 40/10.

†renniraukn *n.* swiftly moving draught animal 7/14.

reri see **róa.**

rétt *adv.* right(ly) 3/4, 9/2.

rétta (tt) *wv.* make right or straight; stretch 42/2; *r. dóma sína* issue their judgements or set up their courts 15/32.

réttlátr *a.* righteous (cf. **láta** (2) behave) 20/10.

réttr *m.* law 6/14.

reyna (d) *wv.* try, make trial of 27/27,32, 44/20; attempt, have a go at 39/39; put to the test, prove, find out about by testing 28/12, 40/27 ('now we shall see'), 47/27; *reynt er* it is decided, a decisive result has been obtained 40/31.

reynd *f.* reality, what is found out about the nature of a thing by experience 19/37 (dat. pl., 'in reality').

ríða (reið) *sv.* (1) ride 13/29, 17/31; with the mount in dat. 13/30, 46/26, 47/2; with acc., ride across, over, or through 15/10, 47/7, 50/16; *r. leið sína* ride on one's way 47/33; *r. braut* ride a path, track 54/25. (2) knit, tie; *r. rœxna á* (adv.) tie knots in (it) 48/21.

rífa (reif) *sv.* tear 49/8, 51/3.

rifja (að) *wv.*, *r. upp* delve into, explicate, rehearse (a subject) 22/20.

ríki *n.* kingdom, realm 4/7, 5/4, 7/3, 8/35; *hann á þar r. er* he rules over a place which 22/32.

ríkiskona *f.* noblewoman 25/3.

ríkismaðr *m.* nobleman, ruler, man of authority or rank 6/10,19, 33/7.

ríkr *a.* powerful (often referring to spiritual or political power or authority) 4/2, 5/29; n. as noun *svá ríkt* such power 36/25; comp. 11/21, 42/29.

ríkuligr *a.* successful, prosperous, glorious 18/24.

ripti *n.* article made of linen; robe? 47/33.

risi *m.* giant 5/6.

rjóða (rauð) *sv.* redden (trans.) 14/38.

rjúka (rauk) *sv.* steam 7/15.

†ró = *eru* (after words ending in -*r*) 19/9, 51/17,34.

róa (rera, røra) *sv.* row 44/25,26,29; go out in a boat 44/9,11.

róðr (rar) *m.* rowing 44/26,27.

rógberi *m.* carrier of slander or (false) accusations 26/34 (see AH *Studier* 66).

rót *f.* (*pl.* **rœtr**) root 17/11, 28/6.

rúm *n.* space (*til* for s-thing) 50/10.

rún *f.* mystery, secret wisdom 53/39.

ryðja (rudda) *wv.* clear, empty; i.e. leave, evacuate 52/26.

rýðr pres. of **rjóða**.

ræfr n. roof ('of which I know the roof'; W and T have *rept*, pp. of *repta* to roof, i.e. 'which I know (to be) roofed') 22/39.

ræxn *m.* knot, knotted loop 48/22.

rœða (dd) *wv.* speak, discuss (*of* about) 54/1.

rœtr pl. of **rót**.

†rǫkstóll *m.* judgement seat 15/40, 35/37.

rǫst *f.* an indefinite distance roughly equivalent to a league 25/38, 50/21, 53/1.

røri p. of **róa**.

sá (1) *pron. a.* that, this, it 53/12; he 7/36, 46/19; separated from noun 53/3, 54/25; outside clause 6/30; *þat* anticipating noun clause 3/18, 50/31, cf. 25/38, 45/3 (how), *ok þat er* and how 45/6; anticipating inf. 41/35; *þat er* whatever 29/26, when 9/13; *þat* referring to f. noun 19/28, with pl. vb. 6/2, 7/5 (cf. **þat**); *þeir* in apposition to sg. nouns 5/30 ('these, Vitta and Sigarr'); with (*h*)*inn* and a., *þau in fyrstu* these (are) the first (tidings) 49/20, *sá hinn* 11/31, 12/39, *hafit þat it djúpa* 37/29; *aurinn þann er* 19/15, *sólarinnar þeirar er* of the sun which 13/39; *mannkindin þeim er* the humans to whom 13/8; *engi sá* no person 39/39, 43/24, 45/3.

sá (2) p. of **sjá** 4/4, 37/20, 45/5.

sá (3) acc. of **sár (1)**.

saga *f.* story 40/33, 45/17, 54/35.

saka (að) *wv.* impers., harm; *e-n sakar* s-one is harmed 45/26,27,30.

sakarvandræði *n. pl.* difficult legal disputes, disputes difficult of settlement 26/26.

†salnæfr (rar) *f.* hall-bark: shingles made of bark of trees were used for thatching (the pl. refers to the separate shingles of bark). Sváfnir's (Óðinn's) hall was thatched with shields, so 'Óðinn's hall-shingles' means shields 7/33.

salr *m.* hall 15/25, 18/11; †pl., dwelling, home 12/14.

saltr *a.* salty 11/10.

saman *adv.* together 12/1, 34/13; in common 3/19, 18/19; *fara s.* follow each other without a break 49/23; *koma s.* converge (in a common origin) 10/34; *einn s.* all alone 5/5.

samgangr *m.* union 29/34; confrontation, conflict 50/31.

samna (að) *wv.* gather; *s. til* collect (material) for 50/39 (impers., 'for which material has been being collected, which has been in the making').

samr *a. pron.* (usually declined weak) same 3/24,33,34; *s. sem* same as 32/21; *slíkt sama*, *it sama* as adv., likewise 4/6, 26/30.

samt *adv.* together 53/39; *einn s.* alone 37/21.

sandr *m.* sand 9/14.

sannr *a.* (*n.* **satt**) true 28/8, 34/14; n. as subst. *satt*, *it sanna* the truth 32/12, 42/34; *með sǫnnu* truly 33/32; comp. n. as adv., more accurately 43/37.

sár (1) *m.* tub 14/5.

sár (2) *n.* wound 11/23, 33/10.

satt n. of **sannr.**

sáttr *a.* reconciled, in agreement 26/26; at peace 34/13 (*um* about it? cf. **meir**).

sauðr *m.* sheep 25/39.

saurga (að) *wv.* defile 29/15.

sé (1) pres. subj. of **vera** 11/34, 14/8, 20/21,23. **(2)** pres. 1st pers. of **sjá.**

†seðja (sadda) *wv.* satiate, feed 32/27.

sefask (að) *wv. md.* calm down 37/25.

sefr pres. of **sofa.**

†seggr *m.* man 7/34.

segja (sagða) *wv.* say 7/11, 8/35; speak 37/18; tell (*e-m* s-one) 5/8, 28/11,16; tell (stories) 8/25, 55/5 (*frá* about); *s. spár* make prophecies 21/19; *s. ørlǫg* foretell or pronounce, i.e. ordain, destinies? 21/26; with acc. and inf. of vb. to be understood 16/11 ('these she says (are) the names of the dwarfs'); *s. frá* talk about (it or them) 4/10, 36/30, speak of 10/37, tell of, about 55/2, relate 44/4. Impers. *segir* it says, it it told 6/19, 9/30; *svá er sagt* it is said 10/40; *þá er sagt* it is said that then 38/6; *er þér eigi sagt* have you not been told 15/6; *ef mér væri sagt frá* if I had been told about it (i.e. if I had not seen it with my own eyes) 41/10; *hvat er at s.* what is there to tell 17/9, 34/26; *þat er at s. frá Hermóði at* as for Hermóðr 47/7; *mart er at s.* there is much to tell 18/30; *er gott at s.* there are good things to say 23/15; *eru at s.* are to be told 49/18,20; *svá er at s.* this can or must be said, the story goes 38/23; *þat er (svá, þér) satt (með* sǫnnu) *at segja at* to tell (you) the truth, the fact is that 33/32, 38/31, 43/26,35, 44/35; *en ek hygg hitt vera þér satt at s.* but I think the contrary is correct to report 45/11; *þat má s.* this can be said, I can tell you this 45/2; *fyrst at s. frá* first (there is) to tell about 46/38.

segl *n.* sail 36/19.

seiðberandi *m.* (*pres. p.*) one who practises *seiðr* (sorcery, divination) 10/22 (pl.).

seilask (d) *wv. md.* reach (with the hand) 42/2, 43/21; *s. til* reach out, over 38/11.

seinn *a.* slow; *seint er* it takes a long time 39/33 ('news travels slowly'); n. as adv., slowly 43/12; i.e. never 50/7 (with *gert*); *mér mun seint verða* it will be a long time before I, I will have to wait a long time before I 28/33; *leit seint til þeira* was slow to turn to them 39/31; n. comp. as adv. *seinna* more slowly 43/9.

selja (ld) *wv.* give 28/22; *s. fram* hold out, offer 28/38.

sem *conj.* as 15/13; like 5/9; *sýnask sem, lítask sem* look as though 40/8, 41/20,22; as long as 41/13; correlative with *svá* 4/12,40, with *jafn-* 33/5, *jafnt* 25/38, *samr* 32/21, *slíkt* 6/7, *þeim mun* 46/14, *þvílíkr* 31/35; *þar sem* where 6/4, in a place which 54/10; *hvar sem* wherever 5/23; *hvat sem* whatever 35/18; as rel., who, which 19/17, 42/6; that which (or to the extent that?) 54/30; with sup., as . . . as possible 40/5, 49/1.

senda (d) *wv.* send 28/2, 30/8; *s. eptir e-m* send for s-one 46/25; *s. til* (adv.) send there 10/14, 27/11.

sendiferð *f.* errand, mission 31/21.

sendimaðr *m.* messenger 28/3,18, 48/1.

senn *adv.* at the same time, together 5/2, 7/36, 33/38.

sér (1) pres. of **sjá**.

sér (2) dat. of **sik**.

sess *m.* seat, bench 24/34.

sét *pp.* of **sjá**.

setberg *n.* flat-topped mountain 43/4,5.

setja (tt) *wv.* set, put, place 7/6, 12/5, 39/24; set down 7/8; put in position 13/2; establish 34/29; appoint, ordain 6/13; *s. e-m borð* set up (prepare) a table for s-one 42/25; *s. fram* launch 46/24; *s. syn fyrir* make a denial 30/3; *s. til* establish, appoint, ordain as, for (a certain function) 5/28, 30/2,4; *s. þar til landa* (*til þess ríkis*) set up (as a ruler) over those territories (over that realm) 6/1,17; *s. e-t við e-u* thrust s-thing against s-thing 45/12. Md., sit down 13/13; take (up) one's position 15/32, 37/39; *setjask á tal* sit down to discuss 54/36; *setjask til* sit down to 37/7; *setjask upp* sit up 39/6.

sétti *ord. num.* (the) sixth 8/31, 17/34.

sex *num.* six 28/5.

sía *f.* molten particle 10/8, 12/7, 13/40.

siðaðr *a.* (*pp.*) having morals of a certain kind; *rétt s.* of good life, righteous, virtuous 9/2.

síðan *adv.* afterwards 24/25, 27/40; again 39/2; (ever) since 48/22; *s. at kveldi* the following evening, that evening 38/18; *s. er* as conj., since 27/35, *s. er . . . þá* after 3/34.

síðar *adv. comp.* later (with dat. of the amount of time) 31/24, 35/33.

síðarst *adv. sup.* last of all, finally 3/2, 13/25; in the rear 39/38.

siðlátr *a.* virtuous, of good life 53/13.

síðr *adv. comp.* less; *eigi at s.* none the less 3/15.

sifjar *f. pl.* relationship, bonds of affinity 49/30.

sifjaslit *n.* breaking of the bonds of affinity 49/26; the word usually has the more specialized meaning of incest.

síga (seig) *sv.* sink 37/20.

sigr (rs) *m.* victory 25/11, 30/35, 36/29.

sigra (að) *wv.* defeat 5/5, 9/29; be victorious over 13/21.

sik, sín, sér *reflexive pron.* (refers to subject of clause) himself, herself, itself, themselves; *á ǫxlum sér* on their shoulders 14/5; *fyrir sjálfum sér* for themselves (individually) 22/24; *sér* respectively, in each separate instance 22/18, for himself 44/21; *sér til kaups* as his payment 34/32; *til sín* to stay with him 33/6. At 27/28 *sér* refers to the logical subject (*úlfinum*), cf. **sinn**.

silfr *n.* silver 20/2,5, 26/30.

silkiband *n.* silken (silky) band 28/21,29.

silkirœma *f.* silken ribbon 28/17.

sin *f.* sinew 28/6.

sindr *n.* slag, clinker 10/2.

sinn (1) (*n.* **sitt**) *reflexive a.* (generally refers to subject of clause) his, her, its, their 3/34, 6/19; one's 36/22; their own 22/23; at 27/28 refers to subject of inf. (*hann,* acc.); at 42/29 to logical subject (*honum*); *sinn* (sc. *maðr*) *í hverju* one (man) in each (throne) 8/17.

sinn (2) *n.* time, occasion 30/9, 41/16; *annat. s.* next time 43/28; *it fyrsta s.* the first time 27/29 (*er* that), for the first time 36/37; *eitt sinn, einu sinni* once 21/5, 25/29, for once 38/6; *at sinni* on this occasion, for the time being 41/5.

sinni *m.* companion; pl., company (?) 50/20.

sitja (sat) *sv.* sit 8/16, 18/30; sit fishing 44/14,30; remain idle 36/10; be positioned 9/28; *s. fyrir* be present (already?), lie in wait? 8/15.

sjá (1) *pron.* this (rarely that); *sjá . . . er* s-one who 36/35.

sjá (2) (sá, *pp.* sét) *sv.* see 4/4, 7/27; perceive 6/10; find 41/14; understand 28/14; look (*til* towards, at) 28/37, 41/15; *sáttu = sátt þú* you saw 43/4; *sjám* let us see 42/11; *ek sé eigi* I cannot see 46/1; *sjá sik* set eyes on himself, i.e. open his eyes, become conscious 39/2; *sá mann ok lék* saw a man playing 7/35; with acc. and inf. 39/24; *sjá e-n sitja* see s-one sitting 47/23; impers. *sér* one can see, there is visible 45/13; *sjá má (mátti)* one can see (could be seen) 3/17, 41/29; *má sjá* can be seen 43/40; *þat er sá augnanna* (as for) what could be seen of the eyes 37/20. Md. *sjásk at* be afraid about 33/3; *sjásk fyrir* hesitate, be wary or cautious 25/13; *sjásk um* look around 54/32.

sjafni *m.* a word for love 29/33.

sjaldan *adv.* seldom (i.e. never) 36/10.

sjálfr *a. pron.* self, himself, themselves 4/11 ('among themselves'), 6/7; yourself 8/3; itself, on its own 31/22; itself, the very 52/36; †*sjálfgi* not herself (see **-gi**) 21/26; *sjálfra þeira* their own 7/22; *fyrir sjálfum sér* for themselves (individually) 22/24.

sjár = **sær.**

sjau *num.* seven 7/35.

sjaundi *ord. num.* (the) seventh 8/31, 17/34, 29/31.

sjávargangr = **sævargangr.**

sjóða (sauð) *sv.* cook; pp. *soðinn* 32/10,17, 37/7.

sjón *f.* sight 13/7, 37/21, 45/3.

sjónhverfingar *f. pl.* optical illusions, magical deceptions, false appearances 7/27, 42/38.

†**sjǫt** *n.* dwelling 14/38.

skaði *m.* harm, injury, destruction, loss 27/26, 46/14.

skáld *n.* poet 7/11, 34/22.

skáldskapr *m.* poetry 25/21,22 ('poetry is called *bragr*').

skalf see **skjálfa.**

skáli *m.* hall, building 37/34,35,39, 38/12.

†**skálmǫld** *f.* age of swords 49/33 (*skálm* f., short sword).

skammr *a.* short 10/17, 18/25; n. as subst., a short distance 48/35; *eiga skamt til* to be a short distance from 48/23; n. as adv., a short way 38/2; comp. *skemri* 3/36.

skapa (að, *p.* skóp 3/1, textual note) *wv.* create 3/1, 11/28; make, shape 13/5, 20/28; ordain, determine, shape (*e-m* for s-one) 12/11, 18/13. Md. impers., develop, come about 10/36.

skapari *m.* creator 3/14.

skapker *n.* vat 33/14.

skaplyndi *f.* character, nature 21/10, 26/38.

skapt *n.* handle 23/9, 39/6.

skarpr *a.* sharp; comp., tougher 28/40.

skaut *n.* corner (as of a square cloth) 12/5.

skegg *n.* beard 28/5,9.

†**skeggjǫld** *f.* age of battle-axes (i.e. of warfare) 49/33.

skeið *n.* race, course (both the race and the ground over which it is run) 40/15 ('a good course for running'),17,23; *s. nokkvor* races over a certain distance 40/10.

skemtun *f.* entertainment 34/3, 45/23; *skemtunar sinnar* for his (i.e. Gylfi's) entertainment 7/2.

†**skepja (skapða)** *wv.* create 16/4.

skera (skar) *sv.* slaughter 37/6.

†**skerða (ð)** *wv.* bite pieces (notches) out of, damage, diminish 19/3 (object understood).

skíð *n.* ski 24/17.

skíðfœrr *a.* able to ski, good at skiing 26/21.

skilja (lð) *wv.* understand 3/16, 4/13; perceive, deduce, tell 6/30, 28/13; realize 48/27; *svá skilðu þeir* they deduced, it was their understanding, interpretation 4/14; distinguish: impers. *hví skilr svá mikit* why is there such a large difference 21/1. Md., part from one another 43/26.

skilnaðr *m.* parting 42/28.

skilning *f.* understanding 4/13.

skin *n.* shining 4/5, 14/25, 24/27.

skína (skein) *sv.* shine 9/33, 51/40; impers. 50/15.

skip *n.* ship 34/18, 36/13; boat 44/25, 45/1.

skipa (að) *wv.* (1) with dat., organize, establish 6/12,14; md., be arranged, be organized 9/39 ('what were things like?'), 15/34 ('take shape'?). (2) with acc., occupy, man 36/18; *eigi er þrøngra at s. hana en ganga í hana* it is not more crowded when it is occupied than when it is being entered 33/32; fill (*e-t e-m* a place with people), allot (people a place) 21/29.

skipta (pt) *wv.* with dat., share out, apportion 18/23 (object understood), 27/15 (*með* among, between); divide 48/37; impers. *e-u var skipt* s-thing was divided, separated 13/2. Md., become separate, distinct, disperse 4/12.

skipun *f.* organization, arrangement (government?) 15/20.

skírr *a.* bright, pure 20/5, 24/23.

skjálfa (skalf) *sv.* tremble, shake 37/37, 46/30.

skjall *n.* the skin round the white of an egg 19/18.

skjalla (skall) *sv*. with dat., crash on 44/19; *s. á* bang against 44/39.

skjóta (skaut) *sv*. shoot 24/17; with dat. object, push, shove 29/5,7; *s. (e-u) á e-n* or *at e-m* shoot (a missile) at s-one 45/24,30, 46/4,6; *s. e-u út* launch (push into the water) 44/24; impers. *e-u skýtr upp* s-thing shoots up, is raised up, emerges (*ok er þá* and (it) is then) 53/34.

skjótfœri *n*. speed in running 43/11.

skjótleikr *m*. speed in running 40/13.

skjótr *a*. quick; n. as adv., fast 14/8, 44/27; soon 28/8,28; quickly, immediately 38/6, 40/14; comp. n. as adv. *skjótara* more quickly 39/39; sup. *skjótast at segja* to put it most briefly 22/21.

skjǫldr *m*. (*pl*. **skildir**) shield 7/29,30, 49/34.

skógr *m*. wood, forest 14/19, 35/20.

skóklæði *n. pl*. footwear 29/23.

skolla (d) *wv*. hover; keep one's distance? refuse to have anything to do (with s-one)? waver, change one's mind? 28/33.

skór *m*. shoe 26/15, 50/39,40.

skorta (t) *wv*. impers. *e-t skortir til* s-thing is lacking for s-thing, the lack of s-thing is an obstacle 31/23; *eigi skortir e-n e-t* s-one does not lack s-thing, s-one has plenty of s-thing 42/25.

skósveinn *m*. valet, chamberlain 31/10.

skot *n*. missile 46/7.

skriðr *m*. (fast) movement 44/26 (ironic understatement).

skrifa (að) *wv*. write (down) 6/26.

skulfu p. pl. of **skjálfa**.

skulu (skal, skylda) *pret. pres. vb*. (1) indicating necessity, obligation, or duty: ought, should 25/8, 51/1; must 13/29; have to 17/40, 25/24; subj. *skyli* ought 8/12; impers. *skyldi* one needed to 43/1; *hvert er fara skal* wherever it is (required) to go 36/20; in 'gnomic' statements *skal* indicates what is proper or normal, the 'gnomic' shall 8/25, 17/7, 21/1, 23/30. (2) indicating future time: shall, will 9/1, 20/8; *skaltu = skalt þú* 28/17; indicating purpose or intention (subj.) 19/16, 49/12, be about to, try to 38/23, 42/40, be going to 41/19; be supposed to 25/7; future in the past, should, would 23/39, 34/35, 39/2; *skyldu hafa* were to have 44/20; with inf. understood *skyldi* would be 34/37; impers. *nú skal segja þér* now you shall be told 42/34; *eigi skyli* one would not, no one (nothing) would 48/34; *eigi skal fara með hann* it is not to be sailed 36/20. (3) indicating permission: were to 3/15, might 6/7, may 30/1, 39/36.

skutilsveinn *m*. serving boy (or man) 40/36,38.

ský *n*. cloud 12/27,40.

†**skygnask (d)** *wv. md., s. um* be carefully looked round 8/12.

skykkjum *adv.* (dat. pl.) in shakes, with heaving movements 37/37.

skyldr *a.* obliged, under a duty (to do s-thing) 36/31; (*e-m*) *er skylt* it is necessary, proper, a duty (for s-one) 21/6,11, 36/30; *skyldir þjónustumenn* bondservants 37/26.

skyn *n.* understandiing; *kunna s.* (*e-s*) understand, know details, the true nature (of s-thing) 22/18, 25/8; *kunna mesta s.* have the greatest understanding, perception 46/15.

skyndiliga *adv.* hastily 38/39, 44/5.

skynja (að) *wv.* understand, deduce (*af* from, by) 6/26.

skynsamliga *adv.* reasonably, carefully, sensibly 37/17.

skynsemð *f.* wisdom, understanding 4/14, textual note.

skynsemi *f.* wisdom, discernment 22/20 ('it requires great wisdom', or 'it would be very instructive, brings great understanding, it is a matter of great interest').

skýtr pres. of **skjóta**.

slá (sló) *sv.* strike 38/6; *s. e-n hǫgg* strike s-one a blow 39/1; with dat. *s. e-u út* throw, pour s-thing away 49/15; impers. *var slegit eldi í* it was set fire to 46/34.

slátr *n.* meat 40/4,6,7, 43/9.

slefa *f.* saliva 29/9.

sleikja (kt) *wv.* lick 11/10,11.

sléttr *a.* smooth 28/16, 40/15; level 54/32.

slíkr *a.* such 27/33; *slíkt . . . sem* as much . . . as 6/7; n. as subst. *slíkt* such things 36/11; n. as adv. *slíkt sama* similarly 4/6.

slíta (sleit) *sv.* break (trans.), tear apart 28/21,26, 51/28; *s. af* tear off 44/23; *s. upp* pull up, pluck 45/37.

slitna (að) *wv.* break (intrans.) 28/23, 50/1.

slyngja (slǫng) *sv.* with dat., fling 51/4.

slœgð *f.* cunning 27/1.

smár *a.* small 8/36, 35/32.

smíð *f.* structure, construction, work of skill 12/21, 15/9,14; (the work of) building 35/24.

smíða (að) *wv.* make (out of some material), shape 4/14, 8/37; fashion, work (a material) 15/28; *hvernig varð fjǫturrinn smíðaðr* what did the fetter look like 28/15; *varð ekki svá smíðat* not as much building was done 35/25.

smíðarkaup *n.* reward or wages for building work 35/30.

smiðr *m.* builder 34/30, 35/5.

smjúga (smaug, smó) *sv.* creep, squeeze 39/28.

snarr *a.* swift; sup. n. as adv. 49/1.

sneri p. of **snúa**.

snertiróðr (rar) *m.* (short) spurt of rowing 44/29.

sníða (sneið) *sv.* cut 50/40.

snimma *adv.* early 34/29.

snotr (rs) *a.* wise, clever, sensible 30/7.

snúa (snera) *sv.* turn 39/20; *s. til leiðar* bring about 13/1; with dat., turn, direct 29/31. Md., turn and go 8/5, 44/21; direct o-self 50/37; fly (into a rage) 50/2; writhe 51/24; *snúask aptr* turn back 40/18,24, 43/32; *snúask eptir* turn (aside) after, follow 3/5; *snúask til ferðar* set off 42/26.

snær *m.* snow 49/21.

soðinn *pp.* of **sjóða**.

sofa (svaf, *pres.* **sefr)** *sv.* sleep 11/1, 24/10.

sofna (að) *wv.* go to sleep, fall asleep 38/20, 39/3,4.

sól *f.* (the) sun 3/35, 13/2; with def. art. 13/39, 14/8, 20/8, 49/37, 54/20.

sólskin *n. pl.* (periods of) sunshine 14/40.

soltinn *a.* (*pp.* of *svelta*) hungry, starved 43/8.

son, sonr *m.* (*pl.* **synir**) son 4/36, 5/9; the son 24/25, 37/9; pl., †descendants, race 10/28, 12/37.

sortna (að) *wv.* grow black (i.e. be extinguished) 52/29, 54/6.

sótt *f.* sickness 45/22.

sóttdauðr *a.* who has died by sickness 27/16.

sótti p. of **sœkja**.

spá *f.* prophecy 21/19, 27/25, 29/15.

spádómr *m.* the gift of prophecy 5/18, 7/25; pl., prophecies 27/8.

spákona *f.* prophetess 5/7.

spánþak *n.* shingle roof (roof with overlapping wooden tiles) 7/29.

spara (ð) *wv.* save; md., save for o-self 41/18.

spekð *f.* wisdom 4/14, 17/16.

speki *f.* wisdom 3/16, 4/25, 5/17, 25/20; branch, kind of learning 27/1.

speni *m.* teat 11/7, 33/13.

spenna (t) *wv.* with dat., gird on, put round, fasten 23/7; *s. sik e-u* gird o-self with s-thing 38/4.

spilla (t) *wv.* with dat., spoil, destroy, injure 35/12, 49/30; md., be spoiled 15/31.

sporðr *m.* tail (of a fish or snake) 27/14, 43/21, 49/3; end (of bridge) 20/3.

spori *m.* spur 47/21.

spotta (að) *wv.* mock, make a laughing-stock of 44/36.

sprakk see **springa**.

spretta (1) (tt) *wv.* split (trans.); *s. á* (adv.) *e-u* make a split in (s-thing), split (s-thing) open with s-thing 37/12.

spretta (2) (spratt) *sv.* spring 3/21, 44/10.

springa (sprakk) *sv.* burst; be overcome by shock 46/33.

spurall *a.* having a questioning nature 29/39.

spurning *f.* question 32/11.

spurt *pp.* of **spyrja**.

spyrja (spurða) *wv.* ask (*e-n* s-one; *ef, hvárt* whether) 8/2,20, 35/11, 38/13; learn, find out (by asking) 3/33, 8/22; *spyrðu = spyrr þú* you ask (*at* whether, or imagining that) 33/6; *s. hverjum* ask with whom 31/11; *eigi er nú fróðliga spurt* that is not an intelligent question 15/5; with gen., ask s-thing 33/29, learn, hear s-thing 39/33; *s. e-n e-s* ask s-one s-thing 36/33; *s. e-n nafns* or *at nafni* ask s-one his name 7/36, 8/3; *s. til e-s* get information about 6/5.

spyrna (d) *wv.* kick 28/39; *s. fœti á* kick (with the foot) against, at 46/36; *s. við (e-u)* kick out (against s-thing), push with the feet (against s-thing) 27/29, 44/40.

spǫlr *m.* rail, bar 39/28.

staðr *m.* place 4/24,28, 20/25 (pl.); position 12/11,18; *í þeim stað* that place 15/24 (cf. place-names formed with preps., see *Two Icelandic Stories*, ed. A. Faulkes, London 1967, p. 96, note to 2/85–6); *í tvá staði* into two sections 48/37; *gefa, nema staðar* stop 7/7, 10/3, 49/3; *gefa e-u stað* or *staðar* stop s-thing 5/25, fix s-thing 12/9.

standa (stóð) *sv.* stand 19/26, 45/38; imp. *stattu* 8/24; pres. p. *standandi* (yet still) standing 51/11; be situated 15/22; extend 17/11; *s. af. e-u* arise from s-thing, come from s-thing (*e-m* for s-one) 10/4,10, 27/9; *s. at* stand by 46/34; *s. til hjarta e-m* stick in s-one's heart 52/18; *s. undan* come from under 20/31; *s. upp* get up 37/13, stand up 50/22; *s. við* withstand 43/23.

stara (ð) *wv.* stare 45/4.

stattu see **standa**.

steði *m.* anvil 15/27.

steðr pl. of **stoð**.

stefna (d) *wv.* direct one's steps, make for (*í, móti*) 39/18, 50/28.

steikari *m.* cook 32/13.

†**steindyrr** *f. pl.* doorway(s), entrance(s) in rocks (i.e. to dwarfs' dwellings) 51/19.

steinn *m.* stone 3/28, 11/11; rock 15/37.

sterkleikr *m.* physical strength 13/21.

sterkliga *adv*. mightily 38/3.

sterkr *a*. (*acc. sg. m.* **sterkjan**) strong 15/8, 20/26; mighty, powerful 35/5; stout 44/33; comp. 27/31; sup. 22/31.

steypask (t) *wv. md.* plunge 45/12; fall in ruins 49/36.

stíga (steig, sté) *sv*. step 38/26, 50/38; *s. stórum* take large steps 38/18; *s. á* mount 46/21; *s. af* dismount from 47/19; *s. upp* mount 47/20.

stigr *m*. path 54/21 (pl.).

stikill *m*. point 41/14.

stilla (t) *wv*. control, moderate, regulate 4/1, 23/29.

stjarna *f*. star 12/17, 49/39, 52/32.

stjórna (að) *wv*. with dat., rule, control 8/35.

stjórnari *m*. controller 4/1.

stjórnarmaðr *m*. ruler, governor 15/19.

stjúpsonr *m*. stepson 26/20.

stoð *f*. (*pl.* **steðr**) support, post, pillar 20/1.

stólpi *m*. pillar 20/1.

stórliga *adv*. arrogantly 39/15.

stórmenni *n*. (collective) great (big) men 42/6.

stórmerki *n*. notable thing 18/28; mystery, sacrament 3/13.

stormr *m*. storm 4/7 (perhaps an error for *straumi*, see **straumr**).

stórr *a*. great 5/38; large 33/30; important 45/18; dat. pl. as adv., mightily, with large steps 38/18; comp. *stœrri* bigger 39/13.

stórsmíði *n*. mighty piece of work 27/33 (pl.).

stórtíðindi *n. pl.* important events 22/27.

stórvirki *n. pl.* mighty deeds, achievements 23/10, 40/34, 55/4.

stótt 2nd pers. sg. p. of **standa**.

straumr *m*. current 53/26.

strjúka (strauk) *sv*. rub, stroke (*of* over, i.e. with the hand) 39/6.

strǫnd *f*. shore 12/23, 13/4.

stukku p. pl. of **støkkva (1)**.

stund *f*. a period of time; an hour 23/11; pl., time, ages 3/4, 55/1.

styðja (studda) *wv*. support; pp. 26/29.

†**stynja (stunða)** *wv*. groan 51/18.

stýra (ð) *wv*. with dat., control 13/34, 14/3; steer, be captain of 50/8, 51/33; (have at one's) command 34/2.

stýrandi *m*. (*pres. p.*) controller 11/17 (see AH *Studier* 25).

styrkr *a*. (= **sterkr**) strong 26/11.

stǫng *f.* pole (for two people to carry s-thing between them) 14/6 **(see note)**.

støkkva (1) (stǫkk) *sv.* fly, shoot (in a spray) 10/31.

støkkva (2) (kt) *wv.* sprinkle, bespatter (*e-u* with s-thing) 14/25 (future).

suðr (1) *n.* south 4/16,21.

suðr (2) *adv.* south (*frá* of) 20/21.

suðrhálfa *f.* southern region 9/25.

sumar *n.* summer 15/1 (pl.), 21/1.

sumr *a. pron.* some 3/19, 14/2; pl., some of them 6/23 (sc. *tóku kvánfǫng*), 12/10; some people 3/4, 18/24, 26/34.

sund *n.* sound, strait 7/8 (i.e. Øresund).

sundr *adv.* apart 28/28; *í s.* apart 28/26.

†sundrborinn *a.* (*pp.*) of different parentage or descent 18/17.

sunnan *adv.* from the south 9/31, 51/38.

sunnanverðr *a.* southern, southerly 20/7.

svá *adv.* so 31/14; such 21/3; thus 15/11; this 44/31; as follows 9/22; likewise 5/18; also 6/19, 40/7, 48/13; similarly 43/6; *svá eru ok dýr* it is also thus with animals 3/22; *svá hart ok yfir* 47/21 see **ok**; *svá . . . ok* thus . . . so that 31/33; *þat . . . svá . . . hvárt* it (should be tested) in the following manner, whether . . . 47/26; *en svá* than this (than you) 40/22. With *at*: so that, so . . . that 3/11,16; such . . . that 54/12; thus . . . that 3/13, 4/14, this, that 3/29, this . . . that 20/21, 44/35; as follows, that 42/20; to such an extent that 4/20; *sterkr svá at* so strong that 20/26; *vitr svá at* so wise that 25/13, cf. 23/15–16; sufficiently . . . to 32/12; . . . enough to 43/25; in such a way that 7/14; in such a way as to 35/13; so much that 49/40; of such a kind that 49/23; such that 22/33; it being the case that 53/35; when 31/36; in asserverations, so . . . inasmuch as 34/1. With *sem*: (just) as 6/19, 42/5; thus . . . as, in the way that 6/14; like 10/2; corresponding to 7/10; in proportion as 4/12; as much as 35/25; to the same extent as 42/1; as . . . as 4/39, 28/17; as if 14/8, 28/25; as though (= that) 41/7; in the form of, in the pattern of 7/29; in the way in which 48/22; having assumed the appearance of 44/7; such . . . as 40/33; *svá sem hon er sterk* (*þá*) strong as it is (yet) 15/9; *svá lítinn sem þér kallið mik* (*þá*) little as you say I am, however little . . . (nevertheless) 42/7, cf. 21/17; in accordance with the fact that 47/38; *svá sem . . . svá* just as . . . so also 10/10, in proportion as . . . so 4/23; *svá . . . sem . . . at* this . . . which . . . that 38/23; *svá . . . ef . . . sem* this . . . if . . . that 41/19; *svá langt upp sem hann mátti lengst* as far up as the furthest he could 42/2.

svaf see **sofa**.

svalbrjóstaðr *a.* (*pp.*) cold-hearted 21/10.

svalr *a.* cool, cold 9/15.

svanr *m.* swan 19/30, 24/8. Originally the male swan (the female being *álpt*), but normally only found in poetry. See AH *Studier* 47–8.

svar *n.* reply 31/13.

svara (að) *wv.* answer, reply 8/2,18; *s. øngu* make no reply 41/12.

svardagi *m.* oath, vow, solemn promise 45/20.

svartr *a.* black 13/23, 14/40 (dark); comp. 19/38.

svásligr *a.* delightful 21/8.

†sváss *a.* dear 52/40.

svefn *m.* sleep 25/37.

sveinn *m.* boy 41/35; servant (follower?) or son 46/20 (T, W, and U have *son*(*r*) here; *sveinn* normally has the meaning 'son' only in poetry, but at 47/23 Hermóðr is called brother of Baldr).

sveinstauli *m.* little boy 39/34, 40/16.

sveiti *m.* sweat; *fá sveita* to sweat 11/1; †blood? 12/30 (cf. 11/36).

svelgja (svalg) *sv.* swallow 41/4.

sverð *n.* sword 26/1, 29/7.

sverja (svarða) *wv.* swear (an oath) 35/17.

sviði *m.* burning pain, severe pain 33/10.

†svigi *m.* stick 9/32, 51/39 (cf. **læ**).

svima (svam) *sv.* swim 15/10.

svipting *f.* sharp pulling back and forth, wrenching, jerking 42/18.

†svæfa (ð) *wv.* lull to sleep (metaphorically), i.e. settle 26/33.

syðri *a. comp.* more southerly 4/17, 10/8.

syn *f.* denial (cf. **synja**) 30/3.

sýn *f.* sight; dat. pl., in appearance 19/36,37, 26/38.

sýna (d) *wv.* show 28/20; md., seem, look, appear (*e-m* to s-one) 28/27, 40/8, 41/3, 43/19.

syni dat. sg. of **sonr**; **synir** nom. pl. of **sonr**.

synja (að) *wv.* refuse; *s. e-m at* refuse to let s-one (do s-thing), prevent s-one from 35/30 (i.e. forced him to leave the world).

systir *f.* (*pl.* **systr**) sister 25/33.

systkin *n. pl.* brother(s) and sister(s) 13/38, 27/7,8, 29/12.

systrungar *m. pl.* cousins (on the mother's side), sons of sisters 49/29.

sæfarar *f. pl.* sea journeys, seafaring 23/30.

sæing *f.* bed 27/20.

sæla *f.* happiness, prosperity 3/15.

sællífr *a.* having a blissful life 21/7.

sær, sjár (*gen.* **sævar, sjávar**) *m.* sea 6/16, 9/14; *sævarins* to do with the sea 4/9.

sæti *n.* seat, throne 15/22,32, 20/6, 31/7; place (in a hall, for sitting, eating, and sleeping) 42/22.

sætt *f.* agreement, reconciliation; *hvat varð um þeira s.* how did they get on together 11/20; means of agreement, terms, pledge of truce 23/34; (payment in) settlement, atonement, indemnity 37/25.

sættask (tt) *wv. md.*, *s. á þat at* come to an agreement that, settle on this, that 23/39.

sættir *m.* reconciler, bringer of concord (with gen., between) 25/19.

sævargangr, sjávargangr *m.* surge of sea 3/6, 50/7.

sœkja (sótta) *wv.* pursue 14/12; prosecute, press, achieve, gain 28/1; make one's way (*fram* forward, i.e. advance; *upp* ashore) 50/3,17; *s. at e-u* (*s. e-t*) attend s-thing 46/38; *s. til e-s* obtain s-thing 8/1. Md., be advanced, progress 35/8, 44/27.

sœmð *f.* honour 46/4.

sœri *n.* oath 35/6, 36/5.

sǫk *f.* cause, reason 3/32, 5/21; *þessi sǫk er til er* this is the reason why 31/33; lawsuit, dispute 26/33; *fyrir e-s sakar* because of, for the sake of s-one 31/16; through, out of s-thing 49/25; as far as s-thing was concerned, to judge from s-thing 28/22; as a result of or as regards s-thing 36/26; *sǫkum e-s* because of s-thing 4/20, textual note.

sǫngr *m.* (*dat.* **sǫngvi**) song, music 24/8.

søkkva (sǫkk) *sv.* sink 38/35, 39/5, 52/30.

søkkvask (kt) *wv. md.* (let o-self) sink, slide back 45/8.

†**-t** *neg. suffix* with vbs. 18/19.

tá *f.* toe 50/40.

taka (tók) *sv.* take 7/4, 11/35; receive 28/33; accept 37/25; obtain 45/20; get 27/11; bring out 40/37; catch 14/15; capture 49/5; take hold of, grasp 45/37; reach, touch 43/21; perform, undertake 40/17; *t. sér* (. . . *sonum sínum*) find o-self (for their sons) 6/22; *t. kviknun* come to life 15/34; *t. at* with inf., begin to 41/4, 42/17; *tók ok leysti* went and undid 38/14, similarly 48/28 (cf. **fara**); *t. e-t af* choose s-thing: *þann* (sc. *kost*) *ætla ek yðr betra* (sc. *vera*) *af at t.* this alternative is I think the better one for you to choose 39/17; *t. til at* set to work to 35/2; *t. til e-s* touch s-one, pick s-one up 46/9; *t. e-t til* undertake s-thing 40/34; *t. um* get one's hand round 49/2; *t. undir e-t* take hold underneath s-thing 41/40; *t. upp* pick up 13/5; *t. upp hǫndum* put out (up) one's arms 31/4; *t. við e-u* take possession of 4/39; *t. við e-m* oppose s-one, stop s-one's advance 6/16.

tal *n*. conversation, discussion 34/34, 54/36.

tala (1) *f*. speech, account 43/30.

tala (2) (að) *wv*. talk; md. *talask við* talk together 53/39.

talaðr *a*. (*pp*.) spoken, having speech of a certain kind 23/19.

talðr, taliðr see **telja**.

tár *n*. tear 29/27 (pl., cf. note to 29/26), 48/5.

taumr *m*. rein 46/26.

tennr pl. of **tǫnn**.

telja (talða, *pp*. **taliðr, talðr)** *wv*. reckon, count 3/34, 26/34; trace 3/32, 6/18; number, enumerate 18/36; recount 23/10; declare (with *at*-clause) 37/16, (with acc. and inf.) 27/32. Md., say that one is, consider o-self 27/37.

tíðast see **títt**.

tíðindi *n. pl*. tidings, news, information 12/20, 19/32, 32/33; account(s), tale(s) 23/10, 37/1; events 13/11, 45/14; *þat er til tíðinda* this (noteworthy event) takes (will take) place 49/40.

tiginn *a*. noble, of high rank; sup. 29/24.

tigna (að) *wv*. honour (*af* with) 4/25, 5/20.

tignarnafn *n*. (honourable) title 25/3.

tigr, tøgr *m*. (set of) ten; *fjórir tigir* forty 22/33; similarly 22/36, 33/35.

til (1) *adv*. too 10/35, 41/9.

til (2) *prep*. with gen., (1) direction or distance: to 3/23, 4/18, 17/36, 40/24; towards 17/15, 43/32; about 6/5; to the home of 37/5. (2) purpose: for 3/22, 9/28, 47/32; as 28/14, 30/4; for the purpose of 22/23 (2); to obtain 23/32; to indicate 34/15; giving rise to 22/24; *til þess at* in order that 4/9, to this effect that 45/20; *þar til landa* over those territories 6/1; *gott til* plenty of 37/32. (3) time: until 25/26, 35/10; *til þess er* until 43/34. (4) as adv., direction or destination: to that place 10/14; up to it 41/40; there, to them 27/11; up to me, them 42/7,19; *til hvar* towards where 46/4; *þar til er* to where 6/16, (time) until 47/19; purpose, for it 35/19; *þar til* for them or in addition 15/27; *vera til* be available 4/30; *til at* for this (purpose) that 43/21, in order to 13/39, so as to 12/9, enough to 27/23, designed to 48/28; *til er* for this that 31/33.

tilkváma *f*. coming, arrival 15/31.

tilvísun *f*. guidance, direction 46/6.

tími *m*. prosperity, success 6/8.

títt n. of **tíðr** *a*. frequent; of concern (to s-one); *hvat er t. um þik* what is the matter with you, what are you up to 38/37; as adv., eagerly, strongly, quickly 38/34, 43/8; sup. *tíðast* 40/5.

tíu *num*. ten 4/38, 5/2.

tíundi *ord. num.* (the) tenth 8/32, 17/35, 29/39.

†tjúgari *m.* snatcher, destroyer 14/34.

tól *n.* tool 15/28.

tólf *num.* twelve 4/30, 5/1, 6/13.

tólfti *ord. num.* (the) twelfth 8/32, 30/4.

topt *f.* site (of a dwelling) 24/24 (pl., collective?).

traust *n.* support, reliability, protection, help 26/17.

traustr *a.* reliable 28/17; comp. 28/22.

tré *n.* tree 17/10, 33/12; wood 15/29; log 13/5.

tréna (að) *wv.* harden, dry up, die 19/16.

treysta (st) *wv.* use (all) one's strength on, pull hard at 28/23. Md., rely on (with dat.); *treystask sér* be confident, be safe 15/16.

†troða (trað) *sv.* tread (trans.) 9/37, 52/3.

trog *n.* utensil (characteristically of wood and square or oblong in shape) such as was used for separating cream from milk; a large kitchen tray for serving food 40/3,6,7, 43/9 (in many stories such a utensil is associated with trolls and monsters).

tros *n.* brushwood, rubbish 39/9.

trúa (1) *f.* (*gen. sg.* **trú**) belief, faith 11/16, 34/2; *þat veit t. mín at* by my faith 22/17, 28/10, 31/38, 33/8, 42/36, 43/12. This expression is not recorded in other early texts but becomes common in romance sagas; it is apparently a hybrid of *þat veit guð* and *par moi foi* (cf. *þat veit guð ok trú mín, Strengleikar*, ed. R. Cook and M. Tveitane, Oslo 1979, p. 94). It probably originated in learned style rather than in colloquial usage. See AH *Studier* 20–21 and *Medieval Scandinavia* 4 (1971), 34–5.

trúa (2) (ð) *wv.* believe 4/8, 6/9; with two acc., believe s-one to be s-thing 10/37; *t. e-u* believe s-thing 36/31,36; *t. e-m at* trust s-one to, have faith in s-one that 25/16, 40/26; *er ek munda eigi t. at vera mætti* which I would not have believed could happen 43/13; *t. á* believe in 21/12; pp. *rétt trúaðr* orthodox 3/5. (Cf. AH *Studier* 18.)

trúnaðr *m.* good faith, integrity 15/12, 25/28.

trúr *a.* reliable 34/31.

tryggr *a.* (*n.* **trygt**) safe 35/6.

trǫll *n.* troll, monster 14/35, 35/8.

trǫllkona *f.* troll-wife 14/20.

tún *n.* (enclosed) dwelling, courtyard; pl., courts 34/9.

tunga *f.* language 4/12, 6/25,27,30, 22/22,23; tongue 18/36.

tungl *n.* heavenly body (cf. **himintungl**); in sg. usually = the moon 13/34, 14/3,16, 35/13,30, 49/38; at 14/24 the word could be pl., and at 14/34 probably means the sun. See note to 14/14–7.

tveir *num.* (*gen.* **tveggja**) two 3/2, 13/5, 48/32.

týhraustr *a.* valiant as Týr 25/12 (or divinely valiant? see Týr in index of names. The compound is not found elsewhere in Old Icelandic, but cf. *týframr* 'divinely bold or excellent', *SnE* I. 306 (*Haustlǫng*), and *týmargr*, *Hkr* III. 53 (Þjóðólfr Arnórsson), where the first element may be simply an intensive like *regin*-).

týna (d) *wv.* with dat., lose 14/25 (future); forget 3/13. Md., perish, be destroyed 9/1.

týspakr *a.* wise as Týr 25/14 (not elsewhere in Old Icelandic; see under **týhraustr**).

tǫng *f.* tongs 15/27.

tǫnn *f.* (*pl.* **tennr**) tooth 3/28, 11/38.

tøgr = **tigr**.

úlfliðr *m.* wrist (wolf-joint) 25/18.

úlfr *m.* wolf 14/14, 24/6; often = Fenrir, e.g. 25/17, 27/23, 28/20, 32/9, 50/13,37, 51/3, 52/8,14.

ull *f.* wool 25/39.

um, umb *prep.* with acc., over 3/3, 4/21, 6/24, 17/31; across 34/32; through 5/4; throughout 49/24; round 6/17, 23/7, 27/12; concerning, with (regard to) 4/34, 38/38; about 40/34, 54/1; *um fram* see **fram**; of time, during 35/24, 48/18, in 37/5; with dat. 22/36 = **of** (4). As adv., around, round 8/8,12, 54/32; about it 34/13 (or *meir um* the more?).

umhverfis *prep.* with acc., around 12/24, 13/29.

umsjár *m.* the surrounding sea, ocean 45/11 (cf. 6/16–17, 12/2,22, 27/12; and see AH *Studier* 33).

una (ð) *wv.* with dat., be content with; *u. e-u illa* find s-thing hard to bear 42/33.

†und = **undir** 19/6.

undan *adv.* away (from some threat) 11/24, 14/12, 35/23 (vb. of motion understood); prep. with dat., from under 20/31.

undarliga *adv.* strangely, wonderfully 20/28; surprising(ly) 41/31; *u. spyrðu* you are asking a strange question 33/6.

undarligr *a.* surprising 14/11, 23/5; marvellous 33/26, 54/20.

undinn *pp.* of **vinda**.

undir *prep.* with acc., under 11/1, 12/5; with dat., beneath 12/10, 13/9; dependent on 25/27; as adv., underneath 48/34.

undr *n.* marvel 35/4, 43/12; *u. mikit er* (it is) a great marvel that, how strange that 31/35.

undrask (að) *wv. md.* be amazed at 3/18, 7/20.

ungmenni *n.* young person 44/12.

ungr *a.* young 5/22, 25/25; sup. *in yngsta* the youngest 30/35.

unnit *pp.* of **vinna**.

†**unnr** *f.* wave 9/15, 51/26.

†**unz** *conj.* until 10/32.

upp *adv.* up 3/21, 7/3; ashore 37/30; aboard 44/32; (go) up 41/14; *upp frá* above 8/16, 20/21,23.

uppfœzla *f.* fostering; *vera at uppfœzlu með* be brought up by 4/37.

upphaf *n.* beginning 9/9, 15/19, 37/3.

†**upphiminn** *m.* the sky above 9/17.

uppi *adv.* up; current, in remembrance 5/19; *u. á* up on top of 33/12.

uppspretta *f.* spring 10/1.

úr *n.* misty rain, condensation, moisture 10/3,7.

urð *f.* heap of stones, scree 11/38.

urðu p. pl. of **verða**.

út *adv.* out 7/7, 8/23, 28/19.

útan *adv.* (on the) outside 15/23; round the edge 12/22 (1); back (to shore) 44/17; *ú. um e-t* round the outside of s-thing 12/2; *þar ú. um* around it 12/22.

útar *adv. comp.* further out, on the side nearer the doors; *ú. frá* beyond 37/10; *ú. á bekkinn* further down the bench (towards the doors, where the lower-ranking seats were) 40/2; further out to sea 44/30.

útarliga *adv.* far out (from land) 44/14; towards the outside, at the edge 45/38.

úti *adv.* outside, out of doors 54/32.

útlausn *f.* ransom 46/18.

útlendr *a.* foreign, alien, not native 9/27.

útvegr *m.* escape, way out 14/12.

uxi *m.* (*pl.* **øxn**) ox 7/3, 44/22,23.

vá p. of **vega**.

vaða (**óð**) *sv.* wade (with acc., in or through s-thing) 17/36, 45/13, 53/16,25.

vaðr *m.* fishing-line 44/33, 45/8.

vaka (**ð**) *wv.* be awake 39/10.

vakna (**að**) *wv.* wake up 38/5,28.

vald *n.* power 6/7, 43/29 (*á e-m* over s-one); authority 27/14.

valda (**olla**) *irreg. vb.* with dat., cause, be the reason for 7/23; be the cause of, be responsible for 18/27, 48/12; have power over, rule 26/4.

†**valdýr** *n.* slaughterous (or carrion) beast (i.e. Fenrir) 52/16.

valkyrja *f.* valkyrie (lit. chooser of the slain) 30/34, 46/39.

valr *m.* the slain in battle 24/31, 30/36, 34/11; *falla í val* die in battle 21/28.

†**valrauf** *f.* spoils, plunder (lit. from the slain); *v. vineyjar* (descriptive gen.) plundered island of meadows 7/19.

†**valtívi** *m.* god of slain 9/34, 51/41 (either gen. sg. = of Surtr, or gen. pl. = of the Æsir; and either with *sverði* or with *sól*; if the latter, *sól* could be dat. in apposition to *sverði*, and *sól valtíva* could be a kenning for sword (cf. *SnE* ι. 208); *skínn* would then be impers.).

†**vályndr** *a.* evil-natured, hostile 15/2.

ván *f.* hope, expectation; *e-m er v. e-s* s-one can expect s-thing 29/13; *kvað illra svara vera v.* said one could expect unpleasant replies 31/13; *sem v. var* as was to be expected 37/23, 48/16; *þess meiri v. at* it was more (very, quite) likely that 40/12 (cf. **líkr**).

vandahús *n.* wattled house 53/14.

vandliga *adv.* carefully, in detail 22/20.

vándr *a.* wicked 9/4.

vandræði *n.* difficulty, trouble, strait, fix 27/2; *tvau v.* a dilemma 28/37.

vangi *m.* cheek, side of the head 39/7.

vanr *a.* accustomed 6/15 (to), 40/37 (*at* to).

vápn *n.* weapon 8/7, 36/18.

vápngafigr *a.* (= -*gǫfugr*; thus W and PE) splendidly, gloriously armed 32/30.

vápnlauss *a.* without a weapon 31/33, 46/2.

vara (ð) *wv. impers.*, *e-n varir* s-one expects 42/5.

várar *f. pl.* plighted troth 29/38.

varðveita (tt) *wv.* keep 25/24.

vargr *m.* wolf 14/21, 46/26, 49/8 (perhaps not synonymous with *úlfr* in spite of *Heiðreks saga* 81: *vargr* often seems to have associations with the supernatural or with shape-changing, and also means outlaw, accursed criminal. In *Strengleikar*, ed. R. Cook and M. Tveitane, Oslo 1979, p. 86, *vargúlfr* is used to mean werewolf).

†**vargǫld** *f.* age of wolves (or criminals) 49/35.

varka see **vera**, **-k**, and **-a**.

varla *adv.* hardly 7/28.

varliga *adv.* scarcely, i.e. not quite? 43/20.

varnan *f.* (pre-)caution, taking care to avoid (*ef* lest) 50/5.

varr *a.* (*f.* vǫr) with gen., aware (of s-thing) 29/40.

várr *poss. a.* our 8/28; †pl. *órar* 10/33.

vásk md. p. of **vega**.

vatn *n.* (*gen. sg.* **vaz**) water 3/21,22, 19/15, 33/5; pl. *vǫtn* 18/6; lake 7/9, 11/37 (pl.), 28/19.

vaxa (óx, *pres.* **vex)** sv. grow 3/24, 4/20, 27/13; *e-m vex* there grows on or in s-one 3/25, 38/5; *óx* it grew, there was growth 10/32.

vaz gen. of **vatn**.

vazdrykkr *m.* drink of water, water to drink 33/9.

vaztir *f. pl.* fishing-ground 44/28.

vé *n.* sanctuary, dwelling-place of a god 26/4, 29/14, 54/5.

veð *n.* pledge (*e-m* to s-one) 17/20, 25/17, 28/35.

veðr (1) pres. of **vaða**.

veðr (2) *n.* weather, esp. wind 15/2 (pl.); gen. pl. *veðranna* relating to the weather (winds) 4/9.

vefja (vafða) *wv.* wrap; *hann má v. saman* one can fold it up 36/21.

vega (vá) *sv.* fight, wield a weapon (*við* against) 52/8,14; *v. með* fight against? 33/39 (W and U have the more usual *við* here); kill 48/13; *v. í* pierce, cut into 44/38; md., wield itself, fight on its own 31/22.

†**veggberg** *n.* cliff 51/20.

veggr *m.* wall 20/1.

vegr *m.* way, direction; *á hvern* (*hverjan*) *veg* each way 50/21, 53/2; *hvern veg frá sér* in every direction from himself, i.e. all round him 54/31; *of veg* forward, on his way? 52/15; distance 39/33 (1); manner 21/31; *annan veg en* otherwise than 39/33 (i.e. 'can it really be true?').

veiðr *f.* hunting, fishing 23/30.

veita (tt) *wv.* give 3/15; pay 46/3; *v. sín á milli* exchange 29/37; *v. e-m atgǫngu* make, bring an attack against s-one, attack s-one 35/17.

vekja (vakða) *wv.* wake (trans.) 24/13, 50/23.

vel *adv.* well 18/26, 31/19; heartily 28/18; highly 40/12; a lot 25/4; thoroughly, successfully 48/1; easily 20/29, 39/15; without hesitation, with propriety 11/18.

velli dat. sg. of **vǫllr**.

vendi dat. sg. of **vǫndr**.

†**véorr** *m.* protector (i.e. Þórr) 52/28 (or perhaps 'encircler', i.e. Miðgarðsormr; but Þórr is called Véorr in *Hym* 11, 17, 21).

vera (var) *sv.* be 3/10; pres. for future 14/26; with suffixed neg. *vara* 9/14, suffixed pron. *erumk = eru mér* 24/3, suffixed pron. and neg. *varka* 24/4 (see **-k, -a**); *ertu = ert þú* 21/21; *verit hafa* have been in existence 4/4, have lived 4/33; *þar hafi verit* it was 48/10; *næst var þat* the next thing to happen was 11/6; *þat eru* it consists of 50/39; *þetta eru* these are 12/20; *aldri er* there can never be 32/9; *þér er at* it is for you to 37/2;

þat er at segja this is to be told 47/7; *vera mun at segja* no doubt there are to be told 45/16; *hvat er* what is up 38/37, 51/14; *sem um þenna mun vera* that the case will be with this one 41/23; *er honum* serves for him as 32/25. With pp. forming passive 4/16, 5/24, forming perfect of intrans. vbs. 3/2, 9/41; *v. at e-m* be forthcoming from s-one 44/12; *v. frá* be descended from 10/18; *v. fyrir* be there (in the way) 48/33; *v. við* enjoy, possess 3/16.

veraldligr *a.* worldly, textual notes to 3/15 and 4/34.

verða (varð) *sv.* happen 3/9; take place 37/36; become 6/23, 27/32; turn into 10/2; turn out to be 21/4, 28/16; come to be 14/23 (future), 32/8; turn out 42/29; come, be produced 33/20; come into being 9/39, 10/14; appear 37/31; exist 43/24,25; *e-m mun seint verða at* it will be long before one 28/33. With pp. forming passive 28/14, 48/13, 50/7, impers. passive 35/25,26,28, 48/14; with *at* and inf. need to, have to 27/36; *v. af* be caused by 28/9, result from 44/26; *v. at* turn into 49/11, fulfil the role of, become (the instrument of) 23/34, 29/16, md. reciprocal (to each other) 49/28; *v. fyrir* meet, become subject to 18/27; *v. til* give rise to, be the origin of 22/18, offer o-self for, undertake 46/20.

verðr *a.* with gen., deserving (of s-thing) 15/14, 35/15; worth, of value to observe 50/5; *minna vert* less impressive 43/17; *meira vert* more significant 45/17.

verja (varða) *wv.* defend 38/1, 43/28.

verk *n.* work 34/38, 35/26; labour 38/25; deed, act 15/22, 46/11.

verr *adv. comp.* worse, less (well) 32/1.

verri *a. comp.* worse; n. as subst. or adv. 27/10.

verst *adv. sup.* worst; with least equanimity 46/14.

verstr *a. sup.* worst 53/29.

verǫld *f.* world 3/10, 9/29.

vestan *adv.* from the west; *fyrir v.* with acc., west of 45/35.

vestr (1) *n.* west 4/16,18.

vestr (2) *adv.* westwards 7/7.

vetr *m.* (*pl.* **vetr**) winter 21/2, 35/8; year 3/34; *tíu vetra* ten years old 4/38.

vex pres. of **vaxa**.

vexti dat. sg. of **vǫxtr**.

við *prep.* (1) with acc., with 34/35; against, in competition with 40/10, 42/8, (in opposition to) 31/33, 52/8; in contact with, in connection with 23/9; against, on 27/28, 52/36; by the side of 18/12, 25/35; near 25/36; at 49/3. (2) with dat., against, in contact with 45/10, 50/9,10 (touching?). (3) as adv., with (in possession of) 3/15; in reply 15/5, 25/29, at him 35/21.

víða *adv.* widely, in many places 5/4; extensively 5/27; sup., in most places 3/13.

viðarteinungr *m.* shoot of a tree 45/35.

viðbragð *n.* (re-)action, push, (quick) movement (against s-thing), touch 46/29.

†víðir *m.* ocean 24/14.

viðr *m.* tree 33/17, 45/22.

víðr *a.* wide, large 7/18, 50/21 (with gen. of extent); extensive 43/33.

viðskipti *n. pl.* dealings 42/31.

víg *n.* battle 24/30, 34/12, 50/34; †*vígi at* in battle 52/39; pl., killings (in battle) 30/36.

vígja (gð) *wv.* consecrate, bless 37/14, 46/34.

†vígþrot *n.* end of (or in?) battle 54/9 ('when V. fights no more').

vík *f.* (*pl.* **víkr**) bay 7/10.

vili *m.* (*dat.* **vilja**) wish 4/2, 7/21.

vilja (ld) *wv.* (*3rd. sg. pres.* **vil, vill**) want, wish 3/12, 6/7; *viltu = vilt þú* 41/29; be willing 21/5, 28/38, 31/19; be desirous (to) 46/17; intend (to) 41/11; be going (to) 38/20; try (to) 29/7; *v. eigi* refuse 25/17, 47/30; *v. ekki* (with inanimate subject) will not 41/14 (inf. understood); with *at*-clause, desire 30/26 (with subject of clause preceding), 50/7 (with adv. *seint* preceding clause).

villieldr *m.* wildfire (magical, deceptive fire?) 43/9.

vín *n.* wine 32/24,29.

vinda (vatt) *sv.* twist, weave, entwine (*e-u* with or out of s-thing) 53/23.

vindbelgr *m.* bellows 14/2.

vindlauss *a.* without wind, still 10/12.

vindr *m.* wind 4/6, 14/26, 20/31, 49/22.

†vindǫld *f.* age of wind 49/35.

†viney *f.* meadow-island 7/18 (descriptive gen. with *valrauf*).

vinna (vann, *pp.* **unnit)** *sv.* do, achieve 8/34, 45/15; perform, commit, bring about 36/8, 46/8; *v. eið* swear an oath, give a solemn promise 45/34; win 40/20,27; *v. sigr á* win victory over (it) 36/30. Md. *vinnask e-m til* last s-one for it (i.e. for drinking) 41/13, be sufficient for s-one (*at* so that) 43/20.

vinstri *a. comp.* left 11/1.

virða (ð) *wv.* value; *v. mikils* value highly 29/14; *v. e-t vel* judge s-thing leniently, favourably, consider s-thing acceptable 21/5.

vísa (að) *wv.* with dat. *v. e-m til* direct, show s-one to 42/21, direct, point s-one towards 46/4.

vísindi *n. pl.* knowledge, science, learning 5/19, 17/17; lore, sources 12/11 (see note).

víss *a.* wise, well-informed 32/12; *verða v. e-s* find out about s-thing 29/40, 32/35; pl. †*vísir e-s* those well-acquainted with s-thing, frequenters of 51/20; n. *víst* certain 44/17; n. as subst. *at vísu* indeed, certainly 28/13, *til víss* for certain 35/27; comp. *því vísari at* the wiser, the better informed, inasmuch as 7/25.

vist *f.* food 32/23,24, 33/5; lodging-place 53/8 ('mansion': *vist* translates *mansio* at *John* 14.2 in *Heilagra manna søgur*, ed. C. R. Unger, Christiania 1877, I. 249); pl., provisions 27/15 (or lodgings?), 32/5, 37/33.

vit *n.* intelligence 6/11; consciousness 13/6.

vita (veit, vissa) *pret. pres. vb.* (1) know 3/30, 8/13; understand 13/14, 51/21; realise 18/40; imagine 37/18; *veiztu = veizt þú* 34/27; *v. e-t með e-m* share (be privy to) the knowledge of s-thing with s-one 29/23; with acc. and inf. 20/11, 23/26; with inf. understood, know s-one or s-thing to be s-thing: *sá maðr er vér vitum mestan* the greatest being we know (of) 11/18; *ask veit ek ausinn* I know an ash (that is) laved 19/20; *míns veit ek mest magar* I know my son's (to be) the greatest 22/40; with *at* and inf., be able to, have the knowledge to be able to 21/3, 36/36 (*tíðindi* is object of *segja*); *v. til at* know about this, that, find out that 27/7; pp., proved, confirmed, tested and found true 45/23; *vitaðr e-m* marked out, destined for s-one, allotted to s-one 53/3. (2) face 53/15; *v. upp* face upwards 39/5; be on the side facing 10/11; *þat er vissi til norðrs ættar* the part which faced in a northerly direction 10/6.

vitandi *a.* (*pres. p.*) conscious 15/36; *margs v.* having wide knowledge 18/31.

vítishorn *n.* sconce-horn, forfeit horn 40/37 (*víti* n., punishment; a *vítishorn* was a large horn which a feaster would be required to drain as a forfeit if he offended one of the rules of the house. Cf. *ÍF* v. 254, 269 and VIII. 162).

vitja (að) *wv.* with gen., visit, go and find; *e-s er at vitja* s-thing is to be got, found 33/10.

vitkask (að) *wv. md.* come to o-self, recover one's wits 46/16.

†**vitki** *m.* wizard 10/20.

vitni *n.* that by which an oath is sworn, witness, attestation 35/6.

†**vitnir** *m.* wolf (= Fenrir) 33/39.

vitr *a.* wise, intelligent 7/20, 25/13; sup., wisest, cleverest 23/18, 48/26.

væl *f.* trick, wile 27/1, 43/28,40; device (*til at* designed to) 48/20,27; trickery, cunning 28/27 (cf. AH *Studier* 85–6, *vél*).

vælræði *n. pl.* trickery, scheme(s) involving deception 27/3.

vængr *m.* wing 20/31 (*honum* his), 20/36.

væni *n.* prospect, expectation; *þótti ǫllum ills af* (adv.) *v.* they all thought evil was to be expected from them 27/9.

vænn *a.* likely, promising; *e-m er vænt at* s-one is likely to be successful in (s-thing), s-one is to be expected to (be able to do s-thing) 43/11.

vænta (t) *wv.* with gen., expect, think likely 4/3.

væri p. subj. of **vera**.

værr *a.* comfortable, pleasant 26/6.

vætta (tt) *wv.* impers. *e-n vættir* one expects, supposes 36/27 (*fár maðr* is the subject of the *at*-clause: 'I guess there are not many men who can . . .').

vǫllr *m.* (*dat.* **velli**) flat open uncultivated ground, plain 40/15, 50/17; pl., fields, open grassy landscape (as opposed to forest) 39/24, 43/33, 50/27.

vǫlva *f.* prophetess 10/18.

vǫmm *f.* blemish, disgrace 26/35.

vǫndr *m.* (*dat. sg.* **vendi**) stick, thin rod 46/5.

vǫrðr *m.* guardian, watchman 25/36, 26/5.

vǫrn *f.* defence 30/2; *v. þar fyrir* defence protecting it or them 18/11.

vǫtn see **vatn**.

vǫxtr *m.* growth, size, stature; dat. sg. *vexti* in size 39/13.

yfir *prep.* (1) with acc., over 17/11, 47/21, 48/32; all over 18/7, 32/39 (after noun); across 15/10; through 5/24; over (to) the top of 7/28; on top of 10/4; above 12/5, 49/12; round 44/37. (2) with dat., over 17/11, 27/15; above 19/26 (with *brunni*). (3) as adv., across, on top 10/3; *þar y.* across it 12/3; *y. upp* up over (the top) 39/25.

yfirkominn *a.* (*pp.*) beaten 36/40.

yfirkonungr *m.* supreme king 4/31 (cf. **hǫfuðkonungr**).

†**ymja (umða)** *wv.* whine, groan, resound, make a noise; be in uproar? 51/12,16.

ýmiss *a.* (inflected **yms-**) various 29/28, 30/8; n. as adv., variously 21/8.

ymr *m.* noise 38/1.

ynði *n.* enjoyment, bliss 20/18.

yngstr sup. of **ungr**.

yrði p. subj. of **verða**.

þá (1) acc. sg. f. and acc. pl. m. of **sá (1)** 3/1, 5/7, 10/40, 12/26.

þá (2) *adv.* then 3/12, 5/2; after that 11/33; at that time 9/8; afterwards 23/39; by then 40/6; by now 38/29; now 38/30 (1); just then 38/39; as a result 25/25, 38/24; therefore 40/2; moreover 4/7. Introducing main clause after subordinate clause (cf. **ok**): *er . . . þá* 3/4, 4/38; *síðan er . . . þá* 3/34; *nú er . . . þá* 43/14; *áðr . . . þá* 11/29; *hvar sem . . . þá* 5/24; *til þess at . . . þá* 4/10; *þat er . . . þá* 37/20; *þeir menn er . . . þá* 18/27 (anacoluthon), cf. *allir er . . . þá fara allir* 26/26; *ef . . . þá* 18/23, 21/5, 28/32; *þótt . . . þá* 36/30; *heldr en . . . þá* 28/35; *svá (. . .) sem . . . þá* 15/9, 22/22, 42/7; *er . . . þá . . . nú* 41/26. Anticipating subordinate clause: *þá . . . er* 13/1, 15/17; *þá . . . at* (= if) 14/9, 43/26; *þá . . . ef* 40/40; *þá . . . áðr en* 46/31; *þá er* as conj., when 11/6, 25/25; *þá er . . . þá* 3/9,26, 9/41–10/2.

þaðan *adv.* from there 6/24, 9/4; from them, that, him 5/37, 10/16, 19/24; about that 33/11; as a result 14/25; *þ. af* from it, from there 9/22, from them 13/8, from that origin 14/22, as a result of this or from then on 13/11, by means of this 12/12, by means of them or from that beginning 15/28; *þ. braut* away from it 50/35.

þak *n.* roof 7/28, 20/1.

þakðr *pp.* of **þekja**.

þakka (að) *wv.* thank (*e-m e-t* s-one for s-thing) 28/18.

þangat *adv.* to that place 17/31; in that place 33/10; *þ. er* as conj., to where 44/22.

þannig *adv.* thither, in that direction, or in the same way 10/3; towards it 39/29; (in)to it 37/39.

þar *adv.* there 4/23,25; *þar var* there was there 6/4; *þar hafi verit* it was 48/10; to that place 17/18; to him 10/33; to them 42/24; *þar fylgði* accompanied them 10/1; *þar hvergi* nowhere there 43/31. With preps. (advs.) equivalent to a pron.: *þar á* on it 46/24; *þar (. . . .) af* from it 11/6,40, about that 11/35, as a result 13/21 (therewith?), 32/35; *þar eptir* behind there 37/27, in accordance with that 23/17; *þar allt . . . fyrir* round all those places 18/11; *þar með* therewith, as well 4/7, in addition 24/27; *þar næst* next (to him) 8/19; *þar ofan í* down in it 43/4; *þar (. . .) til* thereto 13/16, for them or in addition 15/27; *þar . . . upp* up there 3/21; *þar útan um* around it 12/22; *þar yfir* over it 12/3. With adv. phrases: *þar á ǫngulinn* onto that hook 44/34; *þar fyrir durum* in front of those doors 33/27; *þar í hásæti* in that throne 13/13 (cf. 20/6); *þar í jǫrðu* there in the earth 16/7; *þar í sal* in that hall 24/33; *þar í ǫndugi* there on a high-seat, in the seat of honour 47/23; *þar innan lands* in that country or those countries 6/22; *þar til hans* to him 6/19; *þar til þess ríkis* to that kingdom 6/17. With conjunctions: *þar sem* (to) where, to a place which 6/4; *þar (. . .) er* where, in (to) a (the) place which 6/12, 7/1, 31/25, while, as 7/17; *at þar er* to where 38/27; *þar fyrir er* over that place which 5/36; *þar til er* to where, until 6/16, 47/19.

þarmar *m. pl.* guts, intestines 49/9.

Glossary 159

þat n. of sá (1). Often refers to a m. or f. noun, e.g. 10/2 (= ár 9/41?) 13/17,20, 15/7,25, 19/28, 29/9, 35/9, 38/12, and sometimes precedes a pl. vb., e.g. 6/2, 7/5, 11/3, 14/14, 50/39 (cf. sá). In some cases þat is in the nature of an indefinite subject, or refers to a whole phrase or concept rather than to a specific noun.

þegar adv. immediately 8/6, 44/18; as conj., when, as soon as 42/23, þ. er 36/19.

þegit pp. of þiggja.

þegja (þagða) wv. be silent 37/2 (see vera).

þekja (þakða) wv. roof (trans.; e-u with s-thing) 7/30, 20/5; cover? pave? 47/9 (see Gjǫll in index of names).

þiggja (þá) sv. receive, get 34/38; obtain 45/32.

þing n. assembly, parliament, judicial assembly 30/2; meeting 45/24,29, 50/23.

þingvǫllr m. assembly plain 50/17, textual note.

þinull m. the rope along the (top) edge of a net 48/36.

þjóð f. a people, nation 4/12, 22/23, 29/29; race of beings (gods, giants, etc.) 46/38.

þjóðland n. country 4/31.

þjóna (að) wv. with dat., serve, be subservient to 21/17; attend 29/21; act as servant 30/23. The word perhaps has overtones of religious service, see AH Studier 71, 86.

þjónustumaðr m. servant 37/26.

þjǫkkr a. thick 26/15.

þó adv. yet 3/20, 12/10; however 9/25; nevertheless 21/5; as conj., and yet 30/16, 33/3.

þola (ð) wv. endure, suffer 33/10; þ. e-m e-t put up with s-thing from s-one 39/15.

þora (ð) wv. dare (with inf.) 31/9.

þorrit pp. of þverra.

þótt (1) conj. although 9/1, 21/19; even if 34/32, correlative with þá 28/7 (þóttu = þótt þú), 36/28 (2); þ. eigi sé even (to those who) are not 44/3.

þótt (2) pp. of þykkja 36/28 (1).

þraut f. difficulty, trial, danger 26/17.

þrekvirki n. deed of strength, heroic achievement, mighty exploit 35/5, 45/15.

þreskǫldr m. threshold 27/20.

þrettándi ord. num. (the) thirteenth 30/6.

†þreyja (þráða) wv. suffer love-longing 31/29.

þreyta (tt) *wv.* struggle, try hard (with inf., to do s-thing) 39/27; *þ. á e-t, at e-u* strive at s-thing 41/13,25; *þ. e-t við e-n* contend, compete at s-thing with s-one 40/35, 43/10; *þ. skjótfœri e-s* contend with s-one's speed 43/11.

þriði *ord. num.* (the) third 3/26, 5/35, 11/12; *inar þriðju* the third kind 18/16.

þrír *num.* (*n.* **þrjú**; *dat.* **þrim, þrimr**) three 4/16, 17/11, 34/31, 41/2; *þrjár* for three (nights) 31/29.

þrjóta (þraut) *sv.* impers. *e-n þrýtr e-t* s-one runs out of s-thing 41/5.

†þryngva (þrǫng) *sv.* press; pp. *þrunginn e-u* swollen, loaded with s-thing 36/9.

þræll *m.* slave 27/19.

þrǫngr *a.* crowded; comp. n. as adv. *þrǫngra* 33/32.

þumlungr *m.* thumb (-piece) 38/13.

þungi *m.* heaviness, weight 10/7.

þungr *a.* heavy 53/26 (i.e. difficult to cross? strong? viscous?); n. as subst. or adv. 48/34.

þunnvangi *m.* temple 39/5.

þurðr *m.* decrease, lessening 43/15.

þurfa (þarf, þurfta) *pret. pres. vb.* need 25/37, 32/24; with *at* and inf. 22/23, 38/9, 40/20; *Þórr mundi eigi þ.* at there was no point in Þórr . . . 42/20; impers., be necessary (always with neg., there is, was, will be no need) 3/21, 26/12, 37/18, 41/5.

þurr *a.* dry 48/5 (i.e. no tears at all).

þverra (þvarr, *pp.* **þorrit)** *sv.* decrease 41/16.

þvers *adv.* abruptly, at a sharp (right) angle 39/20.

þvertaka (-tók) *sv.* refuse absolutely 29/35.

því dat. sg. n. of **sá (1)**, therefore, for this reason 10/35, 23/2, 29/38; *af því* for this reason 4/8; *því næst* next 27/30, 35/29; with comp., *því harðara er . . . því skarpara* the harder . . . the tougher 28/40, similarly 42/16; *því vísari at* the wiser inasmuch as 7/25; *því framar at* so far ahead that 40/18.

þvíat *conj.* because 4/13, 6/9, 18/4.

þvílíkr *a.* such 39/16, 41/32; suchlike 3/36; similar 43/28; *þ. hǫfðingi sem Freyr er* such a lord as F. is 31/35; n. as subst., such a thing 41/37.

þýða (dd) *wv.* make equivalent (*á móti* to), interpret as (corresponding to) 3/28.

þykkja (þótta) *wv.* seem (*e-m* to s-one) 5/24, 12/3, 32/1; be considered (to be) 40/40, 49/37; impers. with nom. (sometimes pl.) and inf., (*e-m*) *þykkir* one thinks 28/37, 44/25, *þykki mér* I think 25/27, 40/26; *eigi þótti* *mér goðin gera* I do not think the gods made 15/12; *þótti mér þeir hafa* I think they had 13/1; *eigi þótti mér hitt minna vera vert* I do not consider that was less significant either 43/17; with inf. of vb. to be understood, one considers s-thing to be s-thing 6/11, 8/8, 27/9,28, 32/11 (see note), 40/22, 42/29, 49/38; *er eigi mun lítilræði í þ.* who will not think in it (to whom it will not seem) s-thing beneath his dignity 42/10; *er lítit mark mun at þ.* in which there will seem little significance 41/36. Md. (with inf.), think that one 6/26, 22/23, 39/35 (impers. or subj.?).

þyrma (ð) *wv.* with dat., spare, show mercy to 49/25; impers. passive *e-u varð eigi þyrmt* no respect or reverence was shown for s-thing 35/28.

þyrstr *a.* thirsty 41/4.

†þytr *m.* howling 24/6.

þǫgull *a.* silent 26/15.

þǫkð pp. f. of **þekja**; **þǫkðu** p. pl. of **þekja**.

†æ *adv.* always, for ever, continually 10/35, 19/12,26, 32/31.

ætla (að) *wv.* think, be of the opinion (that) 11/17; with acc. and inf. 43/37, with inf. of vb. to be understood, think s-thing is s-thing 39/17; pp. *ætlaðr* (be) intended (to be) 41/20. Md. *ætlask fyrir at* plan to, resolve to 43/32.

ætt *f.* (1) direction, region 10/6 (cf. **átt**). (2) family line 5/37; stock, tribe 14/23; ancestry, descent, origin 5/8, 14/18, 18/19, 47/11; race 11/23, 36/2 (dat.); *álfa, Ása ættar* (gen. sg.) of the race of elves, Æsir 18/16, 23/32; *kominn af þeira ætt* descended from them 13/15; *sem hon átti ætt til* in accordance with her ancestry 13/23. Pl. (lines of) descendants 3/9, 13/11; generations, family lines 3/2, 10/33; dynastic lines 6/22; ancestry (of their families), genealogies 3/33; race 10/16, 13/16; *ættirnar* the races (of mankind) 9/39.

ættaðr *a.* (*pp.*) descended; *vel æ.* of good parentage 18/26.

ættmaðr *m.* descendant 10/40.

œðask (dd) *wv. md.* become frantic, go mad 35/22.

œrit *adv.* (quite) enough, amply; i.e. only too 26/11, (pretty, very) 39/30.

†œrr *a.* raving 21/21.

œsa (t) *wv.* stir up, make (more) violent 20/27.

œztr *a. sup.* highest 8/27, 21/16, 29/18; most eminent, best 34/17.

ǫðli (or **øðli**?) *n.* fatherland, inherited land 7/13 (partitive gen., with *djúprǫðul*; often emended to *óðla* adv., swiftly).

ǫðrum dat. of **annarr**.

ǫfundarorð *n. pl.* words of envy or malice 18/33.

ǫl *n.* ale 30/33.

ǫld *f.* age, time 15/30; *allar aldir* all ages 8/35, 20/10, 53/7; *fyrr mǫrgum ǫldum en* many ages before 9/20; †pl., mankind, men 54/19.

ǫlgǫgn *n. pl.* drinking vessels, utensils for ale 30/24.

ǫnd *f.* breath, spirit, soul 9/1, 13/6.

ǫndugi *n.* seat of honour 47/23.

ǫndurdís *f.* ski-goddess 24/18 (cf. *Hkr* I. 22, *SnE* I. 318).

ǫndurguð *n.* ski-deity 24/17 (cf. *SnE* I. 266 (Ullr), 310).

ǫndverðr *a.* the beginning of, the early part of (a period of time) 34/29.

ǫngull *m.* hook 44/33,34.

ǫrk *f.* ark 3/7.

ǫrn *m.* eagle 18/30, 20/30, 51/27.

ǫxl *f.* shoulder; *á ǫxlum e-m* on s-one's shoulders 14/5, 32/32.

øng- see engi.

ørindreki *m.* messenger, envoy 47/36 (cf. eyrindi, reka).

ørlǫg *n. pl.* fate(s), destiny (-ies) 15/20, 18/23, 21/19; *segja ø.* make prophecies or pronounce, i.e. decide, destinies? 21/24.

†øróf *n.* a huge number; *ørófi vetra áðr* (it was) many many years earlier than 11/27.

øruggr *a.* safe, secure 34/31 (*fyrir* against).

†ørviti *a.* out of one's mind 21/22.

øxn see uxi.

Index of names

Accents are printed over vowels in proper names only when their length is certain.

Aurgelmir m. primeval giant, identified by Snorri with Ymir, 10; otherwise known only from *Vm* 29–30

Aurvangar m. pl., 16 (*Vsp* 14; *aurr* m. 'mud', *vangr* m. 'field')

Austri m. a dwarf, 12, 16 (*SnE* I. 314–16)

Austr Saxaland n. East Germany (Saxony), 5; cf. *Saxland*

Austrvegr m. eastern parts, 35 (often pl.; usually means east of the Baltic, Russia; *SnE* I. 270, 336, 516, 522, *Hrbl* prose, *Ls* 59; in *Ynglingatal* 9 (*Hkr* I. 36) and *Skj* A I. 240 (*Hkr* II. 145) for Sweden)

Báfurr m. a dwarf, 16

Baldr m. = Beldegg, 5; a god, 17, 23, 26, 45, 46, 47, 48, 53 (*Vsp*, *Grm*, *Ls*, *Bdr*, *Hdl*, *Sǫgubrot af fornkonungum* 11, *Málsháttakvæði* 9, *Skj* A II. 132, *Skj* A I. 595). The name may be related to OE *bealdor* 'lord' (cf. *Freyr*). There is little evidence for the worship of Baldr (see AH *Gudesagn* 40–1), though he is mentioned in an Old High German charm (see *MRN* 122–3). *Baldrsbrá* (see 23/17) is the Icelandic name for the scentless camomile (*matricaria*), but the association of this with Baldr is probably due to folk etymology

Báleygr m. a name of Óðinn, 22

Barey f., 31 (? *barr* n. 'barley', *ey* f. 'island'; W and T have the form *Barrey*. Possibly the same as Barra in the Hebrides, though *Skm* has the form *Barri* and describes the place as a grove, *lundr*.)

Beðvig m. = OE Bedwig, 5

Beldegg m. = OE Bældæg, 5

Beli m. (acc. and gen. Belja) a giant (?) killed by Freyr, 31 (*þeir Beli* = Freyr and B.); *bani Belja* = Freyr, 52 (*SnE* I. 262, 482)

Bergelmir m. a giant, 11 (*Vm* 29)

Bestla f., 11 (*SnE* I. 244, *ÍF* VIII. 253; cf. *Háv* 140)

Biaf m. = OE Beaw, 5

Bifliði, Biflindi m. names of Óðinn, 8 (cf. *Grm* 49 and *Blindi*; Bifliði is not found elsewhere)

Bifrǫst f. a bridge, 15, 17, 18, 20, 25, 34, 50 (*Forspjallsljóð* 9, *PE* 372; in *Grm* 44 and *Fm* 15 called Bilrǫst; see AH *Studier* 51–4). Cf. *Ásbrú*

Bifurr m. a dwarf, 16

Bil f., 14, 30. See A. Holtsmark, 'Bil og Hjuke', *Maal og Minne* 1945, 139–54. Bil is frequent in kennings for 'woman', e.g. *Od* 33

Bileygr m. a name of Óðinn, 22

Bilskirnir m. a hall, 22 (*SnE* I. 252, 256)

Bjárr m. = Biaf, 5 (cf. *SnE* I. 484)

Bláinn m. a dwarf (? cf. *SnE* II. 469) or a name for Ymir?, 16

Blíkjanda Bǫl n., 27 (*blíkja* sv. 'gleam', *bǫl* n. 'misfortune')

Blindi m. a name of Óðinn, 22 (cf. *Biflindi*, *Grm* 49)

Borr m. father of Óðinn, 11, 13 (spelt *Burr* in Codex Regius *Vsp* 4; cf. *Hdl* 30, *Egils saga*, *ÍF* II. 169)

Bragi (gamli) m. 9th-century Norwegian poet, 7, 34 (see notes to 7/12–19 and 34/16–24; cf. *Hákonarmál* and *Eiríksmal*, *Skj* A I. 66 and 175; *Skj* A I. 1–5, *Skáldatal*, *SnE* III. 270)

Bragi m. god of poetry, 25 (cf. *bragr* in glossary; *Ls* 12–13, 18, *Sd* 16; see *MRN* 185, AH *Gudesagn* 48–9; *SnE* I. 208 etc.)

Brandr m. = OE Brand, 5

Breiðablik n. pl., 19, 23

Brimir m. a hall, 53 (in *Vsp* 37 Brimir may be the name of the owner of the hall rather than of the hall itself, and in the Codex Regius of *PE Vsp* 9 (cf. 16/5 above) Brimir seems to be another name for Ymir). Cf. *SnE* I. 226

Brísingamen n. a necklace, 29 (mentioned in various mythological contexts in Old Icelandic (*SnE* I. 264–8, 304, 312; *Þrk* 13, 15, 19; *Sǫrla þáttr*, *Flateyjarbók* I. 275–6; cf. note to 24/32–7). See also *Beowulf* 1198–9, and note in ed. F. Klaeber, 3rd ed., Boston 1936, p. 178 and references there.)

Búri m., 11 (*SnE* I. 244)

Býleistr m. brother of Loki, 26, 51 (in some MSS Býleiptr; see also *SnE* I. 268, *Hdl* 40)

Byrgir m. a spring or well, 14

Fjǫrgvinn—(*contd*)
is presumably basing his information
on *Ls* 26, where Frigg is called
Fjǫrgyns mær, though there *mær*
may mean wife rather than daughter,
and Fjǫrgynn may be a name of
Óðinn. The f. *Fjǫrgyn* is a name for
Þórr's mother Jǫrð in *Hrbl* 56
and *Vsp* 56, and is found as a
synonym for 'earth' in scaldic verse

Fjǫrm f. a river, 9, 33 (*Grm* 27)

Fólkvangr m., 24; pl. Fólkvangar, 24

Forseti m., 26 (known only from *SnE*
and *Grm*, cf. *SnE* I. 208, 260, 556; a
Frisian god Fosite is mentioned by
Alcuin, *Vita Willibrordi* I, ch. 10
(*Patrologia Latina*, ed. J. P. Migne,
Parisiis 1844–64, 101, 700), and there
is a Norwegian place-name Forset-
lund. See AH *Studier* 75–7, AH
Gudesagn 300, 304)

Frakland n. land of the Franks, 5

Fránangrsfors m. a waterfall, 48 (*PE*
122)

Freki m. a wolf, 32. Cf. 51/35, *Vsp* 44

Freovin m. = OE Freawine, 5

Freyja f. a goddess, 24, 29, 34, 35, 47
(*Ls* 30–2, *Þrk*, *Od* 9, *Hdl* 6, *Flateyjarbók* I. 275; appears frequently in
Skáld). As a common noun *freyja*
means 'lady'

Freyr m. a god, 24, 28, 31, 36, 47, 50
(appears in many poems; originally a
common noun, 'lord', cf. OE *frea*,
friega; see AH *Gudesagn* 44–6)

Friallaf m. = OE Frealaf, 5

Friðleifr m. (1) = Friallaf son of Finn,
5. (2) son of Skjǫldr, 6 (*SnE* I. 374,
378)

Frigg f. = Frigida, wife of the 'historical' Óðinn, 5; a goddess, wife of the
mythical Óðinn, mother of Baldr, 13,
21, 29, 30, 45, 46, 47, 52 (cf. *Hkr* I.
12, *PE* 76; Paulus Diaconus, *Historia
Langobardorum*, I. 7–8, see *MRN*
72–3; the second Merseburg charm,
see *MRN* 122–3; AH *Gudesagn* 60)

Frigida f. = Frigg, 5; there is presumably an association with Phrygia in
the author's mind (in W (*SnE* I. 20)
the association is made explicit; cf.
Hauksbók 155). According to Servius, commentary on *Aeneid* I. 182,

and later writers Phrygia was named
after a daughter of Aesopus

Frioðigar m. = OE Freoðegar, 5

Fróði m. = Frioðigar, 5

Frosti m. a dwarf, 17

Fulla f. a goddess, 29, 47 (*SnE* I. 208,
304, 336, 346; appears in a number of
kennings in scaldic verse. She is called Frigg's *eskimær* (cf. 29/23) in *PE*
76, but in the second Merseburg
charm (see under *Frigg*) Volla is said
to be Frigg's sister)

Fundinn m. a dwarf, 16

Gagnráðr m. a name of Óðinn, 10/26,
textual note (*Vm* 8–17)

Gandálfr m. a dwarf, 16

Ganglari m. a name of Óðinn, 21 (var.
Gangleri, Gangari)

Ganglati m., 27 (*ganga* sv. 'walk', *latr*
a. 'lazy'; name of a giant at *SnE* I.
555)

Gangleri m. assumed name of Gylfi, 7,
8, 9, 10, 11, 12, 13, 14, 15, 17, 18, 19,
20, 21, 22, 23, 25, 28, 29, 31, 32, 33,
34, 36, 43, 45, 48, 49, 53, 54. Also a
name of Óðinn, see *Ganglari* (*ganga*
sv. 'walk', *-leri* a. 'weak, weary')

Ganglǫt f., 27 (cf. *Ganglati*)

Garðrofa f. a mare, 30

Garmr m. a dog, 34, 50. Cf. *Vsp* 44, 49,
58, where Garmr may be the same as
Fenrir, while Snorri evidently
assumes they are different. Cf. also
Mánagarmr

Gautr m. a name of Óðinn, 22 (*SnE* I.
530; cf. *Bdr* 2, 13; common in scaldic
kennings)

Gavir (or Gavér?) m. = Gevis, 5 (cf.
the *þula* of sea-kings, *SnE* I.
548, var.; Gevarus in Saxo Grammaticus, book III)

Gefjun f. one of the historical Æsir in
Sweden, 7; one of the mythical goddesses, 29 (*SnE* I. 208, 336; cf. note
to 7/4 and *Vǫlsa þáttr*, *Stories from
the sagas of the kings*, ed. A. Faulkes,
London 1980, p. 57)

Gefn f. a name of Freyja, 29 (*SnE* I.
350, 557; common in scaldic kennings, cf. *SnE* II. 489)

Geirahǫð f. a valkyrie, 30 (Geirǫlul,
Geirrǫmul *PE*)

Geirrøðr m., 21 (see *Grm*)
Geirvimul f. a river, 33 (*Grm* 27)
Gelgja f. a rope, 29 (cf. *SnE* II. 431, *Egils saga, ÍF* II. 144)
Gerðr f., 31 (*Skm, Hdl* 30, *SnE* I. 208; *Hkr* I. 24; common in kennings for 'woman')
Geri m. a wolf, 32
Gevis m. = OE Gewis, 5
Gils m. a horse, 17 (*Grm* 30, *SnE* I. 482, sometimes written *Gísl*)
Gimlé n., 9 (*Gimlé eða Vingólf*), 20, 53
Ginnarr m. a dwarf, 17
Ginnungagap m. mighty (or magic) abyss, space, 10, 11, 17 (see *ginnunga* and *gap* in glossary and cf. AH *Gudesagn* 24)
Ginnungahiminn m. mighty (or magic) heaven, firmament, 12
Gipul f. a river, 33 (*Grm* 27)
Gjallarhorn n., 17, 25, 50 (*Vsp* 46; cf. *gjalla* sv. 'resound')
Gjǫll f. (1) a stone slab, 29 (cf. *SnE* II. 431). (2) the river separating the world of the living from the world of the dead, 9, 47; *Gjallar brú* the bridge over the river Gjǫll, 47 (*Grm* 28; cf. *gjalla* sv. 'resound', and compare the bridge in *Grettis saga, ÍF* VII. 173 and note; SG *Kommentar* 199; *Skj* A II. 114, 115, 404)
Glaðr m. a horse, 17 (*Grm* 30, *SnE* I. 484)
Glaðsheimr m., 15 (*Grm* 8)
Glapsviðr m. a name of Óðinn, 22
Gleipnir m. a fetter, 25, 28 (*SnE* II. 431–2)
Glenr m., 13 (*SnE* I. 330)
Glitnir m., 19, 26
Glóinn m. a dwarf, 16 (*Glói* Codex Regius of *PE*)
Glora f. = Lora, 5. Cf. Hlóra, *SnE* I. 252
Glær m. a horse, 17 (*Grm* 30, *SnE* I. 482)
Gná f. a goddess, 30 (common in kennings for 'woman')
Gnipahellir m., 50 (*Vsp* 44, 49, 58)
Góinn m. a serpent, 19
Grábakr m. a serpent, 19
Gráð f. a river, 33 (*Grm* 27)
Grafvitnir m., 19
Grafvǫlluðr m. a serpent, 19

Gramr m. a dog, 34/24, textual note
Grímnir m. a name of Óðinn, 22
Grímnismál n. pl. 'the speech of Grímnir', the name of an eddic poem, 22, 30, 33
Grímr m. a name of Óðinn, 21
Guðólfr m. = OE Godulf, 5
Guðr f. a valkyrie, 30 (Gunnr *Vsp* 30, *HH* II 7; common in scaldic kennings)
Gugnir see *Gungnir*
Gullinbursti m. a boar, 47 (cf. *SnE* I. 262–4, *Hdl* 7)
Gullintanni m. a name of Heimdallr, 25 (not recorded in extant verse)
Gulltoppr m. a horse, 17, 25, 47 (*SnE* I. 264, 480, *Grm* 30)
Gungnir m. Óðinn's spear, 50 (sometimes written *Gugnir*; cf. *Sd* 17, *SnE* I. 242, 340–2, II. 134)
Gunnþrá f. a river, 9 (cf. *Grm* 27 and *Gunnþró* below)
Gunnþráin f. a river, 33 (cf. *Grm* 27, Gunnþorin)
Gunnþró f. a river, 33 (*Grm* 27, cf. *Gunnþrá* above)
Gylfi m., 6, 7; cf. *Gangleri*
Gyllir m. a horse, 17 (*Grm* 30, *SnE* I. 482)
Gymir m., 30 (*Skm, Ls* prose and 42, *Hdl* 30, *SnE* I. 326)
Gǫll f. a valkyrie, 30
Gǫmul f. a river, 33 (*Grm* 27)
Gǫndlir m. a name of Óðinn, 22
Gǫpul f. a river, 33 (*Grm* 27)

Hábrók f. a hawk, 34
Háleygjatal n. list (i.e. genealogy) of the men (jarls) of Hálogaland, 6. This was a poem by Eyvindr Skáldaspillir, a Norwegian poet of the 10th century, preserved fragmentarily in *Skáldskaparmál* and kings' sagas (*Hkr, Fagrskinna, Flateyjarbók*; see *Skj* A I. 68–71). It traced the ancestry of earl Hákon (d. 995) back to mythical times.
Hallinskíði m. a name of Heimdallr, 25 (*Hkr* I. 204)
Hamskerpir m. a horse, 30 (cf. Hamskarpr, *SnE* II. 487)
Hangaguð m. a name of Óðinn, 21 (*SnE* I. 232)

Haptaguð m. a name of Óðinn, 21 (cf. *hapta beiðir*, SnE I. 248, *hapta snytrir*, SnE I. 308)

Hár m. a name of Óðinn, 21; one of Gylfi's informants, 8, 9, 10, 11, 12, 13, 14, 15, 17, 18, 19, 20, 21, 22, 23, 25, 28, 29, 31, 32, 33, 34, 36, 44, 45, 48, 49, 53; weak form *Hávi*, 8 (High, the high one, cf. *Háv* 109, 111, 164; but in some cases the name Hárr may have been intended, i.e. 'hoary', though other etymologies have been proposed, e.g. *Háarr*, 'high ruler'; cf. *Vsp* 21 and the dwarf-name *Hárr*; note also *Ágrip*, ed. F. Jónsson, Halle 1929, p. 1, *Flateyjarbók* I. 564)

Hárbarðr m. a name of Óðinn, 22 (cf. *Hrbl*)

Hárr m. a dwarf, 16 (Hánarr *Vsp* 13; sometimes written *Hár*, see under *Hár*)

Hati m. a wolf, 14 (see note to 14/14–17; there is a giant called Hati in *Helgakviða Hjǫrvarðssonar*, PE 173–5)

Hávi see *Hár*

Heiðrún f. a goat, 33 (*Grm* 25, *Hdl* 46–7)

Heimdalargaldr (rs) m. name of a lost poem, 26 (*SnE* I. 264; *galdr* m. 'incantation')

Heimdallr m. (gen. Heimdalar), 25, 26, 47, 50, 51. Often mentioned in early sources (e.g. *Húsdrápa*, SnE I. 240, 266, 268; *Hdl* 35–8; *Rígsþula*, prose introduction, PE 141; *Vsp* 1, 27; *Ls* 48; *Þrk* 15; *Sǫgubrot af fornkonungum* 11) but there is no evidence that he was the object of a cult

Heingestr m. = OE Hengest, 5

Hel f. (1) the abode of the dead, 9, 47, 48 (cf. *Niflhel*). (2) daughter of Loki, 27, 46, 47, 53. It is doubtful which is the appropriate meaning at 48/9 and 50/19 (companions of Hel or (company of) inhabitants of Hel?—presumably the same as the *fíflmegir* at 51/34, though Snorri may have devils or an army of dead men in mind). The name is personified only in Icelandic: elsewhere it is always a place. In most Norse poems it can be taken to mean the place, but the context is

often ambiguous, as e.g. at *Vsp* 43, *Grm* 31

Helblindi m. (1) brother of Loki, 26. (2) a name of Óðinn, 21

Helgrindr f. pl. gates of Hel, 9, 47 (cf. *Heiðreks saga* 16)

Helvegr m. the way to Hel, 9, 46, 47, 52 (*Heiðreks saga* 35, *Vsp* 47)

Heptifili m. a dwarf, 16 (Hepti, Víli PE)

Heremóð m. = OE Heremod, 5. Cf. *Hermóðr*

Herfjǫtur f. a valkyrie, 30

Herjafǫðr m. a name of Óðinn, 32 (*herr* m. 'host, army'; *Vsp* 43, *Vm* 2, *Grm* 25, 26)

Herjan m. a name of Óðinn, 8, 21 (*Vsp* 30)

Hermóðr m., 46, 47 (see *sveinn* in glossary: he is listed with sons of Óðinn in *SnE* I. 554, II. 636. He appears as a prominent inhabitant of Valhǫll in *Hdl* 2, *Hákonarmál* 14 (*SnE* I. 236), *Málsháttakvæði* 9 (*Skj* A II. 132), *Sǫgubrot af fornkonungum* 11, but does not seem to have the nickname *inn hvati* elsewhere. He is perhaps identifiable with the Heremod of *Beowulf* 901, 1709 and OE genealogies, see *Heremóð* and textual note to 5/13)

Herran m. a name of Óðinn, 8 (cf. *herra*, 'lord', often used of Christ; *harra*, var. *herra*, appears in a kenning for Óðinn in *Skj* A I. 168)

Herteitr m. a name of Óðinn, 21

Hildr f. a valkyrie, 30 (cf. *Vsp* 30)

Himinbjǫrg n. pl., 20, 25, 26

Himinhrjótr m. an ox, 44 (cf. *SnE* I. 484)

Hjálmberi m. a name of Óðinn, 21

Hjúki m., 14 (not mentioned in surviving poems)

Hleðjólfr m. a dwarf, 16 (Hlévangr, -vargr PE)

Hleriði = Loriði, textual note to 5/9

Hliðskjálf f., 13, 31; with art., 20, 48 (see prose introductions to *Grm* and *Skm*; *Akv* 14, SnE I. 242, *Skj* A I. 168; AH *Studier* 39–42)

Hlín f. a goddess, 30, 52 (= *Vsp* 53; *SnE* I. 556). The name does not appear elsewhere either in the Prose or Poetic Edda, though it is common in scaldic verse in kennings for 'woman'. See note to 52/5.

Hlǫðyn f. a name for Jǫrð, mother of Þórr, 52 (the first vowel is sometimes taken to be *ó*; cf. *SnE* I. 474, 585, *Hkr* I. 256)

Hlǫkk f. a valkyrie, 30 (common in kennings for 'battle' and 'woman')

Hnikarr m. (1) a name of Óðinn, 8, 21 (cf. *Rm* 18 ff., *SnE* II. 142, 417, 472). (2) = Vingenir, textual note to 5/11

Hnikuðr m. a name of Óðinn, 8, 22 (*SnE* II. 472)

Hnoss f. daughter of Freyja, 29 (*SnE* I. 556-7, *Hkr* I. 25)

Hoddmímir m., 54 (*hodd* n. pl. 'hoard')

Hófvarfnir m. a horse, 30 (*SnE* II. 487)

Hríð f. a river, 9 (*Grm* 28)

Hrímfaxi m. a horse, 13 (*Vm* 14, *SnE* I. 484)

Hringhorni m. a ship, 46 (*SnE* I. 260, 581)

Hrist f. a valkyrie, 30 (common in scaldic kennings)

Hróðvitnir m., 14 (*Grm* 39; cf. Hróðrsvitnir in *Ls* 39, which looks like a name for Fenrir, and *SnE* I. 591)

Hroptatýr m. a name of Óðinn, 22 (cf. *Háv* 160, *SnE* I. 234-6)

Hrymr m. a giant, 50, 51

Hræsvelgr m. a giant, 20 (*hræ* n. 'corpse', *svelgja* sv. 'swallow')

Hrǫnn f. a river, 33 (*Grm* 28)

Hugi m., 40, 43 (personification of *hugi* m. 'thought'; cf. *Huginn*. Hugi is also a personal name in *Orkneyinga saga*, *ÍF* XXXIV. 95, *Hkr* III. 222-3, *Skj* A I. 442, and *Flóamannasaga*, ed. Finnur Jónsson, København 1932, pp. 25, 57, in each case relating to non-Scandinavians and in the first three corresponding to the name Hugo.)

Huginn m. a raven, 32, 33 (cf. *hugr*, *hugi* m. 'thought', and *Hugi* above; *SnE* II. 142, 417; in verse often used as a common noun for 'raven')

Hugstari m. dwarf, 16 (Haugspori *PE*)

Hungr (rs) m., 27. Cf. the kennings *Heljar diskr*, *askr* for 'hunger' in 13th-century poems, *Skj* A II. 46, 146

Hveðrungr m. apparently a name for Loki; son of H. = Fenrir, 52 (see 27/5 and cf. *Ynglingatal* 32, *Hkr* I. 79, where Hel is described as the daughter of Hveðrungr. The name also appears in *þulur* among names of giants, *SnE* I. 549, and names of Óðinn, *SnE* II. 472.)

Hvergelmir m. a spring or well, 9,.17, 18, 33, 53 (*Grm* 26; *hverr* m. 'cauldron', in Iceland a hot spring. Cf. AH *Studier* 49-50)

Hymir m. a giant, 44, 45 (cf. *Hym*; also *Ls* 34, *SnE* I. 312, *Skj* A I. 24. In *Gylf* the MSS frequently omit the *H*, making the name identical with *Ymir*.)

Hyrrokkin f. a giantess, 46 (cf. *SnE* I. 260, 551)

Hœnir m., 23 (*SnE* I. 208, 266-8, 308, 352; *Vsp* 18, 63; *Rm*, prose introduction; *Hkr* I. 12-13; *Sǫgubrot af fornkonungum* 11)

Hǫðr (rs) m., 26, 45, 46, 53 (*SnE* I. 266, 554, 556. In *Vsp* 32-3 Hǫðr is killed in vengeance for Baldr's death; cf. *Vsp* 62, *Bdr* 10-11.)

Hǫll see *Bǫll*

Hǫrn f. a name for Freyja, 29 (*SnE* I. 348, 557; common in kennings for 'woman')

Hǫrr m. a dwarf, 16 (Hár *PE*)

Iðavǫllr m., 15, 53 (*Vsp* 7, 60; AH *Gudesagn* 30)

Iðunn f., 25 (*SnE* I. 208-12, 266, 304, 312, 336; *Ls* 16-18)

Indriði m. = Einriði, textual note to 5/10

Ingi m. a dwarf, 17 (Yngvi *PE*)

Irides m. = Einriði, textual note to 5/10

Ítrmann m. = OE Iterman, 5

Ívaldi m. a dwarf, 36 (*SnE* I. 264 = *Grm* 43, *SnE* I. 340). *Synir Ívalda* perhaps means 'descendants of Í.', and may be a kenning for dwarfs in general

Jafnhár m. a name of Óðinn, 22; one of Gylfi's informants, 8, 9, 10, 11, 17, 21, 36 ('equally high', cf. *Hár*)

Jálg, Jálkr m. names of Óðinn, 8, 22 (*Grm* 49, 54; cf. *Ǫlgr*, *Ólgr*, *SnE* II. 472, 556)

Miðgarðr m. the rampart surrounding the world of men and protecting it from giants, 12, 13 (*undir Miðgarði*: under the protection of M.?), 14, 34, 44, 52 (*Vsp* 4, *Hrbl* 23, *Hdl* 11, 16, *SnE* I. 400). The original meaning may have been 'middle-earth', the world of men situated between Ásgarðr, the world of gods, and Útgarðr, the world of giants; it may retain this meaning in *Vsp* and at 14/19 (at *SnE* I. 400 it is a synonym for 'ground'). Cf. OE *middangeard*. The original meaning of *garðr* was 'enclosed land' (*gerða* 'to enclose'). The fact that in *Grm miðgarðr* is said to have been made from Ymir's eyelashes or eyelids (12/35–7) may have led to the assumption that the word referred to an enclosing rampart or palisade rather than to the enclosure itself

Miðgarðsormr m. the midgard serpent which lies in the sea surrounding *Miðgarðr*, 27, 43, 44, 45, 50, 54 (*SnE* I. 226–8, *Hym* title)

Miðjarðarsjár m. the Mediterranean sea, 4

Mímir m., 17, 50; *Mímis brunnr*, 17, 50. *Mímr*, 51, is apparently an alternative form of the name (also in *Vsp* 46, *Sd* 14); cf. *Hoddmímir*. There is another account of Mímir in *Ynglinga saga* (*Hkr* I. 12–13, 18). *Míms vinr* means Óðinn (*SnE* I. 238, 250, 602), and Mímir appears among names of giants in *SnE* I. 549. It has been suggested that he is the son of Bǫlþor(n) mentioned in *Háv* 140 (SG *Kommentar* 38, 151)

Mist f. a valkyrie, 50

Mjǫllnir m. Þórr's hammer, 23, 35, 37, 38, 46, 53, 54 (*SnE* I. 274, 284, cf. 342–4; *Hym* 36, *Ls* 57, 59, 61, 63, *Þrk* 30)

Móðguðr f., 47 (cf. *Skj* A II. 114, *Gjallar man*)

Móða m. (var. *Móði*) one of the descendants of Tror/Þórr son of Munon, 5; the name probably chosen because of its similarity to that of Móði son of the god Þórr.

Móði m. son of the god Þórr, 53, 54

(here written *Megi* in R); cf. *SnE* I. 228, *Hym* 34. Common in kennings for 'man'.

Moðsognir m. a dwarf, 15 (cf. *Vsp* 10)

Móinn m. a serpent, 19

Mundilfœri m., 13 (*Vm* 23; the third vowel appears in MSS with *o*, *ǫ*, *a*, *e*, *æ*; cf. *Svaðilfœri*)

Muninn m. a raven, 32, 33 (cf. *muna* pret. pres. vb. 'remember', but see *MRN* 58, 294; *SnE* II. 142, 417; used as a common noun for 'raven' in scaldic verse)

Munon, Mennon m., 4. Cf. Memnon in accounts of the Trojan war, whose name appears as *Men(n)on* in *Tms* 71–2, 108, etc.

Muspell m., 9, 10: the name of the world of fire, apparently the same as *Muspellsheimr*, 10, 12, 13; but earlier in Norse mythology the name of a person (who presumably lived in Muspellsheimr, unless the first element of that name is a descriptive gen., cf. *Yggdrasill*), 36 (*á* = owns). Elsewhere in *Gylf* the name always appears in the gen. with *lýðir* (51), *megir* (15, 50), or *synir* (15, 32, 50; these are presumably all giants). Besides *Vsp* 51 (quoted at 51/30) the name is found in poetry only in the phrase *Muspells synir* in *Ls* 42. The quantity of the first vowel is uncertain. The name is probably connected with the words *muspille*, *mudspelle*, *mutspelli* in Old Saxon and Old High German Christian poems, where they mean the end of the world or doomsday (the second element means 'destruction', the first is perhaps from Latin *mundus* 'world'). It was probably therefore originally an abstract noun, which in eddic poems was personified, and finally in *Snorra Edda* became a place (through misunderstanding of the originally possessive gen. in *Muspellsheimr* as descriptive gen.?)

Mǫðvitnir m. a dwarf, 16 (Mjǫðvitnir in T, W, U, and *PE*)

Naglfari m. (1) husband of Nótt, 13. (2) a ship, 36, 50; Naglfar n., 50, 51 (the

ed., Boston 1936, see note on p. 144); further references in SG *Kommentar* 165

Rekkr m. a dwarf, 16 (Reginn *PE*)

Rerir m., 5 (*Vǫlsunga saga*, see under *Siggi*)

Rindr f., 26, 30 (*SnE* I. 236, 266, 322, 470, *Bdr* 11; AH *Gudesagn* 130; Saxo Grammaticus, book III, I. 70ff.)

Rota f. a valkyrie, 30 (otherwise mentioned only by Egill, *ÍF* II. 149, and Hallfreðr, *SnE* I. 432, in kennings for 'armour'; cf. *SnE* II. 486)

Rǫskva f., 37 (*SnE* I. 252, 254)

Saðr m. a name of Óðinn, 21

Sága f., 29 (*Grm* 7; common in scaldic kennings)

Sanngetall m. a name of Óðinn, 21

Saxland n. Saxony (i.e. Germany), 5, 6. Cf. *Austr Saxaland*; *SnE* I. 456.

Scialdun m. = OE Scealdwa, 5 (cf. *Skjǫldr*)

Sekin f. a river, 33 (Sœkin *Grm* 27)

Selund n. Zealand, 7 (Sælund W; sometimes f., e.g. *Hkr* I. 158; later Icelandic Sjáland, e.g. *Hkr* I. 163, 272; cf. *Hkr* I. 15)

Sescef m. = OE *se Sce(a)f*, 'this aforementioned Sce(a)f', 5 (cf. *Reliquiæ Antiquæ*, ed. T. Wright and J. O. Halliwell, II, London 1843, p. 173)

Sessrúmnir m., 25 (not found in verse; cf. the ship-name, *SnE* I. 581)

Síarr m. a dwarf, 16 (Svíurr *PE*)

Sibil f., 5 (cf. Virgil, *Aeneid* VI 10, 98; a *Sibilla spákona* is mentioned in *Katerine saga*, *Heilagra manna søgur*, ed. C. R. Unger, Kristiania 1877, I. 404. In *Hauksbók* 185 the name Sibilla is used for the queen of Sheba)

Síð f. a river, 33 (*Grm* 27)

Síðhǫttr m. a name of Óðinn, 22

Síðskeggr m. a name of Óðinn, 22

Sif f. = Sibil, wife of Tror/Þórr son of Munon, 5; wife of the god Þórr, 26 (*SnE* I. 252–4, 270, 304, 336, 340–2; *Hrbl* 48, *Hym* 3, 15, 34, *Þrk* 24; used as equivalent of Juno in *Tms* 3–4, 10–11, 88 and *Breta sögur*, *Hauksbók* 233)

Sigarr m. = OE Siggar, 5

Sigfǫðr m. a name of Óðinn, 22

Siggi m., 5 (Sigi T, W, U, and *Vǫlsunga saga*, ed. R. G. Finch, London 1965, pp. 1–2)

Sigtúnir f. pl. Sigtuna (in Sweden), 6 (sometimes Sigtún n.; cf. *Hkr* I. 16 and n.)

Sigyn f. wife of Loki, 27, 49 (*Vsp* 35, prose at end of *Ls*, *SnE* I. 208, 310)

Silfrtoppr m. a horse, 17 (Silfrintoppr T, W, and *Grm* 30; cf. *SnE* I. 480)

Simul f. a pole, 14 (cf. Simul, a trollwife, *HH* 42, *SnE* I. 552)

Sindri m. a hall, 53 (but in *Vsp* 37 it is the name of the ancestor of the owners or inhabitants of the hall, presumably a dwarf; cf. *SnE* I. 340 and n.)

Sinir m. a horse, 17 (*Grm* 30, *SnE* I. 480)

Sjǫfn f., 29 (*SnE* I. 556, otherwise found only in a few kennings for 'woman'; cf. *SnE* II. 490. See AH *Gudesagn* 61–2)

Skaði f., 23, 24, 49 (cf. *SnE* I. 212–14, 262, 336; *Grm* 11, *Skm* prose introduction, *Ls* prose, 49, 51, *Hkr* I. 21. Her function at 49/11 may have been determined by association with *skaði* m. 'harm', but she had loved Baldr (*SnE* I. 212–14). In *Grm* 11 (24/23) she is called *skír brúðr guða*)

Skaðvígi m. = Scialdun, textual note to 5/13

Skeiðbrimir m. a horse, 17 (*Grm* 30, *SnE* I. 482)

Skafiðr m. a dwarf, 16

Skeggjǫld f. a valkyrie, 30

Skíðblaðnir m. a ship, 34, 36 (cf. *SnE* I. 262–4, 340–2, *Hkr* I. 18)

Skilfingr m. a name of Óðinn, 22 (also a general term for 'king', see *SnE* I. 522–8, *Hkr* I. 53)

Skinfaxi m. a horse, 13 (*Vm* 12, *SnE* I. 484; *skin* n. 'shining', *fax* n. 'mane')

Skírnir m., 28, 31, 50 (*Skm*)

Skirpir m. a dwarf, 16 (Skirfir T, W, U, and *PE*)

Skjǫldr m. (1) son of Heremóð, = Scialdun, 5. (2) son of Óðinn king in Asia, 6 (*SnE* I. 374, 522, *Hkr* I. 15; *Skjǫldunga saga*, see Introduction, p. xxiii, note 12)

Skjǫldungar m. pl., 6

Skrýmir m., 38, 39. Cf. *Útgarðaloki*; in
Ls 62 Skrýmir could be the name of
Þórr's knapsack.

Skuld f. a norn, 18, 30 (*Vsp* 20; at *Vsp*
30 Skuld is the name of a valkyrie,
and the identification of the two may
be due to Snorri; cf. *SnE* I. 557 and II.
490. There is a witch called Skuld in
Hrólfs saga kraka, ed. D. Slay,
Copenhagen 1960, 33 etc., esp. 110.
Cf. *skulu* vb. 'must', *skuld* f. debt)

Skǫgul f. a valkyrie, 30 (*Vsp* 30, *SnE* I.
234, *Hkr* I. 193)

Skǫll m. a wolf, 14 (see note to 14/14–
17)

Sleipnir m. a horse, 17, 34, 46 (cf. *SnE*
I. 268, 480, 484 n., *Sd* 15, *Bdr* 2, *Hdl*
40)

Slíðr f. a river, 9 (*Vsp* 36, *Grm* 28
(Slíð))

Slíðrugtanni m. a boar (= Gullinbursti), 47 (cf. *SnE* I. 264)

Snotra f., 30 (otherwise only mentioned
in a *þula*, *SnE* I. 556)

Sól f. personification of the sun, 13, 30
(*Vm* 23, *SnE* I. 556)

Suðri m. a dwarf, 12, 16 (*SnE* I. 300,
314)

Sultr m. (= hunger, famine), 27

Sumarr m. personification of summer,
21 (*Vm* 27)

Surtalogi m. the flame of Surtr (Surti),
20, 53, 54 (*Vm* 50, *SnE* I. 228)

Surtr m. (Surti as first element of a
compound), 9, 50, 51, 52 (also *Vsp*
47, *Fm* 14). His nature is never speci-
fied. He allies himself with giants,
but perhaps can more appropriately
be described as a demon (of fire).
The name is used for a giant in general in scaldic verse

Svaðilfœri m. a horse, 35 (*Hdl* 40; the
third vowel appears in MSS with *a*,
e, *o*, *ǫ*; cf. *Mundilfœri*)

Sváfnir m. (1) a serpent, 19. (2) a name
of Óðinn, 7 (*Grm* 54; cf. *SnE* I. 222,
where Óðinn turns himself into a
serpent)

Svarinshaugr m., 16 (cf. *HH* 31, *HH* II
prose after v. 13; *haugr* m. 'grave-
mound')

Svartálfaheimr m. the world of the
black elves (see *heimr* in glossary and

cf. *døkkálfar*), 28 (*SnE* I. 352; *svartálfar* also *SnE* I. 340, but neither mentioned in poetry. See *ljósálfar* in glossary). *Svartálfar* are perhaps the
same as dwarfs (see AH Studier 37)

Svarthǫfði m., 10 (*svartr* a. 'black',
hǫfuð n. 'head')

Svásuðr m., 21 (*Vm* 27)

Svebdegg m. = OE Swæbdæg, 5

Sviðarr m. a name of Óðinn, 8 (cf.
Sviðurr, which is the form W and U
also have here)

Sviðrir m. a name of Óðinn, 8, 22 (*SnE*
II. 472)

Sviðurr m. a name of Óðinn, 22 (*SnE* I.
530, II. 472; cf. *Sviðarr*)

Svinn f. a river, 33 (cf. *Veg*; Vegsvinn
Grm 28)

Svipall m. a name of Óðinn, 21

Svipdagr m. = Svebdegg, 5 (cf. *SnE* I.
394)

Svíþjóð f. Sweden, 6, 7

Svǫl f. a river, 9, 33 (*Grm* 27)

Sylgr f. a river, 9 (*Grm* 28)

Syn f., 30 (*SnE* I. 556 and in kennings
for 'woman')

Sýr f. a name of Freyja, 29 (*SnE* I. 557
and in scaldic kennings)

Sæhrímnir m., 32

Sæmingr m., 6 (*Hkr* I. 21, *SnE* I. 554;
ancestor of the jarls of Hlaðir. In *Hkr*
I. 4 son of Yngvi-Freyr)

Sœgr m. a tub, 14 (AH *Gudesagn* 26)

Søkkvabekkr m., 29 (*Grm* 7)

Tanngnjóstr m. one of Þórr's goats, 23
(otherwise mentioned only in a *þula*,
SnE I. 589)

Tanngrisnir m. one of Þórr's goats, 23
(otherwise mentioned only in a *þula*,
SnE I. 589)

Thracia f. Thrace, 4, 5 (cf. *Tms* 71–2,
Hauksbók 155)

Troan, f., 4 (see *Tms* 9/19, 56/22
(*Hauksbók* text); the name is supposed to originate in a misunderstanding of a Latin phrase like *ux-
orem troianam filiam Priami* in one of
the sources of that saga)

Trógranni m. = Ítrmann, textual note
to 5/13

Troja f. Troy (dat. *Troja* and *Troju*), 4,
6, 13, 55 (cf. *SnE* I. 226–8. Only the

references in the prologue are included in U)

Tror m., 4 (cf. Tros (grand)son of Dardanus (Dictys Cretensis, *Ephemeridos belli Troiani libri*, ed. W. Eisenhut, Leipzig 1973, pp. 8, 100), written Thror in *Stjórn*, ed. C. R. Unger, Christiania 1862, p. 82)

Týr m., 25, 27, 28, 29, 50 (cf. *Hym* 4, 33, *Ls* 37–40, *Sd* 6. The word is also a common noun meaning 'god'. See *MRN* 180–2).

Tyrkir m. pl. Turks (i.e. Trojans), 6, 55 (*SnE* I. 226, *Hauksbók* 155). The Trojans are commonly called Tyrkir in *Trójumanna saga*: both were inhabitants of Asia Minor, but there may also have been association with the name Teucri. Cf. Ari's genealogy at the end of *Íslendingabók* and *Fornmanna sögur*, XI, Kaupmannahöfn 1828, p. 412, which is derived from the lost *Skjǫldunga saga*.

Tyrkland n. Turkey, land of the Turks (i.e. Trojans) 4, 5 (*Hkr* I. 14, 27)

Uðr m. a name of Óðinn, 21 (cf. *Þuðr*)

Ulixes m. Ulysses (Odysseus), 55

Ullr m., 26 (*SnE* I. 208, 266, 420, 484; *Grm* 5, 42, *Akv* 30; often mentioned in scaldic verse. He was the object of widespread cult in the north though he is not prominent in surviving mythology)

Urðr f. a norn, 18; *Urðar brunnr*, 17, 19 (*SnE* I. 428, 446; *Vsp* 19, 20, *Háv* 111: cf. *urðr* m. 'fate' and OE *wyrd*; and the vb. *verða* (p. pl. *urðu*))

Útgarðaloki m., 39, 40, 41, 42, 43, 44; cf. *Skrýmir*. Útgarðaloki is not mentioned in poems, but cf. Thorkill's voyage in Saxo Grammaticus, book VIII, I. 245

Útgarðr m., 39. Contrasted with Ásgarðr, Miðgarðr: *út* often means 'beyond the sea' (cf. 12/23 and note). Not mentioned in poems (cf. *heimr* in glossary)

Váfuðr m. a name of Óðinn, 22

Vafþrúðnir m. a giant, 10 (*Vm*)

Vakr m. a name of Óðinn, 22

Valaskjálf f., 20 (*Grm* 6)

Valfǫðr m. a name of Óðinn, 17, 21 (also *Vsp* 1, 27, *Grm* 48)

Valhǫll f. the palace of the historical Æsir in Sweden, 7; the mythical palace of the gods, 21, 30, 32, 33, 34, 45 (cf. *Hkr* I. 20, 193–4, and *Ásgarðr*; *Vsp* 33, *Grm* 8, *Hdl* 1, *HH* II prose after v. 38, *Akv* 2, 14; *valr* m. 'the slain', *hǫll* f. 'hall')

Váli m. (1) son of Loki, 49; presumably a deduction from *Vsp* 34 (he does not appear elsewhere) which is only in the *Hauksbók* text, and the correct reading perhaps ought to be *Váli* (nom.) rather than *Vála* (gen.), and if the verse is genuine at all it maybe refers to Váli son of Óðinn. Compare the prose passage at the end of *Ls*. At *SnE* I. 268 Loki is said to have a son Áli (the footnote giving the reading of W as *Váli* is erroneous); cf. the alternation Áli/Váli for Óðinn's son. (2) son of Óðinn, 26, 30, 53, 54 (*SnE* I. 208, 266; *Hdl* 29, *Bdr* 11, emendation). (3) a dwarf, 16 (*Náli PE*)

Ván f. a river, 29 (*Grm* 28, *SnE* II. 432; cf. *ván* f. 'hope')

Vanadís f. a name of Freyja, 29 (cf. *Vanir* and *dis* f. 'lady', often of supernatural or semi-divine nature)

Vanaheimar m. pl. the land of the Vanir, 23 (Vanaheimr *Vm* 39, *Hkr* I. 10, 13, 27; cf. *heimr* in glossary)

Vanir m. pl. a race of gods different from the Æsir, 23, 30 (*SnE* I. 216, *Vsp* 24, *Vm* 39, *Skm* 17, 18, *Þrk* 15, *Alv*, *Sd* 18, *Hkr* I. 10–13)

Vár f., 29 (*Þrk* 30, also in kennings for 'woman'. Vár and Vǫr are not disuished in U, but both are included in the *þula* in *SnE* I. 556)

Vásuðr m., 21 (not mentioned in surviving poetry)

Vé m., 11 (cf. *Véi*, *Ls* 26, and *Hkr* I. 12, 14; see under *Vili*)

Veðrfǫlnir m. a hawk, 18

Veg f. a river, 33 (cf. *Svinn*; Vegsvinn *Grm* 28)

Veggdegg m. = OE Wægdæg, 5

Veratýr m. a name of Óðinn, 22 (*Grm* 3)

Verðandi f. a norn, 18 (*Vsp* 20; pres. p. of *verða* sv. 'happen', cf. *Urðr*)

138 ff. See also *Grm* 30–2; AH *Gude-sagn* 32–3)

Yggr m. a name of Óðinn, 22 (*SnE* I. 236, 470; *Vm* 5, *Hym* 2, *Fm* 43; common in scaldic kennings. Cf. *ugga* wv. 'fear', *yggt* n. a. 'fearful', *Atlamál* 1, *PE* 292 (in MS altered from *yggr*))

Ylgr f. a river, 9 (*Grm* 28)

Ymir m. a giant, 10, 11, 12, 15. See *Vsp* 3, *Vm* 21, 28; cf. *Aurgelmir, Bláinn, Brimir, Hymir*.

Ynglingar m. pl. descendants of Yngvi, kings of Sweden and Norway, 6 (*SnE* I. 522, *Hdl* 16; cf. *Ynglinga saga*)

Yngvi m. son of Óðinn, 6 (*SnE* I. 234, *Hkr* I. 34; cf. *SnE* I. 522, *Rm* 14, *HH* 55. Perhaps the same as Yngvi-Freyr, *SnE* I. 554, 555, *Hkr* I. 4, 24, 25, 280, and Ingunar-Freyr, *Ls* 43, *Hkr* II. 421. Cf. *Fornmanna sögur* XI, Kaupmannahöfn 1828, p. 413 (Ingifreyr), and Arngrímur Jónsson's version of *Skjǫldunga saga*, see Introduction p. xxiii, note 12 (Ingo); also Ari's genealogy in *Íslendingabók*, *ÍF* I. 27. Freyr, however, is son of Njǫrðr, and so is Yngvi-Freyr in those genealogies that include him)

Þekkr m. (1) a name of Óðinn, 21. (2) a dwarf, 16

Þjálfi m., 37, 40, 43 (*Hrbl* 39, *SnE* I. 252–4, 296; also *SnE* I. 274–6. The name was also apparently held by historical persons, see e.g. *Hkr* III 224–5 (but see footnote) and S. B. F. Jansson, *Swedish Vikings in England, The Evidence of the Rune Stones*, London 1966, p. 15)

Þjazi m., 23, 24 (*SnE* I. 210–4, 306, 382, *Hrbl* 19, *Ls* 50–1, *Hdl* 30)

Þjóðnuma f. a river, 33 (*Grm* 28)

Þjóðólfr inn hvinverski (from Hvinir) m. 9th-century Norwegian poet, 7 (see note to 7/31–4)

Þorinn m. a dwarf, 16

Þórr m. = Tror son of Munon, 4; = Ector (Hector), 55 (cf. *SnE* I. 226–8); one of the companions of Óðinn king

in Asia on his migration to Sweden, 55; a god, son of the god Óðinn, 17, 22, 23, 26, 30, 35, 36, 37, 38, 39, 40, 41, 42, 43, 44, 45, 46, 48, 49, 50, 53. Cf. *Ásaþórr, Ǫkuþórr, Vingeþórr, Vingnir* (see note to 22/30–1). He frequently appears in poetry, and in *Skáld*

Þriði m. a name of Óðinn, 21 (*SnE* I. 292); one of Gylfi's informants, 8, 9, 10, 12, 21, 37, 53. Cf. S. Nordal, *Snorri Sturluson*, Reykjavík 1920, p. 114, and references under *Hár*.

Þróinn m. a dwarf, 16 (cf. Þráinn and Þorinn, *Vsp* 12)

Þrór m. (1) a name of Óðinn, 22. (2) a dwarf, 16

Þrúðheimr m. = Thracia, 5 (*Grm* 4; cf. *Þrymheimr, Þrúðvangar*)

Þrúðr f. a valkyrie, 30 (*SnE* II. 490; in various kennings for 'woman'. Cf. Þrúðr daughter of Þórr, *SnE* I. 252–4, 300, 304, 426, 556)

Þrúðvangar m. pl., 22, 43 (*SnE* I. 276; *þrúð-* 'might', *vangr* m. 'field, plain'. Cf. *Þrúðheimr*)

Þrymheimr m., 23, 24 (*SnE* I. 210 (in Jǫtunheimar, see *SnE* I. 212). Always written Þrúðheimr in U; *þrymr* m. 'noise', *þruma* f. 'thunder')

Þuðr m. a name of Óðinn, 21 (Þundr *PE* (Codex Regius), Þuðruðr as one word W and U)

Þul f. a river, see *Fimbulþul*.

Þundr m. a name of Óðinn, 22 (*Háv* 145; cf. *Þuðr*)

Þviti m. a stone, 29 (*SnE* II. 431)

Þyn f. a river, 33 (*Grm* 27)

Þǫkk f., 48 (*þǫkk* f. 'thanks')

Þǫll f. a river, 33 (*Grm* 27)

Æsir m. pl. see *Áss*

Ǫkuþórr m. 'driving Þórr', a name of Þórr, 22, 23, 37, 39, 55 (*SnE* I. 226–8; not found in poetry. See note to 22/30–1; *aka* sv. 'drive (a chariot)'; generally written *Aka-, Aku-* in T and W)

Ǫrmt f. a river, 17